NIGHT DOGS

ALSO BY KENT ANDERSON

Sympathy for the Devil (1987)

NIGHT DOGS

KENT ANDERSON

BANTAM BOOKS

NEW YORK TORONTO LONDON SYDNEY AUCKLAND

NIGHT DOGS
A Bantam Book / January 1998

Originally published by Dennis McMillan Publications December 1996

Book design by Laurie Jewell.

Library of Congress Cataloging-in-Publication Data

Anderson, Kent.
Night dogs / Kent Anderson.
p.   cm.
ISBN 0-553-10764-X
I. Title.
PS3551.N3744N54   1998
813'.54—dc21   97-35529
CIP

Published simultaneously in the United States and Canada

Bantam Books are published by Bantam Books, a division of Bantam Doubleday Dell Publishing Group, Inc. Its trademark, consisting of the words "Bantam Books" and the portrayal of a rooster, is Registered in U.S. Patent and Trademark Office and in other countries. Marca Registrada. Bantam Books, 1540 Broadway, New York, New York 10036.

PRINTED IN THE UNITED STATES OF AMERICA

BVG   10 9 8 7 6 5 4 3 2 1

*This book is dedicated to the memory of
Officer Dennis A. Darden, Badge #403
Portland Police Bureau.*

*Killed in the line of duty
while working alone.*

ACKNOWLEDGMENTS

Jan Foster & Sgt. Helen Foster

Jim Bellah

J.T. Potter and all the other good cops
who worked the Avenue

John & Linda Quinn

James & Julie Durham

Chas Hansen

Robert & Arlene Morris

Howard Smith

Mark Christensen

John Milius

And, of course, Judith

FOREWORD

IT'S THE MID-SEVENTIES, and America's trying to ignore
its ignominious second-place finish in the Southeast Asian War
Games, a loss we suffered because we lacked a clear purpose, an
iron will, and the necessary courage of the Vietnamese. The
American Dream has taken a severe beating, and everything
seems to have gone to hell. The rich are getting richer and more
self-righteous, the poor more desperately poor, and nobody seems
to remember the losses or the lessons of the Vietnam War. Caught
between the hopeful hangover of the sixties and the looming
eighties' decade of unrestrained greed, the various governments
are as confused and indecisive as they were during the war, plus
they have cut services to the bloody bone, and the streets are filled
with the hopeless and the hopelessly insane.

The American center did not hold. Domestic relations have
become disaster areas, neighborhoods free-fire zones, and the cities are fistfighting themselves to the death. Even our pets turn on
us as domestic dogs revert to a more elemental stance, gathering

in protective/aggressive feral packs, and sometimes must be destroyed, since the street cops can't shoot their owners.

Or so it seems, particularly to a young Vietnam vet police officer named Hanson. The only people who have even the vaguest notion of what's actually happening are the men and women in the trenches, the street cops.

As he works the mean streets of North Precinct, Hanson sees himself as the last line of defense, the thin blue line that prevents the criminal and the crazy from destroying the middle-class neighborhoods. Hanson also seems to be one of the few who actually care about the street people, as much caretaker as cop as he dispenses justice rather than law among his charges. On these streets, Hanson is the philosopher-king, mucking out the bloody stables with his bare hands.

Complicating Hanson's chores are the battles within himself. He hates liberals with an intelligent passion, partly because they don't understand the dynamic of the street and partly because he sees his own liberal heart as both foolish and weak. Like many men who ask too much of themselves, Hanson would love the relief of a connection with another human being. But he has enough trouble just talking to himself. So he relies on conversations with his cop partner, the occasional visitation from an old Vietnam War buddy who has moved from pain pills for his war wounds to dealing cocaine, and his irregular love-life, which revolves eccentrically around a woman who seems more depraved than the drug-addled streetwalkers on his beat. Mostly Hanson talks to his dog, Truman, a small wizened mutt he saved from a death at the pound after the demise of his ancient owner, against the advice of his cop cohorts.

It's a lonely life when the job is the *only* life, and when the job is bloody, confused, and dangerous, so is the life. But somehow Hanson survives. The street scenes are at the heart of this novel— moments of courage and compassion, snapshots of anger and understanding, scenes that flash on the brain like unexpected bolts of lightning. Through it all Hanson maintains his pride and sense of duty, but most of all he never condescends to the people on his beat. Throughout the novel, no matter what the anger, the violence, or the epithets, Hanson treats his charges with respect and dignity. They know it and return the favor. This is the way life is for a good street cop. And the way it should be. Hanson is the sort of police officer desperately needed on the street.

There has never been a police novel like this. The writing is as strong as the material: the minor characters are as brilliantly drawn as the best graffiti, the dialogue as solid as a brick through a plate glass window, and the prose as sharply precise as a linoleum knife across the throat.

Night Dogs is not just a fine book, it is an important book. It reminds us of important things, of a time too many people prefer to forget, the loss of faith and purpose after the war; and it reminds us that those people who live on the rough edges of society are people much like us, people with hopes and dreams, with disappointments and endurance; and they deserve the same respect we usually reserve for ourselves. Read this novel, enjoy, think, and rest easy in your domestic peace.

James Crumley
Missoula, October 1996

AUTHOR'S NOTE

THOUGH SET IN PORTLAND, where I was a police officer in the mid-seventies, *Night Dogs* is a novel, a self-contained fictional world, and I have altered streets and landscapes to serve that world. All characters, events, and dialogue are products of my imagination.

I'm proud to have been a member of the Portland Police Bureau, and I have been as honest as I know how in writing this book. Some readers may find it disturbing or "offensive." The truth sometimes affects people that way.

Things are much worse now than they were in 1975.

NIGHT DOGS

PROLOGUE

EVERY JUNE 15TH out at North Precinct, "A" relief and graveyard shift started killing dogs. The police brass and local politicians only smiled if they were asked about it, shook their heads, and said it was just another one of those old myths about the precinct.

The cops at North Precinct called them "Night Dogs," feral dogs, wild and half-wild, who roamed the districts after dark. Their ancestors had been pets, beaten and abandoned by their owners to breed and give birth on the streets. Some paused only long enough to eat the afterbirth before leaving the newborns to die. But there were others who suckled and watched over their mewling litters. Gaunt and yellow-eyed, their gums bleeding from malnutrition, they carried them, one by one, to some new safe place every few nights, out of instinct. Or out of love. You might call it love, but none of the cops at North ever used that word.

Survivors were lean and quick, pit bull and Doberman in their blood, averaging fifty or sixty pounds. Anything smaller eventually starved to death if it wasn't first run down and killed by larger dogs, cornered by children with rocks and bats, or caught in the street by flaring headlights after the bars closed. A quick death the only good luck those dogs would ever know before they were plowed into reeking landfills or dumped in the "Dead Animal Bin" behind the Humane Society gas chamber.

Night Dogs carried a scent of fear and rot in their fur, and the cops at North Precinct claimed they could smell them in the dark—stalking the chain-link fences of restaurant parking lots on graveyard shift, prowling supermarket Dumpsters or crouched, ears back, in the shadows of McDonald's dark arches. When the winter rains came and food got scarce, they ate their own shit and each other.

They waited for night in fire-gutted, boarded-up cellars of abandoned homes the neighborhood had used as garbage dumps, then set on fire and watched burn as they sat on their porches with quarts of Colt .45 and King Cobra Tallboys, waiting for the fire trucks.

Most of the cops would have let the dogs live their wretched lives, but too many were crazy, vicious from inbreeding, putrid food, brain damage. Some thought just the stress of everyday survival made them that way. Everybody had a theory, but in the end it didn't matter.

When Radio sent a patrol car on a dog bite, to "check for an ambulance," they usually found some kid too young to have been afraid. Blacks, whites, illegals up from Mexico, always lying absolutely still, trying to distance themselves from the pain that hurt them worse if they cried. Their eyes gave away nothing, pupils huge and distant in their bloody faces as if they had just seen a miracle.

Sometimes the dogs attacked grown men, even cops, as if they wanted to die, growing bolder and more dangerous in the summer, when people stayed out after dark, and rabies began to spread. It came with warm weather, carried by the night wind and nocturnal animals gone mad—prehistoric possums with pig eyes and needle teeth, squealing in the alleys. Rats out on the sidewalks at noon, sluggish and dazed. Raccoons hissing in the nettles and high grass along polluted golf course creeks. Feral cats, bats falling from the sky, dreamy-eyed skunks staggering out of the West Hills, choking on their own tongues, their hearts shuddering with the virus they carried, an evil older than cities or civilization— messengers perhaps, sent by some brooding, wounded promise we betrayed and left for dead back when the world was still only darkness and frozen seas.

Late one night at the police club, some of the cops from North were talking about it. They'd been drinking for quite a while when a cop named Hanson said you couldn't really blame the dogs.

Well hell, who *do* you blame then?

Someone back in the corner slammed his beer down.

Fuck blame. Just kill 'em.

ONE

PORTLAND, OREGON
MAY 1975

I T HAD BEEN raining all week, spring drizzle, almost a mist, and neither of the two cops who got out of the patrol car bothered to wear a raincoat. The dispatcher had sent them to "check on the welfare" of an old man who lived alone, to see if he was dead. One of the neighbors had called. She hadn't seen him in a week and she was worried. She was afraid to answer her door, she said, what with all this crime.

Just above his gold police badge, Hanson wore a yellow "happy face" pin that he'd noticed in the bottom of his locker before roll call that afternoon. He'd picked it up back in December, off the body of a kid who'd OD'd in a gas station bathroom, sitting on the toilet. The needle was still in his arm, half-full of the China White heroin that was pouring in from Southeast Asia, through Vancouver, B.C., and down the freeway.

As the two cops walked around to the back of the old man's house, Hanson kept an eye on the windows and checked the safety snap on his holster, out of habit, as he did dozens of times during the shift.

The ragged hedge of rose bushes bordering the backyard had been battered by a freak thunderstorm the night before, and the yard was covered with rose petals, pink-veined and translucent as eyelids on the wet grass. The whole yard smelled of roses.

Dana, the big cop, knocked on the door with his flashlight and shouted, "Police." Hanson picked up a rose petal, smelled it, then put it on his tongue. "Police," Dana shouted.

The windows were locked and warped and painted shut, but they managed to break one free and force it open an inch or two.

"I guess he isn't just away on a trip," Hanson said when the smell drifted out.

When Dana kicked the backdoor, the knob fell off and the little window shattered, sucking a greasy curtain out through the splinters. He kicked again and the door shuddered. A shard of glass dropped onto the concrete stoop.

"Maybe you're too old for this," Hanson said.

Dana smiled at him, a little out of breath, took half a step back and drove the heel of his boot into the door. The frame splintered and the door swung open in a spray of dust and paint chips.

A burner on the electric stove in the kitchen glowed sullenly, its heat touching Hanson's cheek through the hot sweet air. Dirty dishes were piled by the sink where gray dishwater rippled with mosquito larvae.

"Police," Hanson called, "police officers," breathing shallowly as they walked into the living room.

Thousands of green flies covered the windows like beaded curtains, shimmering in the gray light as they beat against the glass.

The old man was in the living room, lying on his back. His chest and belly had ballooned, arching his back in a wrestler's bridge, as if he was still struggling to raise up off the floor. His eyes and beard and shaggy hair sparkled silver-white, boiling with maggots, and broken capillaries shadowed his face like brutal makeup. He was wearing a set of one-piece long underwear that buttoned up the front, and he was so swollen that all the buttons had torn out, ripping open from neck to crotch.

The old man's chest and belly were waxy, translucent, mottled with terrible blue bruises where the blood had pooled after he died. One foot had turned black as iron. The two cops stood over him, breathing through their mouths. The furnace hummed beneath the floor, pumping out heat. Flies droned and battered the windows. Something brushed Hanson's leg, and he spun around, reaching for his pistol.

It was a small dog, his muzzle gray with age, the fur worn off the backs of his legs. He looked up at them without fear, with the dignity that old dogs have. Both blind eyes were milky white.

"Look here," Dana said. "It's just the po-lice." He knelt down and slowly moved his hand to stroke the dog's head. "Been hot in here, hasn't it?" He went into the kitchen and brought back a bowl of water which the dog lapped up slowly, not stopping until it was all gone.

They turned off the furnace, then beat the flies away from the front windows and opened them. Hanson saw the envelope taped to the wall above the telephone. Where the address should be were the words, "When I die please see that my daughter, Sarah Thorgaard, gets this envelope. Her phone number is listed below. Thank you." It was signed, "Cyrus Thorgaard." Beneath his signature he'd written in ink, "I'd appreciate it if you'd look after my dog Truman."

Hanson called the number and a man answered. "Hello," Hanson said, "this is Officer Hanson from the police bureau. Could I speak to Sarah Thorgaard, please?"

"That's my wife's maiden name. She's not here."

Out on the sidewalk, a man wearing a black vinyl jacket and plaid bell-bottom pants stood looking at the house.

"What's the problem?"

"I'm afraid her father is dead. At his house on Albina Street?"

The man on the sidewalk started to walk away, then stopped and looked at the house again. The phone droned in Hanson's ear.

"Looks like a natural death. There's an envelope here addressed to your wife. We could bring it by your house if you'd like, Mister . . . ?"

"Jensen. I'll come and get it."

"He's been dead for quite a while, sir. Maybe . . ."

"I'd rather not have a police car in my driveway. I can be there in ten minutes."

"That'll be fine," Hanson said, watching the man out front walk away down the block. He hung up the phone and went into the bedroom. The covers on the bed had been thrown back, and he wondered if the old man had gotten up just so he wouldn't die in bed. Books filled the wall-to-wall glass-fronted bookcases, and magazines were stacked on the floor beneath them—*Scientific American*, *Popular Mechanics*, *National Geographic*, something called *Science and Design*, published in England, many of them dating back to the thirties. Hanson picked one up and thumbed through it. The old man had bracketed paragraphs and underlined sentences in pencil. Down the margin of one page he'd written, "This kind of easy ambiguous conclusion is the heart of the problem. They're afraid to make the difficult decisions."

Some of the books went back to the 1800s. Hanson picked up one with the word "STEAM" embossed in gold letters across the leather cover. A golden planet Earth spun beneath the word "STEAM," powered through its orbits by two huge elbow pipes, one sticking out of the Pacific Ocean, the other rising from North Africa, both of them pumping golden clouds of steam. The book was filled with flow charts and numerical tables, exploded diagrams of valves and heat-return systems, fine engravings of steam boilers. It was as if the book contained all the rules for a predictable steam-driven universe, a world of order and dependability.

Photographs covered one wall, old photographs where the hands and faces of people passing in the background were streaked and blurred by their movement. The old man, alive, looked out at Hanson from them, his age changing from twenty to fifty, a mustache there, a beard in one, looking out from the beams and pipes of a power plant, standing by a Ford coupe on a dirt road, holding a stringer of trout, looking out from each one as if he had something to tell him, something that Hanson had been trying to figure out for a long time. A double-barreled Winchester shotgun with exposed hammers stood propped in the corner next to the bed. Hanson picked it up, brought it to his shoulder, then lowered it and thumbed it open. Brass-cased buckshot rounds shone in the steel receiver.

Hanson looked out through the bedroom door at the old man. He thought of the thunderstorm the night before, and imagined lightning, like flash powder for old photos, blazing through the house, lighting the room for an instant, freezing it in time. The old man, the dog, and the green and gold curtains of flies swarming the windows.

Dana's voice came up through the floor, calling him down to the basement.

"He made this," Dana said, spinning the chrome-silver wheel of a lathe. "Hand-ground those carbon steel blades. Look," he said, slapping the cast-iron base, "the bearings, the bed, everything. The best craftsmen make their own tools.

"That's a forge over there," he said, pointing. "He could melt steel in that. In his basement. And come on over here," he said. "Look at this work bench . . ."

"Hello?" It was the medical examiner at the top of the stairs, his face flushed, wearing a wrinkled gray suit. He looked like a salesman down on his luck. "It's a ripe one all right."

The sun had come out and the grass was steaming. Dana helped the ME unload the gurney from his station wagon, and Hanson pulled out the body bag, the acrid smell of rubberized plastic, like the dead air leaking from a tire, stunning him with memories for a moment.

They tucked the body bag under and around the old man, like a rubber sleeping bag, and zipped it closed. Hanson slipped his hands beneath the bloated shoulders and the ME took the feet.

"Real easy now," the ME said, "easy . . ."

It sounded almost like someone sitting up suddenly in the bath-tub. The weight shifted, pulling the body bag out of their arms and onto the gurney where it shuddered and lurched from side to side.

The ME said, "Damn.

"Damn," he said again. "What a week. Monday I had to police up a skydiver whose chute didn't open. That's a stupid so-called 'sport,' if you ask me. And the *next* day there was the son of a bitch—pardon my French—out in the county, who shot himself in the kitchen and left the stove on. The body popped, exploded, before I got there. One hundred and nineteen degrees in that trailer house. That's official. I hung a thermometer. I mean, is that some cheap, thoughtless behavior, or what? People just don't think. If you want to kill yourself, fine. That's your business. But show a little courtesy to others. The world goes on, you know."

A supervisor had to cover any situation involving a death, even if it was a natural, and Sgt. Bendix was out in front of the house, standing by his patrol car, nodding and listening to the man in khaki trousers and blue dress shirt who had driven up in a gray Mercedes. The ME drove off in his county station wagon as Dana and Hanson walked over to them. Hanson's wool uniform was still damp, heavy and hot in the sun. It would be another month, he thought, before the department switched over to short-sleeve shirts. Bendix watched them come, tapping his own chest as he looked straight at Hanson. "The happy face," Dana said.

Hanson glanced down at the yellow face that smiled from his shirt. "Mister Happy Face says, 'If you like everybody, everybody will like you.'" He took it off and dropped it in his breast pocket.

They nodded to Mr. Jensen as Bendix introduced him.

"He was a smart man," Jensen said. "An engineer. I guess you could call him an inventor. Not that he ever made much money.

"This used to be a nice neighborhood," he said, looking at Hanson. "My wife grew up here."

Hanson nodded.

"We had the money to move him out of this neighborhood and put him in a home. I mean a nice place. Where he could be with people his own age. He wouldn't even talk about it," Jensen said, looking at the house where a seedy robin in the front yard cocked his head and studied a patch of dead grass.

"In denial," Sgt. Bendix said.

The robin pecked the grass.

"A refusal to come to terms with his own mortality," Sgt. Bendix said. "Quite common at his age."

The bird flew off when Aaron Allen's bloodred Cadillac pulled out of an alley down the block, stolen radio speakers duct-taped inside all four doors booming through the neighborhood. It sat there shuddering, the tinted windows rolled up, then crossed the street and disappeared into the mouth of the opposite alley.

"He said he'd shoot anyone who tried to move him," Jensen said.

"What about the dog?" Dana said.

"What?" Jensen said.

"An old dog, about *this* big."

"That dog's still alive?"

"Correct. Sir."

"Well, what *about* it?

"Sergeant," he said, turning to Bendix, "can your people take care of that for me?" He looked at his watch. "I have a funeral to work out. And I'm going to have to think of something to do with that house and all the *shit* in it . . ."

"We'll take care of it, Mister Jensen," Sgt. Bendix said.

"Can we do that?" he said, turning to Dana and Hanson.

"Sure," Dana said.

"I'll get the envelope," Hanson said.

The envelope was taped to the wall just below a large framed document that declared Cyrus Thorgaard to be a member of "The

International Brotherhood of Machinists." It was printed in color with gilt edges. The fine engraving in each corner showed men at work—turning a silver cylinder of steel on a lathe, measuring tolerances with calipers, others standing at a forge, yellow and gold clouds of heat and smoke rolling over them. The center of the document was dominated by a huge black and silver steam engine tended by powerfully built men wearing engineer's caps.

"Do me a favor and get the rest of that asshole's information? I'm afraid I'll say something that'll get me some time off."

"You're gettin' awful sensitive in your old age," Hanson said, peeling the envelope off the wall.

"You know what's gonna happen to that?" Dana said, looking at the document. "You know what he's gonna do with that, and the tools, and the books? All of it? If the neighborhood assholes don't set the place on fire first. After ripping off anything they can trade for dope."

He looked out the door at Jensen and Bendix. "He's gonna shit-can it. He won't even take the trouble to give it away. He'll just pay somebody to haul it to the dump."

The dog stood staring up at the cops, listening.

"You come on with us," Dana said, kneeling down to stroke the dog's head. "It'll be okay."

After Jensen and Sgt. Bendix left, Dana took a hammer and a handful of nails from the basement and went around back to nail the door shut and board up the window.

Hanson walked through the house turning off lights and closing the windows. He pretended not to hear the dog following behind him, trying to keep up. He took another look around the bedroom, kneeling at the bookcases to read the titles on the lower shelves, touching the spines. He looked one more time at the photos, half hoping for some revelation, but the sun had moved, throwing them into shadow, and it would only get darker. It was too late now to do anything but finish closing the house up.

After several false starts, the dog hopped stiffly onto the bed, found his place at the foot and curled up.

"I guess you think it's all gonna be okay again *tomorrow* morning," Hanson said to the dog. "One more night and when you wake up Mister Thorgaard will be asleep there just like always." If the dog heard him, he didn't open his eyes.

"You're on your own now," Hanson said, then looked away, as if he'd heard something in the other room.

"It's a hard world out there," he said slowly, as if he was just now remembering the words, "for dogs, too."

Tendrils from the overgrown shrubbery covered the front window, snaking through the wooden frame into the room, jamming the window open, and Hanson had to pull the brittle vines free with his fingertips. His eyes went wide for a moment when he gashed his knuckle on the weather stripping, but that was his only reaction and he continued to clean the dead shrubbery free. He worked his hand farther into the frame and pulled out a nest of leaves, rotten sash cord, and cotton mattress stuffing. The three desiccated baby mice looked like they were wearing Halloween masks. Insects had eaten through their eyes into the tiny skulls, and the empty sockets were huge, inscrutable mummy eyes.

Hanson tossed the nest out the window, and through a gap in the shrubbery saw the man again. He had a nappy, half-assed Afro. The bell-bottoms covered his shoes, cuffs ragged from scraping the sidewalk, and the vinyl jacket was buttoned up to his neck, the cuffs snapped. To hide needle marks, Hanson thought.

The man looked up the street and took a half-smoked cigarette from behind his ear. "Just looking," Hanson said, trying again to close the window.

"Always *looking*," he said over his shoulder to the dog. "For something easy they can walk off with. Or a *purse* to snatch, or some old man they know they can knock down for his social security check. Whatever. The old guy eats dog food and day-old bread for the rest of the month."

The dog listened now, his cloudy blind eyes serene in the face of Hanson's anger.

"Unless he breaks his hip falling on the sidewalk and dies of pneumonia. Dumped in some fuckin' charity ward. All alone. Lying there till his lungs fill up and he *drowns*," he said, pulling on the window, then slamming it with the heel of his hand. The man on the sidewalk flipped the cigarette onto the yard and turned to walk away.

"Fuckin' *lookers*," Hanson grunted, "waiting for it to get dark. Walking around or sitting in their junk cars. Waiting . . ." he said, straining to close the window.

"God *damn*," he said, spinning and stalking across the room to the doorway where he looked back at the dog.

"I'll be right back."

"Hey," Hanson called. "You!" pushing through the screen door. "C'mere.

"You looking for somebody, my man?" Hanson said, walking up on him. "You lost?"

"I ain't doing nothing."

He had a poorly repaired harelip that gave him a slight lisp.

"New in town?"

"I'm . . ."

"Maybe I can help you find an address."

"I'm takin' a *walk.*"

"I know what you're doing. What's your name?"

"My name?"

"Yeah. What do your *buddies* call you?"

"Curtis, man. They call me Curtis. But you're not . . ."

"Curtis *what?*"

His throat worked like he was going to throw up, choking up his own name, "Barr."

"Let's see some ID."

"ID?"

Dana's hammering, at the back of the house, echoed through the neighborhood. Hanson stepped in closer until their chests were almost touching, smelling marijuana smoke, old sweat, and a sour stink like rancid meat, an odor that rides the air in prison. "You want to show me some ID," Hanson said, his eyes *on him* now, "or you want go to jail?"

"Jail?"

Hanson glared at his head as if he was trying to set the lopsided Afro on fire with his eyes. The hammering stopped.

"Why you always gotta *fuck* with somebody," he said, pulling up one leg of his bell-bottoms. "I mean . . . *shit.*" He unzipped his boot, pulled down his sock, and took out a wallet.

"Photo ID," Hanson said.

He peeled off a sweaty driver's license.

"This is expired," Hanson said, holding it with the tips of two fingers. "What's your current address?"

"Same as it says there."

"Lemme see *that,*" Hanson said.

"See *what?*" Curtis said, closing the wallet. "I done *showed* you . . ."

"The property receipt," Hanson said, indicating the yellow piece of paper just peeking out of the wallet. "Let's see it."

"Oh, *man* . . ."

"Let's see it."

The city jail had issued him the receipt the night before. He'd been released that morning.

"This says your name is *Quentin* Barr. Which *is* it, then? Curtis or Quentin?"

"Curtis is, you know, my nickname."

"What were you arrested for, *Quen*-ton?"

"It wasn't, they said. You know. Burglary, but I didn't . . ."

"Where's your hat?" Hanson said, studying the receipt. "It says here you had a 'brown suede cap.' "

"I don't know, officer. They lost it."

"You should file a complaint," Hanson said, handing the yellow receipt back to him. "Don't walk on this block anymore."

"Say *what?*"

"Look at me," Hanson said softly.

The hammering started again, louder, the echo ringing off houses across the street. Quentin looked at Hanson's ear, over his shoulder, down at his chest.

"I said, *look* at me."

Finally, he did, with the eyes of a whipped, limping animal that will bite if you show any weakness.

"Not this block," Hanson said. "If there's a burglary, or attempted fucking burglary, *anything* on *this* block, I'm gonna look for you. Quentin."

Quentin opened his mouth, his throat working silently.

"That jacket must be awful hot," Hanson said. "Seems like you'd want to roll up the sleeves."

Quentin tried to smile, his upper lip twitching.

"Good-bye," Hanson said. "Have a nice day. Sir."

THE OLD DOG seemed unconcerned when they put him in the patrol car, as if he had been expecting them all those days and nights alone in the house with the body.

The dog sat up in the backseat of the car, behind the cage, as they drove through the ghetto, past the porno movies and burned-out storefronts, the winos passed out in doorways, junkies wandering, dreamlike, in the sun.

Hanson took the happy face out of his pocket and smiled down at it. "Mister Happy Face says, 'If you keep smiling everything will turn out fine.'"

He pinned it back on his shirt.

"Jesus," he said, gesturing out the window where black and red graffiti spooled along the broken sidewalks and the windows of abandoned stores, "It's all going to shit. Like, faster than before."

"Since that China White started coming down the freeway," Dana said.

"Sometimes I wonder what's gonna happen. You know? What's gonna happen next?"

"Just gonna get worse," Dana said, eyes on the street.

"Yeah," Hanson said, as they passed a bag lady screaming at the sky, "I know. But then what happens?"

"Then it's the end of the world. The cockroaches take over."

ZURBO, HIS FOOT in a cast, was working the desk at North, watching the little TV he'd brought from home. As Hanson reached to open the precinct door, he saw Zurbo's eyes in the silver convex mirror down the hall. Like all good cops, Zurbo watched everything, all the time.

"You looking for the Animal Control office?" Zurbo said, his back still to them, as they walked in with the dog. "This is *North* Precinct. We just *shoot* 'em up here," he said, pulling the sawed-off double-barreled shotgun from beneath the desk.

Hanson heard the sound of distant helicopters, the unmistakable shudder of Hueys.

"Zurbo, that broken toe's *got* to be healed by now. I think you're milking disability," Dana said.

"Hey, the doctor knows best. I'm just a dumb cop."

"Getting paid eleven dollars an hour to watch TV. My tax dollars at work," Hanson said, glancing at the TV.

"What's with the mutt?" Zurbo said.

"How about taking care of him till end of shift?" Dana said, setting the dog down on the dark red tile.

"He better not shit on the floor."

"If he does, *I'll* clean it up."

The TV volume was turned down, almost drowned out by radio traffic from North and East precinct patrol cars. The early news was on, footage of helicopters rising from the American Embassy in Saigon, Vietnamese civilians in white shirts trying to hang on to the skids, dropping back to the roof, one by one, as American soldiers, shadows in the chopper doors, drove rifle butts down on their hands.

Zurbo raised up and looked over the counter.

"Fuckin' dog's *blind*," he said.

"I think that's against the Geneva Convention," Hanson said, nodding at the shotgun.

"Over there, *in*-country maybe, but back here in The World you can use it on civilians. No problem. Why don't I call Animal Control to come and get him?"

"We'll pick him up at the end of the shift."

"Okay. If you can handle the desk for a minute, in a professional fucking manner, I'll see if I can find a blanket for Barko there."

On the TV, a reporter looked into the camera, shouting over the roar of helicopters.

"Been showing that all fucking night," Zurbo said.

Delicate women on the roof raised their arms to the departing helicopters, the rotor blast tearing at the folds of their silk *ao dai*, whipping their long black hair.

"Shit," Zurbo said. He punched the TV off with the muzzle of the shotgun and limped out from behind the desk. He bent down to look at the dog, and shook his head. "He's gotta be over a hundred, in dog years."

"Helen's not gonna let me keep that dog," Dana said as they pulled out of the lot to cover Larkin at a family fight, on the way to their district. "You, on the other hand . . ."

"I don't need a dog. You're the one who told him, 'It'll be okay,' not me . . ."

Five Sixty Two, Larkin said over the radio, people screaming in the background, *can you step it up a little?*

Hanson snatched up the mike. "On our way," he said, flipping on the overheads and the siren as Dana accelerated through a red light.

Hanson smiled, his eyes bright, as if remembering some childhood prank. "They eat 'em," he said. "In Hong Kong."

"What?" Dana said, rolling his window up against the siren.

"Dogs. People eat 'em in Hong Kong."

———

That was the week there were so many moths, millions of them. Word at the precinct was that they swarmed that way only once every seven years, though someone else said it was because of the new nuclear plant up north. A long stretch of road back to the precinct was lined with a monotonous, evenly spaced row of new streetlights, those big brushed aluminum poles that rise, then bend over the road like a hand on a wrist. The moths covered those lights like bee swarms, throwing themselves at the yellow bulbs again and again until they crippled a wing and fell to the street so that the puddles of light on the asphalt below the streetlights were heaped with thousands of dead and dying moths.

Each time the patrol car passed beneath one of the lights that night, on the way back to the precinct at the end of shift, the tires made a fragile ripping sound, as though the street was still wet with rain. The sweet stink of the old man's corpse hung in Hanson's wool uniform the way cigarette smoke hangs in the hair of the woman you're sleeping with. Dana kept their speed steady, and the ripping sound continued as regularly and softly as breathing.

Hanson looked out at the night. He adjusted his handcuffs where they were digging into the small of his back, then reached down and touched the leather-bound book he had slipped beneath the seat of the patrol car, the one that showed the Earth spinning itself through golden clouds of steam.

"I can take the dog," he said.

TWO

JUNE 1975

THE PRECINCT HEADQUARTERS rose like a cliff-face north of the river, massive blocks of stone quarried at the turn of the century by convicts long dead now, their crimes forgotten. Black iron straps barred the windows looking out on the flagpole and a granite slab hewn from the same quarry, a monument to bad habits, carelessness, and dumb luck, brass plates bolted down its face, the names of officers killed in the line of duty.

North was the last of the original precinct buildings now that East Precinct had moved into a renovated supermarket, responsible for "the Avenue"—the poor, mostly black, children and grandchildren of cheap labor shipped in by the trainload from Chicago and Atlanta to work in the shipyards, building the destroyers and liberty ships that would defeat Hitler and the Japanese.

The sergeants and lieutenants at North were there because they'd screwed up somewhere else. North was not a good place to build a career. The crime rate, especially violent crimes and crimes involving firearms, was the highest in the city, and rising every year. More crime meant more police-suspect confrontation and more opportunities for things to go wrong. The rest of the city was white and didn't really care what the niggers did as long as they did it to each other, but they were quick to call the police "racists," and the local newspaper was run by East Coast liberals. The safest way to ride out a two- or three-year command exile to North was to stay in the office, do as little as possible, and avoid anything not clearly covered in the *Manual of Rules and Procedures.*

The patrolmen who worked out of North, the street cops, asked to be assigned there because the Avenue was where the crime was, and they liked the work. They were the troublemakers, hot dogs, bad boys, adrenaline junkies back from Vietnam, overtime specialists making sixty grand a year. "Supercops" with something to prove, afraid they were queers or cowards. True believers, racists, sadists, manic-depressives using adrenaline and exhaustion to keep their demons at bay. All seemed sane as long as they walked the streets with a gun—most of them good cops.

HANSON TOOK THE stone steps two at a time, the black Pachmeyer grip of his Model 39 patting the small of his back, and pushed through the frosted glass door with "NORTH PRECINCT" stenciled in black letters. He walked down the hall past a map of North Precinct clumped with color-coded pushpins marking the locations of crimes committed that calendar year.

"Hanson. Could I have a word with you?"

"Yes, sir," Hanson said, turning and walking to the open door of Sgt. Bendix's office, "at your service."

Bendix was talking on the phone. "That's the policy as of now. Access and egress will remain open only to Native Americans with valid ID, who are sober. That's straight from the deputy chief . . . At least one quarter Indian blood," he said, looking under the piles of paper on his desk. "Exactly. No one can," he said, hanging up the phone. Certificates from regional law enforcement schools, for fingerprinting, photography, and polygraph administration hung on the wall behind him, beneath an Associate of Arts diploma in psychology from the local community college.

"Come in," he said, opening and closing desk drawers, looking for something, "have a seat. Just put that on the floor," he said, nodding at the box of blue flyers from the police supply store he owned a part interest in.

Hanson took the box off the chair and sat down while Bendix finished working his way through the drawers. The flyers advertised a *Summer Sale* featuring fingerprint powder, nylon ankle hobbles, and a transparent clipboard made of "ballistic Plexiglas."

"I was going over the stat-sheets today," he said, giving up his search, "and noticed that you and Dana are both way down on moving violations. In fact, you're low man on the totem pole."

"It gets pretty busy out there. Not much time to look for movers."

"Lieutenant Pullman was asking me about it. Let's keep him happy."

Hanson stood up and gave Bendix a two-fingered, Boy Scout salute. "We'll try to snag a few for the lieutenant," he said, then walked down to the report writing room. He'd come in early, as he usually did, to page through crime reports from the graveyard and day shifts to catch up with what had happened in the precinct during the past sixteen hours.

He thumbed through the clipboards of crime reports, the usual family fights and burglaries and purse snatches with useless suspect information—"Male Black, 16 to 18 yrs, 5'10", med bld, blk & brn, dark clothing."

But one of the reports stopped him—an unemployed electrician, M/W, 30, Vietnam veteran, a Marine with two Purple Hearts. Having filled out the paperwork and observed the two-week "cooling off" period required for the purchase of a handgun, he'd gone back to the Kmart where he picked up the gun and a box of half-jacketed, hollow-point ammo. Then he went out to his Ford 250 pickup in the parking lot—lic #312-BOL—loaded the gun, stuck the barrel in his mouth, and fired one round. The clerk who rang up the sale said that he seemed cheerful, that he smiled and said, "Have a nice day," when he left with the four-inch Colt Python .357 Magnum/ser # 95623.

Before he and Dana were issued the double-action 9mm automatics Hanson had carried a Python. Top of the line .357 Magnum, heavy frame, ventilated rib, factory-tuned trigger pull. A beautiful weapon. They'd melt the ex-Marine's Python down with the next batch of confiscated weapons piled up in the property room—the plastic-handled Rhones and RGs, cheap .25 automatics, 7-Eleven holdup guns that might just *click* when you pull the trigger, or surprise you and go off in your hand without warning.

The kind of junk weapons half the cops at North carried in their briefcases, "throwdown guns," just in case they shot someone who wasn't armed after all.

The property room dumped the guns in 55-gallon drums—old breaktop thirty-twos with pitted barrels and peeling chrome plating, hacksawed shotguns with wired-on stocks, cutdown twenty-twos, WWII Lugers, broomhandle Mausers and Jap Nambus frozen with rust. Spring-loaded tear gas pens bored out to fire a single twenty-two, as likely to go off in your pocket as anything else. Army surplus flare guns and five-dollar starting pistols—along with the switchblades, butterfly knives, bayonets, machetes, case cutters, bolos, and hawk-billed linoleum knives. Pieces of pipe, hammers, hatchets, telescoping whip-batons and brass knuckles that would break your fingers if you hit anything very hard.

The city was planning to cast the melted weapons into an antiviolence monument. Hanson imagined some abstract sculpture titled "Wings," or "Peace."

Call it *Doom*, he thought, glancing up at the clock, imagining the Marine in his pickup, his cheeks exploding around the muzzle, flame venting up his nose, searing the backs off his eyeballs, blowing his teeth out. Call it *Welcome Home, G.I.*

He hung the clipboards back on the wall and rinsed out his coffee cup, studying a water-spotted poster above the sink. A well-done cartoon of two snarling, muscle-bound cops squeezed into a speeding patrol car, the left front wheel rolling over the head of a Doberman, his tongue and eyes popping out in a spray of blood that formed the word "SQUISH." The list of rules for this year's Night Dog Hunt was typed out below the cartoon.

1). Dogs may be taken by patrol car, nightstick, or a combination of the two. Shotgun and handgun kills are acceptable, but we do *not* encourage the discharge of duty weapons in violation of departmental regulations.

2). In a two-man car both officers can claim one-half point each per kill, or one officer can claim a whole point.

3). Each kill *must* be verified by another district car. Only CDKs, *Confirmed Dog Kills,* will be counted.

"Summer*time*," Hanson sang, "and the livin' is easy," taking the stairs to the locker room.

Thirty minutes later, afternoon relief was checking out their patrol cars, sirens yelping, overhead lights flashing blue and red in the sun as Hanson filled in his roll call notes.

```
HANSON #487
NORTH ''A'' RELIEF

6-15-75/Tuesday
Dist. #562 W/Dana F.
Sgt. Bendix/Shop #39 (mirror still not fixed)
Sunny & warm (my vest still wet from last night)

Movers—Bendix says we're ''low man on the totem
pole.''

Check status of comp time.

Fox W/DEA so-called Task Force—list of half-
assed drug dealers they are ''surveilling'' & says
''don't hassle them.'' FUCK HIM.

Armed robbery of Plaid Pantry on Lombard St. M/W
w/SEX tattooed on middle finger of left hand.
blu&white short bed PU, poss. Chev. primer on
pass door.

Call Falcone?
```

Hanson inked out "Fuck him," in case the notebook was ever subpoenaed, and put it in his hip pocket. He took the shotgun from under his arm and worked the action, smiling at the *snack snack* of oiled steel. Two cars over, Zurbo threw his briefcase in the trunk of one of the new Novas, while Neal flashed the overhead lights, bleeped the siren and checked the PA system.

"Zurbo," Hanson shouted, loading the shotgun with red, double-00 buckshot rounds, "you guys working selective enforcement on graveyard again?"

"Need the OT."

"And the first confirmed Night Dog kill of the season," Neal said. "Hey," he said, "remember Ira Foresman?"

"Ira *Fore*-skin. He's back in the joint, isn't he?"

"Just got out. Three *days* ago," Neal said, laughing.

"He was fucked-up, pissing on the side of the bus station last night. We popped him for indecent exposure, and CCW. Had a sharpened screwdriver in his pocket."

Zurbo shook his head.

"Two hours of overtime by the time we finished processing him," he said. "Another twenty-nine bucks on my next paycheck."

"Let's go," Neal said. "I gotta pick up my dry cleaning before five."

They drove over the curb and up the street, Zurbo's voice ringing from the loudspeaker on the roof of the patrol car, "Surrender, and you won't be harmed. We are your friends. Trust us, we're police officers."

Hanson locked the shotgun into the steel cuff under the dash, taped the hotsheet on the glovebox, then thumped the spit-and-snot-smeared Plexiglas cage with the heel of his hand to be sure it was latched. When he sat down, stale cigarette smoke seeped out of the broken-down bench seat, mixing with odors of motor oil, urine, sweat, and the sour stink of vomit.

The little phallic plastic and aluminum ozone generator mounted on the dash didn't filter the odor. It didn't seem to do anything at all. They'd been installed in the patrol cars the month before, and were supposed to fill the car with stress-reducing positive ions.

Last year there had been talk of using federal funds to install radio beacons in all the patrol cars to mark their location on a big electronic map at Central Precinct. The police union had killed that plan. They didn't want some deputy chief coordinating police cars like a general in a helicopter, a practice that had gotten a lot of soldiers killed in Vietnam.

With the war over, it seemed like the government had more money than it could spend. Having lost the war with Vietnam, they decided to fight "the war on crime" and, most recently, "the war on drugs," funding almost any crackpot proposal that came in the mail. Before the ozone generators, there had been the water-filled, energy-absorbing rubber bumpers for patrol cars. A pair of them weighed six hundred pounds, cutting acceleration and gas mileage in half. The compressed-air net launchers—"The Immobilizer" / *Less than lethal, humane and more acceptable to the public*—never reached the precincts.

"Let's try for a couple movers," Dana said, opening the door and getting behind the wheel, "before things get busy."

Hanson picked up the radio mike and cleared from the precinct, "Five Sixty Two, low man on the traffic totem pole, is out there."

Five Sixty Two clear . . . the dispatcher responded, *at . . . four ten* P.M. . . . *other car calling?*

They stopped for the light at Greeley where a blind kid in a Black Liberation T-shirt crossed the street in front of them, his head twitching with palsy as he tapped his way across with a white cane. Hanson closed his eyes, pretending he was blind, until the car began moving again.

"I ran into Officer Falcone downtown last weekend," Hanson said. "She was with some citizen who looked like a used-car salesman."

"You gonna call her, or what? Want me to chaperone?"

"You got to think it through before you go to bed with a police officer. You know, taking off our guns and nightsticks, our steel-toed boots, pulling down our baggy uniform pants. 'Here, momma. Lemme help you outta that bulletproof vest.' *Ugh ugh.* Going at it like a couple of armadillos."

They turned away from the river and took the freeway where Hanson checked license plates against the list of stolen cars on the hotsheet taped to the dash. A massive system of overpasses and on-ramps arced above them, the hum and throb and echo of traffic like thunder. The sideview mirror sagged on its broken mount, chattering against the passenger door.

"What kind of *panties* would you wear with uniform pants? Or do the women all wear jockey shorts?"

The chromed lug-nuts of a tractor trailer spun past as they took the exit ramp into the district.

"We should get some coffee and plan our day. I need to wake up. We'll still have time to try for a mover or two."

"An excellent suggestion," Dana said, "we need a plan."

They drove south on Union Avenue, watching passing cars, parked cars, license plates, drivers, passengers, pedestrians— watching their hands and eyes, how they reacted to the police car.

"See that little storefront?" Dana said. "The way it's zoned, we could put three apartments upstairs. The owner wants sixteen thousand for it. Helen thinks he'll come down."

"My partner, the slum landlord."

"Without rental property, taxes would kill us," Dana said as they watched doors and windows, the reflection of the patrol car gliding across plate glass storefronts and the clerks and customers inside. They glanced down alleys and side streets while they listened, their windows rolled down.

"Look who's here," Hanson said, his eyes on the vibrating rearview mirror. "LaVonne."

"In Luther's old Eldorado," Dana said.

"We need to fuck with LaVonne."

Dana looked at him. LaVonne Berry was one of the names on Fox's DEA list.

"It's our district," Hanson said. "It's our *job* to fuck with LaVonne. I don't care about fuckin' drugs. He can sell all the drugs he wants, but he's an *asshole.* Remember how he broke Ira Johnson's arm with a tire iron? For *nothing.* Fox and his DEA buddies can find somebody else to 'surveille.' That's not even a real word."

Dana slowed the patrol car so the Eldorado had to pull alongside them at the next stoplight. The side and rear windows of the car were tinted black, but the driver, a muscular young black man in a gold tank top, had his window down.

"He's gonna ignore us. Doesn't even see the po-lice car, he's so cool," Hanson said. He stared at LaVonne, concentrating on his left ear. "LaVonne," Hanson whispered, his voice lost in the street noise, "here we are."

LaVonne's neck muscles tensed, brought his head slightly to the left.

"La-*vaaaahn.*"

Dana, his eyes on the stoplight, laughed.

"La-*vaaaahn.* Just a . . ." Hanson crooned as the light turned yellow for the cross street, ". . . *quick* look."

LaVonne slowly turned his head, meeting Hanson's eyes and mean smile. He mouthed the words, "Fuck you," and looked back at the light. It turned green, and his tires squealed for an instant as he accelerated. Dana pulled in behind him, turning on the overhead lights, and Hanson gave radio the license plate and their location. They followed him for a block and a half, the blue and red lights flashing off his tinted rear window. Finally Hanson bleeped the siren and the Eldorado bumped over the curb into the lot of an out-of-business auto supply store, where LaVonne got out, locked the car, and leaned back against the door.

"Maybe I can talk him into going to jail," Hanson said.

"Hi, LaVonne," Hanson said, walking up to him. He shook his finger at LaVonne. "I saw you peek at me back there." LaVonne watched passing cars as if Hanson wasn't there. Dana leaned over the trunk, looking into the back window.

"Got any dope in the car?" Hanson said.

LaVonne's dark, stretch-marked biceps bulged as he *slowly* crossed his arms, tilted his head, and spit on the sidewalk.

"We heard a rumor that you're selling dangerous drugs."

"I don't got the *time*, Hanson."

Dana moved around to the rear door and bent down to look in the window, shielding his eyes with his hand. LaVonne pretended not to notice, but Hanson saw the tension in his neck and eyes, and stepped closer.

"Some of that *Viet*namese heroin is what we heard."

"Can't see a thing through these tinted windows," Dana said, looking up as Fox and Peetey drove slowly past in their van.

"Could we just take a quick look inside?"

"You got a search warrant?"

"To be perfectly honest, no, but . . ."

"Then I got nothing to say to you."

"But you could *consent* to a search."

Dana pulled on the door handle, shaking the car, while Hanson kept talking, "And put those rumors to rest, once and for all."

LaVonne looked over the roof of the car at Dana. "You want to keep your hands off my car."

"Or you could confess," Hanson continued, "and start a new life. Get your GED in the joint, and when they let you out, hey, go to college. Get a degree in . . . psychology maybe. Study the human psyche. We need . . ."

LaVonne spit on the sidewalk in front of Hanson. "You finished then?"

"Promise me you'll think about it."

"Think about *this*," he said, cupping his crotch. "I got business to take care of," he said, reaching for his keys.

"It'll just take me a minute to write you this citation," Hanson said, pulling his citation book out. He flipped the pages back and started writing. "You're looking buffed, looking *bad*. Working out in the joint, right?"

"Citation for *what?*"

"Back there where you squealed your tires?" he said, inclining his head, still writing, "It's called 'excessive noise—tires.' When the tires spin," he explained, speaking slowly as if LaVonne was retarded, "you're not in complete control of the vehicle." He looked up and smiled at LaVonne. "It's a moving violation."

"It's a motherfuckin' *shame*, is what it is. It's some mother-fuckin' . . ."

"What color is your vehicle?" Hanson asked him, tapping his pen on the citation. "I don't know what to put here in 'color of vehicle' box. Orange?"

"Ocher," Dana said.

" 'Ocher'?" Hanson said. "Never heard of it."

"Persimmon," LaVonne said. "It's called persimmon."

"He says, 'Persimmon,' " Hanson told Dana, giving him a look, sweating with the rush of adrenaline, absolutely happy.

"Go ahead and *write* the motherfucker. I got places to go," LaVonne said, spitting again, almost hitting Hanson's boot.

Dana walked to the front of the Eldorado, pausing to look through the windshield, studying the grill, the bumper, keeping LaVonne off balance.

"You're welcome to go to court and present your side," Hanson said, filling in more boxes on the citation, "but if you spit on my shoe, you're gonna go to jail."

"You ain't shit without that badge and gun."

Hanson grinned. "Oh . . . I think I am," he said, stepping close, looking at LaVonne's bloodshot yellowish eyes, *into* them, past the brown-flecked iris, through the black pupil into his brain. "I think I'll live forever." He shifted his stance just a little, picturing blood and snot spooling out of LaVonne's broken nose. "You know what I mean?" he said, imagining LaVonne's split lips and bloody pink teeth, seeing it, thinking pain into his face and fear into his eyes, moving still closer until he could smell his breath. LaVonne leaned back against the car and looked at the sky.

"Here you are, Mister Berry," Hanson said, handing him the citation, which he folded once and put into his pocket.

"Thanks for your cooperation, sir," Hanson said, giving him a little salute, "and you have a nice day." LaVonne got into the car and they watched him drive off, just as Fox and Peetey pulled up behind the patrol car.

"Hey," Hanson told Dana, "that woke me right up. And look here," he said, waving the citation, "mover."

Fox, wearing wraparound sunglasses, watched them come up the sidewalk. He was tall, six-two at least, and wiry. He combed his black hair into a ducktail that barely passed department regulations.

"Didn't you guys get the word?" he said, looking down at them from the passenger window.

"What word is that?" Hanson said.

"Not to fuck with LaVonne Berry. We're running a deal with the DEA—and don't want to spook him."

"We really needed a mover."

Fox stared at him.

"Gosh," Hanson finally said, "I'll bet the junkies and whores just *swoon* when you look at 'em hard like that. I know it has that effect on *me*."

Dana put his hand on Hanson's back, to move him along. "Sorry, guys," he said. "It was my fault."

Fox shook his head. He took off his sunglasses and smiled at Dana as if they were a couple of old soldiers. Dana was well-respected in the department, and a lot of people couldn't understand how he got along with Hanson. Fox looked over at Hanson with red-rimmed eyes. "When I was your training officer," he said, "I thought you might turn into a good cop. I was wrong. You think it's all a joke. It's not, buddy."

Fox nodded at Dana, told Peetey over his shoulder, "Let's go," and leaned back into his seat as the van pulled away.

"Let's try for another mover before we tell radio we're clear," Hanson said. "I'm really getting into this traffic enforcement."

Down the block a blue-gray 4-door Dodge pulled away from the curb, and they watched it maneuver through traffic until it closed up with Fox's van. It wasn't anybody from one of the local agencies.

THE HOLLYWOOD MARKET, a little mom and pop grocery store, had a For Sale sign in the window, and Dana wrote the

phone number down on his clipboard as they drove past. The
market had been closed for months, ever since the owner, Mr.
Constanzo, had been hog-tied and shot in the back of the head.
Mrs. Constanzo, raped and pistol-whipped into a coma, was almost dead when the cops got there. She'd been locked in the tiny
bathroom while a crowd looted the store, carrying off or destroying any evidence the killers might have left.

"The insurance people must have finally settled with Missus
Constanzo," Dana said, clicking his pen closed and putting it back
in his pocket.

Hanson backed the car into the vacant corner lot at Union and
Dekum, where they could see the stoplight for both streets, but
south- and westbound drivers couldn't see the patrol car until
they were almost in the intersection.

"How many movers you got this month?" Hanson asked.

"Three."

"I got two. No way I'm gonna get ten this month."

"Got's to, young man, got's to," Dana said. "Goofy Larry's
gonna get real nervous and a pain in the ass if we don't. You saw
him looking in the door at roll call."

"Goofy Larry" was Lt. Pullman's nickname. He'd been in
charge of a hostage situation at Central Precinct a couple of years
before, and one of his men had killed a hostage—the forty-eight-
year-old grandmother of the gunman—as she ran screaming out
the backdoor. He'd shot her in the head with a 12-gauge shotgun
slug, the size of a golf ball. It looked bad on TV. That had gotten
Lt. Pullman transferred to North, and now he was trying to work
his way up to captain and out of there. They sat through the cycles
of the stoplight, watching first one street, then the other, traffic
starting and stopping. The light changed from green to yellow, and
Hanson talked to a red VW bug south on Union. "Okay. Okay,
come on now," he said, leaning forwards, hand on the gearshift,
"come on. Blow it . . ."

The car rolled to a stop.

They watched traffic west on Dekum.

South on Union.

A young white guy, driving a van with "DEWEY THE LOCK
DOCTOR" painted on the side, stopped at the light and pointed at
Hanson.

"Ambushing innocent citizens?" he shouted.

"Nobody's innocent, Dewey," Dana said on the PA.

When the light turned green he waved and drove on. The light turned yellow.

"How's that dog working out?" Dana said.

"Truman?"

The light turned red. They looked up Union.

"It's nice to have somebody to talk to," Hanson said.

Five Eighty, Radio said.

"Five Eighty," the district car answered.

Uh, Five Eighty, we've got a report of a naked man standing in the street at Seventeen and Killingsworth, holding something between his eyes.

"What was that last part?"

The radio buzzed as the dispatcher keyed his microphone in the communication center, laughter echoing in the background, *Uh, Five Eighty. That's what it says on the card here. 'Holding something between his eyes.'*

Right. We'll check it out, Five Eighty said. A moment later he added, *and let you know.*

They heard Aaron Allen's radio, then saw the old Cadillac, northbound on Union. The drip-marked, $39.95 paint job had faded, oxidized paint eating through the finish like a rash. The vinyl top was cracked and brown, sloughing off the roof, the tail fins scabbed with crumbling body filler. It reminded Hanson of a dismembered body that had turned up in the river the summer before.

The thumping bass echoed off the boarded-up storefronts behind the patrol car, getting louder as the Cadillac approached the intersection. *"Dum-*dum, *Dum-*dum, *Dum-*dum," Hanson said, in time with the radio, imitating the shark's theme from *Jaws,* the movie that was playing everywhere that summer.

None of the four kids in the car was older than fifteen. Lithe and graceful as dancers, street kids without fathers, consciences, or any sense of a future, they supported themselves with purse snatches, burglaries, shoplifting and strong-arm robberies.

The light turned yellow.

"Come on, you little fucker," Hanson hissed. "Shit," he said, when the car, big as a cabin cruiser, lurched to a stop, rocking on its worn suspension, the feral children jerking their heads and shoulders to the radio, like striking snakes, the DJ shouting over the music.

"*. . . you understand what I'm sayin'? This the worl' famous, the legendary, one an' only, Wardell makin' the scene. Get down witch me, I'm gon' set. You. Free. All the way till midnight, when Mister Jones keep his appointments, takin' you through the night . . .*

The supreme team request line open, an' I'm talkin' to . . . say what, baby? 'Raylene?' Talkin' to Raylene. On the worl' famous. How you doin', Raylene? Uh, huh. No, baby . . ."

Aaron looked over at them, his shark's eyes black as rivets.

The light turned green, and they drove off, Wardell the DJ talking through some kind of echo box. "*. . . supreme-eme-eme-eme team-eme-eme and the sex machine-ine-ine . . . get it up now, check it out, uh-huh . . .*"

Hanson checked the license number against the number on the "Aaron Allen" index card in the shoebox full of mug shots. There was no mug shot. They needed a court order to take a juvenile's picture, and they were almost impossible to get.

An old patrol car, police markings bleeding through a coat of flat black paint, crossed the intersection trailing blue smoke. The driver, a white guy, stared at them from behind army surplus tanker's goggles.

"Equipment violation," Dana said. " 'Excessive smoke.' Not a mover."

"Looks about like a North Precinct car," Hanson said.

They'd watched the light through two more cycles when Hanson said, "Here comes Mister 'Excessive Smoke.' "

He was a block away, back straight, chin up, striding stiffly towards them like he was counting each step. The afternoon sun flashed off a big silver belt buckle and the steel-tipped toes of his black cowboy boots glowed like live coals.

"Looks like a fat third grader who got big," Dana said.

"That's kinda what I looked like when I tried to march," Hanson said. "My drill instructor in basic training said I marched like I had a Baby Ruth bar up my ass."

He was big and very pale, wearing black pants and a long-sleeved black shirt buttoned up to his chin, white salt stains showing under the arms. His blond hair was shaved to a boot-camp fuzz, and he wore a small transistor radio on his belt, a wire going to one ear.

"They just let him *out* of somewhere," Hanson said, keeping one eye on the stoplight.

"A different kind of an individual," Dana said. "He's plugged into a whole different place."

At the corner he looked up and down the Avenue, executed a right face and crossed the street.

"Oh, good," Hanson said, as he unholstered his pistol and held it out of sight, just below the open car window.

"Crazy people can't resist you," Dana said, holding his pistol between his leg and the door. "The psychotic's friend. I'm not sure what that says about you."

He walked straight to Hanson's side of the car and leaned in the window. Behind the scratched plastic lenses, his watery blue eyes were dilated.

"Yes, sir," Hanson said, watching the man's small, pale hands, "what can I do for you?"

"You know the drill," he said, cutting his eyes across the Avenue to an out-of-business gas station where a pair of yellow cabs were parked side by side, their drivers talking. "We can't talk about it here on the street." His breath smelled like burnt popcorn.

"Why not?"

"I know I don't have to tell you that," he said, pulling the goggles down around his neck.

He jerked his head towards the cabs, and when Hanson only looked at him he said, "You went to the academy, correct?"

Hanson nodded, breathing through his mouth. The burnt smell of the man's breath strong in the car.

He snorted, then looked at Hanson as if he was waiting for the *real* answer.

"Would you please step back from the car just a little?" Hanson said.

Dana opened his door and put one foot on the pavement.

"You really don't remember me, do you? Okay. Fair enough. Fine. But don't you think . . ."

He turned away from the window, pulling the goggles on as a black kid passed by on the sidewalk, wearing an old high school letter jacket that didn't fit, a big letter "C" on the back. When the kid had passed, the man looked at Hanson through the goggles as if to say, *"Now,* do you understand?" Finally, he sighed and asked Hanson, "What does your manual say about *that?*"

"About what?" Hanson said.

"Okay. Fine. Disregard. For now. But, don't you think it's a *little* irregular . . . two nigger cabdrivers just happen to be across the street?" He looked over the top of the car at the cabs, took the earplug out, tapped it on the side of the patrol car, and put it back in, listening.

"Critical incident drills," he said. "Okay?"

"Critical incident drills?" Hanson said, glancing over at Dana, arching his eyebrows.

"You guys just don't get it, do you?" he said, then looked at his feet and snorted. He leaned into the car window and tried to smile, but it was more like a grimace, as if his teeth hurt, teeth the color of dirty motor oil. "What is another name for . . ."

Dana had gotten out of the car and stepped back to the rear door. "What's *your* name, brother?" he said, over the roof of the car.

He looked back at the cabs, pulled out his wallet and, holding it down below the window, flipped it open just long enough for Hanson to see a novelty store "Special Investigator" ID card with a postage stamp-size photo of him in one corner.

"They call me Dakota," he said, snapping the wallet closed and putting it back in his pocket. He looked at Hanson. "I understand," he said. "It's been a long time."

One of the cabs pulled out of the parking lot and he said, "No more time. I shouldn't have stopped."

He backed away from the car like a gunfighter, executed a crisp left face, and walked down the street.

Hanson shrugged. "I've never seen the guy before."

"Strange sort of fellow, wouldn't you say," Dana said, holstering his pistol and getting back in the car.

"Woo woo," Hanson said, fanning the air with his hand, "getting his orders from the radio."

Five Sixty Two. Can you take an unknown problem in the Safeway at Union and Killingsworth?

"Just like us," Dana said, picking up the microphone. "On our way," he said. "Who's our complainant?"

The complainant hung up. Said he was in the produce section.

THE REPORT-WRITING room smelled like coffee, the big urn bubbling while the afternoon relief finished their paperwork and graveyard shift drifted down from the locker room.

"Hanson," Lt. Pullman said, looking in the door, "could you come down to my office for a minute?"

"Yes, sir," Hanson said, following him down the hall.

In the office, Hanson held up LaVonne's citation, shaking it. "Working on movers, sir."

"Have a seat," Pullman said, nodding approval of the citation. "I'm glad I caught you. You did an excellent job on that 7-Eleven shooting," he said, pulling the report from beneath a stack of old "Officer Safety Bulletins" that came in whenever a police officer was killed somewhere in the line of duty, black-bordered teletypes summarizing the incident and pointing out, after the fact, all the ways the dead cop had fucked up. "Your college background is evident in the reports you write."

"Thank you, sir."

"You did an excellent job on the search warrant last month as well. Not many patrolmen could have done that."

Hanson nodded and edged towards the door.

Other unit calling? Radio said on the monitor in Lt. Pullman's office.

"College, in addition to your Special Forces training and experience. A new breed of police officer. With a bright future.

"What's the problem with you and Detective Fox? Off the record."

"Just a personality conflict, sir."

"I, for one, would like to see you put that aside and work *with* Fox in this war on drugs we're trying to fight. Make use of your expertise and potential."

Hanson nodded.

Five Forty, go ahead.

"I'd like to have you on board."

Upstairs, Zurbo turned on his tape player, the soundtrack from the movie *The Vikings.* "Who sails with *Ragnar?*" he shouted, his voice coming down through the ceiling. His locker door boomed as he slammed a forearm into it.

Annoyed, Lt. Pullman glanced up at the ceiling, then looked back at Hanson. "Give it some thought."

"Yes, sir," Hanson said.

"Thanks for coming in."

Copy, Five Forty. You'll be jackpot with two adult males at . . . eleven forty three P.M.

———

Across town, on skid row, Dakota's room was dark, smelling of candlewax and burnt plastic. The only light came from the blinking police scanner, the volume low, *Copy, Five Forty. You'll be jackpot . . .*

Up on the third floor of Central Precinct, the radio monitor hissed from the back wall of Narcotics and Vice, Fox's office . . . *jackpot with two adult males at . . . eleven forty three* P.M.

Fox leaned back in his chair, studying the computer screen. He cleared the screen, typed in Hanson's name and social security number, and pressed ENTER.

HANSON STOPPED OFF at the Police Athletic Association bar, planning to have a couple of beers and go home, but he saw Debbie Deets sitting alone in the corner booth, and half an hour later he followed her home.

Debbie was a cop groupie, a civilian employee who worked in Records, a job she'd taken so she could be around cops. She loved cops, and she was famous for her blowjobs. Fair-skinned, she had short dark hair and full lips, a pretty girl who tended to put on weight, especially during the winter, but managed to lose it again each summer when she wore hot pants and halter tops.

She lived with a roommate in one of the new apartment complexes designed for "swinging singles," a gated cluster of redwood-and-cedar apartments so new they still smelled of plaster and raw wood. It was called "Habitat 2," the name carved in a spotlighted cedar log at the entrance, and it reminded Hanson of the elaborate add-on cluster of gerbil cages Zurbo had set up in the garage for his daughter.

The living room was furnished with chrome and glass; grainy, polyurethaned pine; a slice-of-burl coffee table; and high-tech erotic prints of women and sports cars. Debbie smiled and put her finger to her lips as they walked past her roommate's bedroom. Hanson noticed that her "mood ring" had turned black.

She put on a John Denver tape and brought him a Heineken beer and a frosted mug. She examined the leaves of the fern hanging in a macrame basket, then mist-sprayed it with a little brass atomizer, while he thumbed through an issue of *Playboy* he'd picked up on the night table.

"You know," Debbie said, holding up fern fronds and spraying them, one by one, "they've hooked plants up to polygraphs and they show signs of intelligence. Isn't that amazing?"

Hanson smiled at her and nodded, sitting at the foot of her waterbed, rocking slightly as he thumbed through the magazine, trying to remember the last time he'd been there.

"Really," she said, "they respond to . . . stimulus," pushing him back onto the gurgling, bucking mattress. "You entertain yourself," she said, pulling off his shoes. "I'll be back in a minute."

While she was in the bathroom, Hanson looked over the mirrored bookcase built into the headboard of the massive bed. *The Total Woman. The Sensuous Woman. I'm OK, You're OK. Jonathan Livingston Seagull.*

"Sun-*shine*, on my *should*-ers, makes me *hap*-py . . ." John Denver sang. *A real sensitive motherfucker*, Hanson thought.

He looked in the nightstand drawer and found *The Save-Your-Life Diet, Dr. Atkins' Diet Revolution*, and *Discovering Energy and Overcoming Stress*.

"Sun-shine, in my *eyeeeeees*, can make me *cry*-yi-yi . . ." he sang along with the tape, pulling out *The Joy of Sex*, a well-worn copy with a coffee-cup ring on the cover, and thumbed through it—soft-edged but realistic drawings of couples and threesomes, absolutely relaxed, almost lethargically fingering, fondling, sucking and penetrating one another. "Good hand and mouth work practically guarantee you a good partner," the book said.

He studied a couple into "mild B&D," the text assuring him, "Chains create a tied-up and tingling look—fashionable now, and they look good on naked skin. The idea of being beaten unquestionably turns some people on, and if it does, you should try it."

"Well?"

Debbie was wearing a red string-bikini, three triangles of Lycra, strings tied in bows on each shoulder and hip. She turned around, giving him a view from behind. "I've been working on my tan," she said.

"You look great," Hanson told her, and she did.

"Doing research?" she said, nodding at *The Joy of Sex*. "I'll join you."

Afterwards, she lay with her head still in the hollow of his thigh. She tipped her head, put her lips against the base of his belly, and blew a long raspberry against it. He felt her muffled giggle against his belly. "Well," she said, "how was it . . . how *are* you? Was that good?"

"Great," Hanson said, looking at the Happy Face coffee mug on her dresser, doubled in the reflection of the pink, tinted mirror. "Whoa. Yeah."

"*Giving* pleasure turns me on," she said.

Hanson fell asleep listening to the wind moan through the corridor between units. The aluminum windows buzzed each time one of the big trucks downshifted to take the hill out on the freeway.

He woke up, hung over, to the sound of shouting, and Led Zeppelin's "Whole Lotta Love," pounding through the wall from the other bedroom. He got up, wrote Debbie a note, and slipped out into the living room. A white guy with a bushy blond Afro and a gold chain around his neck was laying on the sofa in his underwear, smoking a cigarette.

"How you doin', man," he said. "You happen to be heading towards the east side?"

"Sorry," Hanson lied. "Gotta go downtown."

"No problem. Have a nice day," he said, and Hanson stepped outside and closed the door.

To the east, out by the airport, aircraft, stacked up and waiting to land, floated like UFOs.

THREE

THEY STOPPED FOR coffee at the Town Square without notifying Radio. They both had packsets, little walkie-talkie radios, on their belts, so they could monitor radio traffic inside.

The Town Square was cool and humid, like the inside of a refrigerator that needed cleaning. It was "mother's day," the day that welfare checks came in the mail, and the bar was crowded.

"Look here," a woman at the bar said, "better act right, ya'll. It's the *po*-lice."

No one looked, watching the TV on the shelf over the cash register. The fuzzy picture throbbed with unnatural blues and greens, warping then flopping back into shape every few seconds as Godzilla lurches through exploding oil tanks, backhanding high-rise apartments into plaster dust and twisted girders.

"Yeah!" someone at the bar shouted, "The rent? You want the rent, motherfucker? My man Godzilla got something for *you*."

A hundred Japanese movie extras run in place, screaming, as chunks of concrete rain down. One of them points up, his mouth working nonstop—without a sound—until a measured English voice finally issues from his throat, "Look. The monster comes."

"*Run*, you gook motherfuckers," someone shouted from a table in the corner. "*Didi* fucking *mau.*"

"Should of drafted old Godzilla. Sent him to The 'Nam. We'd *own* that fucked-up country now."

The movie cut to a news anchor, looking up from his desk, his tie loosened. "Coming up at six," he said, "charges that the United States *abandoned* its allies in Vietnam, and," he went on, smiling now, "a look behind the scenes at a Las Vegas . . ."

Hanson walked around the divider that separated the bar from the lunch counter, its plastic flowers fuzzy with grease and dust, studded with the sparkling bodies of dead green flies. "*Good* afternoon, Gladys," he said as he sat down at the counter.

Gladys looked up from a *Watchtower* magazine, her harlequin-frame glasses magnifying her eyes.

"Hello, Hanson. Coffee?"

"Yes, ma'am, if you would."

"And coffee for me," Dana said, sitting down.

"Two coffees," she said.

When Hanson heard Fox's voice on the packset, he turned up the volume and stared at it.

Go ahead Bravo One.

"Could we get a meet with the district car at Mississippi and Fremont?"

Five Six Two?

Hanson picked up the packset, looked at Dana, then spoke into it, "Uh, we're quite a ways off the district," he lied. "Out by the airport . . ."

You're the only car available, Five Six Two. Bravo One wants to talk to you on channel three.

Hanson held the mike against his leg. "But we don't want to talk to *them*," he said.

"Switching to three," he said, turning the channel knob on the radio. "Here," he said, handing the packset to Dana, "*you* talk to him, okay?"

"Bravo One. Five Sixty Two. What's up?" Dana said.

Uh, Five Six Two. We've got a deal going down in your district, and we could use a little backup.

Hanson rolled his eyes, and shook his head "no."

"We *are* a ways off," Dana said.

We'll wait. In the back of the Mor-4-Les lot on Union.

Dana shrugged. "Give us fifteen minutes."

"We got a *deal* going down," Hanson said, imitating Fox. "Da-da *da-da daaaah*-da," he hummed, the theme from the TV show *Police Story*. "Shit," he said.

Fox and Peetey didn't have to live in the district like he and Dana did, eight hours a day. They'd drive in from the freeway with search warrants to kick in doors, insult and humiliate suspects and their families, trash houses looking for dope, then drive away. Hanson didn't want the neighborhood to think they worked together, that he and Dana were no different from the narcs.

Gladys set their coffee on the counter.

"Thanks, Gladys," he said, but she'd gone back to reading her *Watchtower*, the cover a montage of disasters—fiery volcanos, tidal waves cresting above cowering bathers, blue-green monsoons, fissures splitting a highway, swallowing family sedans, and the words, "THE END OF THE WORLD: WHAT THE BIBLE TELLS US."

Pharaoh came through the lunchroom door, wearing his yellow hard hat, talking to himself, "It ain't done. Ain't done yet, never done. I *been* knowin' that," and sat down next to Hanson.

"How you gentlemens makin' out?" he asked Hanson.

"Doin' all right, Pharaoh. How about you?" Hanson said.

"Pharaoh know the way, Hanson. I got my eye on *you*."

"On me?" Hanson said, looking at Dana, raising an eyebrow. "Is that right?"

"That's exactly right."

"What you looking for?"

"That don' make a bit of difference to anybody but me, so don't you worry about it. Worry don't do no good. I just do my work ever' day, and heed the call when it comes. That way, don't you see, I'll earn my reward."

Pharaoh put in a twelve-hour day, six days a week, pushing a Safeway cart up and down Union Avenue. He kept a broom jammed in the frame of the cart and it rose above him like a flag as he collected beer and pop bottles.

"How much is the chili?" he asked Gladys.

"How much was it *last* time?"

Pharaoh looked at Hanson, smiled, and shook his head.

"Forty cents," Gladys said. "Like it always is."

"Gimme some o' that chili then. If it's not too much trouble."

"Not a bit of trouble," Gladys said.

"We better get back on the street," Dana said.

"You young gentlemen be careful out there. You brave and got the will, but don't be *too* brave. You might whup the demons, but Satan takes many shapes and guises."

FOX AND PEETEY were waiting in their windowless van in the parking lot, dressed in their narc costumes, Fox in a fatigue jacket and wraparound sunglasses, Peetey wearing a red and white polka dot cap, his ponytail sticking out the back. He was shirtless, wearing a cheap Mexican vest to show off his chest and arms, and to hide the pistol stuck in the back of his jeans.

"Thanks for rolling by, Dana," Fox said when they pulled alongside, ignoring Hanson. "We've got a guy dealing out of an apartment around the corner. One of my informants made a buy from him, and I've got a warrant."

"What's he selling?" Dana asked.

"Grass for sure. Probably some heroin. He left his place about fifteen minutes ago—I had my informant call him about a buy—so we're gonna go on in and wait for the asshole to get back."

"Okay," Dana said. "We'll follow you."

"His *informant*," Hanson snorted as they followed the van around the corner. "Some junkie or wino who'll tell him whatever he wants to hear. He's been using Riley 'the Retard' Marx as a snitch."

A Ford Pinto with no windshield and four flat tires was parked in front of the cinder block apartment building where silver duct tape zigzagged across cracked windows, and others had been replaced with the sides of cardboard boxes—SEAGRAMS, CLOROX, NEW IMPROVED CHARMIN.

They slipped in through the back and walked past closed doors down the shotgun hallway towards the common bathroom at the end of the hall where a radio was playing.

"*. . . no doubt* about *it. Have no fear, Wardell is here, an' he say, check* this *out . . .*" his voice fading into the twitchy, ominous beginning of "The Theme from Shaft."

Fox stopped at room 216 and rapped softly on the door. "Robert," he called. "Robert."

He smiled and said, "Time for a surreptitious entry." He pulled a little zippered wallet out of his pocket, a set of lock-picking tools, like strangely shaped, oversize typewriter keys, and sorted through them.

". . . who's the black private dick, who's a sex machine to all the chicks? That's right, uh-huh, Shaft . . ."

The doorjamb had been splintered and repaired and repainted half a dozen times, and looked like it was held together with bent nails and wood putty. "Let me try, John," Hanson said, lifting the door by the doorknob and pushing it open. "How about that?" he said, looking at Fox.

"That's just fine, but he'll probably notice that the door's been forced," Fox said, pointing to some pieces of dried putty that had fallen on the floor. "*I* could have done that if I'd wanted to be sloppy."

"Let's just *sweep* it away," Hanson said, brushing the dust into the room, "and go inside."

". . . Shaft. He's a bad muh-tha . . . Watch your mouth . . ."

The four of them went inside and closed the door of the small room. It smelled of old sweat, stale cigarette smoke, rotting food and roach spray. More like a bus station than a place to live. Styrofoam burger containers and pizza boxes lay on the scarred dresser and the unmade bed. A *Playboy* centerfold girl pouted from the water-stained wallpaper above the bed.

Down the hall, someone flushed the toilet. The radio got louder, ". . . *an' you know* what? *That Mister* Jones *is one* bad *muh-tha . . . huh. You know what I'm saying. Check him out. Mid-night to morning. Takin' you through the dark . . .*"

"Okay," Fox said, "here you go," pointing to an ashtray on the gouged and cigarette-burned dresser. There was enough marijuana in the ashtray to make one generous cigarette.

Hanson laughed.

"Just an indicator," Fox said. "Where there's smoke, there's fuckin' fire. Believe me, I've been doing this job long enough to know," he said. They tossed the mattress, emptied the closet on the floor, and dumped dresser drawers full of wadded-up dirty clothes.

"Hey," Hanson said, "Fox. How come you gotta dump the guy's clothes on the floor? Can't you just open the fucking drawers and look through them? We gotta come down here and get *along* with these people every day."

"I'm not gonna put my hands in that shit," Fox said, turning around. "Fuck these people. Look at this. What did I tell you," he said, holding up a hypodermic syringe.

"Oh *no*," Hanson said, throwing his arms out. "You've got *proof*. This guy uses illegal *drugs*. You know what?" he said, stepping closer, "if I had to live in a dump like this, I'd shoot as much heroin as I could find."

"You're fucked up, man," Peetey said, "John's right. You're fuckin' weird."

"And you're fuckin' dumb as they come," Hanson said.

"Fuck you." Peetey dropped his big shoulders and took a step towards Hanson.

"Fuck *you*, stupid," Hanson said.

"Forget it," Dana said, stepping in between them.

"Cool it," Fox said, looking out the window. "Here comes our man."

His footsteps came slowly down the hall, and when he stepped through the door Fox yelled, "Freeze."

"Freeze, motherfucker," Peetey screamed as they both pointed guns at his face.

"Freeze!"

He wore black trousers and a T-shirt with the words "I'M A PEPPER" across the front. His eyes went wide, and Peetey threw a body block into him, slamming him back out the door and bouncing him off the hallway wall. Fox holstered his pistol, while Peetey kept his High Power pointed at the man's head. Fox grabbed a double handful of his T-shirt and bounced him off the wall again.

"Man," the guy said, standing as passively as he could, fighting the urge to raise his hands for protection, "man, don't hurt me. Don't hurt me now."

"Get your hands behind your back," Fox said, turning him around and handcuffing him. "You have the right to remain silent. Anything you say . . ."

"You the *police?*" he said, twisting around to look at Fox.

"Who the fuck you think we are?" Peetey said.

"Man, I don't know."

"Shut up," Fox said. "I'll do the talking. Anything you say can and will be held against you."

"Hey," Peetey said, jabbing him in the chest with his finger, "is that true? Are you a *pepper*, man?"

"You have the right to . . ."

"Hey, *fucker*, I asked you a question. Are you a pepper? Are you?"

"If you cannot afford an attorney . . ."

"You better *answer* me, asshole. Are you a pepper?" Peetey went on, shoving him, *"Are* you? *Well? Are* you?"

"Yes, sir. Okay."

"Okay *what? Say* it. 'I'm a pepper.' "

"I'm a . . . pepper."

"I couldn't *hear* you, man."

"I'm a pepper."

"All *right,*" Peetey said, smiling, "the man's a pepper."

"Understanding your rights," Fox went on, "are you willing to talk to me?"

"What?" the man said, looking from Peetey to Fox.

"Jesus Christ," Fox said, "you dumb . . . under*standing* your rights . . ."

"Hey, John," Hanson said, "if you want to keep fuckin' with him, I think we'll go."

Dana stood at the door with his hands in his pockets.

"We need you to transport this guy. We can't transport him in the van."

"You all done, Peetey?" Hanson said.

Peetey just looked at him.

"Fine. Let's go. I'll see you down at the jail."

"Okay," Fox said, "he's under arrest for possession of marijuana, sale of marijuana, possession of a controlled substance, and for resisting arrest."

"You need anything out of your room?" Hanson asked the man.

"I got some cigarettes. I didn't resist *arrest.* How did I resist arrest?"

"Where are the cigarettes?"

"Top drawer of the, uruh, the dresser."

Hanson found the pack of Kools. "Let's go," he said.

Back at the patrol car he told him, "I'm gonna search you. You got any guns or knives on you?"

"No, sir."

"You got any razor blades or shit in your pockets that's gonna cut me?"

"No, sir."

Hanson found a handful of change, a half-smoked cigarette, a folded page of newspaper, and a scratch-off sweepstakes game from McDonald's. He'd won a free order of fries. Hanson unfolded the section of newspaper, checking it for more dope. It was the want ads. Two janitor's jobs were circled with pencil. He stuck the paper back in his pocket and opened the patrol car door. "Get on in. Watch your head," he said, then closed the door.

"I'll tell you something," Fox said in a low voice, walking up to Hanson. "Irregardless of what your personal feelings about me are—and I couldn't care less—you *don't* argue with another officer in front of a prisoner. Save it till later. It looks *real* bad. It puts *every* police officer's life in jeopardy on the street if it looks like we're . . ."

"Fuck you. And if you charge this guy with resisting arrest, don't expect me to back you up in court."

"Fine. I knew I couldn't depend on you. A lot of people know that. You're a fucking weirdo. You've got no business in this job if you can't do the work, and I'll tell you . . ."

"Why don't you suck my dick instead?"

"End of conversation. I'm a professional, Hanson. We *will* discuss this later."

Hanson puckered his lips and made a loud kiss. "I love it when you look tough, John. Bye-bye."

Dana got out of the car. "Let's just unload this guy and get back on the street," he said.

"How do you work with this guy?" Fox said.

"We'll meet you at the jail," Dana said.

Hanson got in the car, picked up the mike and said, "Five Sixty Two's jackpot with one adult male."

Five Sixty Two. Jackpot.

"Hey. Hey, man," the prisoner said from behind the Plexiglas shield. "Hey," he said, leaning forwards, his hands cuffed behind him, trying to keep his balance as Dana pulled the patrol car out onto the street.

"Shut up," Hanson said, filling in the arrest report.

"Hey," the prisoner said, "I didn't resist arrest. I didn't do anything but get beat up. I didn't even know it was the police till they had me handcuffed."

"Who the fuck did you *think* it was, the fucking KGB?"

"I never heard of *them*, officer."

"I don't think they're gonna charge you with resisting arrest," Hanson said.

"But what'd they arrest me *for?* I didn't *do* anything."

"You're under arrest for possession of marijuana, possession of a controlled substance, and sale of marijuana."

"Man, I didn't sell anything."

"Yeah, you did. Think back."

"I didn't . . . Oh, *man*. That dude on Sacramento. He kept wanting to know if I could get him some weed. Every time I saw him he's wanting some weed. The dude wouldn't leave me alone. I think he's a little, you know, *retarded* or something."

"He wear a funny hat?"

"Yeah. You know him?"

"Riley Marx."

"I bought an ounce of weed, turned around and sold it to him. I didn't even make any *money*."

"But you kept a little for yourself, right? The stuff in that ashtray."

"I took out a little. For my *trouble*."

"He dropped the dime on you, so I guess that makes you stupider than he is. See this paperwork I gotta do?" he said, holding up the clipboard. "Maybe that makes me stupider than *both* of you."

He filled in some more boxes on the arrest report. At a stop sign a couple of black kids on bikes waved. *"Po*-lice," one of them said. They looked at the prisoner. Hanson forced a smile and waved back as they drove off.

"I'm sorry you got to do the paperwork, officer."

"Look," Hanson said, glancing at the prisoner over his shoulder, "you know how it works. Just be cooperative at the jail. Do what they tell you to do. If they charge you with selling it, tell the public defender what you told me. Tell him you sold it to a guy who works for the police. Say it was entrapment."

"Say what?"

"Entrapment. *Entrap*ment, okay? But if you say you heard that from me, I'll say you're a liar and that you resisted arrest."

They passed Fox and Peetey on the stairs after they'd dropped off the prisoner.

"Why don't you people just stay off my district?" Hanson said.

"Come *on*," Dana said, putting an arm around Hanson and hustling him past.

"We'd *like* to," Fox said behind them, "but you don't seem to be able to take care of it by yourself."

"I'm glad it's the weekend tomorrow," Dana told Hanson. "Why don't you get laid or something?"

In the patrol car, Hanson said, "Do you think Peetey and I had a meaningful exchange back in that room?"

" 'Fuck you,' " he said, in a low voice.

Then in a higher voice, " 'No. Fuck *you*.'

" 'Oh yeah? Fuck you *first*.' "

They both laughed. "You know, Dana, communication is very important. Communication is the key ingredient in any kind of work. I read that in the Sunday paper. Ka-moon-i-kay-shun. Yeah. You got to ka-moon-i-cate with people if you want to succeed. Eee-yi-eee-yi-yo."

FOUR

IVE SIXTY TWO. Can you go?

His eyes on an alley just ahead, Hanson pulled the mike off the face of the radio and brought it to his mouth. "Five Six Two," he said, a kid on a red bike down the alley doing a wheelie next to a green Dumpster as they passed.

Uh . . . Five Sixty Two . . . we've got a psychologist down there at Good Sam Hospital who says one of his patients just called him. Said he's on his way there to kill him . . .

Hanson looked over at Dana. "Sounds like a good idea to me," he said, "one less psychologist on the fucking payroll."

Dana laughed.

Complainant's name is Doctor Ellis.

"Okee-doke," Hanson said, "we'll go talk to the doctor."

Five Sixty Two's got the call. Five Eighty?

"After we kill all the lawyers," Hanson said, hanging up the mike, "we go after the shrinks."

"Five Eighty's got the cover," Zurbo told Radio. "Be advised, though, we're a ways off."

Five Eighty's got the cover.

"Bravo One's loose. We'll roll that way." It was Fox.

Hanson looked down at the dented face of the radio speaker. "Fuck off, Bravo One," he said.

Copy, Bravo One.

" 'Bravo One's loose,' " Hanson said, lowering his voice the way Fox did when he talked on the radio. " 'We'll *roll* that way.' Fucker gets his lines from TV shows. He thinks this is *Police Story*. He thinks he's on *Kojak*."

Dana laughed again.

"And the assholes in prison get their tough-guy criminal lines watching the same shows. Then, don't you see, when they all hit the streets they can . . . communicate."

"Maybe you could *pretend* to be more normal," Dana said.

Hanson snorted, then keyed the microphone. "You got a description on the bad guy?"

Black male, six one, two hundred pounds, probably wearing army fatigues. Claims he has a gun. Name is Marcelle Million . . .

Hanson laughed. "Mar*celle*."

. . . Make that Mill-on, not Milly-un, like a million dollars, Radio said, spelling the name.

"Why does Marcelle want to kill this psychologist?"

Complainant says Millon is a Vietnam veteran with some kind of 'stress syndrome' it says here . . .

"*Syndrome*," Hanson said, as Dana worked the patrol car through the blocks in the direction of the hospital. "Fucking shrinks don't know what something is, so they call it a 'syndrome.' " He looked up at a mug shot stuck in the drooping sun visor, an escaped convict who'd shot a state cop with his own gun the month before.

"Millon," he said, flipping the sun visor up. "Do we know a 'Millon' from somewhere?"

"I don't think so."

Hanson sat back, propped one knee against the padded dashboard, and laced his fingers behind his head.

"You've got all these professional veterans like this guy probably is. They can't hack it, so they say, 'It's not *my* fault. It was the war. I've got a "syndrome" because the army *made* me do all that bad stuff. I'm a *victim*.' "

"I don't know," Dana said. He took the on-ramp to the freeway

and accelerated as Hanson rolled his window up against the wind.
"*Some* of 'em must have gotten pretty bent out of shape over
there."

"What I think," Hanson said, looking over at him, the graying
crew cut and wire-rim glasses in profile as he drove, "is that most
of them were fucked up before they went. And nobody *made* 'em
do anything. They could have refused to do it and gone to jail.
They *did* it, and they won't accept responsibility for their ac-
tions."

"Maybe."

" 'Oh doctor,' " Hanson whined, " 'I have these *nightmares.*' "

"I think maybe you need to get laid or . . ."

"I hate that touchy-feelie *victim* shit," Hanson said. "Put on a
crybaby show like that for the asshole liberals so they'll pat you
on the head and say, 'poor baby.' "

"You're hell on those liberals," Dana said.

Hanson laughed. "Oh doctor . . . *doctor*," he sang, "doctor
feel good . . ."

They were pulling into the lot behind the hospital when they
saw him walking up the hill, a big black guy wearing green fatigues and a floppy bush hat.

"Now why do I think that's our guy?" Dana said.

Glossy squares of paper on his arms and chest and thighs fluttered like ragged feathers, flashing as he walked, catching the sun.
Photographs. They could see that as he came closer. Three-by-five
snapshots, eight-by-tens, the pictures from his wall, pinned to his
fatigues.

"*Millon,*" Hanson said. "It's Millon."

HANSON HAD BEEN working alone that night. Dana had
taken the day off on comp time to pick out a Christmas tree and
meet with his accountant. It was a slow night in Five Sixty Two,
just barely raining so that he had to turn the windshield wipers
on, then off, every minute or so. He'd been thinking about trans-
ferring to East Precinct.

Helen was after Dana to retire and Hanson didn't want to start
over with some new guy. He could make sergeant if he just got his
act together, straightened up a little and . . .

Five Six Two . . . uh, we've been holding some kind of ongo-

ing neighborhood problem over in Four Eighty's district for a while now. They're still out on that stabbing and East is a little short on cars tonight.

"I can go," Hanson said. "What's the address?"

It was a two-story apartment complex in a district just across the precinct border from North, the kind of neighborhood where, when things were slow, they'd cruise the streets looking for cars that had been stolen for joy rides, then abandoned when the gas ran out, hoping to poach one from the East Precinct car.

A beefy young white guy in jeans, motorcycle boots, and a Harley Davidson T-shirt opened the door to apartment seven.

"Good evening," Hanson said, "what can I do for you?"

" '*Good* evening'?" he said, looking up at the drizzle hissing past the porch light. "Right. Whatever."

He had a gold hoop in one ear and a carefully trimmed Fu Manchu mustache. The urban pirate look, Hanson thought.

"It's been over an hour since we called you people. Next time I'll handle it myself."

"What's the problem?" Hanson said.

"Tell him, Steve," a woman said, stepping into the doorway. "I'm tired of that guy's shit," she said, jabbing her cigarette at the door, then sucking on it as if it was her only source of oxygen.

She was wearing tight shorts and a sleeveless, black T-shirt with no bra. In her early thirties, she was five or six years older than Steve, lean, with short black hair. The tattoos started at the hollow of her throat, curling and twining over her collarbones, spilling down the ridged cleavage into the scoop neck of her shirt and out onto her shoulders. Every inch of skin Hanson could see, from the throat down to the collar of her shirt, was covered with tattoos, black and purple, dark green, orange and maroon, the colors of bruised and rotting fruit. Her arms and legs were pale and untouched.

"That's what I'm *trying* to do," he said, looking down at her, stroking his mustache to show he wouldn't be hurried. "There's this *soul* brother who lives upstairs," he said, turning back to Hanson.

"He's been driving us batshit with that pounding," the woman said, "for *days*."

How many hundreds of hours, Hanson wondered, trying not to look down her shirt, had someone worked on her with a stinging electric needle, stitching ink under her skin and beading it with blood.

The TV was on in the room, divers with spotlights kicking down through dark water and silver bubbles.

"Did you talk to him? Ask him to keep the noise down?" Hanson asked Steve.

"Ha," the woman said, exhaling smoke, "you mean like a conversation? An exchange of ideas?" she said, pushing past Steve and looking out at the dark courtyard. "With some stupid nigger in this for-shit neighborhood? Not fuckin' . . ."

"Cool it," Steve said, pushing her back inside. "I'm *talking* to the man, okay?"

"*Talk* to him then," she said. "I can't sleep with the noise."

"I'll *handle* it," he said, slamming the door behind him.

"I'm fuckin' *sick* of it," she shouted through the door.

"Mother*fucker*," he muttered. "Look, my fiancée has a nervous condition, and that fuckin' *brother* up there has got her on my case, okay?"

"Which apartment?" Hanson asked.

"Right above us, man, fourteen. Go in the door down there, and take the stairs."

"I'll talk to him."

"I'm not prejudiced, either. I'll fuck a man up I don't care what color he is, and I'll tell you one thing right now . . ."

"Tell him later," the woman yelled from inside.

"I'll go talk to him," Hanson said.

"This '*for-shit*' neighborhood was good enough for you a month ago," Steve yelled.

The door slammed behind Hanson when, out of habit, he stopped to write down the license number of the green Pontiac in the space numbered for their apartment, then crossed the muddy courtyard.

He took the interior stairs to the second-floor hallway where it smelled like a week's worth of burned suppers, the doors identical except for the numbers. Down the hall a radio was playing. He imagined a game show where the contestant had to choose which door to answer. If he opened the right door, he'd find a pretty girl in a bikini draped across the hood of a new car, but if he opened the wrong one he'd find a pack of hungry Dobermans or a naked man with a shotgun.

Shotgun Hall. *That would be the name of the game show,* Hanson thought as he knocked on the door to number fourteen.

It sounded like someone was moving furniture in the apartment. He knocked again. "Police officer," he said.

The sounds stopped. After the click and snap of hardware and locks, the door cracked open the width of a safety chain. The man who looked out at Hanson had an acne-scarred face and was wearing an OD army hat. For an instant Hanson thought he knew him.

"Howdy," Hanson said, "can I talk to you for a second?"

"You got some ID?"

"Well," Hanson said, holding the front of his shirt out, "I've got this badge and uniform. I left my special hat back in the car."

"Anybody can get a police uniform," he said. "You got some kind of ID card? Photo ID?"

Hanson took out his wallet, found his ID card and held it up. "See," he said, "it's me."

When the man leaned closer, to read the card, Hanson got a glimpse of a death's-head on his shirt. "Okay," he said, "what's the problem?"

Hanson nodded at the pin on the army hat. "Hundred and First Airborne?" he said.

"Yeah," the man said, "who were you with?"

"Uh, Fifth Special Forces."

"Uh-huh," he said. "Sure you were."

Hanson laughed. "It's gotten to where I *feel* like a liar when I say that.

"Hey, I *knew* some guys from the Hundred and First."

"That right?" Millon said. "Where?"

"Down at Phu Bai when they were still there. I was up, you know, Cam Lo, Dong Ha, and then keep going. North of there. An A-camp."

Millon put his face closer, looked up and down the hall, then unhooked the chain. "Come on in," he said. "Can't be too careful, you know what I'm talking about? Everybody's a Vietnam veteran now. Seem like it's one in every bar. Half of 'em claim they Green Berets. Wait," he said, hooking the lock again. "You not CIA, are you?"

"They wouldn't have me."

"Come on in."

As soon as Hanson stepped through the door, Millon closed it, locked it with a deadbolt, and dropped a two-by-four into a pair of iron brackets attached to the reinforced door frame. "Hanson," he said, reading his name tag. "I'm Millon."

He was wearing jungle boots, baggy OD fatigue pants, and a T-shirt with a grinning death's-head on the front, and the words "KILL 'EM ALL AND LET GOD SORT 'EM OUT." He looked, Hanson thought, like someone who's been on twenty-four hour alert, his camp under siege for a long time.

The only furniture in the apartment was a broken-down sofa and a TV set with a screen full of static, hissing like grease in a skillet. Newspapers and magazines and books were stacked neatly, precisely, on both sides of the sofa. Dozens of photos, snapshots and curling Polaroids, the colors fading, were thumb-tacked to the wall above the sofa. Soldiers saluting with cans of beer in Vietnamese bars, their arms around Vietnamese whores with beehive hairdos. In others the soldiers are shirtless, wearing bush hats and baggy fatigue pants, leaning against the gun tubes of 105 howitzers, grinning as they eat out of C-ration cans, and posing with M-16s on some bleak fire base, the blowing red dust turned metallic orange now, and some of the figures fading from the emulsion.

It was hot in the room, and Millon smelled like rotten onions. The two windows had been reinforced with two-by-fours, bars bolted across them. Hanson said, "Glad to meet you," looking for weapons in the folds of Millon's fatigues.

The small dining room nook across the room had an arched ceiling. A Silver Star medal on a red, white and blue ribbon hung from the peak of the arch, centered, as if it could ward off evil. "Silver Star?" Hanson said.

"Uh-huh," Millon said, rubbing his eyes.

"They don't just hand those out," Hanson said.

"What? What's *that* mean?"

"Not many guys *get* Silver Stars."

The ceiling and walls of the nook were papered with aluminum foil, throwing light like an evil force out into the rest of the room. A plywood sleeping pallet was raised above the floor on two-by-fours, and the floor was completely covered with a checkerboard of cardboard-backed, plastic picture frames, dozens of them, face-down like tile.

"My stateside bunker," Millon said. "I been working on it. Gotta scrounge some sandbags and standoff wire."

"Right," Hanson said. He glanced at the locked door, wondering if he was going to have to shoot Millon before it was over.

"What you want with me?"

"The people downstairs called to complain about the noise," Hanson said. "I guess from when you put all this reinforcing on the doors and windows." The TV hissed, blue static twitching across the screen.

"Shit," he said, smiling, his eyes bloodshot with fatigue. "The tattoo bitch sent you. She the *reason* for this," he said, gesturing from the windows to the plywood bed. "I got to get some sleep. I tried sleeping out in my car, but *she's* out there at night, three, four in the morning, with her clothes off. Walkin' those tattoos around. Some nights I'll go to the window, and she's right underneath it, looking up at me. I put that up last week," he said, pointing to a convex truck mirror he'd mounted on the window frame, "so I can look down without, you know, exposing myself."

Hanson thought about using the packset to call for another car, but knew that whatever was going to happen would be over before they could get there, even if they could get through the door.

"I'm just gonna say this," Millon said, "no other way to do it. The tattoo bitch down there? Her old man—*she* put him up to it— shooting beams from a laser up here at me. I know it sounds like I'm, like it's hard to believe, but that's what's goin' on. Nine days now . . ."

He went silent and began scratching his chest, like something had stung him, digging his dirty nails in hard enough to draw blood through the T-shirt, staining the death's-head.

He stopped scratching and went on, as if he'd never paused. "Always late at night, when the others are asleep."

"Why would he do that?" Hanson said.

"She *tells* him to do it. They hit me in the feet. And here," he bent and patted the backs of his legs, "and in the ass. In the balls," he said, lowering his voice. "That's what she likes. Yeah," he said, his voice lower, "sometimes in the balls. Blue and yellow fire. That's why I built this," he said, walking into the glow from the aluminum foil.

Hanson followed him, scanning the room in overlapping patterns, looking for weapons. The foil reflected the jumping blue TV glow, like an ice cave.

Millon picked up one of the frames from the floor and held it out at arm's length towards Hanson. It was a cheap mirror and

Hanson saw the side of his face and the barred door behind him in its rippling silver reflection.

"I got these for one eighty-nine at the Kmart," Millon said. "I told 'em it was for a, you know, *art* project. Had to go back in the warehouse to get enough. They reflect some of the laser beams back. Some of 'em. I thought *that* might help too," he said, pointing at the TV. "Leave it on for interference."

He carefully fitted the mirror back in its place. "They don't work too good," he said, adjusting the other mirrors. "Don't work at *all* most of the time. Not heavy enough to stop the beams. Some nights I leave before dark and walk all night. Got a regular route, through the parks."

He stepped back to study them, then turned to Hanson.

"I know you think I'm . . ." he began, almost saying *crazy,* ". . . lying."

"Where would these people get a laser?" Hanson said. "Why would they go to all the trouble? They're just ordinary assholes."

Millon began scratching his chest again. "What I'm supposed to do? Look at my *place,* man," he said, sweeping his arm across the barren room, the TV screen lighting then shadowing his face. "Would I make this up, motherfucker? Huh? You think I'd tell you this if it wasn't true? Act a fool for some white fuckin' cop? I *know* how it sounds."

Hanson watched the vocal cords working in Millon's neck. A good punch, straight into the throat, would stop almost anybody. But you couldn't ever be sure with a crazy person.

"I thought you might help me out. That's why I told you the truth. I had some friends over there who were white boys. First time in my life. But the war's over now and everything back like it always was."

"I'll go talk to them," Hanson said.

"You won't talk shit," Millon said, "white motherfuckers."

Hanson unsnapped his holster. He'd take a lot of heat for killing an unarmed black man, but he wasn't going to fight a psychotic as big as Millon in a locked room. If he got out of this, he decided, he was going to carry a little throwdown gun from now on.

"Open the door," Hanson said. "I'll tell him to stop the lasers."

Millon must have heard the *snap* of Hanson's holster, or understood the look in his eyes. He walked to the door and lifted the timber out.

"You're not gonna tell him shit, are you?" he said, his back to Hanson.

"I give you my word."

Millon turned and looked at him, cradling the heavy beam in his arms as if he was trying to guess its weight.

"Put that down, let me out, and I'll tell him to stop."

"She'll just get another one to do it for her."

"I can't do anything about that now. Call me if she does."

Millon propped the timber against the wall and began working on the locks. One of the photos closest to Hanson caught his eye. Millon looked young and happy, just like anybody else that age, standing with a couple of white guys, the three of them holding an American flag at shoulder height, smiling over the top of it. A Huey gunship was lifting off a landing pad in the distance just beyond the entrance to the fire base, an archway with a sign that said,

WELCOME TO FIRE BASE DAVY CROCKET
"When you're in the right—
Don't Never Quit."

On the way to the stairs, Hanson kept his eye on the door, the clicking locks followed by a *boom* as the beam slammed home.

In the patrol car he began filling out a miscellaneous report form, not much more than a formality, listing the date and time, the heading, "Neighborhood disturbance." Below that, in the lined SUMMARY section, he wrote, "RE: Millon."

He clicked his pen a few times and wrote, "First name refused."

It wasn't even his district. He could have called for a backup and dragged Millon to the University Hospital and filled out all the forms and hoped the intern shrink on duty would admit him. But he'd probably act sane once they got to the hospital, and the shrink, who'd been on duty for twenty-four hours, half-crazy himself from exhaustion, would decide that Millon posed no danger to himself or others. He hadn't really *done* anything, there weren't any beds available anyway, and Hanson would have to take him back home. Besides, it was much too late in the shift to get involved in all that paperwork. Millon was Four Eighty's problem anyway.

It was a dark night, no moon or stars, the streetlights all broken. The drizzle hung over everything like a heavy fog, and Hanson imagined for a moment that he was drifting through space in the patrol car, alone in the universe. He put the pen in his pocket and looked down the rainswept, empty street before pulling the mike off the radio.

"Five Sixty," he told radio, "going to channel three for a record check."

THE WOMAN ANSWERED the door. Hanson looked down at her and their eyes locked. "Well?" she said, taking a drag off her cigarette, her breasts swelling against the soft black cotton of her T-shirt. The hooded porch light flapped in the wind, squeaking and throwing shadows. Hanson saw hollow eyes and open mouths moving down beneath the top of her shirt, then thought it must be shadows from the porch light.

She took the glowing cigarette from her lips and, her eyes still on Hanson's, blew smoke out of the corner of her mouth. She leaned closer, the shirt falling open, and said it again, softly, almost a whisper, "Well?"

Only the sides of her breasts were tattooed, the tips pure white, like islands in a midnight ocean of undulating dragons.

Hanson's face was wet from the cold mist, and a drop of water rolled down his neck. She ran a hand up into her hair, her breasts shifting, a tuft of hair showing under her arm. Hanson wondered what her skin tasted like.

"The guy's a little crazy," he said, imagining the taste would be salt and green tequila.

"Tell me something I don't know."

"He hasn't been sleeping much," he said. A hook-billed raven on her shoulder seemed to preen when she flicked ashes off the cigarette. "That might be the problem."

"He keeps his lights on all night," she said.

"He says you all are shooting laser beams at him."

The woman snorted.

"I told him that was hard to believe."

"Now why would you say that?"

Hanson smiled. "Can I talk to your fiancé for a minute?"

"Steve," she called, turning her head. "Steve!" she shouted, looking back over her shoulder, the tendons in her neck cording like snakes down into the T-shirt. "The cop's back."

She took another drag off the cigarette and turned to Hanson, looking him in the eyes again as smoke bubbled out her nose. "You think you're really something, don't you?" she whispered.

Hanson looked up as Steve came to the door, barefoot.

"So what's his problem?" he said.

The woman's cigarette smoke drifted out into the fresh, damp air and over Hanson's face.

"He's crazy," the woman said.

"Who? The nigger or the cop."

"The nigger says we're shooting *lasers* at him."

"Right," Steve said. "Go on inside. It's cold out here. I'll take care of it."

"Don't you *tell* me what to do, motherfucker."

"I'm not, goddammit, I'm . . . okay. Please? How's that?"

"You *better* take care of it," she said, going inside and stretching out on the tape-patched Naugahyde sofa that faced the door.

"Did you *tell* him?" Steve said.

She hung one leg down on the floor and hooked her other foot over the back of the sofa, straining the material of the shorts, hiking them up her long, pale legs to where green and gold palm fronds flickered in the hollows of her thighs. She smoked and watched Hanson.

"If you *are* shooting laser beams at him, would you promise not to do it anymore?"

"What the fuck are you talking about?" Steve said.

"Lasers," Hanson said. "Stop shooting him with lasers." If he licked her thighs, Hanson thought, they'd taste like the sting in your nose when someone punches you in the head, the copper taste and black stars.

"Let's close the door," he said, reaching past him to pull the door shut.

"I ran your name, Steve, and found *several* outstanding warrants for your arrest. Two counts of possession for sale of a controlled substance . . ."

"I took care of those," he said.

Hanson smiled. "No, you didn't. Then there's one count of furnishing a controlled substance to a minor, and one count of sodomy with a minor."

"What?" he said, his eyes cutting left and right, poised to run.

Hanson stepped on Steve's bare foot with his steel-toed boot, grabbed the collar of his leather jacket, and pulled him close.

"You *better* not run from me, Steve. I'll shoot you, no problem."

"I don't know *nothing* about sodomy with a minor. I swear. The possession for sale, yeah, but I'm not no fuckin' child molester, man."

"I believe you, Steve. She probably looked older, but that doesn't make any difference under the law. But, hey, this is your lucky night. I'm willing to forget about it if you'll do me a favor."

"What?"

Hanson lifted his boot, and let go of the jacket.

"All you have to do," Hanson said, "is promise me you'll stop shooting lasers. Just say, 'I'll stop shooting lasers.' " He smiled and nodded, as if he was speaking to a child. "Just say it."

"I'll stop?"

"I'll stop *shooting lasers.* Shooting lasers. I'll stop shooting lasers. All four words. A complete sentence. I'll stop shooting lasers. Now . . ."

"I'll stop shooting lasers."

"Great. Good job, Steve," Hanson said. "Good night, now," he said, backing down the steps. "But I'll be checking back. I'll have those warrants in case you let me down."

He walked back upstairs, up the urine-stinking stairwell where winos could sleep and junkies could wait for people to come home with their social security checks.

He knocked on the door. "Millon." He knocked again. "Millon. I talked to them. He said he'd stop." He put his ear to the door and heard the roar of the ocean and his own pulse. No light showed under the door, not even the TV. "I told him to stop. You can get some sleep now. Go talk to the VA, to a shrink. Tell him what he wants to hear and get some of that fuckin' disability money. Okay? Millon?"

He unlocked the door of the patrol car, then looked up at the second floor of the apartment building, counting windows until he came to Millon's. He thought he saw a shadow, someone looking down at him, then it was gone as a car hissed past on the wet street, and the convex mirror in the window flared in the headlights.

He got in the car and finished the report form, writing, "Problem solved upon departure."

———

When the barmaid at the PAA flicked the lights on and off at two
A.M., he left with Judy Bellah, one of the girls who worked in
Records, and went to her apartment. She was small, with short
dark hair and pale skin. When they went to bed he turned off the
lights so he could see tattoos coil her breasts, ripple along her ribs,
whip her belly and flare inside her thighs like black lights.

NOW HANSON WALKED across the hospital parking lot towards Millon, matching him pace for pace across the yellow parking stripes. They stopped a car width apart, the number "28"
showing through oil stains in the empty parking space between
them. Millon went bowlegged, arms loose at his sides, like a gun-
slinger. Bravo One, the old UPS step-van Fox was driving, clattered over a speed bump somewhere behind him. He could just see
Dana, behind and to his right.

"Remember me?" Hanson said, tapping his name tag with his
left hand.

"I don't know you."

A gust of wind brought the smell of honeysuckle over the
asphalt and rattled the photos of APCs, tents, helicopters cork-
screwing red dust on bleak fire bases, snapshots of bunkers, concertina wire, whores in miniskirts and white plastic boots, and
soldiers—leaning against tanks, saluting with cans of beer,
crouching by out-of-focus howitzers, their hands over their ears, a
nimbus of dust coming off the big gun tube, all of them fluttering
in the parking lot like a documentary, the name tag MILLON
blinking on his chest.

"Millon? Come on."

"Millon's gone."

"That's you *there*, isn't it?" Hanson said, nodding at a five-by-
seven high on his chest, "next to that one-oh-five?"

"That *was* me. That's right." His eyes on Hanson, he moved his
hands like a signalman, quick and precise, to his chest and arms
and thighs, holding each position for a moment before snapping a
photo with his finger and moving again, touching his own image
each time, a ritual as practiced as genuflecting.

"That's me. And that's me. That's me *there*. And there," he
said, his arms slashing up and down, the fingers striking photos
like snakes. "Da *Nang.* Quang *Tri.* Cam *Lo.* Dong *Ha.*"

"I've been to all of those places," Hanson said.

"Then you *know* my name."

"What's your problem with this psychologist?"

Millon broke eye contact for a moment, looking over Hanson's shoulder. "All those *police* to kill one sorry ass nigger?"

A holster strap snapped behind Hanson, and Millon looked back at him.

" 'Problem'? No problem. I'm gonna kill *his* sorry ass."

"It's not worth it, man. Put your hands on your head, turn around so I can handcuff you, and I promise I'll look out for you. I give you my word."

"Motherfucker took all I had left. My *heart,* man. I didn't have *much* left, and he takin' the rest every time I tell him anything.

" 'How you *feel* about that?' he says. I tell him and he takes it away. Gives me some pills. 'Why you feel like that?' he says. I tell him and he says I'm wrong. 'War's over,' he says. 'Come home.' What I'm gonna do back home? You tell me."

Beyond the hospital, just a speck in the sky, a Huey helicopter crossed the sun, the faraway pounding of its rotors a whisper. They both glanced towards the sound for an instant, a reflex.

Another patrol car squealed around the hospital, bounced into the parking lot, and skidded to a stop. Two doors opened and slammed closed. More boots scuffed the asphalt and the stink of burning brakes mixed with honeysuckle.

"How were you planning to kill him?"

"I didn't *plan* shit. I'm gonna shoot him. That's *one* thing I know how to do."

"You must have a gun then," Hanson said. When this thing went to court he wanted that on the record. That Millon said he had a gun.

Millon snapped his finger at a photo on his shoulder. He flicked his index finger on his thigh.

"Have you got a gun?" Hanson said.

Millon reached into the loose-fitting fatigue jacket with his right hand, where it was unbuttoned over his chest. "I'm not playing," he said, pain flaring in his eyes, the faint oiled *click* of a shotgun safety behind Hanson.

"He took my heart, man."

Hanson thought of those mystics who claim they can tear out their own beating heart, then replace it and leave no scar.

"My heart."

Hanson almost expected to see the bloody, veined heart, shuddering in his hand. He slipped his pistol out of the holster and held it against his leg. *"Wait,* now," Hanson said. "Don't do this."

"You better kill me before I kill you," Millon said.

Hanson thumbed the safety off his pistol, slowly, so it wouldn't click. "Put it back," he said, looking at the bulge in his jacket as if he might see through the material, so hard his eyes hurt. The camouflage pattern seemed to darken, shift, a different pattern seeping through like dusk in the jungle.

"You better *kill* me."

"You didn't tell me your name was 'Marcelle,'" Hanson said.

Millon smiled. "Yeah, I remember you, Hanson."

"Come on," Hanson said, "we can still get out of this."

"Too late for that now," he said, the smile gone. "I did what you told me to do that night. Outside the door. Remember?"

"Millon," Hanson said, "look at me . . ."

" 'Go see one of those Vee Aye shrinks,'" Millon said, a fair imitation of Hanson's voice. " 'Tell him what he wants to hear.'

"Tell him *this*," he screamed, pulling a bloody fist full of gleaming metal from his jacket. Across the lot behind him, dozens of sparrows exploded from the weeds behind a littered chain-link fence.

The *pop* of handguns seemed distant, but Hanson smelled the gunpowder as he dropped into a crouch, bringing his pistol up into a two-hand grip, never taking his eyes off Millon's chest, the sequence of movements so practiced and familiar and smooth it was almost relaxing as he *squeezed* the trigger and the gun bucked in his hand.

The shotgun behind him was much louder, the concussion clapping his ear like a sucker punch, but didn't interfere with his concentration, his sight-picture on Millon's chest as he pulled the trigger and the pistol bucked again, the empty brass casing arcing end-for-end out of sight. He *tasted* the gunpowder when the shotgun went off the next time, the wadding on fire as it blew buckshot past him.

Millon blinked in surprise, black freckles erupting from his face and forehead. The bush hat blew away and photographs exploded off his fatigues. He tripped on his own feet and went down, bucking in convulsions on the asphalt, kicking the oil-stained number twenty-eight.

Hanson ran towards him, pistol in his hand, as Zurbo came in from the left and Dana from the right. Fox, wearing khaki pants, cowboy boots, and a light leather jacket, lowered his model 29. His partner, the weightlifter, Peetey, dropped a clip out of his .45. His reddish hair fell to the collar of his blue tie-dyed shirt and embroidered red vest. He looked like a brutal clown.

Fluid weeping from buckshot wounds streaked Millon's face and eyelashes like smeared mascara. His eyes, already blind, but still alive, looked up at the windows of the hospital. Buckshot pellets had driven photographs into the fabric of the fatigue jacket so they seemed like part of the camouflage pattern, pink froth bubbling slowly through one Hanson remembered from the apartment.

As he knelt over him, a Zippo lighter, blood-smeared and pocked with buckshot, slid out of Millon's breast pocket and tumbled to the asphalt. They'd sold millions of them to soldiers in Vietnam, an enamel figure of Snoopy, the cartoon beagle pup on one side, wearing fatigues and a helmet, a cigar in his mouth, bracing an M-16 on his hip. Engraved on the other side was a parody of the 23rd Psalm that had been popular in Vietnam, "Yea, though I walk through the valley of the shadow of death, I will fear no evil, *for I am the baddest motherfucker in the valley.*"

Hanson knelt down to look at the ball of foil and mirror shards Millon had pulled out of his jacket instead of a gun. He'd packed it like a snowball around the Silver Star, its red, white and blue ribbon sticky with blood.

He touched Millon's arm with the back of his hand—no one would notice—calling up the real ending of the 23rd Psalm, "Surely goodness and mercy shall follow me all the days of my life, and I will dwell in the house of the Lord forever."

"Motherfucker was dead when he hit the pavement," Zurbo said.

Millon's eyes were completely dead now, opaque and gluey as the eyes of a fish in a supermarket, but the sucking chest wound still bubbled with air left in his lungs.

Hanson stood and thumbed the safety on his pistol up, dropping the hammer, his hand cramped like a claw around the grip, little rainbows of oil and Hoppes #9 rising from the hot steel slide.

A Raven .25 automatic skidded across the blacktop, into the bloody folds of Millon's fatigue jacket.

"It was a good shooting," Fox said, "just the way it happened. *Any* way you look at it. Right?" He looked at each of the other cops, one at a time. Hanson, like the others, nodded. "But you know how it would go. 'Police kill unarmed black man.' The niggers will go crazy, and the asshole mayor wants to get re-elected.

"It was a good shooting. Let's just make it easier for every-body," he said, nodding at the throwdown gun, the cheap, nickle-plated Raven half-hidden by Millon's jacket.

"You were kinda slow there, Hanson. That nigger would have *shot* your ass if I hadn't punched his ticket. I always heard you Green Berets were some kind of bad asses. But then, you can't believe half the shit you hear."

Hanson holstered his pistol and flexed his hand, working the cramp out.

"Don't bother to thank me or anything."

"Fuck you, Fox. He won the Silver Star."

Detectives came and cordoned off the shooting scene with yel-low plastic ribbon, the words "POLICE LINE DO NOT CROSS" printed in black over and over across it. The sun was going down by the time the ME loaded the body up and rolled it to his station wagon.

The hospital rose above them like a cliff face, windows dark or lighted in random patterns. In one lighted window on the third floor, a ribbed rubber bellows pumped up and down in a glass cylinder, swelling and collapsing like a lung kept alive in a jar.

Detectives interviewed them about the shooting, one at a time, up on the sixth floor of Central Precinct in the Internal Affairs office. Talking quietly down the hallway where the janitor swung the droning chrome buffer in arcs across the marble floor, and later by the shuddering Coke machine in the lunchroom, they made sure that their stories all matched. The important thing was to keep the details simple and consistent. As they waited in the hallway, detectives and patrolmen off the street stopped to congratulate them. Fuller, who was working overtime making DWI arrests, waved a handful of implied consent forms and Breathalyzer print-outs at them on his way out of the building. "Good work," he said, rubbing his hand through his crew cut, "one more asshole we won't have to arrest again."

Zurbo came out of the office and told Hanson they wanted to see him next, nodding to him that there wasn't any problem.

Hanson pushed the steel door open, its brushed aluminum doorknob big as a softball, into a narrow office that smelled like floor wax and Brasso. The gray siding on the walls had the same dull shine as the floor.

"Have a seat, Hanson," Rivas said.

The gray steel desk against the left wall, where McCarthy sat, was a few feet closer to the door than Rivas' on the right, so there was room to walk between them to the straight-back chair facing his desk. The only other furniture in the room was an aluminum coat rack.

"This shouldn't take long."

Narrow louvered windows, too high to see the street below, ran the length of the outside wall. There were no family pictures or golf trophies on the desks, no posters or cartoons, no framed testimonials from the Elks Club or Rotarians on the walls. Nothing to look at but Sgt. Rivas, a Puerto Rican from New York, sitting across the desk.

He had to look back over his shoulder to see McCarthy, a big red-faced cop who used to ride motorcycles in Traffic Division. They'd had to call McCarthy at home to come in for the interviews, and he looked a little drunk.

Rivas spread his hands on the desk and looked at Hanson. "You got a problem with the way it happened?" he said, his voice echoing slightly in the bleak room. "I hear you might."

"Not me. Who told you that?"

"Nothing anybody said. Just an impression we got from some of the statements. You and Fox, you know, maybe we were 'hearing' something there."

"The guy said he had a gun. He said he was going to kill me. Everybody waited as long as they could before using deadly force. I waited *too* long."

"Maybe you got a problem with deadly force," McCarthy said behind him.

Rivas drummed his fingers on the desk. The thumb and trigger finger on his right hand were scarred and stiff. When he was still a patrolman, he and his partner had been driving to supper when a sixteen-year-old girl, angry at her boyfriend, blew a stop sign and broadsided the patrol car. The window had been open, and when the car rolled it caught his hand between the door and the street. He'd had to qualify left-handed with his revolver to go back to work. His partner, who had been driving, was retired on disability. He shot himself in the head a year and a half later.

McCarthy was breathing like he'd just jogged up a flight of stairs. "Have you thought about that?" he said.

"No," Hanson said, glancing back for a moment, his neck stiff. He tried to filter out the sound of McCarthy's breathing, imagining himself on the bank of the river where he fished as a kid, at the falls.

"Don't you think maybe you should?"

The roar of the water, silver, blue and foaming.

"If you can't handle deadly force, you owe it to the guys you work with . . ."

"I didn't *think* about it," Hanson said, turning in his chair, "because it isn't a problem. I've killed more goddamn people than you . . ."

"This guy?" Rivas said. "You seen his army record? Special Forces. Airborne."

Hanson sat back in his chair. Rivas' narrow-lapeled sport coat was woven with some kind of metallic thread. It hung, shapeless and gutted-looking, from the aluminum coat rack behind him.

"That G.I. Joe stuff isn't the street," McCarthy said.

"What about the contact you had with this individual back in December?" Rivas said.

"Like it says in the report, some neighbors complained about the noise he'd been making. He was a little nuts . . ."

"He thought white people were shooting him in the ass with lasers. I'd say he was a twelve-gauge psychotic," McCarthy said.

"I thought about taking him up to the medical center," Hanson said, "but he didn't act like he was a danger to himself or others at that point. Probably just wasn't taking his medication. I don't think they'd have admitted him."

"He should of been locked up where they *made* him take his fuckin' medication. But the liberals and the ACLU won 'em their fuckin' *rights* to walk the streets and use police officers to put 'em out of their misery."

"You think it was a good shooting?" Rivas said.

"Yes. Absolutely. He wanted to die."

"Then he should have gone off somewhere—out in the fuckin' *county* would have been good—and had the balls to do it to himself. Saved us all a lot of needless documentation."

Rivas smiled at "needless documentation," and looked over Hanson's shoulder.

"Just another inconsiderate motherfucker. I guess you can't expect 'em to learn anything about responsibility on the street, but you'd think being in the *army* would of at least taught him some self-reliance and consideration," McCarthy said.

Out the window Hanson noticed, for the first time, a billboard on top of another building, lit up with spotlights so it seemed to be floating in the night sky. A perfect blonde, her eyes sparkling the same green as her skintight leotard, a sheen of sweat on her face and arms. Turned just enough to show off her muscular thighs and buttocks, and the way the straps of her leotard lifted and separated her breasts, she smiled at Hanson over her shoulder, a glass of milk in her hand.

"Thirty-two entrance wounds, counting buckshot pellets," McCarthy said, getting out of his chair, "courtesy of his white liberal friends. I gotta take a leak."

After he went out the door, Rivas looked down at his hand, tapped the desk, then looked up at Hanson and shrugged.

"What's the problem you got with Fox?" Rivas said.

"No problem."

Rivas thumbed through the statements on his desk.

"Personality conflict," Hanson said. "I don't like him."

"I can understand that," Rivas said. "Can't like everybody. He's gotta be an obsessive-type guy. When he's not on the street, he's over at Detectives running names through the computer. You work with him much out at North?"

"Not much."

"They got a whole different, what do you call it, 'lifestyle,' " Rivas said.

"They turned her lights on," Rivas said, looking out the window. "They put that billboard up a couple of weeks ago. It's enriched my life. She's real 'wholesome,' you know? The lieutenant was pissed, though. Said it was 'psychologically distracting' to have it outside an interview room like this."

He looked back down at Hanson's file.

"The lieutenant took some psychology courses," he said, deadpan. "This file," he said. "I'm impressed. College degree. Couple of Bronze Stars with Special Forces. How'd a guy like you end up here?"

Hanson's personnel file was on the desk. A brick-red folder

with the word "RESTRICTED" stamped on it in black. Rivas tapped it with his finger.

"Impressed, my ass," Hanson thought. "One Bronze Star with a 'V,' " he said. "They hand those other ones out to everybody."

"Oh, yeah? You sure? There's stuff in this file," Rivas said, "the DOD won't release. Flagged in the computer."

"I did a little of the cross-border stuff everybody knows about now. But they keep it classified anyway, for, I think, it's seven years. Just a formality."

" 'Downgraded at seven-year intervals,' " Rivas said. He took out a piece of gum and unwrapped it. "My wife kept telling me that cigarettes will kill you, so I stopped smoking and started chewing gum. Now she says the gum makes me look 'lower class.' "

He looked out at the billboard. "I guess the lieutenant's right," he said. "I spend a lot of the city's time thinking about how I'd lick the sweat off her."

He put the gum in his mouth, chewed it a couple of times, and tucked it into his cheek.

"I was in the army. Nothing like you, though. My last six months in, they made me the classified document custodian at Fort Bliss. This was when the anti-war movement was *hot*, you know? We were getting rid of fuckin' *crates* of classified documents. Run 'em through this big shredder, looked like an old steam engine. It mixed the shredded stuff with water and squirted out this gray paper pulp about like cow shit."

Hanson smiled politely. A printed slip of paper, not much bigger than the message in a fortune cookie, was taped to the corner of the otherwise bare desk. The upside-down words: "TODAY'S VICTIM IS TOMORROW'S SUSPECT."

"This stuff in your file," Rivas said, "I gotta tell you, I even made a few phone calls to DC. It's fuckin' *classified.*"

Hanson looked at the beautiful woman on the billboard, smiling at him, her breasts straining against the spandex leotard straps. "Nothing to it. You know how the army is."

IT WAS A GOOD shooting. They were given three-day administrative leaves, standard procedure after a fatal shooting.

Just like the war, Hanson thought. Take a prisoner or kill enough of them, and they gave you a three-day R&R. He'd felt good about those, but not this one. A nigger who knew the day he got back from Vietnam that he'd outlived his future. Knew he was already dead the minute he stepped off the "freedom bird," as dead as whoever was up there in the third floor of the hospital with the lung-in-a-bottle doing his breathing.

He was drunk when he got home. The shooting interviews and reports had dragged out so that he'd gotten to the club late, but he'd made up for it by drinking Irish whiskey instead of beer.

The dog, Truman, was on the porch.

"Buenas noches, pal. Don't go away," he said, on his way into the kitchen for a beer, "I'll be right back." He came back out and sat down on the porch steps next to the dog.

"Quite a day," he said. "First I helped a guy commit suicide, and then I got to go to Internal Affairs."

He watched the pattern of moonlight cutting through the rafters of the collapsing barn out back, and scratched the bump between the dog's ears.

"You doin' okay?" he said. "Sometimes I worry you're like that guy in the hospital, hooked up to a machine that's keeping him alive when he's supposed to be dead."

He sipped his beer, and looked at the blind old dog.

"Should I turn the machine off? Maybe if you died you could come back with a new puppy body. Start over."

The dog snorted and lay down.

"You must miss old Mister Thorgaard," he said, standing up. "You don't really know me at all."

He took his beer into the front room of the old farmhouse, walking past the big easy chair and the woodstove to the bookcase against the far wall, where he pulled Mr. Thorgaard's book, *Steam,* off the shelf and thumbed through it as he had done maybe a hundred times since that day he'd found it in the dead man's bedroom. The leather-bound volume of flowcharts, mathematical tables, air/fuel efficiency formulas, graphs and steam-return blueprints seemed self-contained and conclusive—Water + Fire = Steam = Energy. He'd read it front to back. From the last page, backwards, to page one. Opened it at random. He'd tried leapfrogging through the pages in multiples of two, four, eight, searching for a pattern. Sometimes he purposely blurred his vision, looking for words or images hidden within the etchings of power plants, steamships plying the Great Lakes, the panoramas of disaster—

the crosshatched black guts of ruptured boilers buried beneath
splintered timbers and the rubble of collapsed chimneys—hoping
to penetrate the fundamental mysteries of fire and water, and find
within them instructions for living honorably in the midst of
madness and brutality, a diagram or formula that would show him
a way to walk, with courage and mercy, through a world where
sometimes, late at night when it was very quiet, he thought he
could hear pain itself rising from the earth to ride the dark, apple-
scented air.

He turned to the table he'd memorized on page fifty-seven:

TEMPERATURE OF FIRE

Appearance	Temperature Fahrenheit
Red, just visible	977
dull	1290
Cherry, dull	1470
full	1650
clear	1830
Orange, deep	2010
clear	2190
White heat	2370
bright	2550
dazzling	2730

Finally, he closed the book and slipped it back in the bookcase,
about to call it a night, when he noticed—dusty and half-hidden
under military training manuals and old issues of the *Shotgun
News*—the walnut box his uncle had carved the year Hanson was
born, his oldest possession. He picked it up, and, turning it, read
the fluted Old English script cut around the sides.

Consider The Lilies Of The Field How They Grow

He put it back down, opened it, and took out the green beret
folded inside, the beret he wore in Vietnam. Not on operations. It
was hot and didn't shade your eyes, ornamental, a useless piece of
equipment when you thought about it. He only wore it when they
went into Da Nang, strutting in their tiger suits, challenging everyone they passed, hundreds, thousands, of Vietnamese and

American soldiers, to get in their way, or look them in the eyes, or just look away too slowly. No one ever did. It was a country where people believed in death. Even in Da Nang, a safe place, you saw fresh corpses in the streets every morning.

He took it out and unfolded it, leather-trimmed green wool, lined with camouflage parachute nylon. A black "flash," the shape of an eye patch above the right eye, the silver Special Forces crest pinned over it, crossed arrows over a dagger, a black enamel flag above it declaring, *De Oppresso Liber*, "Free The Oppressed." Of course they all laughed at that. They knew better than that. If anyone asked them what the Latin words meant, they said, " 'Fuck The Oppressed.' " But it meant something else to them too.

Hanson remembered the day he was awarded the beret, in Training Group, knowing then that he would die before he would let anyone insult the beret, or insult him while he was wearing it. He knew that was adolescent, silly as the beret itself, and he'd never told anyone he'd felt that way.

Folded inside were the badges and medals. Silver American parachute wings. Vietnamese parachute wings, dull silver and black, crudely cast. The Combat Infantryman's Badge, silver with blue enamel, a flintlock rifle in an oak-leaf garland. A dog tag with his name and serial number, blood type—"A-Pos"—and religious preference—"No Pref."

He put the Bronze Star with the "V" for valor and the oak-leaf cluster in the palm of his hand. The cluster looked more like a bug than an oak leaf. He wished he'd won the Silver Star, but the Bronze Star with a "V" was okay. And he felt that he'd earned it, that day, though he'd only done what he had been trained to do, under fire. He had put aside his fear and accepted the fact that if he died, he'd die, but he would not be afraid and he would not fuck up because of fear. He'd killed a lot of North Vietnamese soldiers that day and they'd put him in for the Silver Star, but he'd gotten the Bronze. Of course, other guys had done braver things than what he'd done, and hadn't gotten a medal. Some, mostly officers, had done nothing at all and been given the Silver Star. But Hanson felt okay about the Bronze Star with the "V." It was fair to everyone. He didn't think that the guys who had done more and not been given a medal would say that he hadn't earned his. Even the ones who had been killed. Out there in heaven or eternity, or wherever you go when you die, they would say, "It's okay. He earned it."

Hanson smiled and shook his head, the medals clicking when he folded the beret back over them. Who knows?

He set it aside and took a photograph out of the box. A grainy Polaroid of Hanson, Quinn, Silver and Dawson standing in front of the teamhouse, the shadow of out-of-focus mountains behind them. The four of them grinning, looking *bad*, cradling folding-stock AKs, Thompsons, Swedish Ks, a Car-15. Quinn and Silver were long dead. Hanson had watched them die.

Dawson was probably dead by now, too. Hanson smiled. "Dawson." Everybody called him "Doc," the only black man on the team. Doc was one scary motherfucker. If it'd been him in that parking lot instead of Millon, he'd have taken a bunch of cops down with him.

Hanson placed the photo on top of the beret and took out a color photo of himself, wearing the beret and a pair of aviator sunglasses, grinning, holding up a bloody Viet Cong head by the hair, next to his own head, the two of them looking like those comedy and tragedy masks. "Tragedy," the dead Vietnamese, seemed to be looking down beneath drooping blood-streaked lids, his lips pouting, as if he was ashamed of mankind.

Hanson still couldn't work up any real shame for killing him and holding up the head for a photograph, no more than for holding a dead deer up by the horns. He had planned to have the photo printed on Christmas cards to send back home from the war. He sent the negative to a photo place in Australia, but it must have gotten lost in the mail because it never came back.

He'd wanted to send them all a severed head, not just a photo on a Christmas card. They were pro-war this or anti-war that, and they didn't know anything about it. When he'd first gotten back home and made the mistake of talking about some of the things he'd seen and done, they had looked at him like he was a monster.

Hanson drank the rest of the beer down. Well, he *was* a monster. That was true. There was nothing he could do for that. Too bad, he thought, putting the photos back in the box and covering them with the beret. It was a good thing he'd become a cop. He'd be in prison now, or dead, crazy as Millon, if he hadn't become a cop.

He closed the box, put it back on the shelf and gave it a little pat.

" 'Consider the lilies of the field, how they grow.' "

He'd stopped going to church a long time ago, but he loved the

King James Bible. The sound of the words. " 'They toil not, neither do they spin.' "

The dog came through the door, ears up, turning towards the
sound of Hanson's voice.

" 'And yet I say unto you, that even Solomon in all his glory
was not arrayed like one of these.'

"Learned it in the army," he said to the dog. "Did I tell you I
was in the army? The *brothers* called me 'Pageman' in basic training. I could hide eight or ten pages in my fatigue pockets, sneak
'em out and read 'em while I was standing in formation.

"Couple of the brothers would come up to me, and say, 'Look
here. It's my man. You know my man, Hanson? Uh-huh. Only I
call him *Page*man, 'cause he always got some *pages* in his pocket.
Tears 'em out of a book. Ain't that right?'

" 'That's right,' " I'd say.

" 'You don't mind if I call you Pageman, do you? I mean, I
wouldn't want you to get pissed off an' whip my ass or anything
like that because I call you *Page*man.' I'd smile and say it was
okay with me.

" 'What was it now you told me was in those books?'

" 'Poems. Like I told you, when I read 'em they make me feel
better.'

"He'd grin and say 'Shit,' and slap me on the shoulder like I was
the retarded white boy, and they'd walk off laughing at me.

" 'My man readin' *pomes.'*

"Come on, let's get another beer. The army took my poems
away," he said, the dog following him to the kitchen, "and gave
me a Bible."

He laughed and looked down at the dog. "Captain Decker did it,
Truman . . ."

IT HAD BEEN another hot July night, a month into basic training at Ft. Bragg, when Captain Decker held a three A.M. surprise
inspection. Decker was slightly taller than Hanson, trim and well
built, but his uniform hung on him like a cheap suit, the gaudy
stateside "Missile Command" patch on the shoulder. He was self-
conscious about his small hands, but wore a heavy gold ROTC
ring, from Paterson State College in New Jersey, which made
them look even smaller.

Staff Sergeant Washington followed a pace behind the captain, clipboard in his hand. Washington changed into fresh starched, tailored fatigues three times a day, always looking sharp. He never seemed to break a sweat or even breathe hard when he led the company in P.T. or five-mile runs. They knew, somehow, that he'd had two tours of Vietnam, but he never talked about it.

Decker found the two books, under a towel in Hanson's footlocker, the covers rubber-banded around the torn sections.

"Fuck books," he said, throwing the towel on the floor. "Fuck books in *my* barracks. Look at that. Sergeant Washington?"

"Yes, sir."

Henry Johnson, a black kid who slept on the bunk above Hanson, was standing at attention next to him. He smiled the second time Decker said "Fuck books."

"What *you* smiling at, Johnson?" Sgt. Washington said. "Illegal possession of pornography. Automatic Article 15. Nothing *funny* about it, I can see. Fuck books in Captain *Decker's* barracks. Get down and give me twenty."

Henry Johnson dropped between bunks, counting off his push-ups. *"One* thousand. *Two* thousand."

"You will rue the day, Private," Decker told Hanson, "when you chose to bring that filth into my barracks."

"Sir, it's . . ."

"As you *were*, Private," Washington said, looming over Decker.

"And what happens, Private," Decker went on, "when you become aroused? In a barracks full of young men. What do you think about when you engage in this type of literature? It makes me ill to think of that, Private.

"Do I have a cocksucker in my barracks, Sergeant?"

"Not to my knowledge, sir."

"Back in New Jersey, where I grew up, you know what we called 'em, Sergeant?"

"No, sir."

"We called 'em 'cornholers.' "

"Four thousand, *five* thousand," Henry Johnson shouted, covering his laughter.

"Is that what we've got?"

"I don't know, sir."

"Are you a cornholer, Private," Decker said, looking at Hanson's name tag, "Hanson?"

"No, sir."

"A faggot? A homosexual? Why else would you arouse yourself in a room full of sleeping, naked young men?"

Henry Johnson did push-ups, grinning at the paste-waxed floor as he called them out, *"Eight* thousand. *Nine* thousand."

Decker smiled at Hanson, and stepped closer. "Sergeant Washington," he said, his breath in Hanson's nose, "would you pick up one of those pieces of filth and hand it to me?"

"Fourteen thousand. *Fifteen* thousand."

A drop of sweat rolled from Decker's crew cut down his temple.

"Sir," Hanson began, staring at Decker's left ear.

"You're at attention, soldier," Decker said, as Washington handed him the book.

"Looks like you just about wore this one out," he said, holding it with two fingers. Without taking his eyes off Hanson's face, he snapped the rubber band off. "Some pussy eating going on in here, then? Cunnilingus? Some anal intercourse?" he said, looking down at the book.

"Sixteen thousand," Henry Johnson shouted.

Hanson listened to the rustle of the pages, then risked a look and saw, upside down, the words "Lord," "Jesus," and "Thou" all over the pages. Gerard Manley Hopkins, the nineteenth-century poet and Jesuit priest Hanson had been studying the semester he was drafted.

Decker tilted the book towards the light.

"Seventeen thousand."

He turned the page.

"Eighteen thousand."

He closed the book and looked at the cover.

"Nineteen thousand."

"Are you planning to be a minister, Private Hanson?"

"Yes, sir. I've been thinking a lot about it lately, I've . . ."

"Twenty thousand," Henry Johnson shouted at the floor, then leaped to his feet, snapped to attention next to Hanson and screamed, "Charging Charlie all the *way,* sir."

Decker nodded to him, then turned back to Hanson.

"That's all very well," Decker said. "Nothing wrong with that . . ."

"I've always been religious, sir, but it's only since I enlisted in the army that I began to . . ."

"Listen to what the captain has to say," Washington said.

Decker held up his hand, his eyes on Hanson. "I'll take care of it, Sergeant," he said, holding the book out. "Would you take this for me, please?

"As I was *saying*. That's all very well, but there is a time and a place for everything. Right now we are endeavoring to make a soldier out of you and the rest of these men to defend a country that *allows* freedom of expression and religion. Do you understand that?"

"Yes, sir."

"Do you see what I'm getting at?"

"Yes, sir."

"I misjudged you for a moment, but for good cause. In this army of ours, yours and mine, the Bible is the only book a soldier is allowed to have in basic training. Is that clear?"

"Yes, sir."

"What is the third general order?"

"Sir. The third general order is, 'I will not desert my post until properly relieved,' sir."

"Correct. Keep working hard, Private Hanson."

He looked up and down the formation. He nodded, squinting his eyes, his lips in a tight smile.

"An army is made up of rough men, Private Hanson. But we still need men of God among us."

He turned off the smile, did a right face, and stepped away.

When the captain was finished, he turned the company over to Sergeant Washington.

"Private Hanson will come outside with me. The rest of you people, *dis*miss."

"Gonna be a preacher, that right?" Washington asked him out in the company street. "Gonna spread the word? Work for The Man?"

"Yes, Drill Sergeant."

"Now you might want to tell the captain you 'thinking a lot' about being a preacher. The *captain* might believe it. But you don't want to be telling *me* that bullshit like I'm stupid as he is. *Do* you, young man?"

"No, Drill Sergeant."

"That's good, Hanson. That's better," he said, tapping the rolled-up pages of poetry against his huge open hand. "I don't know what this shit is, but I don't want to see it no more."

"Yes, Drill Sergeant."

"Good. Next time, though, you do *anything* to get Captain Decker upset—I don't care what it is—I'm gonna be pissed off at *you*, and you don't want that. You understand me?"

"Yes, Drill Sergeant."

"I don't want Captain Decker upset, or confused. 'Cause then he might have to make a decision, and maybe *do* something. That means more work for me, and more time I got to spend listening to the captain. I hate that. So don't fuck up no more."

"Yes, Drill Sergeant."

"What you doin' *here*, Hanson? You're not like these other crackers. I mean, shit, you been to *college*. In spite of that, you're even half smart sometimes."

"They drafted me, Drill Sergeant."

"You enlisted. A three-year RA."

"After they drafted me."

"Damn, boy. You could of got an MOS to keep you out of combat without taking that extra year, with that college on your record."

"I had to have three years to take the Special Forces test. I volunteered for infantry. If the fuckers are gonna draft me, then I want to see some war."

For a moment, Hanson thought Sgt. Washington was going to hit him.

"Now ain't that a goddamn shame you had to go to all that extra trouble so you'd have a chance to get your ass shot off—when you don't *have* to go over there at all. Too bad you wasn't born black, Hanson. Then they'd give you all the bad shit you want, all the time. They give it to you for *free*. God *damn*, boy," he said, jerking off his wide-brimmed hat, "you don't know . . ."

He rubbed his shaved black head, like he wanted to hurt himself. It was the first time Hanson had seen him without his hat on. The scar on his temple was purple in the light from the CQ office. He set the hat back on his head and adjusted the chin strap, his eyes distant, as if he'd forgotten Hanson was there.

"Get some sleep," he said, like he was talking to himself, and walked away, his head up, looking sharp, spit-shined jump boots flashing.

"Long day tomorrow," he said.

The next day Hanson went to the chaplain and got a tiny New Testament. It made the chaplain's day. He had a crate full of little New Testaments with black plastic covers that no one wanted.

The only time recruits seemed to visit him was when they wanted an emergency leave or a way to get out of the army for good, and he almost always had to send them away disappointed and angry.

"Thanks very much, sir," Hanson told him, shaking his hand, then saluting the smiling chaplain.

"Feel free to talk to me any time," the chaplain said.

"Thank you, sir," Hanson said. It was the best day he'd had so far since he'd been in the army. It made him feel good to cheer the chaplain up like that. And he was glad to have something to read that he didn't have to hide.

After that, Hanson carried the little book everywhere, memorizing passages in the Carolina sun, in the barracks and mess hall, in the smoky EM club at night, drinking 3.2 beer at a table in back if he could find one or leaning against the wall, out of the way of the sweating, skin-headed boys screaming to each other over the pounding jukebox, their names already typed on manifests for Vietnam.

"**MEMORIZED THE SHIT** out of that little King James Bible," he told Truman, turning off the light. At the stairs he turned and smiled at the dog watching him in the moonlight.

" '. . . how they *grow.*' Yes. Think of it, people. 'They toil *not,*' " he said, slipping into rhythms of the preachers and traveling evangelists of his childhood. " 'Neither *do* they spin. And yet I say unto you, that even Solomon' . . . even *Solomon,*" he shouted to the empty house, "the most powerful king of his time, wise Solomon, so rich he could of dressed hisself in raiments of purest gold . . . 'even Solomon was not ar-*rayed* like one of these.' Little. Lilies.

"Good night buddy," he said, taking the three steps to the landing where he looked out the window, at the branches of the apple trees against the sky.

" 'Take therefore,' " he said, working his memory for the last verse, " 'no thought for the morrow.' "

The lights of a car, way out on the main road, flared over the hill. " 'For the morrow shall take thought for the things of itself.' "

The crowns of the trees bloomed in the dark for a moment as the headlights topped the hill and swept down on them, the car picking up speed now. " 'Sufficient unto the day,' " Hanson said, the headlights flickering through the trees, fading, then gone, " 'is the evil thereof.'

"Well," he said, looking through his reflection now in the dark window, "that's about right, isn't it, Truman? That stuff seems to take care of itself. Not much you can do one way or the other."

He pulled the pistol out of the waistband of his jeans, thumbed the safety off, carrying it upstairs to bed as if he was searching a strange house. He'd clean it in the morning, he thought. He was too drunk to be cleaning guns.

He hesitated at the top of the stairs, then called down to the dog, "Truman, why don't you sleep up here tonight? I'll make you a bed with the sleeping bag. If you want to."

He folded the sleeping bag and put it on the floor by the bedroom window, turned off the light, and got in bed. When he heard the dog limping up the stairs, he went to sleep.

Truman sat on the sleeping bag and looked up, out the window. Of course, he was blind, but he seemed to be watching the moon go down behind Mt. Hood, called "Stormbreaker" by the Indians a hundred years before, thirty miles away.

The mountain had been there from the beginning, its massive west face chipped away by a million years of weather, facing the sea like a stone axe. The mountain blocked the storms coming off the Pacific, split them in half, the worst of them passing harmlessly to the north and south of Hanson's house, like black boxcars full of thunder and lightning.

Hanson moaned in his sleep, and the dog turned away from the window, listening, until he was quiet again. It was late. Some people were already getting up to start another day.

DOWN ON SKID ROW, in his room in the Nordic Seas Hotel, Dakota opens his eyes at the hiss of the scavenger outside, black trousers and shirts floating above him in the dark room on clothes-hangers hooked in the chicken-wire ceiling. The street-sweeping machine turns the corner, much louder now, foraging the gutter, its flashing yellow light dappling the hanging clothes and the walls of the second-floor room as it passes.

When it is gone, Dakota lights a candle stub on the floor and holds a knot of gingerroot over the flame until it blisters and chars, filling the room with sweet smoke, one of his morning rituals. Men with flowing blond hair and sequined capes seem to emerge from the smoke and flickering light, striding out through packs of tigers and great maned lions, black panthers leaping above their heads, through hoops flaming in the shadows.

Dakota sits up, hairless and fish-belly white, and turns on the light with a knotted length of shoelace dangling above him. He pulls on a pair of black boots, the bare lightbulb still swinging from a cord beneath the chicken wire, webbing the ceiling with bloated geometric patterns, glaring off the glossy circus programs and magazine pages that paper the walls, all pictures of Gunther Gebel-Williams, Barnum & Bailey's famous German lion tamer in different costumes and cages.

Naked except for his boots, his chest and thighs and buttocks crawling with scars, livid and thick as night crawlers, he walks a complex pattern around all the other candles on the floor. The votive candles are set in clusters of chicken bones decorated with marbles, coins, bottle caps, and broken glass. Dakota kneels at each one, lights it, then opens the window. Pigeons rustle and coo on the ledge outside where he keeps his food.

Down in the street winos limp and grumble through the murky false dawn, the tips of their cigarettes glowing in the alley. A bottle bongs and shatters against a Dumpster and someone shouts, "How's *that* for 'whaddaya mean?'"

Dakota takes the top off a carton of cottage cheese, smells it, sees that it has turned rancid. He eats it standing up, his eyes on the dark window, ladling in great mouthfuls with a white plastic spoon, chewing methodically, with controlled rage, clots of the stuff running down his neck and naked chest. He scoops the last of the cottage cheese out and washes it down with a two-liter bottle of Pepsi.

Dakota opens the padlock on the bottom drawer of the cigarette-scarred desk and takes out the quart bottle of Popov vodka. He holds it up to the light, studying it, then puts it back. He bought it almost six months ago, and the seal is still unbroken.

He digs through the unopened bottles of Thorazine and Dilantin in the bottom of the drawer, and takes out a dog-eared Gideon Bible he found in a Motel Six in Barstow, California, the nicest room he ever spent a night in. He took the Bible, clean and new-smelling as the room, to remember it by. But the Bible, its tissue-thin pages stained now and reeking of lock-down disinfectant and flophouse hallways, is almost as important as Gunther and the cats.

''**GOOD MORNING, BUDDY,**'' Hanson said, pulling the warped backdoor shut. Truman, who was dozing in the sun over by the garden, thumped his tail twice. The air smelled of apple blossoms. It had been a late spring, and a few blossoms drifted down onto Hanson's hair and the sleeveless sweatshirt he wore.

Stormbreaker, still snowcapped, rose to the west, perfect and patient as death, willing to take him whenever Hanson chose to go.

"What a morning, huh?" he said, kneeling down by the dog.

The mountain was only an hour or so away. A nice drive, he thought, putting his arm around the dog, feeling his beating heart. He'd go in the morning, wearing jeans and tennis shoes and a T-shirt, leave the van where the road ended and hike up to the timberline, then climb up beyond the trees into the real cold.

"But not today," he told Truman. "Hey, who'd take care of you for Mister Thorgaard? Gotta run off this hangover, though," he said, standing and saluting down at the dog.

"Gotta go," he sang, "gotta be," jogging down the dirt road, finding his pace, "airborne . . . *in*fantry."

When his side began to cramp up, he talked to it, "Does that *hurt?* Let's make it hurt a little more," picking up the pace a fraction, thinking that physical pain was the only emotion anyone could really depend on.

The sky was absolutely blue.

He glanced down at his legs, amazed as always at the complex machinery of his knees and ankles and feet, then concentrated on Stormbreaker, on a spot just above the tree line, until he was *up* there, his breath turning to frozen fog, leaving the pain down by the irrigation ditch with the false Hanson. A trick he'd learned so he could keep running when his body wanted to stop.

Valium, he thought. With a quart of vodka. *Sleeping pills.* He came to a road where he ran in place for a few seconds, dancing on the balls of his feet, then turned smoothly and crossed the asphalt, catching up to his own rhythm.

Carbon monoxide. Hook a hose up to the van's exhaust, and run it through the window. A good method. He'd taken a report on one like that a few months before. The guy had done it in the garage on a weekend while his wife was out of town, nailing the garage door shut and stuffing blankets under it. He'd turned bluish-black by the time she got home and found him, and called the police.

Hanson had been sitting on a sofa, finishing a supplemental report, when the wife said, "Do you have any questions I haven't answered?"

She was leaning against the doorway, smiling at him. "Don't get up," she said. "I'll come over there."

She sat next to him, her leg touching his. Ten years older than Hanson, according to the report, she was sexy, with curly black hair and pink lipstick.

She leaned into him, her breast brushing the back of his arm, spreading against his ribs, and looked down at the clipboard on his lap.

"It was just like him," she whispered, sweet liquor on her breath, "taking a coward's way out."

She opened her hand, pressed it down on the clipboard, and he'd gotten an erection, in his wool uniform pants, while the Medical Examiner loaded her husband onto the gurney, pushed it across the room and out the front door. The body had stiffened into a sitting position, his knees pulled up and his arms crossed at his chest as if he'd been leaning on the steering wheel. You could see that even though the body was covered with a gray blanket. Hanson remembered her perfume and the way the lamplight had caught her cleavage when she looked him in the eyes.

HE CROSSED A dirt farm road, past the steel slats of a cattle guard, and back up on the irrigation berm. Death would probably be interesting, Hanson thought. He'd been ready for a long time now.

He laughed, imagining heaven as an old black-and-white movie, where some angel tells God, "That guy Hanson again. He's way overdue. Let's kill him *this* time."

"Take care of it," God says, and the angel is out of sight when God *remembers* something and shouts, "Not *him*. Kill somebody else."

The pounding rolled out of the hills behind him like Judgment Day, unmistakable on the back of his neck. Gunships. A pair of Cobras on his trail, coming up fast. He held his pace, shivering with the old terror and joy as they closed the distance.

A few years before, up in Northern I Corps, on a sunny February afternoon, Hanson had called in a pair of Cobras. He'd been trapped in a bomb crater with a handful of Montagnard tribesmen, surrounded by a platoon of North Vietnamese regulars who were shooting divots of red mud off the lip of the crater and trying to lob hand grenades in on them. When the Cobras arrived on station, Hanson had directed their fire—rockets, grenade launchers, and droning miniguns—laughing, bringing them over in pass after pass.

He ran full-out now, these Cobras above him, *on* him, back for a moment to that afternoon when he had killed fourteen men, the best day of his life.

They boomed over like thunderheads, Black Cobra gunships blotting out the blue sky, miniguns jutting from their drooping noses, so loud now they were all he could hear or smell or taste, the hot rush of burning jet fuel in his nose and eyes like that day in the bomb crater when he'd seen the truth for the first time, like looking into the sun—Kill or Die. All the rest was lies.

FIVE

AFTER HE'D RUN, Hanson called his mother, back in North Carolina, as he did almost every Saturday.

His ninety-five-year-old grandmother was doing okay, she told him, and loved the card he'd sent her. His cousin Lee Ann was getting married again. How was *he* doing, she wanted to know. She prayed for him every Sunday. Good, he laughed. He'd take all the extra credit he could get.

She told him about the retreat her church group had gone to at Camp Good Hope. His aunt Helen had kept them all laughing.

He told her he'd probably be able to fly out for a visit at Christmas.

His sister would be disappointed she'd missed his call, she said, but they could hardly wait until Christmas. It had been too long since they'd seen him. They were so glad he was doing better now than when he left almost four years ago . . .

———

AFTER THE MANDATORY army steak dinner and welcome-home-you're-all-heroes speech at Ft. Lewis, Hanson had taken a cab with four other soldiers, all strangers, to Sea-Tac airport. After a stop at an off-base liquor store, they began swapping war stories and describing the hell they would raise when they got home. None of them had Combat Infantry Badges, but Hanson nodded and smiled at their lies for a few miles, then took out the sweat- and bloodstained copy of *The Collected Poems of W.B. Yeats* he'd carried through the war.

It was a long ride. The war stories and the amount of drinking and fucking they'd soon be doing grew more heroic, their laughter louder as Hanson read.

> *I will arise and go now, and go to Innisfree,*
> *And a small cabin build there, of clay . . .*

At a red light on the outskirts of Tacoma they described what they'd like to do to the woman in the car stopped next to them, groaning and whistling when she rolled up her window.

> *. . . of clay and wattles made:*
> *Nine bean-rows will I have there,*
> *a hive for the honey bee,*
> *And live alone in the bee-loud glade.*

The E-5 from the Americal Division, a big Italian from New York named Dellasandro, began mugging for the three E-4s, arching his eyebrows and rolling his eyes at Hanson. Finally, while the others watched, he said, "That pretty good stuff, Sarge?"

> *Nine bean-rows will I have there,*
> *a hive for the honey bee,*
> *And live alone in the bee-loud glade.*

Dellasandro, who had a thick mustache and was sweating in his uniform, looked at the others and tried again.

"That book you're reading. Must be some hot stuff the way . . ."

"If I kill you," Hanson said, looking up at him, "they'll put me in prison. We're almost home, okay?"

Dellasandro nodded. "Sure, Sarge," he said.

After a few awkward attempts to pick up their camaraderie, they sat back in their seats and looked out the window for the rest of the trip, only radio static and the *tick* of the meter breaking the silence. Hanson felt bad about ruining their homecoming and could only pretend now to concentrate on the book. At the airport they each paid the cabdriver and split up without a word. Hanson caught a standby seat for home on the last eastbound Delta flight.

It was after eleven when he picked up his duffle bag at his hometown airport. His mother and sister weren't expecting him, and he thought about staying the night in a motel, somewhere he could change out of his uniform. He'd stuck his beret in his pocket, but the jump boots and the insignia on his jacket were getting a lot of attention, mostly angry looks, and he didn't know how long he could keep ignoring them. The chirping in his ears was getting louder.

He called from a pay phone and waited out in the parking lot until his mother and sister, who were both crying, picked him up.

He changed into jeans and a T-shirt when he got home, and they stayed up until three, talking and drinking the bottle of Benedictine they'd been saving for him. He drank most of it, but it didn't make him sleepy. After they went to bed, he stood, hands in his pockets, in the middle of the bedroom that had been his, the door closed behind him covered with sunflowers he'd painted late one night, his hands trembling slightly from peyote.

Everything was just like it had been when he'd left for basic training more than three years before, except for the "WELCOME HOME OUR HERO" banner strung from the ceiling. Little tins of greasepaint still lined up along the back of the dresser he'd painted in a reptilian pattern of green and purple scales. As the war had escalated back then, he'd taken LSD direct from Timothy Leary's commune at Millbrook, so new it wasn't even illegal yet, the workaday rituals and moral injunctions of society suddenly absurd through his dilated eyes as he looked in the mirror, painting his face in green and blue tiger stripes or solid white, his teeth and eyeballs yellow and wolflike. Then he'd ride his motorcycle through town, laughing, the headlights of oncoming cars boiling like atomic furnaces in his dilated pupils.

The pictures of who he had been on the walls, grainy, high contrast black-and-white photos taken by a girlfriend who had written him for a while after he went into the army. She married a young professor and moved to Chicago where he heard she'd committed suicide. He had hair down to his shoulders in the photos, his head slightly turned, looking past the camera into the distance, *like Prince Valiant*, he thought. Only his eyes were in focus, the rest of his face fading artistically into the emulsion. He snorted with embarrassment, turning to the line drawing of him, done by a visiting art professor when Hanson had earned money for his tuition by modeling for art classes. A darkly romantic portrait on the opposite wall had been painted over a series of afternoons by an English professor's wife he had been half in love with.

"Salome," the life-size copy of one of Beardsley's decadent, mythical women he'd painted on the wall over his bed, regarded him with heavy-lidded, stone-cold eyes from beneath a headdress of snakes and fork-tongued lizards. A six-pointed star tattoo circled the nipples of her bare breasts, and a fan of real peacock feathers covered her thighs, their iridescent eyes dull now with dust. He looked at it all as if he'd wandered into a stranger's house and been mistaken for the person who lived there, embarrassed and ashamed of himself for going along with the mistake, not wanting to disappoint anyone who thought he was the person they'd been waiting for. But that was who he had been back then. He couldn't change that.

As the sun came up, he looked through the boxes of essays and term papers and letters, then moved to the zebra-striped bookcases, glad to see his books again until he thumbed through them, finding the arrogant, self-righteous notes in the margins, all written in ink. He could hardly believe he'd written those words, but he'd done it, all right. He'd been real sure of himself back then.

He pulled the curtains and got into bed, looking up at Salome frowning down at him just as she had before the war.

"Hiya, Sal'," he said, the jet lag and liquor finally slowing him down. "Remember me? I was a real *sensitive* fucker back then."

He smiled and fluffed his pillow. Outside, people were driving to work. "Even back then. All along," he said to her, "you knew what I was going to find over there, didn't you?" He closed his eyes and went to sleep, the chirping in his ears a bee-loud glade.

He'd been drinking 3.2 beer in that replacement center bar in Tan Son Nhut less than two days before as far as he could figure, counting through the time zones. Sitting at a table with seven other Special Forces troops. When everyone else in the bar began singing "God Bless America," Hanson had organized his table into a chorus line in front of the door, linking arms and chanting, "Ho,

Ho, Ho Chi Minh. The NLF is *bound* to win." Then they'd given the finger to the packed bar shouting together, "Fuck you." Not one of the hundred or two hundred soldiers, who had fallen silent, did anything about it.

In the mornings his mother and sister would be gone by the time he woke up, and he'd take a cup of coffee into the living room where it was cool and quiet, and look out the big window. It was autumn, but the big gray mockingbirds hadn't gone south yet.

When he felt his chest tighten he'd sigh, set the coffee down, and rest his forearms on his knees before the sobbing began. When it was over, and he could breathe, he'd wipe his eyes with his fingers and the heels of his hands and finish the coffee. It only lasted a minute or two and then he was fine. Some sort of tension-reducing mechanism.

At 11:45 he'd walk to a tavern named The Filling Station. It wasn't far, and he found a route where he didn't have to cross many streets. Stan, one of the bartenders, had spent some time on a fire base in Vietnam. He didn't like to talk about the war and that was fine with Hanson. He'd have a bacon cheeseburger and drink beer until three or four in the afternoon, then walk home where he'd pass out and sleep until suppertime.

He and his mother and sister would eat and watch the six o'clock news about the war that was still going on. They were worried about him, but tried not to show it. He hadn't seen his father in years, and didn't ask about him. The last he'd heard, his father was working in a Christian shelter for alcoholics in Charlotte, trying to stay sober.

When the sun went down, he'd walk to The Filling Station, swallows and bats diving and snap-rolling in the dusk, and drink until they closed at midnight.

One morning, two middle-aged men carrying briefcases walked up on the porch and knocked on the door. He knew they'd seen him through the window, so he opened the door and they looked at one another through the screen. Their suits hung on them like hand-me-downs, their shirt collars were dingy, and their hair looked as if it had been cut by a wino. They looked like life had beaten them almost to death and then, on a whim, allowed them to live some more. Hanson wondered if they were messengers from his future.

"Good morning," the big one said. "My name's Lee, and this is

Gus. We're from the FBI." He saw the flash of fear in Hanson's eyes—what did the computers have on him?—and laughed. "That's right," he said, "Free. Bible. Information. F. B. I." He had a belly and a salesman's smile, there to *make the sale for God*. "Let me ask you something," he began.

When Hanson finally tried to interrupt him, saying, "I think about God a lot, every day. I . . ." Lee nodded, ignored him, and went on.

"That's good, thinking about it, because you know what? *Logic* tells us that God exists. Not just faith. No, sir . . ."

Gus listened and nodded. His new false teeth didn't seem to fit right. Hanson couldn't tell if he was trying to smile or adjust the teeth so they wouldn't ache. "You're an intelligent young man. You can see that, can't you, Gus?" Pale and still strung out, Gus managed to nod, swallowing as if he might be sick. He needed a drink. Hanson imagined this was a training mission for him.

"Let me ask you something," Lee said, turning back to Hanson. "What if you were walking through the desert, hot and tired. You want a drink of water. You're dying of thirst. But all it is out there is sand dunes. Everywhere you look it's sand. You're about to give up, but you decide to walk over one more sand dune, up one side and down the other and suddenly . . . there's this *house*. In the middle of the desert. How about that? Just when you were about to give up you find a *house* in the middle of nowhere! Inside there's a kitchen. You turn on the faucet and get a drink of water. There's a bathroom too, with a shower and a commode. Now how did that house get there? It's not possible but it's *there*. You go and get you a co-cola out of the refrigerator. *Somebody* had to *build* that house. It's only logical . . ."

Something about Gus reminded Hanson of his father.

"Everything, don't you see, works together as parts of a logical universe. From the big," Lee said, spreading his arms, "to the small." He brought his thick hands together, cupping them as if he had captured a bird. The skin was dry and splotched with red patches.

"Let me ask you something," Lee said, pressing his palms together as if he was praying, or flattening a hamburger patty. "Do you like hamburgers? Sure you do. Everybody does. Now, just look at an old meat grinder," he said, spreading, then interlacing his fingers, flexing and wiggling them like a ball of snakes. "All the gears have to *mesh* if it's gonna do the job and turn that chuck steak into hamburger. That's the whole story right there. Do you see now what I'm saying?"

Hanson thanked him and promised to think about what he'd said.

"Don't take too long," Lee said, "because the end is coming. Everybody who wanted to could of got on the Ark, even after it first started raining," he said, holding his hands out, palms up like he was feeling the rain, looking up at the sky. "They still could of got on even then."

Gus watched Hanson like he knew him from another time.

"But once those doors slammed shut," Lee said, slapping his hands together and looking grimly at Hanson, "it was too late then, brother."

Hanson managed to slip Gus a twenty-dollar bill while Lee was looking for a pamphlet in his briefcase. When Lee started down the stairs, Gus whispered, "Don't never let 'em do this to you."

"Come on, Gus," Lee called over his shoulder. "Get a move on. We got a whole lot of the *Lord's* work to do."

It was late afternoon and the normally quiet street was busy, people on the way home from their jobs, windows rolled up, breathing cool, artificial air.

Hanson started the gas-powered lawn mower and it exploded with blue smoke until he throttled the choke back. Little stones and bits of mud quivered across the cowling like beads of grease in a hot pan. The roar of the machine swept over him, killing the traffic noise, the next best thing to silence.

He started at the sidewalk, losing himself in the irregular contours of the yard, trying to follow them perfectly, working inward on an ever-diminishing island of grass. Row after row, the ragged grass bent gracefully beneath the mower, emerging in uniform and perfectly parallel rows. The pattern looked like elevation lines on a map, and he thought of how Quinn and Silver would laugh, if they were still alive, to see him doing something as pointless and "American" as mowing the grass with a three-horse-power gasoline engine. It had been years since he'd mowed this yard, and the forgotten smell of fresh-cut grass and gasoline startled him into the past, until some tiny interruption in the relentless press of grass feeding into the mower blade shuddered up through the handlebars, and touched the palms of his hands. Without breaking stride, still mowing, he looked down and saw it, the thing he'd felt, surface in the green wake of the mower. It glistened wetly in the grass, subtle movement flowing through the perfect set of tiny internal organs—intestines, lungs, and tucked down in the purple contour of the liver, the throbbing little heart of a toad, the external body snatched cleanly away, like the skin off a plum, leaving just a bundle of guts that still thought it was alive. Hanson watched the toad's heart, an innocent toad he had skinned alive, beat more slowly, erratically, and finally stop, then he walked back into the house, the lawn mower roaring behind him.

In his bedroom Salome looked down at him from the wall, and Hanson knew who she was, now. Death's sister.

Her brother had been his companion and teacher in the war. Smiling Death, taking the fear away so Hanson could pretend he was brave. If Death was his friend, what was there to fear but an instant or a minute of pain? Death would shepherd him through that to the other side. But now his old friend was angry at him for leaving the war and coming home, betraying his friendship, cheating him on the deal he'd made to die over there. It was too late to go back this time. The war was over.

Hanson left town the next day. He told his mother and sister that he had friends to stay with out west, taking the bus only as far as Asheville where he started hitchhiking to save money, looking over his shoulder. When the trees rustled or dust rose behind him, he stopped to listen and smell the air.

He'd been on the street as a cop for over three years now.

SIX

UP IN NARCOTICS and Vice, Fox was at the computer, scrolling through U.S. Army travel orders for the Republic of Vietnam, alphabetized lists of soldiers and serial numbers. He'd worked his way from January, 1968 to June, 1968. Peetey sat across the room, his feet up on one of the metal desks, paging through a year-old copy of *Guns and Ammo*, watching the back of Fox's head and glancing up at the clock every few minutes.

Finally, he put the magazine down, pulled back his ponytail, and took his feet off the desk.

"Let's hit the street, man," he said. "Find out what's going on."

"It's all in here," Fox said, tapping the PAGE DOWN key, scrolling down through alphabetized names on the still-classified Special Orders dated May, 1968, assigning Special Forces personnel to foreign duty. "Everything we need to know, and I'll find it. All it takes is . . ."

He hit another key, the list of names replaced on the screen by the words: NOT A VALID COMMAND. ACCESS DENIED. SEE DOD SPECIAL ORDER (AR 210-10) and the reflection of the office door opening. ". . . I'm beginning to think I'll *never* access these files."

"Exactly," Rivas said, standing in the doorway to the outer office. Peetey started up from the chair, then caught himself, pretending he'd known Rivas was there all along.

"How's it goin', Peetey," Rivas said, on his way across the room, stopping behind Fox, looking down at the computer screen over his shoulder. "Any luck?"

"These DOD files are *tough* to break into, I've tried . . ."

"I wouldn't *know*," Rivas said, raising his hand, "anything about *breaking into* classified files. And I'm sure you wouldn't want to violate any federal laws.

"Hanson's record speaks for itself. I just get curious sometimes. My wife tells me not to bring the job home, but I get curious. No big deal. If *you* can't access those files, nobody can. Don't waste any more of your time or expertise on it," he said, walking away.

He stopped at the door. "You're due to go on vacation in a week or so, aren't you?" he asked Fox.

"Postponed it for a while. Need to clear some of these cases before I go."

"You work too hard," Rivas said. "Take her easy, Peetey."

"That little spic motherfucker," Peetey said, when the door closed behind Rivas.

Fox watched names scroll down the screen.

"You got a lot of vacation time built up," Peetey said. "If you don't use it . . ."

"I'm planning to take a couple weeks in September," Fox said, his eyes on the screen.

"You going to the same place down there in . . ."

"Panay," Fox said, keying another file, the cursor blinking on a blank screen. "On one of the little islands." He looked up at the clock, flipped through his notebook, typed in a command for yet another name search.

"I'm jealous, man," Peetey said. "You're buying two of 'em?"

"It's more like a *lease*. A two-week lease for a pair of sixteen-year-olds. I give 'em the money and for two weeks they do whatever I want."

"Like what, man? I mean, I gotta ask."

Fox typed in another code and the screen filled up with words— CLASSIFICATION—SECRET—DOD AND USARPAC REG

CATEGORY II—NOFORN—NEED TO KNOW ONLY. PRESS *ENTER* TO CONTINUE.

"What did I just say? *Any thing,*" Fox said, hitting the ENTER key, "as long as it doesn't cause permanent damage. Sometimes you have to pay a bonus."

"Real pros."

"They're not *whores,* like these, *nothing* like some nappy-headed blowjob junkie up on the Avenue who smells like her last fifty tricks, with sores on her mouth.

"These girls are *clean,* like geishas, 'the floating world,' you know? Trained since childhood to give a man pleasure. At the end of two weeks, it's 'bye-bye' girls, whatever name you decided to call them.

"And they say, 'Bye-bye. We aw-rays ruve you.' You never hear, 'Call me tomorrow?' or 'Where were you last weekend?' "

Peetey laughed.

Fox stared at the screen, tapping the PAGE DOWN key, running text down almost too fast to read.

"You know," Peetey went on, "a few times last year, when you were down there in the Philippines? With two girls? And I'm in bed with Trish? I'd look over at her, sleeping, putting on weight while she *sleeps,* man." He shook his head. "I'd think, what if she died? Just *died.* I don't mean kill her, nothing like that. At *all.* But . . ."

"Bingo," Fox said, freezing the names, highlighting one halfway down the screen:

HANSON, C.K. SGT. 240-60-3427—NEW DUTY STATION—ASSN CO. C. 5TH SPECIAL FORCES GROUP (ABN), USARPAC RVN. SECURITY CLEARANCE: SECRET—DOD NAC CENTER>>>

"We're in business," Fox said.

HANSON DROVE SLOWLY down Mason Street, maneuvering through the district to keep the afternoon sun out of his face, while Dana looked through the newspaper real estate ads. He was about to decide whether to jog left on Vancouver when a woman ran out from behind a house, waving her arms, followed by a little girl in a yellow sun dress.

"It's that Topper," the woman shouted. "He's killing her."

"Hurry," the little girl cried. Her eyes were huge and her dark brown cheekbones glistened with tears.

Hanson pulled to the curb, threw the car in PARK, pulled the keys from the ignition, and slid his nightstick out of its holder as he opened and closed the door. Dana was already out. "Where?" he said.

"Does he have a weapon?" Hanson asked, about to pull his packset to call for a cover car.

"Back here," the woman said, turning and running. "Hurry."

The little girl ran behind her, stopped and looked at the cops, then ran some more.

"Does he have a *weapon?*" Dana said.

"Don't *have* no *weapon*. It's *Topper*," the woman said. "In the *back*."

As they ran between houses, Hanson thought he heard cursing and grunting in the back. He kicked through a broken gate into the backyard.

There at the edge of a little garden, in the tomato plants, a brindle pit bull was eating a German shepherd. The shepherd's throat was matted with blood, his stomach torn open, but he was still alive. Her eyes were rolled back to the whites and her front legs twitched as if she were asleep and dreaming of a chase. The pit bull had pulled a translucent blue and gray coil of intestines out of the shepherd and was chewing it, without anger or relish or urgency.

The little girl shrieked and ran towards the dogs. Hanson caught her by the arm, and she fought him, screaming, tearing the neck of her sun dress. The pit bull turned at the noise and walked, stiff-legged and growling, towards them, a length of intestine caught in his teeth, trailing behind him.

Dana shot the pit bull once, square in the chest, and he raised slightly up on his hind legs, then dropped back down, stiff-legged on all fours. He turned and went back to the twitching shepherd and began chewing again, blood pumping out of the bullet hole in his chest. "Hold her," Hanson said, picking up the kicking girl and handing her to a man watching from the back porch. He pushed through the crowd that was gathering, and ran to the patrol car.

Neighbors were walking up the street now, crossing the yard, drawn by the patrol car and the sound of the shot. Hanson popped the magnetic lock on the cuff that held the shotgun against the dashboard, pulled the gun out and ran back around the house. The crowd moved aside when they saw the shotgun.

The pit bull's maul-shaped head was half-buried in the shepherd's stomach, jerking from side to side, worrying something inside loose. The shepherd's jaws opened and closed convulsively, vomiting gouts of blood, shiny as paint, that splashed on the dark leaves of the tomato plants and the brown soil.

Hanson jacked a round into the shotgun and fired into the dogs, pumping another round and another. Each twelve-gauge round fired a dozen lead pellets the size of pencil erasers, hitting the dogs and the fat tomatoes like a killer wind, blowing a red mist of meat and fur and bloody mud and tomato flesh across the garden. When the shotgun was empty, Hanson jacked the action open. The stink of gun smoke mixed with the rich smell of fresh tomatoes. The two dogs looked like something on the freeway after a lot of traffic had run it over.

"We didn't call you all to *shoot* her dog," the woman holding the little girl shouted. "We could of took her to the *vet*."

Hanson looked down at the dogs, his ears ringing. The shotgun was hot in his hands.

"Could I get your name, ma'am," Dana said to the woman, holding his pocket notebook.

"*No*, you can't get my name," she shouted, "what good *that* gonna do anything now? He killed 'em both."

"Ma'am," Dana said, "there wasn't anything we could do for the little girl's dog except put it out of its misery. If I could just have your name . . ."

"*You* don't know that. You could of took it to the vet. That's all you know is how to *kill* something."

"Her guts were torn out and all over the yard, ma'am," Hanson said. "A vet can't fix that."

"Let's get outta here," Dana said, "and write it up somewhere else."

As the two of them walked back through the crowd, a teenage boy, held back by two men, screamed at them, "Why you kill Topper? Why you kill my dog? It was a fair fight, man, till you shot her."

"You *proud* of yourselves?" someone in the crowd yelled.

Hanson snapped the shotgun back into its holder as they drove off.

"Well," Dana said, "I think there's gonna be a whole lot of paperwork on that. What do you think?"

"We're gonna have to write a book on that," Hanson said. "We're gonna have to do some creative writing."

"I don't want to sound critical, my man, but I think maybe you overreacted a little bit. With the shotgun and all," Dana said. "We'll be lucky if we don't have to go to Internal Affairs on this."

"*Fuck* Internal Affairs," Hanson said, wrenching the wheel, fishtailing a little onto Vancouver Street. "You know? *Fuck* them. They can stick it up their *ass.*"

They passed the Muslim Temple and the boarded-up Egyptian Theatre. Dana looked at Hanson, then back at the street. The hot smell of the shotgun filled the car.

All you know is how to kill something.

"One time," Hanson said, "up in Northern I Corps. A few days after we'd been overrun and taken the camp back. The Montagnards were out burning the grass in the perimeter wire, so sappers can't crawl through the wire by hiding in the grass. The 'Yards were being lazy, and they didn't police up all the claymore mines. The grass fire set one of them off. I heard the explosion and saw the smoke in the wire, and at first I thought we were taking mortar fire. Then I ran out there.

"The claymore had caught the squad leader from the One-Oh-One company, dead center, from his hips up into his chest. We weren't good buddies or anything, but I *knew* him, you know? His name was *Kraang*-the-Hawk. We'd been on operations together. I talked to him sometimes. He'd shown me pictures of his family and was always saying how he was gonna take me down to Hue sometime to meet them. He'd had to pay a fortune in bribes to get them out of a Vietnamese resettlement camp.

"They'd gotten a poncho under him and were trying to use it like a stretcher, but it kept slipping out of their hands. I worked my way over to him—kept getting caught on the concertina, the grass burned black and still smoking, burning my feet.

"He was rocking on his elbows. I could see his hipbones, pieces of his fucking pelvis. Rocking up to look at himself. Then he'd slip in the blood and fall back. Splashing blood."

Hanson turned his head at a threatening flicker of movement, a Doberman watching them from behind a chain-link fence. The sleek dog was poised as if he was ready to jump, his ears up, alert, shivering with excitement as they passed.

"Like a bathtub of blood. He humped up again, on one elbow, and reached down there like maybe he could stuff his guts back in. He was, *keening*, is the word, I guess."

Hanson pushed back into the broken-down bench seat. He turned off Haight Street onto Failing, opening and closing his hand. A sound down in his chest, so faint at first that he wasn't aware of it, rose in his throat before he choked it off. Dana hadn't heard the sound, or was pretending he hadn't.

Hanson tried to relax his neck muscles, looking out the filthy windshield at the passing neighborhood. "Then he saw me standing behind him. Carrying my Car-15. And gave me this look. Rolled his eyes up and *looked* at me."

At a stop sign, Hanson took his pistol belt in both hands and tugged at it. "I knew what he wanted." He pushed up out of the seat and *jerked* the belt, heavy with equipment, into a more comfortable position.

"I fuckin' looked away, man. I ran back to the team house and yelled for the medic. The *medic.* Shit. The medic couldn't do anything for him."

They passed a broken-down pickup truck with four flat tires. Its engine and hood had been removed and piled in the back along with a muffler and an old TV set. The blocks were lined with gutted cars that looked as if someone had taken them apart and then couldn't figure out how to get them back together. "We need to tag some of these junk cars," Hanson said, "and get 'em towed.

"We brought a stretcher out from the medical bunker—the grass was still burning—and rolled him onto it. He kept opening and closing the hand that still worked. Making a fist. I wish I could go back, for thirty seconds, and act like a fucking man this time. It's, the truth is, I don't feel bad about anybody I *did* shoot . . ."

Five Eighty.

"Five Eighty, go ahead."

Uh, Five Eighty, take a cold burglary report . . .

"Sometimes," Dana said, "with that kind of damage, the pain's not as bad as you might think. Shock and . . ."

"We had an agreement. Me and Quinn and Silver and Doc. If one of us got real fucked up, lost our legs or balls or faces, whoever was with him would see to it that he was dead before the medevac got there. We got drunk in the team house one night, cut our hands with an NVA bayonet, and made a blood oath."

Hanson looked at the scar on the heel of his hand, a livid knot at the end of a fine white line, like a tiny comet. "A *blood* oath. Like a bunch of Boy Scouts."

Small children playing in the streets waved as they drove past, calling PO-lice, PO-lice, a sound like cooing doves. Hanson and Dana waved back and said, "Hi, young man," or "Hi, young lady, how you doin'?" The cops were already as regular a part of their young lives as breakfast or bedtime.

They drove the blocks for half an hour without getting a call, angling through the district, turning left or right at random, circling back, watching over the district. They looked for trouble, stolen cars and open doors, for people who looked away too quickly or walked wrong when they saw the patrol car, yet it was relaxing, like cruising the neighborhood. Hanson felt at home. It was home.

SEVEN

AFTER FINISHING THEIR reports and taking show-ers at the precinct, Dana went home and Hanson drove across town to the PAA, the Police Athletic Association, a bar for the police and their groupies. The mildewed little weight room in the basement was the only thing "athletic" about the club.

It looked like any working-class bar, with red vinyl booths along one wall, tables and chairs, and a pool table. Willie Nelson was singing "Good-Hearted Woman" on the jukebox as Hanson walked through the door.

When "A" relief got off the street at 11:00 and midnight, the place began to fill up. Most of the off-duty cops wore blue jeans and workshirts and could have passed for loggers or truck drivers. Some of the younger guys, the ladies' men, wore blow-dried hair, suede jackets, sunglasses and cowboy boots. The narcs and vice-squad people looked like hippies and bikers and small-time hoods.

Just inside the door, Farmer, a big homicide detective with a crew cut, wearing a cheap gray suit, was talking to Peetey.

"I'll try, Peetey," he said, "but you know how chickenshit the

DA's office is getting about search warrants. If you don't write it letter-perfect . . ."

"Tell me about it," Peetey said. "The little motherfucker released all that money we seized. Said our probable cause was 'dubious.' "

"Yeah, well . . ."

"Hey," Peetey said, "all we're askin' you is . . ."

"Hanson," Farmer said, when he saw him, "you write a damn good crime report. That 7-Eleven thing was ironclad.

"You know Hanson, don't you?"

Peetey, who was wearing a tight, black, Harley Davidson tank top, pulled his shoulder-length hair back with both hands. "Yeah," he said.

"Peetey and I had a talk just this afternoon," Hanson said, smiling at Fox's partner. "You're looking real authentic tonight, Peetey."

Hanson turned to the detective. "Glad you liked the report. I try to be clear and concise, and get those spontaneous, incriminating statements. Write me a *letter* sometime about what a fine officer I am. Something I can put in my personnel file."

"Yeah . . . Hey, you know LaVonne Berry, don't you?"

Peetey glared down at Farmer, trying to make eye contact.

"I wrote him a mover a couple of weeks ago. 'Excessive noise— tires,' " Hanson said, laughing at the absurd charge.

"You might want to give him a little extra attention," Farmer said. "Peetey tells me he's getting real ambitious. Moving a lot of dope . . ."

"Just a rumor," Peetey interrupted. "Probably nothing to it."

"Sounded pretty solid to me," Farmer said. "Kilos. Up from L.A."

Peetey put his hands on his hips, shrugged his shoulders, dropped his hands back down and flexed his fingers.

"Getting in over his head, if you ask me," Farmer said. "Those people down there eat morons like LaVonne for breakfast."

"Probably just talk. Trying to impress the other assholes. We'll let you know," Peetey said.

"Okay," Hanson said. "I need a letter," he said, turning back to Farmer. "I haven't been getting my movers."

"A mover a day keeps the sergeant away," Farmer said.

"Thank you, Detective *Farmer*," Hanson said, "but write me an attaboy, okay? Something I can hold up and show to the lieutenant when he calls me in. You can do it on city time."

"Tell you what. You write one up, fire it over to me, and if it's not *too* exaggerated, I'll sign it and send it to personnel."

"Excellent idea. Thank you very much *y muchas gracias.* I'll send it over Monday."

Hanson looked at Peetey and shook his head. "Damn," he said to Farmer, "look at those *arms.* I guess I better start bulking up if I want to get any respect."

He gave Peetey a little two-fingered salute and walked away.

It was the only bar where Hanson felt comfortable, where he wasn't afraid to get drunk. Almost everyone in the place carried a gun. They had all seen people killed, some of them having done the killing themselves. They wouldn't get drunk and challenge anyone else without realizing what that could lead to. In the PAA he didn't have to worry much about all that. The cops knew if anyone started trouble, things could get serious in a hurry, and that accounted for the general atmosphere of good manners. An armed society, Hanson thought, is a polite society.

The women in the bar were in their twenties and early thirties. Some of them were cops, but most were cop groupies who worked in Records or Radio or on the EMT ambulances. A few of them, like Debbie Deets, and Sgt. Steele from East Precinct, were good looking, but most were just average. They were likeable women though, tougher than most because of their exposure to police work and cops. They didn't ask for much and they didn't complain.

Zurbo and Neal were sitting over by the window. Zurbo waved at Hanson and pointed at the empty pitcher on the table. Hanson nodded and walked to the bar.

"A pitcher and a glass, please, ma'am," he said to the barmaid, a woman whose husband had been killed in a high-speed chase two years before when his patrol car hit a phone pole. "How's it goin', Kate?"

"Can't complain, Hanson," she said, reaching up for a pitcher. The picture on her T-shirt, a leering, cartoon cop, stretched across her breasts. A cigar stuck out the side of his mouth, and beneath him were the words, "Have a nice day . . . ASSHOLE."

Zurbo was showing Neal a flat leather sap, not much bigger than a shoehorn. He slapped it into the palm of his hand. "Is that a

beauty, or what?" he said, handing it to Hanson. "Ordered it out
of the *Shotgun News*."

Hanson flexed it, felt the smooth lead sewn into the leather,
slapped it into his palm while Zurbo poured himself a beer. Falcone had come in with another woman cop from East Precinct.
She was turned away from him, her short blond hair catching the
blue light from a neon Budweiser sign over the bar.

"Hey, Falcone," Hanson called to her. "What brings *you* up
here?"

She walked over to the table. "Had to cash a check," she said.

"You ought to come by once in a while," Hanson said.

"I'm not much of a drinker."

Hanson thought she was glad to see him.

She smiled at Zurbo and Neal. "Hi guys. How's things up in
Five Eighty?"

"We try to keep 'em under control," Zurbo said.

"How you doin'?" Neal mumbled, then looked back down at
his beer.

She nodded, her smile fading, suddenly uncomfortable. "Gotta
go. See you guys later."

Zurbo watched her walk away. He snorted and shook his head.

"What?" Hanson said. "She's a good cop."

"She's okay for a woman."

"I hear she's a dyke," Neal said. "Her 'friend' there, Bishop, is
definitely a lesbo."

"Any woman who wants to work the street is a dyke. Whether
she knows it or not. That's one fuckin' thing I agree with Cindy
on," Zurbo said.

"Fuckin' shame," Neal said. "Good-looking woman like that
wastin' it on another woman."

Zurbo took a sip of beer, licked foam from his mustache, and
took the sap back from Hanson. "Look at the leather. Full grain
cowhide. Not that cheap split-grain shit. Miller, over at the jail,
has one just like it. Says it works good in the elevator."

"Zurbo's new penis extension," Neal said. "Ooooh. Let me rub
it."

"Hey," Zurbo said, "you're gonna wish *you* had one. Go to a
family fight, right? Room full of hysterical niggers breaking furniture and screaming all kinds of 'motherfuckers' at each other. You
got no room to swing a nightstick in there. Now *this*," he said,

taking the sap from Hanson, "short little swing," he said slapping it into his palm, "side of the knee and Tyrone is *down*. He be on the floor. Elbow, collarbone, if you're pissed you go 'tap' and his jaw's busted. The fucker is eating soup through a straw for six weeks. No fried chicken for a while."

Peetey had cornered Falcone by the stairs, one arm on the doorway, blocking her way. He leaned over her, smiling, just as the song, "Superstition," on the jukebox ended. "Why don't you go fuck *yourself*," she told him, slipped beneath his huge arm and went down the stairs.

"Hey," Neal said, "remember that shooting over on Albina last year. The guy's laying on the floor going, 'Ooh. Ooh,' two thirty-eights in him, bloody fried chicken all over the floor. The guy who shot him, skinny guy, junkie, what was his name . . . ?"

"Sims," Zurbo said, "Eugene Sims."

The window behind their table was open, and a damp breeze came in off the river. The jukebox shuddered, changed gears, and a steel guitar played the first notes of "Tequila Sunrise." Across the river, atop the Lighthouse Rescue Mission, a red neon JESUS bled through the mist. The "E" flickered on and off. Hanson shifted his chair so he could see the steps to the front door directly below.

"Yeah, fuckin' *You*-gene Sims," Neal said. " 'Why'd you shoot him?' Zurbo asks You-gene.

"And he says, 'Cause the nigger put *my* hot sauce on *his* chicken.' Fuckin' jigaboos, man. Like they're from Mars. The other night, me and my little girl Jennifer tried to think of all the names we've got for niggers. We came up with eight."

"Just like Eskimos and snow," Zurbo said. "Whatever's important in your environment, you got a lot of little distinctions."

Neal was pretty drunk, but he thought about that.

"Jennifer *loves* to play name-that-nigger with me," Neal said. "Holds up mug shots like flash cards and I have to give his name, what kind of car, who he hangs around with. She's so fuckin' cute. I'll say, 'sixty nine, uh, *Buick*,' and she'll say, like, 'No, Daddy, try again. Not a Buick.'

"I'll say, 'Pontiac?' And she'll say, 'What color?' "

He laughed. "She loves to play that game."

Falcone and Bishop finally came out the door below. They were laughing. Bishop stepped in front of Falcone, knees bent, slouching, arms hanging down like a gorilla's. Imitating Peetey. Her phony laugh echoed down the narrow street, *har har har*. Hanson smiled. Then Bishop put her arm around Falcone's shoulder and they walked out of sight.

". . . and *then*," Neal was telling Zurbo, laughing, "Hanson bounces him off the car, kicks his legs out from under him, and he goes down. Hanson grabs a double handful of Afro, and the fucker has a *conversation* with the sidewalk. Beautiful."

Hanson, smiling, held up his hand. "You're too kind. I learned everything I know from Dana."

"The old Bear of the Avenue. You should have seen him in the old days," Zurbo said, smiling.

"He hardly ever talks about those days," Hanson said.

"How long's he been with that new wife of his?"

"They been married, I *think* . . . five years. Yeah."

"Huh. Doesn't seem like it's been that long since he was with Peggy. This new one, what's her name . . ."

"Helen."

"She's got a pretty *elevated* opinion of herself."

"She's okay," Hanson said. "Just doesn't understand cops."

"After five years? She doesn't *want* to 'understand' 'em," Zurbo said.

"Dana put the *fear* in 'em, on the Avenue," Neal said. "He was, like, a legend. Back when I came on the department."

"Ah," Zurbo said, throwing a kiss off the tips of his fingers, "street justice. That's the only thing that does any good out there. Hammer the fuckers as soon as you catch 'em. Close the jails. Fire the fucking DA."

"You gotta get 'em right away," Neal said. "Kick their ass. They get the point immediately. You want to stop jaywalking? Shoot the fuckers and leave the bodies in the street. Pretty soon, nobody jaywalks."

"Hey, I see you and Dana haven't signed up for the Night Dog Hunt yet," Zurbo said.

But Hanson was watching Fox's reflection in a window as he walked behind their table. "What can I do for you, John?" Hanson said.

Fox stopped and looked at Hanson through his mirrored sunglasses.

"I lost my temper this afternoon. It won't happen again."

"Well, that's a comfort, John."

"How many beers has it been tonight? A county unit's gonna

pop you for dee-wee one of these nights on that long drive home,'' he said, walking away.

''You guys ought to kiss and make up,'' Zurbo said.

Fox played ''New York, New York'' on the jukebox. Some of the older cops were Frank Sinatra fans.

''Speaking of narcs,'' Zurbo said, ''you got any Valium?''

''The pressure of the job too much for you?''

''Yeah. I can't handle the fuckin' stress. Asking you for Valium is just a 'cry for help.' ''

''Down inside,'' Neal said, ''he's a sensitive, wonderful guy.''

''Who has a pistol match in Seattle this weekend,'' Zurbo said. ''Five milligrams of valium will *smooth* your trigger pull. Just a little edge.''

Outside, the thumping bass of a boombox got louder, bouncing between buildings, doubling and tripling over the DJ's voice ''. . . *like to talk to you all night, baby, but, you know, Wardell got to get outta here, got to get down, and get gone, forgive me, baby, got to va-cate the premises . . .*''

''*I fo'give you, 'cause . . .*''

''*Thank you, baby, an' you gonna check us out tomorrow?*''

''*Uh-huh, I'm . . .*''

''*Good night, baby,*'' Wardell said, cutting her off.

''*Mister Jones be here in about five minutes, taking you through the night like a armed escort. And he told me, he wanted me to, you know how I been telling you all that Mister Jones is a bad . . . ? He says that's wrong, that he's, these are his words, not mine, I respect the man, I want you to know. He says that he's just as scared as, worse than, everybody else. Tol' me he's scared all the time,*'' he said, his voice fading down the street. ''*If that's true, y'all—I been thinking about it—then it's the scared ones you best get out the way for . . . He'll be here in a few minutes, and I'll be back tomorrow with the rest of the Worl' Famous, Supreme Team. Goo'night, y'all, here's the Ohio Players and 'Skin Tight,'* '' his voice lost in the music as it faded away around the corner.

Neal poured himself another beer, shaking his head. ''Fucking Zulu music.''

''No,'' Zurbo said, ''that's *not* Zulu music. Come by my house and I'll *play* you some Zulu music. The Zulu are *warriors,* not a bunch of fast-talking street niggers.''

Two pitchers later, Hanson had stopped paying attention to the war stories about arrests, and fights and car chases, watching his own reflection in one of the windows, looking *through* it at the same time to a glass-and-steel high-rise downtown that cut his face into light and dark grids.

"It's against regulations to carry that sap," Neal told Zurbo.

"Oh. I'm sorry. I guess I'll just let a bunch of garbones stomp my ass so I can tell the lieutenant, on the way to the hospital, 'All according to regulations, sir.'"

"Gotta go," Hanson said, standing up. "Gotta get some sleep so I can fight crime tomorrow."

"Sweet dreams," Zurbo said.

Fox was standing by the door, talking to someone Hanson had never seen before, but it was obvious he was a cop.

"Here he is," Fox told him as Hanson walked up. "A cop with his *own* ideas about justice. A smart guy.

"Say hello to Deputy Inman, Hanson. He works out in the county not too far from that farmhouse of yours."

"How you doing, Inman," Hanson said.

Inman nodded, polite but reserved, like most cops meeting strangers.

"Drive safely," Fox said, when Hanson turned to go down the stairs. "But hey, if anything happens to *you*," he called after Hanson, "we'll be sure to send Animal Control out to take care of that dog."

EIGHT

A FEW MILES OUT of town he ran into a shower. Only one wiper worked, slapping a paste of rain and bug guts across the windshield. "Gotta fix you up with new wipers," he said, peering out the milky safety glass.

He reached over and turned on the radio, but the local stations had either signed off for the night, or were too far away for the broken antenna to pick up. All he could get was rushing static, the same sound military field radios made when no one was transmitting, "white noise."

"Nobody talkin' on the airwaves tonight," he said, glancing in the rearview mirror. "Nothing but white noise out there," he said, as if he wasn't alone. "White noise in the black air. Yin and Yang. Yes. Good and evil. White . . . Rose *Salve*," Hanson sang, holding the last note, imitating a radio commercial he'd grown up with as a kid in North Carolina.

"Welcome to the White Rose Salve Hour. This is the Hoss Man talking. An' you *know* . . . if the Hoss Man says it's so. It is *so*.

"White Rose Salve, my friends.

"People tell me that they can not get along without it.

"Working man? Chapped hands? Try White Rose.

"Cracked teats? A common problem for you dairy farmers. Try White Rose.

"It is a world of uses for White Rose," Hanson went on, making it up now.

"Say, you boys servin' with the army overseas in Vet-nom. You got problems with that M-16 gun jammin' when you shoot them gooks. *Try* White Rose. That's right. Dip your bullets right in the familiar blue and white can and see if that don't help. Lubrication. A world of uses. The Hoss Man says it's so."

Hanson sang the sign-off tune, "So buy a jar of White Rose, White Rose Saaaalve . . ."

The rain came down harder, gusts of wind shaking the van. The doors rattled on rusty hinges, but the little engine was still strong. Lightning flared silently beyond the horizon.

Hanson tried the radio again, steering with one hand, tuning in a voice out of the static just as a gust of wind hit the van broadside, blowing it across the road. Two wheels dropped off the shoulder, headlights catching something back in the trees, its eyes red in the lights for an instant then gone before Hanson wrenched the wheel, bounced back over the shoulder, and fishtailed across the road.

"Jesus," Hanson said, tingling with adrenaline, bringing the van back under control on the rain-slick blacktop.

". . . *out there in the dark, brothers and sisters,*" the voice on the radio was saying, "*storm's just passing through. Mister Jones'* gonna *be looking out the window for that moon . . .*"

Music, all but lost in the static, so faint it seemed to have traveled a long way, replaced the voice.

". . . I can see *clearly* now,
the *rain* is gone.
I can see *all* obstacles
in my way . . ."

The music grew clearer and stronger as a wind coming off Stormbreaker Mountain began to break up the clouds.

Hanson lived thirty miles from the precinct, out in the country, in an old farmhouse he'd bought with no plumbing and no electricity on twenty acres of land. He'd gotten it cheap, through a state auction. He dug an outhouse and took showers at the precinct. He'd read books on plumbing, made friends with a local electrician, and slowly improved the place.

The rain clouds had blown away, but the dirt road to his house was muddy, and the bus skidded off the road, the front fender bouncing off the trunk of a huge Douglas fir. "Whoa," Hanson shouted, "look out," downshifted, hit the gas, and fishtailed the rest of the way to the back of the house, parking beneath more of the big fir trees.

He checked the pebble he'd left on the threshold in front of the screen door. If someone had opened the door, it would have fallen onto the porch. A cheap burglar alarm. He went inside, stood listening for a moment, then, without turning on a light, took a beer out of the refrigerator. The light from the refrigerator threw shadows across the scarred wooden floor of the kitchen, a spiderweb gleaming in the corner. Hanson knelt by the web, tapped it, and the spider appeared. "How's it goin', Legs," Hanson asked it. Realizing it wasn't food that had disturbed his web, the spider loped away into the shadows.

The air was a little chilly that late, out in the country. It smelled of grass and blackberries, a hint of apple blossoms. Nothing like the city.

"Hey, Truman," Hanson called, stepping outside, "you old night fighter. You out there, buddy? Time to come in."

The little dog came out of the dark, hopped stiffly up the two sagging steps, and stood next to Hanson, just touching his leg. The dog stared out at the night with his blind eyes as Hanson knelt to pet him.

"How about this country living, huh? You have a good day, did you? I ran into Falcone at the club, the first time I've ever seen her there. Don't know why I've started thinking about her so much. We were in the same academy class, almost four years ago, and nothing happened. Betty was living here then.

"How you *doin'*, pal," Hanson said, scratching his ears.

"Anyway, Falcone went to East Precinct out of the academy, I went to Traffic for a while, then North, and I just forgot about her. Until lately. Like the song says, 'Love is strange.'

"How about a beer?" Hanson said, standing. "Don't go away.

"Loooove, *whoa whoa*, love is *strange, yea yea* . . ." he sang as he went into the house.

"All that shit stacked up in the front hall belongs to Betty," he called over his shoulder. "I guess I miss her sometimes," he said, flooding the kitchen with light as he opened the refrigerator door.

"She used to hang out with Kesey and the Pranksters when they were just getting started. A few years older than me, but that seemed to work," he said, moving cans and bottles, his voice echoing when he stuck his head into the refrigerator. "I don't know what happened. I think she just . . . I know there's a couple more beers in here. *Here* we go."

Hanson poured a beer into a cereal bowl and set it in front of the dog. "Drink up, pal."

As the dog lapped up the beer, Hanson looked through the branches of an apple tree at the stars and the full moon.

"Hello, moooon," Hanson said, drawing out the word, his smile turning into a grin, "still up there, I see. I'm still down here. Hey," he said, waving his arm, "still here." He looked at his shadow on the wooden planking, then back up just as the tiny blinking light of a high-flying aircraft passed across the moon. "Perfect," Hanson said. *"Perfect,"* remembering Doc. It was the word Doc used when everything suddenly came together just right. Like that time they'd slipped across the border into Laos and set up the claymore ambush on one of those underwater bridges, a foot bridge suspended just below the water so it was invisible from the air.

He and Doc staked claymore mines on both sides of the bridge, beneath the surface of the muddy water, then crawled back into the brush and waited. A lone NVA regular emerged from the jungle on the other side of the river and walked towards them over the bridge. Just as he stepped into the killing zone of the claymores, Doc jiggled one of the detonation wires, making ripples in the brown water. The soldier stopped.

"Uh-oh," Doc had whispered, "what's that *splashing?* Is it a . . . *fish?*" He jiggled the wire again, and the soldier peered down at the water, then squatted for a closer look. When he stiffened, they knew he'd seen the blunt shadow of the claymore, an unmistakable shape, in the muddy water. He stood up slowly, his eyes on the jungle.

"Maybe we're gone," Doc whispered. "Maybe we planted the mines and got tired of waiting. Maybe we . . . fell *asleep."* He looked at Hanson and smiled. "Shhhh," he hissed, "don't wake 'em up," and touched the plastic firing device to his lips. Hanson held the other firing device, stroking it with his thumb. It looked like a fat green clothespin, with a texture like raw wood. When the ends were squeezed together, it sent a tiny electrical charge down the wire to the blasting cap in the mine.

Then the NVA looked directly at where they were hidden. "You *know* we're here," Doc whispered. "Better run. It's the only chance you got."

The soldier spun around—"Perfect," Doc said—and was taking his first stride back across the bridge when the double *thud* of the claymores drowned out Doc's laughter and the soldier vanished in an eruption of smoke and silver-brown water.

Hanson smiled, and remembered how it hurt to smile after a few days out on operations, when his lips were split from sunburn. "Those were the real days, Truman. I was sure I was gonna die over there, but I didn't mind, you know? I just hoped it wouldn't *hurt* too much. When you know you're gonna die, you can do anything you want to.

"Have I told you this before?

"I think God made a little mistake. I'm supposed to be dead. They eliminated my position, but I'm still here.

"Say *what?* Time to go to bed? Okay. I'll leave the door ajar. Come on in when you're ready."

He walked through the kitchen into the living room, smelling the cold wood stove, the burlap he'd stapled to the walls, and the shelves of books. He went to one of the bookcases and pulled out the manila folder of photographs he'd collected since becoming a cop. The largest photo was a group portrait of his academy class. He looked at Falcone, in the front row, and himself, in the row behind her and to the right. Both of them looked much younger, awkward in their new uniforms.

Another photo fell out and he picked it up off the floor. A snapshot Hanson had taken of the interior of a pickup truck two drunk armed robbers had been driving after holding up a 7-Eleven store. Two pistols and a sawed-off rifle on the seat, dollar bills everywhere, beer bottles rolling around the floor. Hanson had talked Dana into pulling it over before the backup cars arrived, "just for fun." Dana had taken the passenger, a Mexican who probably weighed less than 150 pounds, out of the truck and back to the patrol car. The driver, a white guy, was enormously fat, but strong. He had one huge arm around Hanson's neck, pulling him into the truck, choking him, reaching for a pistol, when Dana suddenly reached in, heaved him out, headfirst onto the street, and when he resisted, dislocated his shoulder bringing it back to handcuff him. One of the times Dana had saved his life.

Hanson took another look at Falcone, put the folder back in the bookcase, and went upstairs to bed.

Most of the firing had stopped. There were a few bursts of small-arms fire off to the north, towards the shimmering rice paddy. It was the same old dream. The sweet-blood stink of Vietnam riding the heat, the smell that was always in the dream. Quinn and Silver were dead. Mr. Minh was dead. The dream always started after it was too late to save them, too late to do it all differently.

Sometimes, as he was falling asleep, Hanson tried to trick his subconscious into starting the dream sooner, backing it up just a few minutes each night to where they were alive and he still had a chance to save them, or if that was not possible, to die with them.

He lay in bed, listening. In the jungle he had depended on his ears more than his eyes. On patrol you hear the enemy before you see them.

Helicopter rotors, jet turbines, and small-arms fire had scarred his inner ears, but he had learned to listen through the chirping that was always there now, like a sky full of birds.

He opened his eyes, sat up and swept the pistol off the floor where he always placed it. He listened to the house, straining to hear each room, upstairs then down. The house he had wired and plumbed, whose foundation he had braced with pier blocks, and whose walls were shingled with cedar shakes he'd split himself.

He eased out of bed and went through the house barefoot, two steps at a time. Two steps, then he'd stop and listen, breathing through his mouth. He paused at the kitchen door before stepping through, gun in hand. The dog was waiting, washed in moonlight from the window, looking up at him with eyes white as pearls.

A WINO MIGHT have seen the light go on in the second floor of the Nordic Seas Hotel, but it is almost three in the morning, and they have all passed out hours before, the warm urine that soaks their trousers cold now as they lay curled up behind Dumpsters or beneath bags of trash where there is less chance they'll be seen and set on fire by speed freaks or sleepless psychotics waiting for dawn. They are all asleep, fortified wine and vomit eating

ulcers in their stomachs and throats. Maybe some of them are
dreaming when Dakota turns on the bare bulb in his room.

He opens the padlocked bottom drawer of the desk and takes
out a folder marked "TOP PRYORITY—CLASSIFIDE," thick with
blue stationery, and the Gideon Bible from the Barstow Motel Six.
He studies the unopened quart of vodka, then kicks the drawer
shut.

The stack of blue stationery in the folder is almost an inch
thick, the letterhead dark blue, from the Supreme Council,
Knights of Columbus, Religious Information Bureau. The letter
on top of the stack is almost two years old, addressed to O. Payette
Simpson, 99240, California State Hospital, Bldg. 92, Vacaville,
CA. O. Payette Simpson is Dakota's legal name, given to him by
some flunky in the California welfare system when he was five
days old. The police had found him in the bloody house trailer
where his mother and her boyfriend—not his father—had somehow shot each other to death after he'd been born. He was barely
alive, his mother dead for three days, when they kicked in the
door of the trailer. The police had saved his life.

Once again, he reads the dog-eared three-year-old letter:

Dear Mr. Simpson:

We were pleased to receive your first test, and we are
returning it to you with the score of 83%. This is a
good beginning. With each correction we have given you
a page reference so that you can easily find where you
made your mistakes. We certainly hope and pray . . .

As Dakota reads, Gunther Gebel-Williams guides lions and tigers and black panthers across the walls with his voice and the
touch of his hands, directing them through flaming hoops and
onto candy-striped platforms where they watch him, ears back,
pissing themselves, the urine steaming from their bellies beneath
the circus lights.

Dakota pulls a new blue envelope out of his pocket—he's been
carrying it for days—and slices it open with his case cutter, another letter from the Knights of Columbus. He skips down past
the standard beginning paragraph that ends, "Let's take a look at
your work:

> ''No. 7 is false. You may be surprised because
> there are those today who would tell us that it is
> impossible for a highly educated man, a scien-
> tist, to have a simple faith in God. But they are
> wrong. True faith and true science are not incom-
> patible.''

Gunther Gebel-Williams smiles, his white-blond hair flowing as he runs with the cats, in complete control of the beautiful carnivores who have no natural enemies and fear nothing on earth. Gunther grins, his crucifix swinging and bouncing on his sweaty bare chest.

Dakota riffles the onionskin pages of the Bible, frustrated as always when he finally opens one of the blue letters, his breathing labored now.

> ''No. 9 is false, because, even though a man
> does not believe in the Bible, his powers of rea-
> son, when rightly used, point certainly to the
> existence of God.
> ''No. 21 should have been marked ''T.'' All an-
> gels, whether they are good or wicked, are pure
> spirits. The word 'pure' here means that they
> have no manner of body and need nothing material
> in order to live.''

Across the room Gunther directs a white tiger onto its perch, then touches his forehead in a salute to the beast, who snarls theatrically and paws the air.

The animal tamer pays no attention to Dakota when he stands up and paces the room, finally slamming the Bible against his forehead, pounding a halo of dust over his gleaming scalp.

"Why can't they just *say* it? Give me the answer instead of a riddle," he demands, as Gunther rides a black-maned lion across the center ring.

Dakota stops at a full-page glossy photo of Gunther standing easily in a semi-circle of African elephants. The suspended lightbulb throws a shadow from Dakota's head onto the photo, and for a moment it seems that Gunther is looking out, beyond the glossy paper, until Dakota stumbles out of the light and throws the Bible onto the floor.

Gunther raises his arms and the elephants curl their trunks, spread their ears like palm fronds, and raise up on their hind legs, obeying him instead of trampling and goring him into bloody, sequin-wrapped meat. Dakota picks up the Bible and goes back to the desk to search for the other answers.

NINE

"I'VE GOT THE one guy handcuffed," Hanson told Dana, "and an ambulance coming for the other asshole, when the lieutenant walks in."

"Goofy Larry?"

"Yeah, a few days after they sent him to North. Didn't I ever tell you this story?"

It was another beautiful day. Warm, but not hot, a few high clouds over the ghetto as they passed the Mt. Zion Baptist Church, its pink doors and windows wide open. The choir was practicing, singing "Open My Eyes," backed up by guitar, bass and drums.

They passed the plasma donor center, the Salvation Army Thrift Store, and the Pussycat Theatre.

"So Goofy Larry walks in—I'd done a *great* job . . ."

They both turned their heads, watching a young guy at the bus stop pull something shiny out of his back pocket. An aluminum comb the size of a meat cleaver.

". . . a great job. I was looking like a movie star—and he wants to know why I'm not wearing my hat. I just looked at him, and . . ."

Hanson followed Dana's look out the driver's window to the alley behind the Bon Ton Billiards where a persimmon-orange tail fin, not quite hidden behind a Dumpster, caught the sun. "LaVonne got lonely," Dana said. "Had to come back and see his buddies, when he *knows* about those secret indictments Fox got. Guys like him don't know how to start over somewhere new. They always show up back on the block. Fox should be happy," he said, picking up the microphone.

"Fuck Fox. Let's arrest him ourselves."

Dana took his thumb off the transmit button.

"Just for fun," Hanson said.

Dana jammed the microphone back in its holder. "Don't tell Helen you talked me into this. We gotta do it quick. In and out. You get LaVonne into the car, and I'll keep the others back."

"Woo-woo," Hanson said. "Some fun, huh?"

They drove to the end of the block where Hanson got out of the car. "I'll look for you at the backdoor," he said, and walked towards the pool hall. Up the street, two men sat on a bench at the bus stop, sharing a bottle of wine in a paper bag. When they saw Hanson, they looked around for other cops and tucked the bottle behind them. They were not much older than Hanson, drinking wine in the sun. As he walked by, Hanson looked directly at the half-hidden paper bag. He glanced at their dark, corded arms, checking for needle marks for future reference. There might be a family fight or a disturbance where he would want an excuse to arrest one of them to solve the problem. "Good afternoon, gentlemen," Hanson said, smiling like a shark.

"All right," one of them said. The other one just grunted, and they both looked down at the sidewalk. After Hanson passed, they watched him go into the pool hall.

Hanson stepped sideways through the door and stood there a few seconds, letting his eyes adjust, the figures in dim puddles of light around the pool tables taking on detail. The place reeked of sweat, cigarettes, and marijuana, big overhead fans barely pushing the air.

Conversations stopped in mid-sentence. Men who had been bent over pool tables straightened up and turned silently to watch him. Hanson had arrested some of them, and he knew most of the others. Their mug shots were in the shoebox in the car.

LaVonne was standing back by the plywood bar that Dee Brazzle, the owner, had nailed together. Some of the nails had curled out of the splintered wood, and the bar itself stood a little lopsided on the floor, a piece of red carpet tacked on the front. When Dee had first started selling liquor in the pool hall, without any kind of liquor license, he'd been too obvious about it. Dana and Hanson had warned him, but he hadn't paid attention. So one night they took all the bottles and poured them out on the street. He was more discreet after that, at least when they were around. There was no way to stop it, but there had to be street rules to keep things from getting out of control.

Hanson walked over to the bar. "*Mister* Berry. You're under arrest. Would you please turn around and lace your fingers behind your head?"

LaVonne glanced towards the backdoor, poised to run, just as Dana walked through it.

"Under *arrest?*" he said, his eyes working the room behind Hanson, cutting to the doors and windows. "What the fuck you talking about?"

"Seventy thousand dollars' worth of drug warrants. You know what I'm talking about."

"I took *care* of that."

"Turn around and lace your fingers behind your head."

Dana watched the room.

"What I just tell you?" LaVonne said, taking a step backwards.

"Man *said* he took care of it," Dee said, half drunk as usual.

Dana walked towards them, and LaVonne put his hands behind his head.

"Now ain't this a goddamn shame?" Dee said. He looked towards the front door. "The rest of 'em outside?"

"Carrying any guns or knives today?" Hanson asked LaVonne.

"You the ones got all the motherfuckin' guns," LaVonne said, slipping his hands down to the sides of his neck, his big arms flexing.

"Keep your damn hands up there," Hanson said, pulling his nightstick with his left hand, pointing the handle at his face. "And turn around."

Dana stood facing LaVonne while Hanson moved behind him, pulled his arms down and handcuffed him, patted him down, then reached under the shirt and slipped out an aluminum dagger, the handle in the shape of a naked woman. A cheap knife, the edge crudely ground, as vicious as a prison-made shank. It was warm and damp from being next to LaVonne's skin. Hanson stuck it in his gunbelt and jerked down on the handcuffs. "What's wrong with you, man?"

"I forgot about it."

"Let's go," Hanson said.

"Ow! You breaking my hand," he shouted. "Ow!"

"Why you always gotta hurt a black man?" Dee proclaimed, playing to the customers.

"Ow!" LaVonne shouted. "You and the others gonna beat me up outside?"

Some of the pool players stepped between Hanson and the door, moving in and out of the sunlight coming through the door and dirty windows, holding pool cues at their sides.

"Put down the pool cues and get out of the way," Dana said. "Dee, if anybody swings a pool cue, I'm gonna shoot you right away."

Hanson heard the metallic snap of Dana's holster strap, and he thumbed his own off.

For a moment no one moved, then they laid their cues on the pool tables.

Hanson walked LaVonne past Dana, out the door into the sun, and Dana followed, walking backwards. They put LaVonne in the back and got into the patrol car, moving quickly, but not so they'd look afraid.

LaVonne twisted around and looked out the back window as they bumped over the curb and out into the street. "You all there is?" he said.

"Just like the Texas Rangers, Pilgrim," Hanson said as they took the on-ramp for the freeway and the trip to jail. "Five Sixty Two will be jackpot with LaVonne Berry," Dana told radio.

Five Sixty Two, Fox's voice said over the radio, *go to channel three.*

Hanson switched channels on the radio. "Yessir," he said into the mike.

Where'd you find him? Fox said.

"Hanging out at the Bon Ton."

Why didn't you notify me? There were more indictments coming down that you don't . . .

"Just glad we could help. We're jackpot," he said, hanging up the mike and switching channels.

"Not *too* pissed," Hanson said.

"That motherfucker Fox," LaVonne said. "After he promised me . . ."

"What?" Hanson said. "Promised what?"

"I don't cry to the police."

While Dana took LaVonne up in the jail elevator, Hanson took the stairs to the third floor to pick up some mug shots. Two motorcycle cops, wearing knee-high boots, black gloves, and leather jackets with silver snaps and buckles were on their way down.

"You guys are so *formidable* in your leathers," Hanson lisped, fluttering his hand at them.

They stopped, blocking the stairs, looking down at him, their leather gear creaking in the silence.

Finally, the one wearing sergeant's stripes said, "When are you gonna come talk to me about joining the Reserves, Hanson? We need some new blood." He was a sergeant major in the Army Reserves and Hanson knew he had two Purple Hearts.

"I don't know, Sarge. I'm not a very good peacetime soldier."

"We'll find another war before long. Better than that last one. Then you'll wish you'd signed on," he said as they stepped aside to let Hanson pass.

"I'll think about it, Sergeant Major," Hanson said. "Thanks."

A shotgun hallway down one side of the detectives' offices was lined with little "interview rooms," claustrophobic interrogation rooms, each one with a table that almost filled it up and a few heavy wooden chairs. They were dingy white and stank of sweat and cigarette smoke and fear, the yellowed, sound-deadening tiles on the walls and ceiling stained and torn. Someone was screaming and throwing himself against the solid oak door of the third room down.

Zink and Farmer, their ties loosened, stood in front of the door. Farmer looked at his watch.

"Hiya guys," Hanson said. "What's up?"

They looked at him, then back at the door. "Speeding Bear," Farmer said, running his fingers through his hair. "A drunk, 250-pound speed-freak Indian."

"I know Speeder," Hanson said. "He hangs out down by the Burnside overpass."

Speeding Bear screamed and hit the door again.

Hanson cupped his ear with his hand and leaned towards the door. "Sounds like he's kind of upset."

"He seemed *fine*," Farmer said.

"Yeah, I thought he was okay," Zink said. "We took off the cuffs and told him we'd be right back . . ."

"And he went *off* on us," Farmer said.

"We brought him in with, you know, that punchy old boxer who wears the football helmet . . ."

"Champ?"

"Yeah. They found a body in an airshaft behind that flophouse, the Nordic Seas, where they stay. Some poor old wore-out whore, sodomized, cut all to shit—a razor blade, it looks like—"

"Getting to where every homicide is some kind of, what do you call it, 'cliché.' I'd give it 'murder of the week,' though."

"Murder of the *month*," Zink said. "Easy."

The door shuddered.

"The two of 'em got into a pissing contest over something that happened a year or two ago, and we had to put 'em in separate rooms."

"Most of the time they're buddies, aren't they?"

Hanson nodded.

They looked at the door. "I guess somebody's gonna have to go in there and handcuff him again," Zink said.

"I guess so," Farmer said.

"You can't hardly *hurt* Speeder when he's drunk," Hanson said. "He threw me behind a Dumpster once when I worked downtown. After I wore my arm out hitting him with my nightstick. He just *looked* at me."

Zink put his ear to the door and listened. He knocked, lightly. "Speeder?" he called.

The legs of a chair inside scraped the floor. "Speeding Bear? You okay now?"

"Fuck *you!*" Speeding Bear yelled from inside as the chair smashed against the door. "Fuck *you*, White Eyes!" he screamed.

Zink looked at Farmer. "Let's give him a little more time," he said, "before we go in."

Something slammed against the door just down the hall.

"Fuck ya yourself, ya fuckin' redskin nigger. I'll slap that big Jew nose right off your fuckin' face!"

"That's *Champ*," Hanson said.

The door down the hall *boomed*.

"Sounds like he ran his *head* into the door," Farmer said.

"He likes to charge you, head down," Hanson said.

"Shit," Zinc said. "He's got a plate in his head, and our ass is grass if he drops dead."

"Or if anything happens to another Indian while he's in custody," Farmer said.

"Maybe we should call 911," Zink said.

"Well, guys," Hanson said, "good luck. We better get back out on the district before Sergeant Bendix starts getting nervous because we aren't answering the radio."

"Bendix?" Farmer said. "Sent him to North, huh? I *heard* he fucked up." He laughed. "That must be playing hell with his police-supply business. Being way up there."

"Yeah," Hanson said, "we don't see much of him on the street."

The door boomed and shuddered, plaster dust spraying out from around the frame.

"Gotta go, guys," Hanson said. "Hey," he said to Farmer, "write me that *letter*, okay?"

He cut through the lunchroom which smelled of cigarettes and machine-brewed coffee to the wing that housed Narcotics and Vice. The steel shutters over the front office were open and Fox, his back to Hanson, was working the computer on the far wall, scrolling names. Hanson stopped, trying to read the tiny green words flickering up the screen, but couldn't make them out before they vanished when Fox, seeing Hanson's reflection in the screen, keyed another file.

"It's not a game," he said, his eyes on the screen, watching Hanson. "It's a cancer." He tapped the keyboard as he spoke, scrolling through an old search warrant. "I kept thinking you'd see that."

He touched a button on the desk, and the shutters slowly began to close. "Maybe today was just a misunderstanding. I don't think so, but even if it was, that doesn't undo the damage," he went on, the shutters sliding out of the ceiling, slat after slat, and pivoting into the steel tracks.

"I've cut you a lot of slack," he said, the shutters clattering down over his face, his shoulders.

"But don't . . ." he said, and the shutters closed with a *bang*.

Behind the shutters, Fox looked towards the sound of Hanson's footsteps. When they were gone, he punched his "SEARCH" back on the screen, keying in codes from brittle, brown thermofax copies of pages from a DOD operations manual. Suddenly, the screen filled up with dates and columns of names, with the heading "Special Orders Number 34019. TC 322 UP Assg. to SOA (CCN)."

```
Hanson, John C. 5/7/58
Hanson, Kelly NMI 11/9/42
Hanson, Ken J. 5/5/45
```

Peetey buzzed himself in the backdoor, and sat on the desk across from Fox. "Check it out," he said, reaching under his Mexican vest and pulling out an ancient army .45, all the blueing gone, the worn slide clattering against the frame.

"Where'd you find *that?*" Fox said.

"Down in the property room. One of the guns they were gonna melt down for their fuckin' *Peace* memorial. I just kind of picked it up when Dumbshit down there wasn't looking."

"Looks like it might blow up in your hand if you tried to shoot it."

"Do I look that stupid? Like I'd try to shoot this piece of shit? It's a throwdown gun."

"That they can trace to the property room?"

"It was in a burn barrel with a hundred others. Crossed off the inventory. It doesn't exist anymore."

He popped the clip out and checked the dark, empty chamber. The rounds in the clip were discolored, no two alike—hollow-point, full metal jacket, wadcutter, jacketed hollow-point, round-nosed lead.

"Loaded for bear," he said, sliding the clip back in.

Fox turned off the computer. "I'm gonna go sign for that buy-money. We need to go talk to Ira."

"What a slimy little creep," Peetey said, sighting down the .45.

"They're *all* slimy little creeps, but we need them. And the one thing they want, more than the buy-money, is to be treated like they're *not* slimy little creeps. Don't ever forget that."

Fox stared at him until he looked up from the gun. "Okay," Peetey said, "I got it."

"I'll be right back," Fox said, and Peetey looked back down at the .45. Crazed and cracked, made of some dark, dense wood from Africa or Asia, the grips had been polished by the pressure and sweat of—who knew how many?—frightened, angry hands. A checkered circle carved in the center of each grip was stained reddish-black, like dried blood. Peetey used the lock-blade knife on his belt to scrape away at the stain on one side, then spit on it and rubbed it with his thumb until Fox came back.

"Check out these cool grips," he said, holding the heavy pistol up by the barrel. "Some Nazi must of owned it."

Set in the center of the checkered circle, rusty, pitted and discolored, was a steel swastika.

"That was around a long time before Hitler decided to use it. Thousands of years. As long as the cross."

TEN

THEY PULLED INTO McDonald's and parked next to the battered golden arches glowing in the summer dusk. Miranda and Murry, the two security guards, were at the back of the parking lot, talking to four flashy women in a Bonneville convertible. They were the only black security guards in the district, and the only rent-a-cops the police had any respect for. They had been Marines together, under fire for three days and nights during the Tet offensive in Hue, where they had thought they were going to die. After that, Murry told Hanson late one night at the Top Hat bar, the only people they really trusted were each other.

They earned their pay, taking care of problems themselves, instead of calling the police, like the other security guards, white guys, in the supermarkets and discount stores. Though they earned *their* money too, in a way, for being terrified eight hours a day.

"All you want's a milkshake?" Hanson asked Dana.

"If that wouldn't be too much . . ."

Bravo One is looking for a black over blue Dodge Charger,

Radio said, *unknown California plates possibly registered to James Durham McKiver, white male, ten-thirteen-fifty-one. If located Bravo One requests that you have it towed to the police garage.*

Hanson picked up the microphone, scratched his cheek on the mesh face, then keyed it.

"Is the car being driven by Mister McKiver, and if so, is he wanted? Or is he already in custody?"

This is Bravo One, Fox said. *Be advised that the vehicle is probably being operated by McKiver. There are no wants on the subject at this time. We just want the vehicle seized and towed.*

"What do you want us to tell the man when we take his car away from him?"

Bravo One? Radio asked.

Okay. If you locate the vehicle, just call us. We'll talk to him. Is that simple enough?

"Okee-doke," Hanson said, "simple enough." As he hung up the mike, the radio clattered with the sound of other cars keying their mikes, a gesture that could mean applause, disapproval, or, in this case, laughter.

Dana shook his head. "You should let somebody else fuck with Fox once in a while."

Hanson tapped the date on the hotsheet, " 'June seventeenth, nineteen seventy-five,' " he intoned, a radio commentator's voice. " 'What sort of day *was* it? A day like *all* days, filled with those events that alter and illuminate our times. And, *you* are there . . .' "

"What is that?" Dana said.

"Walter Cronkite. Introducing *You Are There,* a Saturday morning TV show I watched when I was a kid. Last night I was lying in bed, and I remembered the whole speech.

" 'A warm summer evening,' " Hanson went on in his *You Are There* voice, getting out of the car and walking across the lot, " 'and young Officer Hanson con-*tinues* to heap scorn, and disdain on the anti-drug bureaucracy . . .' " Drowned out by Wardell the DJ's voice coming from fifty car radios, ". . . *go to the phone and we're gonna talk to . . . Kim. Kim, what's up, girl? Do you love the Worl' Famous Supreme Team?*"

"*Uh-huh.*"

"*Kim, I'm askin' do you love the Worl' Famous?*"

"*Uh-huh.*"

"Awright! Kim, do you . . ."

A kind of "soul muzak" was playing inside, a slowed-down, instrumental version of James Brown's "I Feel Good," violins and French horns replacing the trumpets and saxophones.

A floor-to-ceiling wall of bulletproof Plexiglas separated customers from the employees and cash registers. Hanson smiled at the cashier, a high school girl wearing her McDonald's tunic and paper hat, and gave her a little salute.

"Yolanda," he said, talking into a voice-activated speaker set in the Plexiglas, "What it *is*?"

The speaker took a couple of seconds to activate itself, losing the beginning of each sentence. That, along with the soupy James Brown, made Hanson feel like he was out of sync with the rest of the world. He was a little hung over, too.

". . . alright. How you doing, *Han*son?" she said, her voice reedy and metallic through the speaker.

"Pretty good."

". . . you need today?"

"How about a Big Mac, medium fries, a milk, and a milkshake for Dana. To go."

". . . right up," she said, opening a paper bag.

A nice girl, Hanson thought. Back in February she'd just taken Everett Birdsong's order for a Quarter Pounder with cheese, when his wife Sheila walked in the backdoor and shot him in the head, then emptied the stolen .38 Special revolver into his body as he went into convulsions on the floor.

Dana and Hanson had been the first cops on the scene. When they got there, people were still standing in line, walking around the body, placing their orders with Yolanda through the blood-splattered Plexiglas.

Hanson put his money in the little revolving door. Yolanda turned the door, took the money, replaced it with plastic foam-packaged food and change, and rotated it back to Hanson.

"Thank you, ma'am," Hanson said. "See you next time."

". . . sure and be careful, Hanson."

Hanson strutted back to the patrol car singing "I Feel Good." He gave Dana the milkshake and took a bite of his Big Mac, breathing the stink of Butzer's day shift cigars, the smell of urine and vomit, and the faint, sweet odor of old blood.

"Um, yumyum," Hanson said, "I don't know how some guys eat this shit every day."

He peeled the bun away from the gray meat patty, watching the pickles, tomato and lettuce slide down through the dripping "special sauce."

"Halfway through one of these things I realize that I didn't really want it. Makes me feel kinda . . . soiled."

"Thanks for sharing," Dana said, taking the lid off his milkshake.

Unknown problem, screaming in the background until complainant hung up, fourteen oh five Sacramento.

"Marx family," Dana said, peeling the wrapper off his straw. *"That's* the 'problem.' "

Six Twenty?

Six Twenty's got it, Falcone said. *Fourteen oh five Sacramento.*

Six Twenty was the East Precinct district just south of them.

Dana shook his head, snorted. "A happy day when they moved down to East Precinct," he said, putting the straw in the overflowing milkshake and bending down to take a sip.

Six Twenty's got the call. Six Forty?

Hanson grabbed the mike. "Five Sixty Two's close. We can go."

Dana looked up at him, the straw in his mouth.

Five Sixty Two has the cover.

"I'll buy you another milkshake," Hanson said, throwing his Big Mac out the window and starting the car. "I want to talk to Falcone."

Dana tossed his milkshake as Hanson backed out of the parking place.

Half a block beyond the address, their headlights picked up Riley "the Retard" Marx, walking away down the middle of the street, his pudgy silhouette in the derby hat unmistakable. "I'll check the house," Dana said, opening the door, "and you can talk to Riley."

Hanson drove up on him, almost nudging him with the bumper. He hit the horn a few times, then leaned out the window. "Hey. Riley. I want to talk to you."

Riley kept walking. Hanson turned on the PA system and whispered into the mike, his voice hissing through the neighborhood, "Riiii-leee."

He turned the volume down and whispered more softly, "Riii-leee. Talk to me or spend the night in the drunk tank. With all those mean men. Remember last time?"

He stopped, but didn't turn around, as Hanson got out of the car.

"Look at me, Riley."

Riley began to moan. He turned around, tears coming to his eyes. "No drunk tank," he said.

"What's going on at your house?"

"They make me be bad in the drunk tank. I can't go there."

"Okay. No drunk tank."

"Promise?"

"I promise. Stop *crying* and tell me what's going on."

"Nothing," Riley said, walking away. In his early twenties, he was moderately retarded, a shoplifter, a purse snatcher, and there'd been complaints that he was exposing himself to girls who had to pass his house on the way to school. His brother Ritchie was doing time somewhere down in California. Rodney, his other brother, had been stabbed to death the year before while trying to sodomize another patient at the mental hospital in McMinnville.

Hanson stepped around in front of him. "Who called the police, Riley?"

Riley looked back at his house as if the answer might be there.

"I see," Hanson said, "it's a mysterious secret, right?"

Riley shrugged and tilted his hat down over his eyes, watching Dana walk up.

"Nobody answered the door," Dana said. "It was quiet except for the TV."

He tilted his head. "Sounds like Duncan's driving," Hanson said, listening to the drone of a patrol car, in a hurry, several blocks away.

Duncan had been on the street less than a year. He had a degree in criminal justice from the community college, and had once made the mistake of declaring his intention to make lieutenant before he was thirty.

"Wear a gun and drive fast," Hanson said, the drone of the engine closing in. "I hear he's got paperwork in to transfer to North."

"I have to go," Riley said, trying to walk around them.

Dana grabbed him by the sleeve of the filthy coat he wore year round. "*Sit* down."

"You can go after you talk to us," Hanson said.

Riley sat on the curb, just as Duncan, his headlights flashing high-low, roared through the intersection up the block, missing Sacramento Street. A few seconds later his tires squealed, yelped twice, the automatic transmission howling, and burned rubber.

"Sounds like the famous and fancy 'locked-brake speed turn,'" Hanson said. "Riley. You want to be a police officer so you can drive fast?"

Six Twenty skidded around the corner, ran up on the curb, bounced back onto the street. Riley jumped up, off the curb, as the patrol car hissed past, slowing, finally coming to a stop down the block in the middle of the street, the smoking brakes almost gone.

"I think I'll go finish that crime report," Dana said.

Duncan jumped out of the car. "My call. I got it," he said, jogging up to them. "What's the problem?"

"We don't know," Hanson said, his eyes on Falcone in her baggy uniform pants and shirt, sagging gunbelt, the heavy holstered revolver smacking her like a gloved hand with each step she took towards them.

"Meet my good friend Riley Marx. He lives at the complainant's address."

Riley was looking at his hand. "I sat in dogshit," he said, wiping his hand on his pants.

"Riley, I'm Officer Duncan," he said, pulling at the notebook in his hip pocket. The pen flipped out of his other hand, but he caught it. "What, uh," he said, "God *damn*," yanking the notebook out, "seems to be the problem?"

Riley closed his eyes and tilted his head back, then brought his feet together, knees locked and back straight, like a high-diver. Extending his arms like wings and leaning back on his heels, he pivoted smoothly away from Duncan and walked off.

"Riley," Duncan said, following him with his notebook and pen, "what's your date of birth?"

"When did you start working Six Twenty?" Hanson asked Falcone.

"I'm just there for the rest of the week."

Hanson nodded. Her eyes were gray-green. The whites so clear they were pearly in the late afternoon light. When he didn't say anything, she went on.

"Until," she said, looking at Duncan, "his partner gets back from vacation. He's kind of excitable, but everybody is at first. He'll be fine."

She sounded a little shaky, but it was probably just adrenaline from Duncan's driving. Hanson tried to think of something to say. Little curls of stray hair clung to Falcone's forehead, and the top of her lip was shiny with perspiration. He smiled at her.

"Somebody cut the seat belts out of our car," she said, flexing her right hand, fine tendons cording and rippling beneath the skin.

"I think I had a death grip on the rollbar," she said, laughing.

A wonderful laugh, Hanson thought. The chirping in his ears was gone.

"What?" he said.

"Should we worry about that guy?" she said, nodding towards Riley who was still walking away, Duncan sidestepping like a sheepdog to block his way.

Someone down at the Marx house screamed, and Riley bolted past Duncan.

"Let him go," Hanson said, "you'd never catch him," watching Riley run between two houses, through a break in a fence, and vanish into the next block.

"We can pick him up later if we need to," he yelled over his shoulder, running towards the house. "I don't think he's ever gone any farther than the freeway."

Dana shouldered the door open, and they followed him into the room where two men and a woman, all in their fifties, sat on the floor watching a rerun of *The Rookies*, never even looking up when they came through the door.

The TV was the only light in the dark room, almost mesmerizing, and the four cops, catching their breath, stared at the screen where two handsome young cops are in trouble. Crouched behind their patrol car, they fire upward. Ricochets whine and chatter and drone around them. The windshield on the patrol car shatters, but The Rookies keep firing.

The people watching TV ignored the real police standing over them, their packsets crackling and buzzing with radio traffic. They didn't seem to notice when a *thud* in the next room shook the house, and the real police threw open the bedroom door.

A shirtless man and a woman in a see-through pink slip were rolling on the floor, panting, their arms and legs locked around each other. They rolled into the wall, grunted, rolled into a wobbly dressing table, toppling it over, the mirror exploding against the foot of the bed, shards of silvered glass raining down, glittering like knives in the filthy green shag carpet.

Dana and Duncan grabbed the man. He didn't resist, standing

passively, keeping his voice as calm as he could, though he was out of breath. "No problem, officer," he said. "It's okay."

The girl leaped up, her hands over her mouth, and squeezed into the far corner of the room, next to a gold-tone plaster floor lamp–telephone table combination, a trumpeting elephant the size of a St. Bernard.

"Miss. Are you okay?" Falcone asked her.

On the other side of the sagging bed, the man put his hands behind his back and turned so Duncan could handcuff him. "Linell Stark," he said. "I got ID in my pocket. Believe me, officer . . ."

"Miss? Look at me," Falcone said.

She looked past Falcone, through the open door at the TV set, panting, her dark nipples straining against the cheap slip. Her lips were bloody and her teeth pink with blood, almost the same shade as the curlers in her hair. Both eyes were swelling shut.

Hanson went into the other room, watching the TV cops move cautiously through a hotel corridor, guns drawn, the soundtrack tense and getting louder.

"Ma'am," he said, tapping the woman on the shoulder, "ma'am. What's going on, ma'am? Missus Marx . . ."

"None of my business," she said, staring at the TV, "Rosetta's man is her business."

"I'm just a neighbor," one of the men said, the light from the television blinking and shifting across his face as he looked at the screen, "come over to watch TV. I don't know a thing about it."

Rosetta screamed, pulling her hair with both hands, the curlers popping off, bouncing around Falcone's steel-toed shoes like pink grasshoppers. She *kept* screaming, keening, breathing in and screaming out.

"Rosetta!" the older woman yelled. "Shut up, girl. We trying to watch our program."

Rosetta slid slowly down the wall until she was sitting on the floor, her legs apart, and her slip bunched up above her waist. Falcone looked down at her, then walked into the other room.

The Rookies stand on either side of a closed door, about to kick it in. On the other side of the door a pair of long-haired bikers, sneering, sweat running down their faces, wait with shotguns.

Hanson felt Falcone come up behind him, smelled her.

"Do you have any idea what's going on?" she asked him.

Hanson glanced back at her. "Things look bad for the police," he said, nodding towards the TV set.

"They gonna get out of it okay," one of the older men said. "I seen this one before. The one that's having trouble with his girlfriend, what's his name . . . ?"

"Chris," the woman snapped. "Be quiet."

"Shhh," Hanson said to Falcone, his finger on his lips, and they walked back to the bedroom where the muscular young black man limped from the window to the broken bed and sat down, a bloodstain the size of a child's hand seeping through his pants at mid-thigh.

"It's all right," he said. "We all right now."

"Linell," Duncan asked him, *"did* the young lady stab you?" He held a steak knife by the blade, the word "SIZZLER" burned into the wooden handle.

"Sizzler," Hanson hissed, *"more* than just a meal."

Falcone smiled, looking away so Duncan wouldn't see.

"Just a little accident. No problem now," Linell said.

Duncan said, "I'd better take a look at that wound."

"Thank you, officer, but everything alright. I'll be fine."

"It's my job to see if you require medical attention. You probably need suturing."

"No, sir. I don't want to take it to court. I just want to go home. These people are crazy."

"Stitches, Linell," Falcone said. "You might need some stitches."

"Let's take a look at it," Duncan said. "Just pull down your pants."

Linell looked at Falcone. "I wouldn't want to, you know, with, uh, the lady . . ."

"That's okay, Linell," she said. "I see stuff like this all the time."

"All right, then," he said, braced himself on his good leg, and pulled his pants down below his red bikini underwear. Duncan crouched down to get a close look. He shone his Kel-Lite at the small stab wound. It looked like a little mouth. When Linell shifted his weight, the mouth puckered and spit a stream of blood onto Duncan's shirt.

Rosetta began pounding the back of her head against the wall, the sound booming through the house like a metronome, shaking her framed high school graduation photo hanging on the wall above her head.

"Rosetta. Come on, now," Falcone said, grabbing her shoulders, but it was like trying to stop a piece of heavy machinery.

"Rosetta," her mother yelled from the next room, "stop beatin' your head against that wall, girl. You *know* what happened last time you started."

"I don't *care*," Rosetta yelled, and slumped forwards like she'd gone to sleep.

Hanson looked out the bedroom door to see how The Rookies were doing. Dana came around the bed and stood behind him, looking over his shoulder.

The Rookies are back in their car, the windshield fixed somehow, their hair still neat, their uniforms clean and pressed. The rookie behind the steering wheel watches his partner as they move through traffic. "Well," he says, as the car takes a freeway ramp, "are you going to swallow your pride and call her? Remember what Dr. Sobel told us in the academy? Almost all relationship problems boil down to lack of communication."

"You're right. We haven't been communicating. Maybe we can talk it out now."

"I think it's worth a try, partner."

The picture freezes, credits begin to roll, then the grinning rookies vanish, replaced by a horse-drawn wagon full of beautiful blond girls in fringed vests and hot pants, dancing across bales of hay with young men who look like surfers in cowboy outfits. They leap and click the heels of their cowboy boots, cans of Dr Pepper in their hands, singing, "Wouldn't you like to be a Pepper too?"

"Let's head for the high lonesome," Hanson said.

"An excellent suggestion," Dana said. "Before Duncan turns a social stabbing into a major police report. I want my milkshake."

They looked back in the bedroom. "You got it under control?" Dana said.

"We'll see you later," Duncan said.

"Thanks," Falcone said.

Hanson smiled at her, hesitated, gave her a little wave, and followed Dana. Out in the yard, he paused and duplicated the wave, holding his hand up as though he was swearing to tell the *"whole* truth" in court. He did it again, and shook his head, thinking it was the way a fag would wave.

"I'll be right back," he told Dana, and jogged back up the porch and into the house. He was grinning when he came out a minute later.

"All set," Hanson said, getting into the car. "Let's go fight more crime."

Dana looked at him, the car in PARK.

"I asked Falcone for a date. She said okay."

After work, Hanson stopped by the police club, but the place seemed dreary, as if some of the fluorescent lights had burned out, depressing, and he left after one beer.

He picked up a six-pack on the way home, poured some in a bowl for Truman, and sat next to him on the back porch, looking out at the night and smelling apple blossoms. It was becoming almost a routine, he thought, a little ritual that he looked forwards to, maybe the best part of his day.

He told Truman about the incident at the Marx house.

". . . hard to figure out what happened, who's the suspect and who's the victim. Lately, it seems like, it's even hard sometimes to tell what's real. Anyway, Linell was okay, works at that Shell station near the hospital. Rosetta was sitting on the porch in that slip, he started talking to her, and she invited him in. He thought he was gonna get laid, but he got stabbed instead."

He laughed. "I almost lost my nerve," he said, "about to get in the car, but I ran back to the house and asked her for a date. A 'date.' Jesus. She said, 'I don't know if that's a good . . . good *idea*,' I think, something like that. Then something changed her mind. She said, 'Why not?'"

ELEVEN

THE WHITE ROLLS-ROYCE had California plates. It was double-parked, the driver talking to a young dude wearing a white bell-bottom jumpsuit and red, stacked-heel shoes, a fashion statement much appreciated by the police. The shoes were difficult to run in and a real handicap in a fight.

"New folks in the neighborhood," Hanson said, as Dana pulled up behind the Rolls. "Guess I'll go introduce myself."

As he approached the car, the young guy in the jumpsuit gave him a glance of cool disinterest, as if he hadn't even *noticed* the police car with the flashing lights.

"Hello," Hanson said, smiling at the driver. "Could I get you to pull over there, out of the street?"

She was a beautiful black woman in her mid-twenties, with high cheekbones and close-cropped hair.

"I'm not planning to be here that long," she told him, and went back to her conversation with the guy in the jumpsuit.

"Ma'am."

Hanson watched her hand tighten on the steering wheel, the

muscles and tendons flexing along the back of her hands and forearms. She wore gold rings on all her fingers, her red nails curving
around the wheel like talons.

"Ma'am."

"What'd I just say? I'm not blocking traffic."

"That's right, my man," the guy in the white suit added, "what
the lady's sayin'. No problem here."

"Not *yet*," Hanson said, giving him The Look. The Look was
full of knees and elbows and nightsticks, car hoods and concrete,
broken noses, broken collarbones and concussions.

"I think I see a problem," Hanson said, holding a hand to his
forehead like a fortune-teller, "unless you wait over *there*," he
pointed across the street, "until I'm through." He stepped closer,
their faces only a few inches apart. "I think that's fair. Is that *fair?*
Do you mind doing that for me?"

"Right. Man just doin' a job. I can dig it," the guy said, walking
away.

The siren on the patrol car blipped and Dana gestured at Hanson through the windshield.

"Gotta go," Hanson told the woman. "Just move the car out of
the middle of the street, okay? Thanks."

He trotted back to the patrol car, his holster, handcuffs
and packset slapping his hips, feeling the woman's eyes on
him.

"Bank alarm," Dana said, "we're covering with Five Eighty.
People's Savings down there on Grand Street." The engine
moaned as it sucked in gas and air.

Dana kept the accelerator to the floor and Hanson watched the
speedometer hit fifty . . . fifty-five. He looked at his watch.
"False alarm," he said. It was closing time for the banks. Someone
had probably tripped an alarm on the way out.

They slowed for an intersection, the siren going *ow ow ow*, as
they both made eye contact with other drivers, and Dana hit the
gas again, roaring through a red light.

"Probably."

Hanson picked up the mike. "Five Sixty Two will take the
northwest corner, okay?"

Right, Five Eighty said, *we've got the southeast.*

Hanson watched the overhead lights race past in the storefront
windows. "I'm getting hungry," he said. "Let's see if we
can't . . ."

Five Sixty Two . . . Five Eighty . . . disregard. The bank called in a false alarm.

"Yeah-yeah," Hanson said, as the car slowed and Dana turned off the overheads. "Five Sixty Two, copy," he said into the mike, as they swung back towards their district.

The Rolls-Royce was still double-parked, the dude in the white suit leaning into the window. But now half a dozen guys were standing in the street, talking to the driver. Three more guys were standing in the street with him.

"That *pisses* me off," Hanson said as they pulled up behind the car. "Now we're going to get *official,*" he said, turning the overhead lights back on.

"Is there some way to write up a double-parking citation so it's a mover?"

Dana shook his head, *no.*

"Well, hell," Hanson said, "we can use the *parking* citation."

"Now ain't *this* a shame?" one of the men said. He was wearing a pair of sunglasses, the lenses not much bigger than postage stamps. "Man," he said, looking at Hanson over the top of the glasses, "don't you got nothing better to do?"

Down the street, a carload of Muslims pulled to the opposite curb.

"Nigger, they get *paid* to fuck with us," said a muscular guy wearing yellow pants, yellow suspenders, and no shirt. His hair was up in bright blue curlers, covered with a transparent plastic shower cap, his way of saying, "I'm so bad, I can wear curlers to, you know, *style* my Afro."

"What it *is*, Hanson?" A younger guy, in a green flowered shirt, asked him. "How come you aren't out arresting bank robbers and child mo-*les*-ters . . ."

"And guys who sell stolen goods out of their seventy-four Plymouth with expired plates," Hanson said. "Thanks, Byron, for reminding me what I'm supposed to do."

Byron smiled, looked at his watch, and said, "Gotta go."

"Miss," Hanson asked the woman, "could I see your driver's license, please?"

"You want to *see* it? Why?"

"Your driver's license, please," Hanson said. *"Por favor."*

"You don't *look* like a Mexican," she said, and the guys around the car laughed. Hanson smiled.

"What *is* the problem?" she said.

"It's against the law to double-park."

"Seem like just about everything against the law," the guy in curlers said. "For black folks."

"What's *your* name?" Hanson asked him.

"My name's *Carl*, man."

Hanson looked at him, but decided to wait for the cover car. By now, dozens of people were watching from the sidewalk, attracted by the overhead lights.

"Here. You want it or not?" the woman said, her green halter top shifting when she held the license out the window. "Now what?"

"Now," Hanson said, reading her name on the license, "I'm going to write you a citation, Asia, uh, Miz Gooding."

"For *what?*"

"For double-parking this Rolls-Royce."

"Fine," she said, "write ten of them. Write a *hundred* citations, 'cause I'm just gonna throw 'em away like any other trash."

"I'll be right back."

"The plate and registration are clear," Dana told him, back at the car.

"How about running this for me," Hanson said, handing him the license.

Radio came back with the news that Asia Gooding had three "failure-to-appear" warrants for traffic violations.

"Now why doesn't that surprise me?" he asked Dana. "I don't think this arrest is gonna go textbook smooth, either. But I'm gonna get *some*thing out of this," he said, writing another citation.

"The gentleman with the blue curlers and motel shower cap may be a problem. Then again, Helen says this job has given me a negative outlook." He picked up the microphone. "Five Sixty Two here . . . could you step up that cover car."

Five Eighty's almost there.

"I better put on my fuckin' hat in case the lieutenant shows up," Hanson said.

She was half-sitting on the hood of the car, her satin shorts hiked up. One of the men lit her cigarette.

"Miz Gooding," Hanson said, tearing the citation out of the book, "this is for double-parking."

She wadded it up and tossed it over her shoulder.

"Okay," Hanson said. "Here's another one, then. 'Failure to yield to an emergency vehicle.' A moving violation."

"You got any more?" she said, throwing it to the street.

"Would you gentlemen please move back to the sidewalk," Dana said, behind Hanson now.

"No more citations," Hanson said, "but I've got some bad news. You have a couple of warrants in the computer, and you're gonna have to come downtown with us and clear them up."

She took a drag on the cigarette and slid off the car, her shorts bunching up like bikini bottoms. "Must be a mistake."

"That's possible, but we still have to go down and clear it up."

"*I'm* not going anywhere."

"Why don't you just pull your car over and lock it up? We'll have it towed to the police lot."

"Don't you hear?" she said. "I'm not going anywhere."

The Muslims, four of them, had crossed the street and were watching, their arms folded across their chests. As always, they wore black suits, white shirts and black bow ties.

Hanson put the citation book in his back pocket and straightened his pistol belt, brushing his thumb across the safety strap of his holster to be sure that it was snapped.

"Please step over to the patrol car."

"I ain't *steppin'* anywhere. Your *momma's* gonna get in that car before I do."

"You're under arrest," he said, gently cupping her elbow with his left hand.

She slapped him, knocking his hat off, and dug her nails into his cheek. When Hanson grabbed her arm, she hit him with her other hand, her cigarette exploding in sparks against his neck.

Hanson hit her on the side of the head with his open right hand and tripped her, but she grabbed his shirt and they both fell to the street where she clawed at his face until he wrestled her onto her stomach and held her down, twining his legs around hers, spreading them so she couldn't get the leverage to raise up.

Someone grabbed his shirt, but Dana pulled him off. A cover car came around the corner, and another. Scuffles broke out around them, while she fought him.

She tried to push up on her hands, but Hanson jerked one arm back and she dropped to the street again, the halter top slipping under her breast when she flailed back at him with her free hand. She was strong beneath him, but he held her down, his face in the crook of her neck, breathing sweat and perfume as she bucked beneath him, his crotch sliding against the seat of the satin shorts, both of them sobbing for air.

She stopped struggling. "Okay," she said, panting, "okay."

"You gonna. Walk to the car. Now?"

"Fuck you."

Hanson kept her pinned while he pulled her arms back and handcuffed her.

"I'm gonna pull your top back up, okay?" Hanson said.

"Do whatever the fuck you want," she said, as he awkwardly tried to slip the halter over her breast, covering her with his chest, hoping no one would see.

"Enjoying yourself?"

"Right," Hanson snorted, "but we gotta stop meeting like this," he said, helping her to her feet.

When she kicked back at his shin, he pulled her arms back, and up, with the handcuff chain, bringing her to her toes, her back arching.

"Ow! Mother*fucker.*"

"Get his badge number," someone yelled.

"Walk to the car and I'll stop," he said, lowering her arms to take the tension off her shoulders and back. She tried to pull away and Hanson raised her back to her toes, keeping her an arm's length away. *"Walk* to the car."

Another cover car pulled up, overhead lights flashing.

Holding her on tiptoes with one hand, he opened the door of the patrol car, losing his balance just enough for her to twist around and spit on him. He pushed her head down, shoved her into the car, slammed the door and leaned on the hood, catching his breath.

Dana was talking to a huge woman in a Hawaiian-print muumuu, one of the community activists. "Yes, ma'am," he was saying, "we understand that . . ."

Behind them, Zurbo and Neal had the guy with the blue curlers. His shower cap was gone and his face was bloody.

"If you under*stand* it," the woman shouted, her enormous breasts flexing beneath the yellow and green material, "then why you got to *act* the way you do? *Shame* on you. Shame on the police."

Hanson touched his cheek, smearing blood on his fingertips. He got in the car and looked at his cheek in the rearview mirror.

"Get his badge number," someone shouted.

Hanson looked down at the three-cornered tear in his shirt where his badge had been. He couldn't find a Kleenex, or a napkin from McDonald's, so he wiped the bloody hand on his sock. Asia was panting in the backseat. "You know," he said, looking at her in the mirror, catching his breath, "you gotta. Bad. Attitude."

"Your *momma's* got a attitude."

"Yeah. My momma," he said, and began to laugh.

"Glad to see you two hitting it off so well," Dana said getting in the car. He adjusted the mirror. "Thought we were going to have to call for more cover until Big Shirley calmed things down. But I think you blew your chance to be Officer-of-the-Week back there." He drove off, and Hanson cleared with radio.

Asia had scooted back in the seat, against the door, her knees drawn up to her chest. "Is all this information correct?" Hanson asked her, holding up her driver's license.

She looked out the back window.

"Could I have your current address?"

"Naw," he said, smiling. "I didn't think so."

She looked around at him.

"You won't be laughing for long," she said.

"You know," he said to her, studying her driver's license, "this picture doesn't do you justice."

"Too late for that shit," she said. "After you towed his car and put your hands all over me. He's gonna tear your white ass *off*."

"Who is?"

"That's all I got to say."

"Who's the car registered to?" Hanson asked Dana.

"On my clipboard there."

Hanson looked down at the clipboard. He picked it up for a closer look, then tapped it. "This one here?"

"At the bottom there."

Hanson laughed and looked back at Asia. She ignored him, staring out the window.

THE MCDONALD'S PARKING lot smelled like grease and asphalt, the grimy yellow arches rising like ghetto rainbows. Murry was talking to a cute girl in a red GTO.

"Hey. What's happinin', *police*?" he said, smiling over the roof of the GTO. "I hear you been beating up women."

Hanson pointed at his chest. "No badge. No name tag. I'm probably gonna get lockjaw from this," he said, touching his cheek. He held up the torn elbows of his uniform shirt. "Ruined my shirt . . ."

"Maybe you should have used your gun on her," Murry said.

"I told him," Dana said, "that he's going to have to learn to *talk* to people."

Miranda, the other security guard, strutted out of McDonald's, grinning. "Hey," he shouted, "Iceman—they all saying, 'Hanson some kind of cold motherfucker. Knocking ladies down.' "

Hanson waited for him to go on.

"You look kinda beat up your own self. Must of been some of her boyfriends did that to you."

"I think it was her whole family," Hanson said. "Everybody in the neighborhood."

"You know what he looks like," Miranda said to Murry, "all scratched up like that? One of those scared recruits takin' fire for the first time. Up in Hue. You know, diving through windows and running into walls."

"Not like *you*, right?" Murry said. "You didn't do anything like that."

"That's right," Miranda said, jogging in place, strutting, tugging on the cuffs of his uniform shirt, "I always looked cool under fire."

"Uh-*huh*," Murry said, "I remember how cool you looked."

"Come on," Miranda said. "We'll buy you a Big Mac."

Hanson ordered last, the other three sitting at a table by the window. He was trying to decide between a Big Mac and a Quarter Pounder with cheese, when a silver Porsche pulled into the "No Parking" zone out front.

"Check *this* dude out," Miranda said, at the table.

"The man's *pissed*," Murry said.

"He's *looking* for somebody."

". . . decided, Hanson?" Yolanda said through the speaker.

"I'll take a Big Mac, I guess, and . . ." Behind the ballistic plastic, Yolanda was looking past him, towards the street. In the plastic, Hanson saw the warped reflection of the man who'd gotten out of the Porsche.

"Here he comes," Murry said.

"Fine-looking suit."

"Got a little limp, looks like."

The man pointed his finger and shouted, "Which one is Hanson?" His voice carried across the parking lot and through the double glass doors, a voice Hanson had heard before.

"What's that little fucker think he's gonna do?" Murry said.

"I believe it's you he wants, my man," Dana said.

On the other side of the bulletproof plastic, Yolanda and the other kids in paper McDonald's caps moved away from the bubbling french fry cookers, back to the big stainless steel refrigerators.

Customers scooped up their food and went out the side doors.

"*Look* at this crazy motherfucker," Miranda said.

"And I left my machine gun at home," Murry said, the three of them pushing their chairs back, and standing up.

"*Nobody* fucks with my shit," the man shouted, kicking over one of the birdshit-spotted plastic tables out on the patio.

Hanson spun the revolving bulletproof serving door.

"Hanson?" Murry said. "You better turn around."

"He's right, my man," Dana said. "Somebody might have to shoot this guy."

The three of them lined up behind Hanson when the man came through the double doors, cardboard Ronald McDonald clown faces swinging on a wire above his head.

Hanson watched the man's funhouse reflection come through the door, in the turning plastic cylinder—*whu whu whu*—and it looked like he kept entering door after door.

"What's the problem?" Dana said.

"My problem's with *him*. You," he said, to Hanson's back.

"What a world, huh?" Hanson said, turning around. "Good to see you, Doc."

The driver of the Porsche looked Hanson up and down, taking in the torn shirt and the swollen scratch along his cheek. "Perfect," he said.

"Your Asia didn't give me much choice," Hanson said. "She's got a bad attitude towards authority."

"I'll bet she *did* have a bad attitude," he said.

"*Officer* Hanson. Never would of thought that."

"What you been . . ." Hanson began.

"I gotta go. This is costing me money."

———

The Muslim patrol had pulled in behind the Porsche, the four Muslims, in white shirts and black bow ties, stood on the sidewalk, arms crossed.

"If you're Muslims," Doc said, walking past them, "why don't you wear turbans, like all the other ragheads, instead of those JC Penney outfits?"

"You're only showing disrespect for yourself, brother," the Muslim-in-Charge said.

"What's this *brother* bullshit?" Doc said, opening the car door. "I'm not your brother."

"*All* brothers. We got to work together."

"I work for myself."

"Got to trust somebody else in this world."

"There was some people I trusted one time," Doc said. He looked at a scar on the ball of his thumb. It was thicker at one end, tailing out as if it was streaking away from his palm. "They're all dead," he said, getting into the car.

He glanced back at McDonald's, but the afternoon sun, poised on the horizon, had turned the windows into fiery black mirrors.

"That was another world," he said, and slammed the door.

Behind the windows, Hanson ate one of Dana's french fries and watched the Porsche drive up the street and out of sight, just as the sun vanished below the horizon. A moment later, the big yellow arches flickered, then filled with light.

TWELVE

FALCONE HAD DIFFERENT days off, so Hanson took Friday night off on comp time. It had been over a year since he had been off the street on a weekend, and almost that long since he'd been out anywhere but the police club. Dana would be working with Norman, a good cop, so he wasn't worried about that. Just a little, maybe.

They'd agreed to meet at a new seafood place in an upscale suburb east of town, the closest thing they could find that was "halfway" between their houses. Falcone had found it in the yellow pages, The Rusty Scupper. When she'd talked to him on the phone, Hanson thought Falcone sounded a little distant, but he might have imagined that. He was excited and nervous as a high school kid, and though he felt foolish about that, he was enjoying it too. He hadn't allowed himself to drink anything at home to relax, afraid of fucking things up.

He'd spent an hour trying on different shirts while Truman watched, and on the drive to the restaurant, he kept smiling, for no reason at all.

He saw her yellow Firebird when he drove beneath the sign that said Docking Harbor into the parking lot, but the five-dollar watch glued to the dash said he was on time. He parked, told himself to be cool, and walked over. She had a clipboard propped against the steering wheel, filling out some sort of personnel forms.

"Hi," he said, looking in the window of her car, "hope I'm not late. You been waiting long?"

"I was early," she said, laying the clipboard on the seat. Hanson opened the door for her.

The gray concrete building was braced with heavy wooden buttresses and half-buried in the hillside like a huge bunker.

"Looks like the Saigon embassy," Hanson said. He was nervous, and the words just slipped out. He reminded himself not to talk about the war. He listened to their footsteps as they walked across the lot, glanced at Falcone.

"Well," he said, "here we are on a date. An adventure."

They walked beneath a nautical-looking sign that said USS CUISINE and through big brass doors where they were met by a hostess in a plaid blouse and blue overalls. Her name tag identified her as JULIE—BOSUN'S MATE. She led them through the ferns, wicker furniture, walls braced with rough-cut timbers, beneath the track-mounted directional lights to a table by a window overlooking the freeway.

Hanson cupped his hand over his ear, leaned against the window, and closed his eyes. "It sounds kind of like the ocean, I guess, if you *wish* hard enough." It was the first time he'd noticed the chirping in his ears all day.

He clasped his hands between his knees, like an intimidated child, and looked around the room.

"I'm not totally comfortable here. Yet. So far." He laughed. "Let's order drinks quick."

When she didn't say anything, he asked, "Are you okay?"

"Sorry. I'm a little preoccupied."

A pretty blond waitress, wearing overalls, hip boots and a stocking cap, came to the table. "Hello," she said, "I'm Sue, your Deck Hand. Can I bring you anything from the engine room?" she said, nodding towards the bar. The barmaid wore a name tag that said CHIEF ENGINEER.

"Yes, ma'am," Hanson said. "I'll have a Scotch and water. A double. Make that on the rocks."

"White wine," Falcone said. "No. I'll have what he's having."

With the drinks, she brought them each an oar the size of a fraternity paddle, with the menu burned into the wood. "Enjoy your drinks, and I'll be back to take your order."

Hanson sighted down his oar as if it was a rifle, swinging it in an arc until it was pointing at a well-dressed couple sitting across the room. The man, wearing a military-cut leisure suit with epaulets, happened to glance over just as Hanson sighted in on him, making eye contact, then looking away. Hanson brought the paddle to portarms, then laid it on the table, feeling a little foolish.

Falcone looked at him, picked up her fresh double Scotch, and drank half of it down.

"Look," she said, "I shouldn't have agreed to come tonight. I don't know *why* I did. It was stupid of me, and I apologize. I don't know how else to say this . . . I'm not interested in you as, in any kind of 'romantic' way."

"Oh," Hanson said, thinking that Zurbo and Neal had been right, feeling like a fool.

He drank most of his Scotch in one swallow.

"If you want to leave now, I'll take care of the check," she said. "Maybe . . ."

"Look," Hanson said, talking more softly, "I don't care about your sexual preferences . . ."

"What?"

"It doesn't make a shit to me."

"Listen . . ."

"Let me finish, okay? You owe me that."

She looked at the ceiling. "Go ahead," she said. She swirled her drink around, drank half of it, set it down, and looked at Hanson.

"It's okay with me. I don't care much for fags, and, you know, lesbians are kind of a pain in the ass. Hard to get along with. But what they want to do is their business . . .

"You said I could finish.

"I'll tell you the truth, though. I feel a little bit foolish—I should have known when I saw you with Bishop—but what the fuck? The thing is, I feel *bad*. I'll go ahead and tell you that. I *like* you. I was kind of *excited* about our," he snorted, " 'date.' Well, shit. We might as well go ahead and eat. I don't have anything at the house but a can of split pea soup that's been there for a year and a half. And dog food." He got the waitress' attention.

"Would you please tell her I want the 'Surf 'N Turf'? Medium rare? I gotta go to the bathroom."

The bathroom was huge and sparkling clean, with expensive-looking green tile, green sinks and urinals, green-tinted mirrors, and piped-in music. Gordon Lightfoot was singing "Sundown." A few urinals down, a guy about Hanson's age, wearing a fancy western shirt and cowboy boots, looked over at him. He looked away the instant he saw Hanson's eyes, zipped his pants, and left.

Hanson walked to the wall full of green sinks. While he washed his hands, he sang along with the Muzak, lowering his voice to imitate Gordon Lightfoot, " '. . . *Sun*down, you better take care, if I *hear* you been sneaking 'round my back stairs.' "

He dried his hands, and was leaving, still singing, when a man with a neatly trimmed beard and a tweed jacket came through the door. " 'Sometimes I think it's a shame . . . that I get feelin' better when I'm feelin' no pain.' Music in the shitter," he said to him. "Gordon Lightfoot. A *manly* singer."

Falcone had ordered another drink, and Hanson remembered her saying she wasn't much of a drinker.

"I'm not a lesbian," she said, when he sat down. "I just don't want to get involved with a cop. I don't date cops."

"I understand," he said, noticing how she was slurring her *t*'s, just a little. Almost enough to be arrested for DWI.

"I don't think you do. But, why should you?"

They went to the salad bar, the hip new thing in restaurants, taking a plate from a spring-loaded, refrigerated stack beneath the sign Chilled Salad Plates.

Hanson stared down through the plastic roof over the salad bar, stirring a bowl of tiny brick-red chips. "What are these things?" he said. "Looks like dried mud."

"Come on," Falcone said. "They're Bac-Os. Textured soybean . . ."

"Artificial bacon. Of course," he said, sprinkling them on his lettuce. "America keeps improving." Across the room, the man with the military leisure suit patted their waitress on the ass with his paddle-menu. She managed a smile that vanished when she turned to walk away.

Back at the table, Falcone said, "I did have a reason for coming here, but I could have called a meet with you down on Fremont Street and taken care of it."

At the next table, two men in their forties were sitting with two very pretty girls in their early twenties. The man wearing an Ultrasuede leisure suit was talking across the table to the guy with the beard and the tweed jacket with patch elbows who'd come into the bathroom when Hanson was leaving.

". . . find a good realtor," the man said. "*He* can stay on top of it. Tell him what you want, then just turn it over in a few years."

"Bishop's been working downtown for Vice," Falcone went on. "She has to dress up like a whore and walk around until some jerk hits on her, then the 'guys' arrest him. Anyway, she says that Fox is really out to get you. She says he's obsessed with it. Running your name in every state, local and federal file he can access. He comes in early and stays late to do it."

"Me and Fox don't like each other. At all," he said, leaning back in his chair when the waitress set down his steak and shrimp platter. "The health food plate," he said. The waitress gave Falcone her shrimp salad. "Enjoy your meal."

"What's he looking for?" Falcone asked him.

"Probably just trolling the files, hoping something turns up that he can use."

"Okay," she said. "I just thought you should know."

"Thanks. Tell Bishop I appreciate it. I *know* he's out to get me, but if she hears anything specific . . . No one will ever know where I found out," he said, taking a bite of steak.

"Why'd you become a cop?" he asked her.

"Remember those white plastic boots a lot of women used to wear?"

"Yeah. Sleazy, but kind of sexy. Kmart boots. 'These boots are made for walkin',' " he sang, " 'an' that's just what they'll do. One a these days these *boots* are gonna . . . *walk* all over *you.*' I must have heard that song five hundred times when I was in Vietnam."

Falcone smiled. The first time she'd smiled all night, Hanson thought.

"Those are the ones," she said. "The ones I wore were Hertz orange. I wore them every day, with matching plastic short-shorts. For a year and a half, renting cars at the airport. Guys kept asking me, 'Are those pants *really* hot?' My boss liked to pat me on the ass every time he walked behind me. A forty-minute commute each way so I could wear those boots and shorts and look cute and stupid. I saw an ad for the police exam, and decided it was worth a try."

At the next table, the guy in the leisure suit said, "Not many people know that."

"He must have been *beside* himself," the girl sitting next to him said. He smiled at her and stroked her leg.

"I'd have said that's his daughter," Hanson said, "but maybe not."

"Call girls," Falcone said.

"I guess that beats walking the sidewalks on the Avenue. Fewer crazy customers. Look at that other asshole. In the tweed jacket with elbow patches. A college professor. No, a shrink, the fucker's a shrink. The way he leans back and sucks on his cigarette, you know, *thought*fully pondering the topic. 'Well, hummm, nothing to get excited about, actually. There are no really serious problems here. We've got paddles,' " Hanson said, holding his up. " 'We've got our *chilled* salad plates. God's up there. Everything is taken care of, and if that's not enough, just turn it over to a realtor and *he* can stay on top of it.' "

"What do you know about shrinks?" she said.

Hanson rotated his plate. "Surf 'N Turf," he said. "Water plus dirt. Equals mud."

"Right," she said. "It's none of my business. We all had to see Dr. Giotto to get on the department."

"I've talked to a couple others over the years," he said, glancing over at the other table.

"Fascinating," one of the women said. The "shrink" smiled at her like she was a retarded child and continued talking.

"First we kill all the lawyers," Hanson said, biting the last of his shrimp in half, "then we go after the shrinks."

"I think they do a lot of good," Falcone said.

He looked out at the freeway, long-distance trucks and commuter traffic. "They take people's hearts. So they can 'function,' and be 'productive members of society.' Producing *what?*"

"I know people who I'm *certain* would have spent their lives locked up, or killed themselves if it wasn't for shrinks, and medication."

"Better to kill themselves than let some slimy, used-car salesman—they're *salesmen*—'Trust me. I can make you happy and successful'—better dead than let somebody like that put their hands on your heart."

The sun was going down in a toxic nimbus of carbon monoxide and smoke from field burning. Cars and trucks on the freeway were beginning to turn on their headlights. Hanson put his ear to the window and listened to the sound of the ocean. *Just tell him what he wants to hear.*

"I don't know anything," Hanson said.

"Look," he said. "I appreciate you going to all this trouble to tell me about Fox."

"No trouble. At all."

"Well," Hanson said, "I guess I'll, you know, go on then."

He reached for the check, but she snatched it away.

"My treat," she said, standing up. "Remember the time in the academy when that DEA guy jumped all over me when I asked him how they came up with their street values? I appreciated you standing up for me like that. Nobody else would have done it."

On the way out, they had to pass the bar, a yuppie fern bar called No Dogs Allowed.

"Let's have one more drink," she said, her eyes showing the liquor now, along with her voice. "As long as we're here. One more, then I've got to go."

"Sure. I'll buy," Hanson said, smiling. "So you won't completely destroy my masculinity by paying for supper."

He knew it was a mistake as soon as they walked through the door. Noisy and crowded. He found a corner table, at least, where he could sit with his back to the wall.

The waitresses were busy, ignoring them, and Hanson went to get their drinks, leaving Falcone at the table.

The bartender was talking to someone at the end of the bar. Finally, he nodded at Hanson, and went back to his conversation. Hanson squeezed in between two guys in sport coats who made it clear, by the way they looked at him, that he was annoying them.

"How are you two guys *doing* tonight?" Hanson said, looking at one, then the other.

"Okay."

"Fine."

They gave him more room and looked away.

The bartender walked slowly over to Hanson. "Yeah?" he said.

"Two shots of Teacher's," Hanson said, keeping his temper, telling himself, One drink, and I'm gone. No problem.

"And a beer," Hanson said.

The bartender set the Teacher's bottle down, sighed, and looked at Hanson. "Bud or Heineken's," he said. "We got 'em both on tap."

"Bud. And make that *three* Teacher's. Sorry."

"That it, then? Or what?"

"Yeah, that's it."

He poured the shots, set them on the bar, and said, "Eight fifty," looking at something over Hanson's shoulder.

Hanson knocked back one of the shots, drank the beer, and felt a little calmer. But he was very careful walking back to the table, stepping out of his way to avoid bumping into people.

A band was setting up on the stage. The singer, in his mid-thirties, looked tired and sick. A guy who's just about run out of chances, Hanson thought, this bar the end of the road.

"Awright," he shouted. The microphone squealed and he twisted it, stumbling but catching himself, panic flaring in his tired eyes for an instant, looking out at the crowd to see if anyone had noticed that he'd almost fallen.

"Awright, now," he said. "We're gonna boogie!"

The other members of the band watched him sullenly.

"We're talking about . . ."

Good luck, pal, Hanson thought.

". . . talkin' about that *Wild Thing* . . ."

The band stumbled into the number, sloppy and loud, like a bunch of strangers shouting at each other.

"Wild thing. You make my heart sing. You make every-thing groo-vy . . ."

Back at the table, it was impossible to talk without yelling. Falcone looked out at the dance floor, gloomy, Hanson thought, almost brooding.

Hanson watched a table of young guys in suits, mid-twenties, laughing and drinking beer. He picked out the one who seemed to be the leader, a good looking, well-built guy who was doing most of the talking.

"Comeon comeon wild thing . . ."

Through the smoke and noise, Hanson focused in on him, his eyes stopping down like gun cameras, wanting to hurt him, make him cry and beg in front of his buddies.

"Wild thing, I said wild thing, I think I love you . . ."

He turned to Falcone, feeling the pistol shift in the small of his back. "Maybe we should get out of here."

In the parking lot, she couldn't find her car keys.

"Why don't you let me drive you home," Hanson said.

"No *thank* you," she said, digging through her purse, the Chief's Special .38 catching the parking-lot lights, "they're in here somewhere."

"Even if they are," Hanson began. "I know you're not used to drinking this much. Let me drive you home. I *promise* that's all it'll be. I give you my word."

She didn't say anything once she was in the van, and fell asleep on the way back to town. Hanson leaned towards her, smelling her hair. He looked at the dashboard watch, and turned on the radio, the volume low.

Mr. Jones was talking.

Falcone lived in an old house perched above the river, probably built in the forties, during the war, when they built up the shipyards. It was cozy, if a little threadbare. It reminded Hanson of a graduate student's house, back in the sixties—thrift-store furniture, tie-dyed throws, brick-and-board bookcases, a wire-spool table.

"I like this house," Hanson said.

"That's very polite of you to say so."

"I mean it."

"It's a little spartan, wouldn't you say?"

"Yeah, but . . ."

"I'm saving my money," she said.

"You should see *my* place," he said, smiling.

"The *farm*house," she said. "I've heard about that. Look, I'll be right back, then you can leave. *Don't* make yourself comfortable."

She walked through a curtain-covered doorway, and Hanson looked over her books—history, anthropology, and biology texts. Books by Edward Abbey, Margaret Mead, the poet Wendell Berry . . .

He was looking at a framed photograph on one of the bookcases when she came back through the curtain.

"Me and Scott, my ex. In happier days," she said.

"I guess I didn't know you'd been married."

"Married once. Divorced once. He kind of *liked* me in those orange plastic hot pants, handing out car keys to middle-aged creeps while they stared at my crotch. And I think ol' Scott was just as glad I couldn't find a job after I got my degree."

Hanson nodded.

"He was in Vietnam too."

"Right," Hanson said. "What did he do over there?"

"Oh, nothing like *you*, from what I've heard . . ."

"I didn't mean . . ."

". . . but it was bad enough. I wouldn't want to go through *that* shit again.

"I didn't tell him anything about the police until I was hired. He couldn't handle it. The gun. Working with other cops all night. We didn't have sex for nine months. Near the end, we even went to a marriage counselor.

"You're right about shrinks," she said. "I was just trying to argue.

"He's got a nice wife now.

"They're sending me to Records," she said. "Next month. They don't really want women on the street."

"You've got a good reputation," Hanson said.

"Spare me the bullshit. You're one of 'em too."

"One of *what?*"

"Men. 'Nice guys' like Scott. Assholes like Peetey. Like Fox. Little boys like Duncan . . ."

"They're not *me*," Hanson blurted out.

"You're the worst."

Hanson walked to the window and looked down at moonlight on the river. Barge traffic. Fountains of sparks up at the shipyard. "I don't know what you mean by that," he said, watching the river, "other than it's time for me to go."

"Goddamn," Falcone said. It sounded like she was tearing one of the tie-dyed throws. "Damn it."

He turned just as she finished ripping her shirt open, and watched as she took it off and threw it to the floor. She fumbled with her pants, almost fell taking them off, threw them on the floor, the belt buckle going *clunk*.

"You want to fuck me," she said, standing there in her bra and panties. "Fine. Why not? Then we're even for that time in the academy. A 'sport fuck' I think you guys call it."

"I don't think it would be much fun."

"That's fine, too," she said, picking up her pants.

"Consider us 'even,' " Hanson said, walking to the door.

"Wait a minute," she said. "Just a . . ." she said, her pants half on, holding them up, limping across the room, looking for something under books and papers piled on the wire-spool table.

"Here," she said, handing him a folder of computer printouts that had been balled up, crumpled, torn, then smoothed out. "Bishop slipped these out of Fox's wastebasket. You hurt his feelings, is what she thinks. He's trying to get something on you about the war, along with anything else."

Hanson took them, his eyes on her bra, and the scar on her breast that was just peeking out. She followed his look down to her breasts, then met his eyes when he looked back up, held them for a moment, then turned away and picked her shirt off the floor.

"I haven't felt this stupid in years," she said, slipping the shirt on. "I'm just gonna *forget* it happened."

"I will too," Hanson said. "No, I won't. But I won't tell anybody."

He walked out the door, stopped, and turned to look at her. "I want you to know. I'm . . ."

"What?" she said.

"Disappointed. No, it's more like . . ." He tripped, and almost fell. "Fuck it."

He looked down at the tree root humping out of the buckled section of sidewalk. "How come Bishop went to all the trouble?" He walked on, more carefully. "She hardly knows me.

"What?"

"I said," Falcone shouted, "I have no idea."

THIRTEEN

THE DOG WAS asleep on the sofa next to Hanson. It was just past ten, and Hanson was reading about the first minutes of the midnight Tet offensive, when NVA sapper units began blowing paths through perimeter wire and minefields, shooting sentries asleep in their bunkers and guard towers, clearing the way for assault troops massed and waiting in the dark of the lunar new year. A holiday truce had been declared, and the Americans under attack initially dismissed the explosions and sporadic shooting as fireworks, welcoming the Year of the Rat.

Hanson had been in many of the places discussed in the book, and he studied the maps, imagining himself on patrol again, down in the whorled contours of hills, rivers sidewinding through them, coiling past villages named *Thon Doc Chin, Cam Lo, Mai Loc,* and on to the edge of the page.

He'd put in a long day working on the foundation of the house, and the floorboards groaned and creaked as the new pier blocks settled beneath them. His arms and shoulders ached, but he knew the pain in his muscles meant he was getting stronger.

He looked at the heavy iron plate he'd been using as a base for the hydraulic jack in the morning. You can trust iron, he thought, to give true weight, and to break your hand if you didn't respect it.

Truman opened his eyes.

The night air mingled apple blossoms, the rot of turned earth, and the metallic green scent of Johnson grass.

A pickup hissed by out on the road.

The floor creaked.

Hanson closed the book and turned off the lamp. He pulled the 9mm from between the sofa cushions and picked up the aluminum flashlight on the way to the kitchen.

June bugs buzzed and staggered across the screen door as he pushed it open and slipped out into the yard, through Johnson grass and blackberry vines into a pocket of cold air under a big Douglas fir where he waited, screened by its branches, breathing softly. The clouds were light gray and dark gray as they bubbled past the tumbling moon. A covey of quail exploded just behind him, and the tree drew blood when he spun around, his heart pounding. When the rush of wings faded away, he heard footsteps in the gravel driveway. He looked slightly away from the sound and saw him, limping out of the darkness.

It wasn't until he got to the back porch that Hanson could see his profile, head tilted as if he was trying to hear something far away. He laughed and looked towards the big fir tree where Hanson was hiding.

"Scary out here in the dark."

"Only people who live around here," Hanson said, pushing through the fir branches and walking towards him, "are rednecks with shotguns, who think *I'm* some kind of liberal. No place for someone of the Negro persuasion to be walking around at night. You might be safer to stay in your car."

"I'm not driving my new Porsche 911 down some gravel road at night and fuck up the paint. What happened to you?"

Hanson touched his cheek and looked at the blood on his fingers. "Birds."

"You like it out here in the woods?" Doc said, looking out the kitchen window as Hanson got a wet cloth from the sink and held it to the cut. "I'd about decided that I'd gotten lost."

He was wearing glove-leather loafers and tan slacks, an off-white linen shirt and a tan jacket. "Don't they pay the po-lice enough to live in town? It's a half-hour drive to the 7-Eleven store."

"I got the house and twenty acres for eight thousand bucks at a state auction. All mine," he said, gesturing across the spartan kitchen. "I put in the plumbing, the wiring . . ."

"I heard some white folks live in places like this, but I never been in one before."

"You like that shoulder holster?" Hanson said. "I'm always afraid I'm gonna shoot myself in the armpit if I get in a hurry."

Doc smiled. "I like a shoulder holster. Gun on my hip spoils the drape of a tailored coat."

Hanson took two beers out of the refrigerator and held one out to Doc.

"Where's Sergeant Major?" Hanson said.

"You got anything to drink besides that beer?"

The dog looked up from the floor as they walked into the other room where Hanson handed Doc a bottle of cognac from a bookcase. "Same stuff I used to buy at the PX in Da Nang. Costs a lot more here. You want a glass?"

Doc drank from the bottle, looking at the dog. "Sergeant Major's MIA in Cambodia. Three years ago. Him and Krause. They're all dead," he said as he took a glass vial from his coat pocket and unscrewed the top. With a tiny gold spoon he scooped out some white powder. His eyes on Hanson, he snorted it, then held the bottle out.

"No, thanks," Hanson said. Behind him, the dog hopped up onto the sofa.

"I had a dog once, when I was real little. One afternoon he didn't come out from under the house when I came home from school. Lady next door told me," Doc said, beginning to smile. "Said, 'Motherfucker got run over—his own damn fault—garbage truck packed his dog-ass off to the dump.'"

Hanson drank from the bottle of cognac. "How'd you get the limp?" he asked.

Doc took another hit of the cocaine and put it in his pocket. He bent down, the butt of his pistol just visible as his jacket fell open, and looked up at Hanson. "I don't show this to everybody," he said, pulling up his pantleg.

His calf looked like it had been built with cuts of day-old meat, marbled with streaks of creamy yellow, then varnished over. He braced himself on the old sofa and pulled up the other pantleg.

"This one isn't so bad, just ugly." The shiny black skin looked like burned patent leather.

"It was a bad night. Took some shit in my back and one arm. 'Peripheral damage,' they called it."

He draped his pantlegs over his shoes, then brushed the back of the sofa with his fingers. "Where'd you find this furniture?"

"Salvation Army Thrift Store. Most of it."

Doc laughed. "I'm glad to see that you made a successful transition to civilian life."

"That your old High Power?" Hanson said, glancing at Doc's legs, then back at his face.

"Just *like* that one. I like a nine millimeter," he said, touching the pistol through the expensive fabric of his coat. He looked down at the meteor-shaped scar on his hand, looked at Hanson.

"Happened on my third tour," Doc said. "Project Omega. The idea they had was to insert two teams outside of Haiphong to take out some SAM sites. You remember Hanadon?"

"Sure," Hanson said, smiling at the memory. "Jump school, Training Group, O an' I at Holabird. His name was always just before mine on the personnel rosters. They even sent us back to Bragg together," Hanson said, his smile fading. He looked at the dog curled up on the Salvation Army sofa. "For that medic training. What's he doing?"

"He stays pretty busy being dead. His team, on the lead chopper, *almost* on the ground when their pilot says, 'abort.' 'Abort.' End of transmission. Then the fuel cells blew. They'd been waiting for us. Motherfuckers *knew*.

"Looked like a normal landing except the whole chopper was *inside* fire, rotors turning through it. That JP-4 burning, you know, like the 180 proof rum we used to get in Da Nang. No flame. Just a blue glow out at the edges, all over that chopper like they were the *chosen*.

"A couple of 'em," he said, "swimming in it. In the door. Trying to swim out of the fire, flames *on* them, in their hair, coming off their tiger suits and packs, rounds cooking off in their ammo pouches and bandoliers, little yellow flashes like Fourth of July firecrackers. That's when our chopper went down, I guess. All I remember is the smell of JP-4 and burning meat."

The faraway whine of a sawmill, so faint and pitched so high it had been part of the silence, stuttered, hesitated, and they listened, heads tilted, as it droned to a stop. A moment later it started up again, slowly, almost a moan, building, the pitch rising until it was gone.

Doc looked up. "Lemme see that pistol you got."

Hanson handed it to him, muzzle towards the wall. "There's a round in the chamber," he said, sitting next to the dog.

"I *hope* so," he said. He popped the clip out and dropped it in his pocket.

"Next thing I knew, I was looking up at a green star, all alone and the brightest thing in the sky. I studied that star for a long time while they walked around in the dark shooting the others. I must of been so fucked-up looking they thought I was already dead. I don't know. They're pretty good soldiers. Should of shot me too."

He pulled the slide of the pistol back and caught the round as it ejected from the chamber.

"Reaction team policed us up. Almost zipped me into a body bag. They shipped me to Japan, then a VA hospital in New Jersey. Casts all the way to my chest, a tube up my dick, hooked up in a bed with ropes and pulleys. People handling me like a piece of nigger meat, talking to me like a dog. I just went and studied that green star, never answered, never even looked at the motherfuckers, and they stopped talking."

He slid the clip into the pistol, chambered a round, and sighted it across the room. He put the extra round back in the clip.

"One of 'em, a 'nurse' named Junior Lott, decided to fuck with me. He'd pull those ropes so my legs went up and down and tell his asshole buddies I was 'Sambo the puppet,' and he was gonna take me on the road. He'd pretend he was my voice, say, 'Uh-oh! Feets, don't desert me now,' and pull those ropes so it looked like I was running.

"This a *safety?*" he said.

"Brand-new design. Only issued 'em to ten people on the department."

He thumbed the safety on and gave the pistol back. "Alloy frame," he said, shaking his head.

"No, thanks."

"You sure?" he said, holding the cocaine out to Hanson. Hanson laid the gun on the sofa and took the vial. The white powder burned his nose like dry ice, and the lights in the room got brighter.

"They screamed in the mornings," Doc said. "Down in the

burn ward. The staff taking their morphine and doing it themselves. Then about eleven o'clock every day, when the sun was *on*
me, heating the cast up, the smell of that greasy meat they were
cooking over in the cafeteria started coming through the window.
I studied that star till they moved me to a wheelchair, and one day
I got 'Junior' by the throat and *almost* killed the motherfucker.
His white faggot face was purple as the head of my dick when they
threw alcohol in my face and showed me a lit match.

"Locked me in a closet with old mop buckets, rats running over
me in the dark, lying in my own shit. After two, three days, I
smelled this other, like the smell in that bomb crater south of the
river, the Song Cam Loc. Where they tried out that new Napalm
B, and we had to . . ."

"Yeah, Doc," Hanson said. "I remember."

". . . had to," Doc went on, "don't be interrupting me, had to
dive into that bomb crater and what was left of those people?"

"I *said*, I remember."

"It was my legs. Gangrene. Janitor found me in that closet, him
and his nephew smuggled me out. Took me to a real doctor who
wanted to amputate this *bad* leg. I told him I'd kill him, and his
whole family, if he did.

"Some kind of bone infection in there now. From the VA they
told me. Sometimes it's not so bad."

Hanson nodded, standing up.

"It's been getting worse," Doc said, as if he was talking to
himself.

"But I'm not *crying* about it," he snapped, stepping in front of
Hanson as he reached for the cognac.

"I know," Hanson said. He thought he smelled burnt gunpowder.

"You *know?*"

"Sure . . ."

"You don't know *shit*."

"Doc, all I'm saying . . ."

"Don't you talk *down* to me, motherfucker."

"I do whatever the *fuck* I want," Hanson said, stepping back.

"Do it, then," Doc said, dropping his shoulder so the coat fell
open.

"Fuck you," Hanson snarled, half-turning, reaching back to the
sofa. The dog was sitting on his pistol, bewildered by the anger in
Hanson's voice.

"That dog's blind," Doc said, his hand on the butt of his pistol.

"It's okay," Hanson told Truman, stroking his neck. "Let's put that away. Okay?" he said, glancing at Doc, his hand poised above the gun.

When Doc nodded, he picked up the pistol and slid it under the sofa cushion. "I know you're not *'crying'* about it."

"Just so you know that."

"You never told anybody about it before. Did you?"

"Forget I said anything."

"If that's what you want."

"All right, then," Doc said.

"How long did it take you to find Junior?"

"Not long. He was working at a 7-Eleven store in Gaffney, South Carolina. Was a couple of years before I got around to it, though."

Hanson took a drink. "This is Truman," he said, handing him the bottle. "Mister Thorgaard's dog.

"How about you souvenir me a little more of that cocaine?"

He snorted some more and looked around the room. "That stuff really turns the lights on. Puts the world in a happier perspective," he said, laughing. "I wonder if this is how normal people feel all the time? All those motherfuckers out there telling each other that everything's fine. 'Just fine. Uh-huh. Okee-doke.' Sometimes I'll see a guy. Some successful-looking *nice* guy, you know? Who thinks he's got it dicked. Having a beer and laughing with his buddies, or waiting in line at the movie with his girlfriend, and I want to grab him by the collar, get in his face and say, 'I've got a little *secret* to tell you, motherfucker. When's the last time you were *really* scared?' "

Doc started laughing, and Hanson couldn't keep from smiling.

"A *third* tour?" Hanson asked him. "What the fuck did you do that for?"

"I was up in Cam Lo one Sunday afternoon. Got laid, had a few drinks. They were closing the camp at Mai Loc and I had a lot of free time. I was on my way back to the camp when a couple of MPs in one of those 'gun jeeps' pulls me over. Said I was speeding. Said Cam Lo was off limits and I was *'out of uniform,* motherfucker.' Said I better 'produce some *eye dee,* motherfucker.' " He laughed and took a drink.

"Told me I was in *deep shit,* motherfucker. They didn't even know the jeep was stolen, and I had about four kinds of contraband in the back. This was about a *traffic* violation.

"I told 'em to go fuck themselves. I didn't have anything to do with their fuckin' army."

"White guys?" Hanson said.

"Sorry-ass, sad sack-looking motherfuckers too. The one with the peckerwood accent tells me, 'You're under arrest,' " Doc said, imitating a white southern accent. " 'Get back in your *vee*-hicle, clear your weapon, and follow us.'

"I told them to suck my black dick, and walked back to the jeep. 'If that's the way you want to play, we can play too. You just used up all your civil rights, nigger,' he says." Doc clapped his hands, laughed, and shook his head. Hanson felt himself grinning.

"Motherfucker's gonna handcuff me. He reaches out to take my *arm*, you know? When I pull it away, he gives me what I guess was his *bad*-ass look, and puts his hand on his .45.

"There's a *war* going on and these two think they're fucking with some barefoot nigger in Alabama or Mississippi or some fucked-up place like that. Hey, we're five miles north of Cam Lo, nowhere fucking Vietnam. Nobody else around except Charlie, who's gonna kill 'em if I don't.

"I ask this fool, 'You gonna shoot me or what?' He says, 'Turn around. Do it *now*.' Like I guess they taught him in MP school."

Doc laughed again, his glittering eyes meeting Hanson's.

"You smoked 'em," Hanson said. "Didn't you?"

"My Car-15 right there in the jeep. Dumb motherfuckers stood there *looking* at me. Eyes like *this*. Mouth open 'Oohhh.' No wonder we lost the war.

"On the way back to camp I started to worry," he said, looking at his legs. "Fuck. Everybody would of thought Charlie did it, but I let myself get worried. I told Sergeant Major that I needed to disappear for a while. He got on the horn to a guy up in Omega. I had to re-up for a year, but the next morning I was *gone*. Omega so classified *nobody* could of found me. All the paperwork's gone now, since the bad ole communists took over."

"It's good to see you, Doc. Sometimes I think I'm crazy, one of those guys who takes a duffle bag full of guns up on a rooftop or a shopping center. As far as I can tell, *nobody* else ever thinks about doing that."

"How'd you end up with the police?"

"Only job I could find. Lucky for me, too. I'd be dead or in prison without it."

"I can give you something a lot better."

"Thanks, but I like the work. It's what I do now."

"The cops?"

"They got *rules*. You can do *this*, but you can't do *that*, 'cause if you *do*, I kick your ass and put you in jail. I'm good at it."

"Fuck their rules. They just made 'em *up*."

"Everything's made up, but these are written down in a book. It's the *law*. Fair or not, it's right there in the book for anybody who wants to see."

"What's the pay?"

"All I need."

"Here's a phone number," Doc said, taking a pen from his pocket. "If you change your mind."

Hanson handed him the book on the Tet offensive. "Write it in there."

Doc looked at the cover of the book, opened it, and began paging through it. When he came to the maps, he stopped and looked at them closely.

"Here," he said, holding the open book out to Hanson, pointing at a spot on one of the maps. "That time we had to find a hole and call artillery down on our own position?"

"Yeah," Hanson said. "I was a little scared that time." When they stopped laughing, Doc held the book at arm's length. "Nothing but a book now."

He wrote a phone number inside the cover and handed it to Hanson. "I'll get the message."

"After I saw you the other day, in McDonald's, I ran your name through the computer."

"You find my name in there?"

"Your name showed up a couple of times."

"I had a little trouble," Doc said. "And it wasn't no police department gonna hire *me*."

The dog clicked across the wooden floor, stopped in front of Doc and looked up at him.

"Old dog like that," Doc said, "ought to just put him out of his misery."

"I promised I'd take care of him."

Doc nodded. "Gotta do it, then." He stopped at the door, as if he was going to say something else, but changed his mind and walked out.

The dog followed Hanson out to the porch where they listened to Doc's steps in the gravel until they couldn't hear them anymore. "It was good talking to you," Hanson called, but there was no answer.

The dog, stiff with arthritis, tried to ease into a sitting position, but lost his balance and landed on one hip. Hanson watched as he gathered his strength and lurched up onto his haunches.

"Is he right? Would it be better if I put you out of your misery?"

He knelt and scratched the old dog's head. "You can't chase rabbits or get in fights. Couldn't be much fun." He smiled and ran his hand down the dog's stiff leg, over the scabby elbow where the hair was worn off. "You're not getting laid a lot while I'm gone, are you?"

The dog stared straight ahead, at what was left of the old barn.

"You haven't gone *deaf* too, have you?

"Am I just talking to myself? Truman?"

The dog looked up at him.

"Okay. I guess we won't shoot you tonight, Pilgrim."

Off to the east, the moonlight broke through a hole in the clouds over Stormbreaker.

"Maybe we'll both know when it's time."

He pulled a splinter off the porch. "Hanadon too."

The clouds opened wider and Stormbreaker, its snowy peak glowing, rose up through them.

"He was half Mexican and half Filipino, a big guy, from down near Salinas. Didn't talk much till he got to know you. Had big brown eyes. Well, we . . . I'll be right back."

He went inside and brought back a can of Oly, poured some in a bowl for Truman, and sat down again.

"We went through a thing called 'dog lab' together. A new eight-week course they were trying out. I thought they'd flagged my orders again. Gonna assign me to Bragg instead of Vietnam, but they were talking about going to four-man teams for cross-border stuff. Out there you'd have to treat your own wounded."

He jiggled the bowl of beer. "You want some of this?" He stuck two fingers in the beer, touched them to the dog's gray muzzle, and let him lick the beer off.

"Down here," he said, "in the bowl.

"I've thought about it. There was no other way we could have learned to treat gunshot wounds like that. You could hang out in an emergency room, hoping one would come in, but even then, all you'd be able to do is observe.

"They had a couple of extra slots, so they sent me and Hanadon up from Holabird with eight senior NCOs. Dog lab," he said, watching Truman lap the beer up.

"I remember Hanadon's eyes. The last day. When we, well, said good-bye. To the, uh, the dogs."

He looked up and took a drink of beer. The moon threw bars of light through the sagging barn out into the blackberries.

"We got plenty of beer. Finish that up and I'll get us another one."

He reached over and stroked the dog's dusty neck. "There were eight of us . . ."

IT HAD BEEN a Friday afternoon, after the first month of classroom work that washed out three senior NCOs, when they walked across Smoke Bomb Hill to the dog lab, one of the WWII barracks behind the old hospital. Eight of them now, seven Special Forces NCOs and Mr. Peshka, a Medical Warrant Officer attached to the class, sent up from Ft. Sam Houston to go through the course and evaluate it.

The green van parked behind the wooden, two-story barracks looked like an armored UPS truck. It couldn't be seen from the gate where a dozen animal rights protesters with hand-painted signs were trying to "educate" two MPs guarding the entrance to the hospital grounds.

The backdoors of the truck were open.

The dogs were in individual cages, turning tight circles against the wire or down on their bellies, ears back, watching. Big dogs, from the Fayetteville pound.

The CO, an orthopedic surgeon who'd been drafted and assigned to Special Forces for two years, walked the men through the truck.

"Do they have names?" Mr. Peshka asked. He had never made a parachute jump or been in combat, a "leg" the others considered no better than a civilian.

Sgt. Krause grinned at "Ranger" Noonan and shook his head.

"Who knows?" the CO said. "When you're assigned a dog on Monday morning, you can give it any name you want. By then we'll have checked 'em over, made sure they're healthy. The staff will induce the trauma about an hour before you get here to begin your procedures. So look 'em over, and I'll see you Monday.''

Hanadon was kneeling in front of one of the cages, cooing to a silver German shepherd who was licking the back of his hand where he had it pressed against the wire. When he saw Hanson, he jerked his hand away and stood up, his back to the dog. ''Hey, bro,'' he said, smiling, ''we made it. Four more weeks of this, a thirty-day leave, and we'll be *in*-country, my man.''

''And what a long, strange trip it's *been*,'' Hanson said. He came to attention and saluted. Holding the salute he began marching in place, singing a line from a popular anti-war song, ''. . . don't *ask* me I don't give a damn—Next stop is *Viet* Nam.''

Krause turned and looked at him from the other end of the truck.

Hanadon laughed softly. ''My *man*,'' he said slapping his shoulder, ''talkin' that shit again.''

''I don't know about ya'll,'' First Sergeant Hicks said, pulling his beret out of his back pocket and putting it on, ''but I believe I'll get a beer. Bein' it's a special occasion and all.'' The others followed him out of the truck.

Hicks was the ranking NCO in the class, the NCOIC. Tall and lanky, his face tan and seamed, he looked like a movie cowboy. He was from Kentucky, and Vietnam was his third war. He'd joined the army when he was fifteen, just in time to get frostbitten toes at the Battle of the Bulge. He won his second Silver Star killing nine Chinese soldiers on a frozen hill near Soduchon, Korea. The cold probably saved his life, clotting the blood from his wound until the bleeding stopped. The medic who found him had to thaw the Syrette of morphine in his mouth, tucking it inside his cheek until it was warm enough to flow through the needle. He'd had two tours of Southeast Asia, grateful for the tropical climate. ''Outstanding location for a war,'' he'd say.

''I'll see you Monday morning then,'' Windley said. He was the only black soldier in the group. His wife and kids lived in Fayetteville.

''Okay, Win,'' Hicks said. ''You tell Leona I said, 'Hey.' ''

''She wants to know are you gonna come to dinner one of these weekends.''

''Whenever she says. Tell her I'm looking forwards to it.''

Out at the gate, the protesters had all piled into the MPs' jeep.

As the MPs watched, stone-faced, obeying their orders, the protesters pretended to be racing into battle, laughing and cheering, making machine-gun noises with the bullhorn.

"I'll tell her," Windley said. He clapped his hand on Hicks' shoulder and headed back towards Smoke Bomb Hill. The rest of them kept walking towards the shadow of the abandoned hospital, its windows dark and broken. Behind them, one of the dogs began to howl. Someone closed the doors of the truck, but the protesters had already looked back and seen them. They waved their signs and shouted, their voices weak against the breeze that had sprung up.

The soldiers stopped and turned towards the gate, red dust swirling around their spit-shined jumpboots.

"Don't those Commie motherfuckers have nothing better to do every goddamned day?" Krause said.

"I disagree with them too," Mr. Peshka said. "Nonetheless, they . . ."

"If they want to let the dogs go, I'll be happy to cut on them instead," Ranger Noonan said.

". . . they have every right . . ."

"They have shit," Krause said. " 'Rights' my ass. 'Rights.' Nobody's got any fuckin' rights unless they've got a machine gun."

Ranger Noonan narrowed his eyes. "I'd trade my dog for that little snapper there in that peace-and-love T-shirt. With the big tits."

"She's about *Hanson's* speed," Krause said.

"How about that, Hanson?" Ranger Noonan said. "Will those hippie girls generally suck a dick?"

"They're pretty broad-minded, Sarge."

"I'd like to strap *her* down and perform a few invasive procedures," Ranger Noonan said.

Candelaria laughed. *"Las palabras bonitas del amor.* Pretty little words of love. You are so romantic, Noonan."

"You got that right, Candle-*air*-ia. They like me because I'm a little bit *different* from what they're used to."

Hanadon grinned at Hanson. Krause and Ranger Noonan were already Special Forces legends, and everybody knew who Candelaria was. Wounded and captured by NVA regulars on his second tour, he'd escaped on the march north, his broken arm in a splint, and hobbled into a Marine fire base at Cam Lo twelve days later.

The demonstrators turned their bullhorn on them, but whatever they were saying was lost in the feedback clatter.

"Dumb motherfuckers," Ranger Noonan said. "Can't even operate their equipment."

"Crybaby civilian cunts," Krause said. "If it wasn't for us and the goddamn police, they'd last about one day before all the assholes on welfare burned their houses down and fucked 'em to death."

"You're exaggerating, of course," Peshka said. "But it is ironic. We're fighting this war to defend their right to protest it."

Krause looked at Peshka as if he was some kind of animal he'd never seen before.

Hicks stroked his mustache, studying the demonstrators. "It's a hard world," he said, half to himself, half to Hanson and Hanadon standing next to him. "For dogs too. Those people never been out in it, so they don't know."

He smiled at the two young soldiers.

"But we don't get paid to worry about that, and I was on my way to get a beer."

"I USED TO wish that First Sergeant Hicks was my father," Hanson said, opening another beer and pouring some in Truman's bowl.

He scratched the dog's ears.

"I need to get you a collar. With an ID tag in case you wander off. Something *bad*, with silver studs."

A car topped the hill out on the road, the engine wailing, winding up, and Hanson spun towards the sound, his fists clenched.

"Mother*fucker*," he yelled as the car caught third gear and boomed past.

"You know to stay back here close to the house, right? And *away* from that road. Truman?"

The dog cocked his ears.

"Look at me."

He looked up, his eyes an ancient glacier blue in the dark, then blind ice-white as ragged clouds blew past the moon and the apple trees filled with light.

"Right," Hanson began, lost in the dog's eyes for a moment. "Good.

"The next, uh, on Monday we scrubbed up and went into the

dog lab. The dogs were real scared. Like a room full of tortured prisoners wondering what we were going to do to them next. I could smell singed fur and blood. And gunpowder, on the back of my throat.

"Look, I'm gonna tell you what happened as true as I can. What I did. I'm not apologizing for anything, or making excuses.

"It was Monday . . ."

THE DOGS WERE strapped to heavy oak tables with leather restraints. They snarled and whined, twisting their heads, trying to lick the gunshot wounds in their shoulders, their tongues lapping empty air.

The staff doctor walked the group from dog to dog, discussing the wounds. They stopped behind a black Labrador who had shit and pissed herself. A stubble of burnt fur darkened the raw tissue at the perimeter of a wound riddled with bone fragments.

"Through and through gunshot wound," the doctor told them. "Seven-six-two by thirty-nine millimeter, full metal jacket round, fired from an AK-47. The kind of wound you're likely to see once you're back in-country."

The Lab rolled her eyes back, till nothing but the whites showed, trying to see the men who had done this to her.

"They couldn't find a way to simulate shrapnel wounds with any degree of uniformity. They tried a couple years ago, but the severity of the trauma was unpredictable and . . ."

Krause snorted.

". . . they killed too many dogs," he finished.

"Just thinking about some personal experience I had with the shrapnel from a command detonated one-oh-five round, sir," Krause said, touching a red, star-shaped scar on the back of his neck. The same artillery round that gave him the scar had killed four of his Nungs, and Lacy, the other American on the operation, driving a piece of the Vietnamese radio operator's jaw up into Lacy's throat, through the roof of his mouth and into his brain.

"You're right, sir," Krause said. "Some bad ole trauma."

Ranger Noonan laughed, and the doctor smiled, moving on to the next table where a big poodle/terrier mix lay shivering, her eyes glassy.

"We'd better get to work on this one or we're going to lose her to shock. Sergeant Windley?"

"Yes, sir," Windley said, "I'll hit her with morphine and get an IV going."

"Good. The rest of you, let's look at this last one."

The German shepherd that had licked Hanadon's hand in the truck snarled and tried to snap at them, blood oozing from the wound as he rocked the table. His muzzle was scarred, one ear chewed off in long-ago fights.

"That old boy's been around the block a couple of times," Ranger Noonan said.

The table rocked and thudded back down as the dog lunged at them, against the restraints, the bleeding worse now.

"I saw you looking at this one," the doctor said to Hanadon. "Take care of him."

While the doctor assigned the rest of the animals, Hanadon put on rubber gloves and tried to inject the morphine Syrette into his dog's neck without getting bitten. Finally, he used a folded blanket to hold the dog's head down, slid the needle into his neck, and squeezed the little silver tube. The morphine quickly took effect as he rigged an IV.

The dog's eyes were dreamy as he shaved a patch of fur over the artery in his neck, stroked it with his thumb to pump it up, and carefully threaded the big needle into it. He shaved the fur around the wound with a safety razor, trimmed away the dead and damaged tissue, and began picking out bone fragments with tweezers.

"There we go," he said, bringing them out like big splinters, pieces of the destroyed shoulder socket, "almost got it. There. It's not so bad. I'm going to call you *Sensei*," he told him. "Old master."

By now, the others were as busy as he was.

"It was some cold motherfucker just *shot* your ass, didn't he?" Windley said to his dog.

"Himmler," Krause said, snapping his gloves on as he looked down at the boxer he'd been assigned. "Put some little round 'hippie' glasses on him and he'd look just like Himmler."

"I'm sorry, Sensei," Hanadon whispered to his shepherd, looking into the pulsing gray eye.

Later he would tell Hanson, "He looks up at me, you know, like 'I sure hope you're my friend.' I never had a dog when I was a kid. My father said, 'Something else to worry about.' "

They watched the dogs around the clock for the next five days and nights, charting their blood pressure and temperature while the wounds drained. They slept on the floor next to the tables, worried about infection, waking up like parents with sick children when the dogs whined in their sleep.

"Goddammit," Krause hissed at three A.M. on the third night, "will you keep that crybaby fuckin' mutt quiet, *Mister* Peshka? Himmler finally got to sleep and you woke him up."

"He's got a *fever*. He can't help it."

Alicia, Candelaria's clumsy poodle-Airedale, almost died after supper the next evening. He was up all night, checking her with his flashlight, crooning to her, *"Pobrecita . . ."*

After five days, when they'd stabilized the dogs, they started the classes again on the second floor of the barracks, checking the dogs every hour where they recovered in individual wire cubicles.

Hanson and Hanadon made beds out of blankets and carpet scraps. Peshka bought a blue velour bed at a pet store for his terrier, Archie. When Ranger Noonan saw it, he said, "Wasn't much of a dog to start with. Now you gone turn him into a faggot."

Ranger Noonan's long-eared mutt, Animal, slept on an army issue poncho liner. "Travel light and freeze at night, by god. You can't make any klicks carrying equipment like that faggot blue bed. Animal, now, he's hard core."

One Saturday, Windley brought his kids by to help fix up an old crib mattress they'd found in the basement for Ladine. The kids were crying when they left.

"What in the world was I thinking about?" he asked Sgt. Hicks. "Bringing those children down here?"

By the end of the fourth week, the dogs were able to hobble around, and they took them for walks on leashes. Even with his ruined shoulder, Hanadon's shepherd was the dominant animal in the group, the "pack leader." Once, when he nipped Krause's boxer, Krause said, "Keep your fucking dog on *that* side of the black tile. I'm not tellin' you again."

Hanadon glared at him, the living legend, while he stroked Sensei.

"Do you *copy*, son?" Krause said, stepping closer.

"I'll take care of *my* dog," Hanadon said, his voice shaky. "You do the same."

"What did you say to me?"

"Come on, Krause," Windley said, "let it go."

"Nobody asked you, Windley. It's time we introduced these recruits to the real world."

"Sergeant Krause," Hicks said from the doorway to the class-room, and that was the end of it.

During class they listened to the dogs downstairs, like mothers listening for a baby in the next room. The dogs were all out of danger by the fourth week, but their lives had revolved around the dogs so completely by then, it had become a habit. On the Wednesday afternoon before they graduated, Ranger Noonan went down to get a *Merck Manual,* and when he came back to the classroom, Candelaria said, "Don't fuck with Alicia."

"Say *what?*"

"Just don't fuck with her."

"I didn't go near your butt-ugly mongrel bitch."

Candelaria stood up. "I can hear, man. I know my dog. You got too close to her. She doesn't like that."

"I think I might *fuck* her the next time I'm down there."

"I've heard that you fuck dogs."

"Nothing to it, son. Ranger Noonan's not particular about what he fucks. Dogs, Mexican whores . . ."

"Little boys . . ."

"Whatever. For an extra dollar, your Meskin whore'll get down on all fours and bark while you . . ."

"As you were, goddammit," Hicks said. "Two more days and we're through. Humor an old soldier."

On the last day they wore civilian clothes. Krause stood out in the red and green patterned silk Hawaiian shirt he'd had tailor-made in Hong Kong on a five-day R&R they'd given him for a prisoner snatch he'd made when he was with CCN on his last tour.

Each of them gave a critique of the class and the lessons learned.

"This was your final outbriefing," the doctor told them when they'd finished. "You've worked hard and applied all you've learned. The proof of that is in the other room. They're all alive because you pulled them through, gentlemen. The last thing you have to do, now that your patient no longer needs you, is to say good-bye.

"You are professionals, the toughest, best-trained soldiers this country has. We'll give you a little time with the dogs, to see once more what you've accomplished, and then you can part without any regrets."

Handlers, draftees from the transient barracks across the post, had the dogs on leashes out in front. The pimply-faced private holding Animal was smoking a cigarette, looking off in the distance, and when Animal pulled against the leash, he jerked him back just as Ranger Noonan walked outside. Noonan took hold of his wrists, drilling him with his gray-green killer's eyes, the handler silently weeping, his face wreathed in stinging smoke from the cigarette trapped in his mouth.

"Spit that fuckin' cigarette out," Noonan said, releasing his grip, the red and white impressions of his fingers turning to bruises on the kid's bony wrists. "I *hate* cigarette smoke and so does Animal, and lemme tell you something, son, you smoke over there in the jungle, and Charlie's gonna kill you," he said, shoving him away.

"Damn," he said to Animal as he straightened a kink in the leash, "no wonder we're losing the war with a bunch of sorry-ass draftees.

"Hanson," he said, "how'd you get scarfed up with all these bottom-of-the-barrel white-trash motherfuckers they're drafting now?"

Flattered, Hanson grinned. "If we don't fight those Communists over there, they told me, we'll be fighting 'em on the beach at Santa Monica," Hanson said.

"Shit," Noonan said. "I'd of thought you were smart enough to stay out of this fucked up army and the for-shit war they got going."

"Don't you know?" Krause said. "He's one of those *sensitive* motherfuckers with a, what you call it, 'death wish,' or some such shit."

He studied Hanson, his tailor-made silk shirt rippling in the breeze, dozens of dinosaurs, green-scaled Tyrannosaurus Rex, their teeth bared in death-grins, stampeding through flaming L.A. palm trees beneath the HOLLYWOOD sign.

"He's gonna end up in one of the *projects*," he told Noonan, "poetry book and all. Shit. And win him a medal, probably."

Noonan laughed. "Then he can go into politics. Hanson, you gonna run for office if they give you a medal?"

"No, sir, Sergeant Noonan, sir. I plan to forsake material goods and help my fellow man."

———

They each took their dog for a walk, spreading out, away from the gate and each other, for a final talk with the animals whose lives they had saved, who would now return to the pound and be gassed.

On the way back to the truck, Sensei, her ruined shoulder strapped in a brace, growled at the protesters, the humans who were there to protect animal "rights." It was when Hanadon gave Sensei back to the handler that Hanson saw the eyes he'd never forget.

When the dogs were back in their cages, they walked towards the NCO club for a last round of drinks. In thirty days they'd all be in Vietnam, except for Mr. Peshka.

None of them spoke, or looked back at the truck, until Mr. Peshka said, "I feel good. You might be able to save your buddy's life with what we've learned. Besides, how many dogs die every day? Get hit by cars. Starve."

"Fuck your 'buddy,' " Candelaria said. "I'd rather save Alicia."

Peshka nodded, pretending he hadn't been insulted and challenged. "Whoever's right," he said, "I've enjoyed serving with all of you. Sergeant Hicks? I'd better go back to the barracks and get a start on that paperwork."

"And fuck you, too," Candelaria said as Peshka walked away.

"They're dogs," Krause said. "I don't believe you people. Special Forces NCOs. Every one of you has two, three tours over there. Except for our two virgins there. How many people have you killed?"

"More than you have, *cabrón*."

"Bullshit! You must be counting that claymore ambush last Christmas, when we were *supposed* to be observing a cease-fire . . . wait a minute. Are you gonna count that main-force company who fucked up and got caught out in the open up in I Corps that time? Get serious. Any pussy with a prick-twenty-five radio could have done that. Mr. Peshka could of done *that*. Fuckin' artillery and gunships. How many have you killed with a *knife?*"

"We've all heard how you stabbed those two prisoners down at Dak To," Candelaria said. "Big man. They should of court-martialed your ass."

"Prisoners?" Krause said, stroking his thumb along the red scar barely hidden beneath the hand-rolled collar of his hundred-dollar silk shirt. "They were in a fuckin' *tunnel*," he said, stepping back, turning, the sun glinting silver-blue off his star-sapphire ring as he peeled the solid gold Rolex watch off his wrist and stuck it in his pocket.

"As you were, gentlemen," Hicks said. "Do it somewhere else. Put that watch back on, Krause. You wouldn't want to lose something that costs as much as a damn automobile."

"Killers," one of the demonstrators yelled from the gate.

"Torturers. Tor-ture-ers."

"I could shotgun every one of those motherfuckers, go home and sleep like a baby," Ranger Noonan said.

"Nazis. Not-Zees," they yelled.

Krause pulled the gold watch back on. "Fuck 'em," he said, and they walked on until Hanson realized that they'd left Hanadon behind, striding out the gate into the midst of the demonstrators, looking them in the eyes, pivoting and sidestepping among them, his open hands at chest level. None of the demonstrators seemed to realize the danger they were in as Hanadon moved like a dancer through *tae-kwon-do* forms, a skill he'd never mentioned to anyone.

"Who called me a torturer? Who said I was a torturer? Was it *you?*" he said, snapping a punch at a demonstrator's face, stopping it a quarter inch from his nose. "Or you?" he said, spinning and driving the edge of his hand to within an inch of another demonstrator's neck.

Hanson could see he was getting angrier, coiling and uncoiling like a snake, poising to throw a kick. His stiff black hair stuck up from a cowlick in back.

"Jeff," Hanson said, keeping his distance. "Jeff." Hanadon spun, his arm cocked, his leg poised to kick, looking at Hanson like he was a stranger. "Come on, Jeff. We don't want to go to jail. Let's get drunk instead. Fuck these people."

Slowly, he stepped in and put his arm around Hanadon's shoulders, turning him and walking towards the gate where one of the MPs, who wore a Combat Infantryman's Badge and a 101st Airborne patch said, "Fuckers showed up with NVA flags last week." He nodded at rust-colored stains on the asphalt. "And balloons full of blood."

Hanadon spun out from under Hanson's arm, towards the protesters, shouting, "What do you know about it? You didn't sit up all night with him. You didn't see him when he'd torn his sutures out, or the look on his face when you came in every morning—

how happy he was to see you. How scared he was the first days, looking up at you. You don't know anything."

"It's just like Nazi Germany, man," a thirty-year-old with a ponytail and John Lennon glasses said. "That's the way *they* started. First it's animals, then they start experimenting with the Jews."

"It's not worth it," Hanson said, pulling Hanadon to the gate. "Go on. I want to talk to that girl for a second. I'll catch up."

It was still early afternoon when they started drinking in the NCO club annex. Hicks and Windley left after a couple of beers, for supper at Windley's house, and Hanson got up to leave too, telling Hanadon he was broke.

"Already?" Hanadon said, since they'd been paid that morning. "I've got plenty of money," he said, pulling a wad of bills out of his pocket.

They were into their fourth or fifth beer when Hanadon said, "Maybe they'll find somebody to take him. They said that happens sometimes. That could happen."

From the jukebox a yakkety sax played, backing up a popular group called Rare Earth as they sang ". . . so get ready 'cause here I come . . ."

Down the bar, Krause snorted. "Who's gonna want a crippled, full-grown dog. Get real. It's a dog. They eat 'em in Hong Kong."

"Come on, Ranger Noonan, let's get a table." He looked at Hanadon and Hanson. "If you two think you want to be Special Forces troopers, you're gonna have to get a whole hell of a lot tougher than you are. Mentally tough. I patched Himmler up, sat up with him at night and wiped his ass while his wounds healed, same as you. He's just a dog. A training device. A means to an end."

Ranger Noonan nodded.

"Nothing more," Krause said.

". . . get ready, get red-ee . . ."

Krause and Ranger Noonan moved to a table and ordered boilermakers—short beers and Jack Daniel's.

The six o'clock news was on when Krause and Ranger Noonan pushed their chairs back, stood up, and began to trade punches. Hooking into each other's shoulders at first, they didn't seem angry. "Ha," Krause said, "not bad. But try *this* on." Then they traded shots to the chest and stomach. They were big men, and the punches rocked them. Walter Cronkite was talking from the

TV, ". . . an ambush in the area north of Saigon, an enemy sanctuary known as the 'Iron Triangle.' Twelve Americans and forty-
seven South Vietnamese were killed, according to initial casualty
figures, and an estimated two hundred Viet Cong were killed in
the firefight and subsequent air strike . . ." but everyone in the
bar watched Krause and Noonan as stick-figure soldiers, each rep-
resenting ten dead men, appeared on the TV, Cronkite's voice lost
in the brutal rhythm of their breathing and traded blows.

They hit each other in the face, blow for blow, taking turns, the
rhythm ragged now, blood spraying their hair and eyes. Ranger
Noonan's nose broke with a *snap*. Finally, a Sergeant Major from
the 82nd Airborne said, "Maybe you two should call it a night."

Krause looked at him, one eye swelling closed, as Candelaria
got up from the bar. "That what you think, Sergeant Major?
Maybe *you* should . . ."

"Hey," Candelaria said, throwing an arm around Krause,
"come on. Let's go into fucking Fayetteville, man. Like the old
days. When we were kids. Go to the fucking Circus Lounge, man.
See if the whores are as hard as they used to be. Come on," he said,
looking at Ranger Noonan, "the three of us."

"Sure," Krause said. On his way to the door, he stopped at the
bar and looked down at Hanson and Hanadon. Blood dripped from
his chin onto the flaming palm trees and grinning dinosaurs,
spreading into the weave of the silk fabric.

"Do you understand now?" he said, blood bubbling from his
nostril. "They're just dogs. Do you *get* it?"

"**. . . HARD TO IMAGINE** Krause dead," Hanson told Truman. "If they can kill him, they can kill anybody.

"It's late," he said. "I better get some sleep. You want to come
inside?"

The dog didn't move, his head resting on his forelegs, his eyes
open.

"Up to you. It is a nice night," he said.

He got up and went inside. "See you tomorrow then."

The screen door banged behind him.

"You got enough water?"

A cricket trilled from the far side of the dark kitchen and was
answered by another one out in the yard.

"They gave me a black and white border collie. You know, the kind they use to herd sheep and cattle. Smallest dog of the bunch. I called her Simone because of the white patches of fur on her chest and feet. Looked like one of those French maid outfits?"

He walked back and looked out the screen. "Come on inside. It'll be chilly in the morning," he said, opening the door. "Come on. I'll worry about you."

The dog pulled himself up and limped inside, wagging his tail while Hanson closed and locked the door.

"Really smart dogs. I always stop and watch when I see one working some of the pastures around here, herding cattle. Working. Like they've got a job to do and want to please their owner."

He fluffed up the dog's blanket next to the cold woodstove, and took his bowl to the sink where he filled it with fresh water.

"You know, I told you, that last day, when I had to keep Hanadon from killing a couple of protesters? The hippie girl with the peace-and-love T-shirt was there. After I got Hanadon back through the gate, I gave her a hundred and thirty-two dollars—all the money I had—and told her about Simone. Asked if she would try to buy her out of that truck."

He set the bowl down by the stove and touched the dog's shoulder. "I never saw her again, though. Whatever happened. It's all I could think of to do," he said, standing up.

"You try to do what's right," he said. The dog's ears were up, following his voice as he walked away across the living room.

"You gotta decide who to trust, then *trust* 'em. Maybe what they tell you to do *seems* wrong, but maybe it's not."

He disappeared through the hall and climbed the creaking steps, his voice hollow through the shiplap cedar walls.

"Maybe it's a hard thing you have to do, so something a lot *worse* doesn't happen. You can't, well . . . shit. Who knows? Good night, pal. See you in the morning."

BACK ON SKID ROW, Dakota unlocks the door to #212. In a room down the hall, Champ sings softly, pausing within phrases, between words, before going on.

"I *don't* . . . wanttoset the world . . . on, *fi-*er . . ."

Sometimes he falls silent for five minutes—ten minutes—so that anyone listening might think he's fallen asleep, forgotten the words, or been overtaken by memories. But when he continues, as he always does, his timing is flawless. It almost seems, sometimes, like he never paused at all.

"I *just* wanttostart . . . a, *flame* in your, heart, and . . . I *don't* . . ."

Dakota turns the plastic lemon to the correct position, takes off his shirt, and lights the pattern of candles on the floor. He lies on the bed watching Gunther and the cats go through their paces in the shadows, listening to the crack of the whip, but he still feels restless.

He goes to his desk, and opens the locked drawer where he keeps the unopened quart jug of Popov vodka, and the stacks of blue letters. They've all been slit open except the one on top. It's just come in the mail. He picks it up, takes the case cutter out of his pocket, then puts the envelope back and locks the drawer.

Back in bed, he slides the case cutter open, pushes the exposed corner of razor blade into his shoulder, and draws down to his sternum, shuddering as he splits the skin. The blood thins out in the sweat on his chest.

Dakota shows his rotten teeth—it looks like a smile—and closes his eyes.

FOURTEEN

DAKOTA FOLDS AND unfolds the computer printout from the Department of Health and Welfare, reminding him of his appointment at the mental health office. He folds it up again and puts it in the pocket of his black shirt.

The police scanner on the desk behind him stops at the sound of Hanson's voice . . . *we'll be out at the property room and Detectives* . . . then continues searching through the police radio frequencies. Dakota stoops down to the plastic lemon, a little squeeze bottle, on top of a cottage cheese-carton lid on the floor. Four peach pits are positioned around the lid at twelve, three, six and nine o'clock. He keeps the nozzle of the lemon pointed at the door while he turns the lid a single revolution. He moves the peach pits clockwise, advancing them one position, takes a last look at Gunther and the cats, touches Gunther and closes his eyes, then goes out the door and padlocks it.

Down the hall, the Chinese manager lets himself out of his chain-link cage. Carpeting runs the length of the hall, gray now with decades of grime, any design long gone.

"Excuse please."

He blocks the hall. "Excuse please," he says to Dakota, and points at the sign hand-lettered on a flyblown piece of gray cardboard, the kind dry cleaners put in starched shirts like a torso. It reads, Rent Must Be Payd Wensday. An identical piece of shirt cardboard, wired on the chain link next to it, list Rules of House.

"You pay rent now."

"Later."

"Pay now."

Speeding Bear slams the door as he comes out of the bathroom down the hall, his fly unzipped. He stops and looks at Dakota for a moment, trying to focus his eyes. "The salmon are waiting, in deep green water," he says, and staggers towards the stairs.

The Chinaman touches Dakota's arm, his yellow fingernails an inch long, thick and twisted.

"You pay rent."

Dakota slaps his wrinkled hand away. "Queer!" he says, looking at his arm as if he'd been burned. "*Fish*-eater gook *queer*. Jerking off with those *queer* magazines."

"Where's all these queers, honey? I'll take all you got."

It is an aging black transvestite, or maybe a transsexual, dark red lipstick on her full lips, bald, shiny patches of fabric showing through her ratty wig, like the fur of an old, sick animal. Her modest breasts are padded and squeezed into cleavage, humping out of a black rubber bustier.

"You're a *big* one," she tells Dakota. "And *shaved* too. You shave anything else besides that big ole head?"

A red-faced sweating man in his fifties comes out of the nearest room, buckling his belt. He is shirtless, his skinny chest covered with crude prison tattoos.

"Come on back to the room, Roxanne," he says.

"I think *not*," she says, running her big mechanic's hands down her hips.

"Aw, come *on*, sweet thing."

"I think I may have found a new love," she says, reaching out to Dakota, stepping back when he reaches into his pocket.

"Excuse *me*," she says. "*You* were the one talking about 'queers,' and you certainly *look* the part in that midnight-cowboy outfit. An' anyway," she says, sliding an index finger into her cleavage, "I seen you looking at these."

Dakota watches, transfixed, until she slips the finger out, puts it in her mouth, her eyes on him, then reaches down and cups her crotch. "An' I got seven inches of black magic, too, honey."

Red-faced, speechless, Dakota turns and walks away.

"Rent due Wensday," the Chinaman shouts, pointing at the sign.

Dakota almost crosses the street to avoid the political rally in front of the Federal Building, men and women holding Vietnam Veterans Against the War banners. On the marble steps of the building, a man in faded fatigues, his shoulder-length hair tied back with a bandanna, is talking into a whining microphone, ". . . bought into the whole John Wayne thing, and I felt *good* when I reloaded my M-60 and killed more gooks as they kept coming in a human-wave attack. That's what they were to me, man. 'Gooks.' I had dehumanized 'em. Just like they *wanted* me to do . . ."

Dakota pauses, then walks on, through the crowd spilling out onto the sidewalk, until his way is blocked by a vet in a wheelchair, wearing a bush hat covered with badges and buttons.

"These medals they gave me, man . . ." the speaker is saying, as Dakota, his breathing fast and shallow, tries to push past the wheelchair.

"You want to take it easy, man?" the vet in the wheelchair says.

Dakota stiffens, looks at the stubs of his legs, leans down and tells him, "I don't feel sorry for you. We didn't win because we lacked the *will*."

Down the block, without breaking his lockstep stride or looking back, he wipes the case cutter on the appointment slip and jams them into his pants pocket.

At the end of the block he glances back, then turns the corner.

"And I wrote this poem about it, for my bros." The speaker continues, reading from a notebook, "My first confirmed kill, his out-thrown arm . . ." ignoring the cluster of people around the overturned wheelchair, until a woman notices the blood on her hands and begins screaming.

HANSON WALKED DOWN the steel-edged concrete steps to the property room in the basement of Central Precinct. The folding steel shutter was pulled down over the counter, a handwritten note taped to it: Gone to lunch—back at 5:30.

The vials of blood in his left hand were warm, two clear glass tubes with red rubber stoppers, labeled and held together with rubber bands. The blood was the color of black cherries, LaVonne Berry and the case number written on the labels in black felt-tip pen.

LaVonne had been found in the trunk of his Eldorado a little before noon. He'd been shot four times in the chest and three times in the back of the head with a 9mm. The medical examiner said that any *one* of the rounds probably would have killed him. Dana and Hanson had been on their way downtown when Detective Farmer asked if they'd swing by the ME's office and pick up the blood.

Hanson held the vials up to the light. Shook them. Tiny air bubbles dislodged from the rim of the stoppers.

"Well, LaVonne," Hanson said, watching the bubbles float slowly back around the stoppers, "you should have listened to us and confessed that day on Union Avenue. No chance for college and a new career now."

He looked around at the sound of high heels coming down the hallway and smiled at the young woman. She read the note on the shutter, then looked at her watch, ignoring Hanson. She was pretty, but too thin, almost gaunt. Probably one of those anorexics, Hanson thought, uncomfortable in the grim concrete basement, alone with a cop. He pointed to the clock on the green concrete wall. "In two more minutes, he's gonna be late. Then we can get *mad*, right?" he said, smiling. He bounced his fist off the counter. "We can shout and pound on the counter." She smiled politely and looked away.

The shutter opened with a clattering of chains, and the clerk looked at them, both his hands on the counter, like a bartender. Hanson gestured towards the young woman, and the clerk took the postcard she had, authorizing the release of property. He walked back into the maze of shelves, like library stacks, except the shelves were piled with guns and knives, radios and baseball bats, car parts and parking meters, toasters and street signs and toolboxes. Hanson looked over at the woman. "Burglary?" he said.

"No," she said. The property-room clerk was stacking boxes

and moving furniture somewhere in the back. It sounded like he was angry. "Actually," she said, "it was a rape."

Hanson nodded his head. "I'm sorry."

She hurried on as if, once started, it was a litany she had to finish. "But it's been a long time, now. It happened on March sixteenth, and I've come to terms with it. I had to accept it to move on."

Hanson wondered if a therapist had told her that it was good to talk about it.

"I'm almost over it, I think. I'd just moved in with a new room-mate on Quimby Street. A nice neighborhood, really. I liked the house," she said. "It had a screened porch and a yard. We *did* get burglarized, of course. But that happened first. They think he must have taken a key. He came back three nights later."

That's when Hanson scared himself, moving to take her hand, or maybe even put his arms around her, he thought later. But he managed an awkward turn towards the counter, almost tripping on his own feet, then stood on tiptoe, as if he was trying to spot the clerk in back, saying, "He must be lost back there. In the stolen TV section."

She'd think he was crazy. Another rapist.

The property clerk came back carrying a brown paper grocery bag with "MARCH 16" in bold felt-tip letters across it and a case number below that. It had been in the freezer and vapor rose from it like smoke in the humid air. It was the clothes she had been wearing when she was raped.

"Did they catch him?" Hanson asked her.

"No." She looked at the bag, shook it a couple of times, and said, "Well, I guess that's the end of it."

She smiled at Hanson. "Bye," she said, turned, and walked off down the hall.

It was all luck and evil out there in the dark, Hanson thought. The police couldn't protect anybody.

He logged in the vials of blood and walked back upstairs. He hesitated at the door, then stepped outside.

The woman was gone. It was hot on the street, stinking of late-afternoon traffic. Down the street, in front of the Federal Building, the emergency lights of an ambulance and a fire truck were all but lost in the glare. Stunted shrubs alongside the base of the building baked in the sun reflecting off its mirrored windows. They were almost dead. Hanson squinted at the traffic going past. He looked at the receipt the clerk had given him for the blood.

The perfect blonde in the green leotard, an icy drink in her hand, smiled down at him from the billboard across the street as he went back inside to find a bathroom where he could wash his hands.

Fox watched him from a third-floor window in the Narcotics and Vice office, then went back to his computer, scrolling names and numbers down the screen. He'd spent the morning there, working the computer. He looked old and sick with fatigue, red-eyed, with two days of beard stubble.

Peetey was looking at the Polaroid photos of prostitutes that covered most of the back wall, squeezing a coiled-spring grip exerciser that squeaked each time he closed his hand over it.

Fox looked out the window again, at the empty sidewalk where Hanson had been. He looked for a long time, as if he'd forgotten where he was, the cursor blinking on the computer screen. "My father died two weeks ago," he said.

The squeaking stopped.

"In the VA hospital up in Tacoma," Fox said.

"I'm sorry, man," Peetey said.

"Why should you give a shit?" Fox said. "I don't. I haven't talked to him in five, almost six years. Called himself *Reverend* Fox, did you know that?"

"No, man. I don't think you've ever . . ."

"Worked at Monk's Auto Upholstery when I was a kid, until he got religion. Got 'The Call,' and sent off for some mail-order divinity degree, joined a little church up in Tenino, and conned his way into taking over. He was a talker when he had to be . . . there's something about *Hanson* that reminds me of him," he said, still looking out the window.

"Got caught with his hand in the till, after embezzling church money for years. To pay for his liquor—I remember how he used to smell, Old Spice aftershave to cover the smell of liquor. He'd take 'pep pills' he bought at the truck stop to straighten him out. He'd listen to his fuckin' Frank Sinatra records, then say he had to go take care of some 'church business.' Hymn-singing whores. It was a sin to smoke, or drink, but it was okay to spread their legs for the *Reverend* Fox . . ."

He closed his eyes and leaned back in the office chair. Peetey squeezed the grip exerciser, his forearm bulging. Finally, he released his grip and started to leave the room.

"He'd come home drunk," Fox said, "after my mother died. Make me get on my knees and *pray* with him. After all those years fucking around on her.

"I'll tell you one thing, maybe I'd get down on my knees, but I'd *think* pure hate at him, and that was a kind of prayer for me. I'd slip out and follow him around town at night, steam his mail open, go through his desk drawers. Sent off to *Popular Mechanics* for plans that showed you how to make a little extension phone, so I could listen in to his phone calls."

"A born detective," Peetey said, laughing.

"This isn't funny," Fox said. "I'm tellin' you what happened. I never told anybody about this before. You think it's funny?"

"No disrespect intended, man."

"I was in high school when I found his other bankbook and sent it to one of the deacons. All they did was fire him. Is that justice?"

"Right. I mean, *hell* no. You oughta go home and get some sleep. You look like a wino . . ."

"What?" Fox said, sitting up, turning to look at Peetey.

It was late afternoon when Hanson and Dana left Detectives, the time of day Hanson hated, when the sun was in his face. They passed a gang of Hare Krishnas at the edge of a little park on their way down the street to the patrol car.

They danced in a circle, saffron robes twisting at their ankles, finger cymbals ringing like spurs. Swaying, their eyes unfocused, heads rolling from shoulder to shoulder, they chanted, "Hare Krishna, Hare Krishna, Krishna Krishna, Hare Rama." The rhythm grew ever faster.

"You ever see a black Hare Krishna?" Dana said.

"Nope."

"Speaks well for black folks," Dana said.

The dancers spun in and out of the circle, their finger cymbals buzzing like a swarm of steel locusts. One of the dancers, gliding round, missed half a beat when he saw them, then closed his eyes and danced away.

"Check out the guy on the other side of the circle. Real pale. *There.* Just spun away."

The sun gleamed on his shaved head, gold earrings, and the pale white streak painted from his forehead to the bridge of his nose.

"Fuckers all look alike to me," Dana said.

Hanson laughed. "Here he comes now . . . look."

"Ira Foresman."

"That's him. Ira Foreskin got religion."

As they crossed the street, Hanson held up two traffic citations. "The ME said LaVonne was shot sometime early this morning, so I dropped a couple of movers on him. Speeding, and Failure to Yield to Oncoming Vehicle. One for you, and one for me," he said, handing him a citation.

"Well, that's real white of you."

Hanson laughed. "Extremely white. And looking good for the lieutenant."

They still had to do a property report and a supplemental report on the blood, maintaining the chain of evidence, but could finish them over their meal break.

It was after six, so cars were parked on both sides of the narrow downtown streets. They passed groups of winos who dutifully stuck their bottles in their shirts or held them behind their backs as the patrol car passed. It had been a hot day, the sun baking them as they had sat or lain on the hot concrete and brick storefronts. Champ, who claimed to have been a prizefighter, nodded a greeting and Hanson waved back. "Champ," Hanson called, "knock 'em down, push 'em around." Hanson had gotten to know him when he'd worked down on skid row as a rookie.

The cops were their friends down there, protecting them from jackrollers, taking them to the emergency room when they had seizures, when they tripped and fell against the curb or through a glass door, when they got knifed in some stumbling argument over a mickey of wine.

Hanson kept a pair of leather gloves in the trunk, just for handling winos who stunk of urine and disease and month-old sweat, who often shit their pants when they passed out. Their skin was crusty with filth and they had sores on their faces and arms.

A lot of cops were heavy drinkers, and maybe that was why most of them were so patient with the winos. They'd curse them and shake them sometimes on the way to the backseat of the patrol car, walking behind and holding them up by the sleeves or shoulders of their shirts, at arm's length as the upscale shoppers at the "Old Town" boutiques watched with disgust. They weren't gentle with them, but they were usually patient. They could see themselves in the winos. Too many more years of working the streets, where it was all despair and hardly ever a happy ending, too many more nights closing up the police club bar, driving home drunk and not remembering the drive home or the last four hours in the club, and they might be the wino.

Hanson had never heard a cop say that, but he knew they thought it, because *he* did. He handled the winos as he might handle his own drunken father. Hanson saw himself in winos lurching down the sidewalk in the brutal afternoon sun, dried spit on their chins, half-blind on Thunderbird or Night Train.

He never saw himself as one of the successful young executives or attorneys who sometimes had to step over a passed-out drunk to meet some slim, well-groomed woman in a fern bar where they discussed racial injustice and human rights over cocktails.

The winos walked the streets like ghosts of things to come, babbling secrets that only they and the cops knew.

Hanson turned down Fourth, an old cobbled street lined with expensive restaurants and high-rise office buildings. The patrol car wobbled over the cobblestones, the radio on the downtown frequency competing with Dana's packset monitoring North Precinct.

A new Volvo, dark blue, was double-parked up ahead on the narrow street, its red hazard lights blinking.

"Right," Hanson said, as they rolled towards the Volvo, "you want to double-park? Just turn on the *blinkers*. That's what they're for. If they're blinking, whatever you do is okay."

A red and white bumper sticker on the Volvo read Question Authority. "Oh," Hanson said, gesturing towards the bumper sticker, "I see *now*. It's a *liberal*. Out here testing the limits of his legal motherfucking rights."

Dana laughed. "My man is hell on those liberals."

"No, no," Hanson said, "not at all. I'm *glad* we have people out here questioning *authority*," he said, jerking the wheel to go around the car, driving slowly past.

The man in the driver's seat of the Volvo had a neatly trimmed beard and was wearing a tweed sport coat. He was smoking a pipe, reading a newspaper spread across the steering wheel. Hanson pulled the patrol car alongside the Volvo and stopped.

"Not real alert," Hanson said, staring at him. "If it wasn't for the police he'd last about one day before they burned down his house and fucked him to death."

"Who's 'they'?" Dana said, his eyes on the driver too.

"You know who. The LaVonne Berrys and Sylvester Hills and Willy Thompsons. Crazy guys like that guy who drives the old police car."

The driver of the Volvo turned the page of his newspaper.

" 'Call me . . . Dakota,' " Dana said.

"Ira *Fore*-skin."

"Ira got religion," Dana said.

"And LaVonne's dead."

Startled, the driver of the Volvo looked up at the sound of their laughter. But he quickly composed himself, regarding them sternly, working that into an expression of superior dismissal, and went back to his newspaper.

"Perfect," Hanson said as they rolled past. "A beard and a pipe and a Volvo. Did you see the way he *looked* at us? Huh?"

Dana laughed again, and Hanson tried not to smile. " 'Question Authority,' " he snorted. "Like we're the fucking Nazis out here and little weenie guys like him are keeping us in line. Let's go around the block," he said, making a right turn. "If that guy is still there he's gonna get a ticket. He *deserves* a ticket."

"Absolutely," Dana said.

Hanson made another right-hand turn. The dispatcher on Dana's packset sent Five Eighty to an address on Fremont Street to take a report on a runaway.

"Sherry North," Dana said.

"Runaway?" Hanson said. "She's been turning tricks down in East Precinct for a year now."

"Her mother must still be trying to claim her for the ADC money," Dana said.

"You know," Hanson said, "I've never known anybody who smoked a pipe that was worth a shit. I'm trying to be objective, and I can't think of *one*. I mean, what do you *do* with a pipe if you have to move quick. Like, 'Hey, come on, let's *grab* that guy.' And what does the guy with the pipe do? He says, 'Uh-oh. Right. Be right with you. Let me tamp my pipe here and uh, where shall I put it?' "

They turned back down Fourth Street. " 'I'd *like* to help,' " Hanson said, " 'but I have to take care of my pipe.' You know, it's

like a guy with a pipe is going through life with a serious handicap."

The Volvo was still double-parked. "What do you suppose this
guy *does?*" Hanson said. "I bet he's some kind of psychologist. Or
a therapist. Hmmm," Hanson said, stroking an imaginary beard,
"certainly there was some trauma involved. How do you *feel*
about that?"

He pulled up behind the Volvo, and put the car in PARK. The
bearded driver studied his paper, ignoring them.

Hanson turned on the overhead lights and they reflected off the
windows of the office buildings. The man looked up from his
paper to the rearview mirror. "Hello, dope," Hanson said. He
picked up his ticket book and got out of the car. Dana got out and
stood at the right rear bumper, watching the back of the driver's
head. They did all their traffic stops the right way, always assum-
ing that the people in the car might have guns.

"Hi there, sir," Hanson said to the driver. "Could I see your
driver's license, please?"

"What's the problem, officer?"

"Well, see," Hanson said, looking to the right side of the street,
then the left, then holding his hands out in front of him as if he
were describing a small fish, "the problem is that you're double-
parked in this narrow street. A *small* 'problem,' true, but a *problem.* Could I see your driver's license, please?"

"Officer," he said, "I'm just waiting for my wife and my daughter. I didn't expect them to take this long, but obviously," he said,
gesturing with his arm out the window, "I'm not causing a major
traffic problem here."

"Daddy."

The driver's daughter and wife had come out of the building.
The daughter was in her early teens and was wearing braces on her
teeth. She was embarrassed that her father had been stopped by
the police, looking up and down the street to see if anyone was
watching. The mother, an older, tougher version of the daughter,
stepped from behind her. They were both thin, and both wore
black. "Get in the car," her mother said.

The girl got in the backseat, looking at Dana and Hanson as if
they might shoot her. The woman got in beside her husband.

Hanson smiled at the two women. "Hi.

"Sir," he said, looking back at the bearded man, "your driver's
license?" The woman stared at Hanson, her mouth a hard line,

holding the look, demonstrating her refusal to be intimidated, before turning away. She spoke to her husband, then looked out the windshield, chin up. Her husband turned to Hanson with new firmness.

"Officer," he said, "my wife and daughter are here now. As I told you, I was waiting for them, as I often do. Obstructing no one. As a matter of fact, your patrol car is the only car I've seen since I parked here two or three minutes ago. Surely you can . . ."

"I have to see your driver's license," Hanson said.

"You don't have to show him anything," his wife said.

"Step out of the car, please," Hanson said, his voice no longer joking.

The driver stiffened, as if he'd just touched the wrong electrical wire, trying not to show it.

"Get out," Hanson said. "Now. I'm tired of fooling around. Out."

He opened the door and stepped out as if he was sleepwalking.

"This is ridiculous," his wife said.

"Da-dee," his daughter cried from the backseat, "Daddy."

"Do you want to step around behind the car, please?" Hanson said.

The man's legs were shaking. Dana approached him from the other side, the two cops dealing with him as they would anyone they were planning to arrest. The daughter was crying in the backseat of the car, and the wife had gotten out on the sidewalk, a notebook in one hand, pencil in the other. She leaned slightly forwards, over the car, trying to see Hanson's badge.

"Badge four eight seven," Hanson said, "my name's Hanson.

"Now, sir," Hanson said to the man, "can I see your driver's license, please?"

On the sidewalk, his wife looked at her watch, then wrote some more in the notebook.

"Better get mine too," Dana said, touching his badge.

"*He's* the one I want," she said.

"Sir," Hanson said, "do you want to show me your driver's license, or do you want to go to jail?"

"You can't be serious."

"Yes, I can. I'm usually a fun guy, but I can be serious. Step back to the patrol car, please."

At the patrol car, the man patted his coat pockets, took out a ballpoint pen, then dropped it by the rear tire. He bent down, fumbling to pick it up. Hanson's eyes were on him when he stood up.

"You need to work on your technique some," Hanson said.

"What's that?" he said, trying to smile, a tiny muscle twitching at the corner of his mouth.

Hanson shook his head, looked over at the wife, at the tearful teenager with braces. "This is your lucky day. Let's see the license."

"He can't do this," the wife said from the sidewalk.

"Shut up," he told her. "Shut up and get in the car."

She folded her arms and glared at him.

"Get in the damn car."

The man took out his wallet and gave his license to Hanson. His hand was shaking.

"Thank you," Hanson said. "Why don't you wait for me in your car. I'll be right with you."

Hanson ran a routine check on the license and began writing out a traffic citation for double-parking. "Dumb fucking little dipshit liberal," he muttered. "Gonna 'question authority.' Jesus Christ. They don't even know what authority *is*. Fucker's living in some kind of dream world. *Authority* is what kicks your ass if you break the rules."

The license check came back clear and Hanson took the ticket up to the Volvo. "Here's a citation for double-parking," Hanson told the man. His wife stared straight ahead through the windshield, and the daughter sat against the far side of the car, pulled up against the door.

The man took the ticket without looking at Hanson. "Thank you," Hanson said, "and here's your license back."

"Can I go now?" he asked, still not looking at Hanson.

"Yes, sir."

"Thank you, officer," he said.

"Good night, ladies," Hanson said. As they drove off, he fished the baggie of marijuana out from behind the rear tire where the man had tossed it, about ten dollars' worth. He kicked it back under the patrol car, folded the ticket into his citation book, and got in the car.

Dana laughed. "I'm glad we're out here doing some quality law enforcement."

"That's right," Hanson said, trying not to smile. "That's exactly right," he said, waving the citation book. "Break the law and go to jail.

"Is double-parking a mover?" he said, thumbing through the list of statutes.

"He was *parked.*"

Hanson stopped turning pages, looked up at Dana, smiled.

"*Double*-parked. 'Double' suggests that the *vee*-hickle was in two different places. A kind of movement, if you think about it. The language of the law can be very subtle."

Dana shook his head.

"Look at 'excessive noise—tires,' for Christ's sake. How can noise be a mover? How stupid is that?"

"Double-parking is not a mover."

"Fuck it, then," Hanson said, tearing the parking citation out of the book and starting another one. "He was jaywalking too."

AFTER HE LEFT the club, Hanson parked down the street from Falcone's house. Only one light was on, in the back of the house, and he wondered if she was home. He fell asleep looking at the tie-dyed sheet she used as a curtain, and when he woke up, the house was dark.

He was halfway home when he thought to turn on the radio, catching the ending of "Stand by Me."

" '. . . when night has come,' " Mr. Jones said, quoting from the song, " '. . . well I won't be afraid.' " He laughed. *"I know what the man's talkin' about. Got to stand by your brothers and sisters. Only way any of us gonna make it through the night."*

FIFTEEN

IT WAS AN elegant Victorian town house built in the nine-teenth century, one of three on the tree-lined street. In recent years before they had been in danger of being torn down, but Dana and his wife Helen had gone into debt to buy all three and slowly refurbish them. Some of the young professionals who had moved out from the East Coast decided they liked the neighborhood and now the town houses were worth a small fortune. Dana had sold the other two houses to an attorney and a psychiatrist.

Dana didn't have to work. He and Helen owned real estate all over the city now. Dana worked because he enjoyed being a cop, after almost fifteen years. He told Helen that the job was a good way to stay familiar with the city and property that came up for sale, and he downplayed the danger on the streets.

Hanson liked the town house, the walls of old brick that had once been covered with plaster, the solid, scarred beams and the restored stained glass windows. Helen met him at the door, ele-gant in gray satin slacks and black blouse. Her black hair was short and she wore big hoop earrings. Besides managing all their real estate, she was an adjunct professor at a private college in the hills just east of town, a heavily endowed school known for its radical faculty and students where she gave seminars in "Radical Economics."

"Officer Hanson," she said, "how nice of you to leave your rustic country home and visit us."

Hanson grinned. "Thanks," he said. "I wasn't able to kill anything to eat tonight anyway. How are things going at that Commie school? You must get tired of listening to all those whining liberals in your classes. Oh," Hanson said, "doesn't injustice just make you *sick?*"

She smiled and patted him on the cheek. "I love you dumb macho types," she said.

"That's right," Hanson said. "I'm not very smart, but I like to dress up in a uniform and beat up minorities.

"How was the coast?"

"I'm *very* pleased with what we worked out. Go upstairs and help Dana," she said, dismissing him with a wave of her hand. "He's still working on that skylight."

"Yes, ma'am," Hanson said, saluting her.

The stairs were handmade, put together with wooden dowels instead of nails, and the full-length mirror on the first landing reflected a vase of orange marigolds.

Dana was wearing blue overalls, standing on a stepladder, trying to bend an aluminum flange with a pair of channel-lock pliers. The hallway smelled of sawdust.

"Doing a little detail work up there?" Hanson said.

"Not anymore," Dana said, putting the pliers in his back pocket and coming down the ladder. "Cheap junk. It's gonna leak. I'd be glad to pay the extra for heavy-gauge aluminum, but they don't *make* it anymore. This stuff," he said, gesturing with his head, "is like something you'd find in a mobile home."

He looked up at the skylight. "But it's not going to rain tonight. Let's get a beer. I'll worry about it tomorrow.

"How does that place of yours do in the rain?" Dana asked as they walked downstairs.

"It's tight," Hanson said, over his shoulder. "It's been out there in the weather for eighty years. I think the rafters and the roof beams have grown together. Like they were grafted. It's probably put down taproots and one of these days the roof is going to blossom."

Dana smiled at Hanson's back. "Seen anything of your friend, Doc?"

"Not lately."

"I know he's an old friend," Dana said, "and it's none of my business, but . . ."

"I know," Hanson said. "You're right."

Helen was in the kitchen slicing tomatoes into the salad. The Siamese cat, Jean Paul, was rubbing up against her leg. She'd bought him in Paris where she'd been attending a seminar. The paperwork to get him into the country had been "staggering."

"How's the French cat?" Hanson said.

"Very well, thank you."

"It's where she's happiest," Dana said, getting two beers out of the refrigerator. "In the kitchen. Tossing a salad."

"Uh-huh," she said. "Did you get that skylight fixed?"

"I *would* have," Dana said, "but I had to stop to entertain our guest."

"What a host you are."

Dana blew her a kiss. "Come with me, young sir," he told Hanson. "I got a *deal* on a new elk rifle. Think about it," he said, walking out of the kitchen. "You ought to invest some money in real estate. Put it to work for you. Think about the future."

"I like to know where my money is," Hanson said. "I can look in my little bankbook and see how much I've got. I'd like to keep it in gold coins under the bed."

"Gold's okay," Dana said as he brought the rifle out of the entryway closet, "but you don't want to put *all* your money in it.

"Ruger number one," he said, handing the compact rifle to Hanson, "in 300 Winchester Magnum. It'll kill anything in North America. Three to nine variable wide-angle scope."

Hanson brought the rifle up to his shoulder, lowered it, then snapped it up again, the hand-rubbed maple stock smooth against his cheek, the blued receiver smelling of Hoppes #9 solvent. He worked the lever-action and the heavy falling block slid open like a tumbler in a huge lock. "Beautiful," Hanson said. "Single shot, but all you ever get is one shot."

He carried the rifle across the high-ceilinged living room to the window, brought it to his shoulder and worked the action, chromed and lightly oiled, the oil like a light coat of sweat. Hanson closed it slowly over the throat of the barrel until it locked with a faint *click*. "Pure sex," he said.

He aimed it out the window, scanning the street through the crosshairs of the scope. The optics gathered light from the gray dusk, showing the trees and passing cars in fine relief. He followed a Chevy, tracking it down the street, crosshairs twitching in the silhouette of the driver's head, then picked up a Cadillac coming the other way. He aimed through the windshield of the big car, into the driver's throat, a heavyset man in a blue shirt, his glasses reflecting the pearly light. When the car passed, Hanson swung the rifle back towards the sidewalk.

"Uh-oh," he said. "Look at this," turning the focusing ring and zooming in with the scope on a cocker spaniel puppy as it came into view from beneath the leaves of a tree up the street, followed by a man in a three-piece suit who had the dog on a leash.

"A guy walking his dog," Hanson said, "and he's got a briefcase. A young professional. Maybe . . . an attorney!" he said, moving the crosshairs from the cleavage of his vest up to his face. As Hanson looked down at him in the failing light, the man's eyes and mouth were shadows.

Dana looked out the window. "That's our neighbor," he said.

"Yes, an attorney," Hanson said. "A fighting liberal from the East Coast. Yes, yes. Someone who really cares about injustice." He slid the crosshairs over to the trotting puppy. "The puppy first," he said, pulling the trigger, the gun dry firing. *Snap.*

He cocked the rifle again. "Oh no! What happened? My puppy blew up. Who could be mean enough to shoot a puppy?"

He talked as he tracked the man in the suit. "Three hundred Magnum," he went on, enjoying himself. "That's a big slug, what? Two hundred twenty grain?"

"Two forty," Dana said.

"Better yet," Hanson said, "and moving fast, about 3200 feet-per-second out of a 24-inch barrel. Am I right?"

"Pretty close," Dana said, laughing.

"Yes, sir," Hanson said, placing the crosshairs over the man's heart, just below the glint of a pen in his breast pocket. "Straighten that guy right up," he said, squeezing the trigger, "lift him onto his toes. Improve his posture," he said, easing the trigger back. *Snap.*

"Perfect," he said, turning from the window, smiling at Dana. "You know how you can tell, the instant you pull the trigger, if it was a good shot?"

He looked over and saw Helen watching him from the kitchen

doorway. "Just kidding, ma'am," he said, coming to attention and going through a little manual of arms with the rifle. "Pre-sent arms. Right shoulder arms. Order . . . arms."

He glanced out the window, then looked again, way up on the next block, at a blond woman in a red dress. He braced the rifle on his left arm and looked through the scope, the shifting image of the street dizzying as he searched for the woman through the optics. Cars in the street had begun to turn on their headlights and they glowed like moons as Hanson swept the scope up the street, passing the woman in red, stopping, then backing up until he had her in the sight picture.

He smiled, tracking her down the street as she walked towards the house. It wasn't quite a miniskirt she was wearing, but almost, and Hanson watched the muscles flex in her calves and thighs. The way her hips and legs moved in the high heels made her look vulnerable and sexy. She was carrying some sort of portfolio under one arm.

He twisted the scope, zooming in on her, moving up from her feet and legs, past her hips—pausing a moment at her breasts— then up to her face. Her hair was red, not blond. Her eyes seemed big in the scope, and for a moment he thought she was looking at him.

"Looks like she's coming here," Hanson said, taking the rifle from his shoulder. Helen walked up behind him.

"That's Sara," she said. "One of my students. She has to drop off a paper."

"Okee-doke," Hanson said, as the woman came up the steps. Suddenly, he held the rifle out to Dana.

"Here," he said, "don't tell her I'm a cop, okay? I get tired of being a cop all the time. I want to be a liberal. A nice guy. Somebody who looks for the *good* in everything?"

"Let's not get carried away," Helen said. "She's just here to drop off a paper. She's not your type, anyway."

"What do you mean, 'not my type'?"

"She's normal."

Dana laughed as Helen answered the door. "Hi," the woman said, a little out of breath, "I'm running late as usual. I've got a plane to catch early tomorrow, and I'm still not packed. I just love this house," she said, looking around.

Everything about her seemed pale—the freckles on her arms, the faded, flaking lipstick on her full lips, smudged eye shadow and the strawberry-blond hair. The arteries and veins in her wrist showed through her skin like bruises as she handed the portfolio to Helen.

"Hi, Dana," she said. "You still working for the army of occupation?"

"Still out there," Dana said.

"For the moment," Helen said.

"Hi," Hanson said.

"A friend of ours," Helen said. "I'd ask you in for a drink, but I know you're in a hurry."

Sara looked at Hanson. "I've got time for a glass of wine," she said. "Probably good for me to slow down for a minute."

"Dana," Hanson said, "why don't you put that gun away. It makes me nervous."

"Sure," Dana said. "I forgot how sensitive you were about firearms."

Hanson smiled at Sara and shook his head. "Dana. Mister Macho."

"Come on into the kitchen," Helen said. Sara smiled at him as they walked past, her dull gold earrings, snakes biting their own tails, swinging as she turned her head. She smelled like straw in the sun. When his eyes met hers, he thought for a moment he might fall down. The high heels made her taller than he was. They both looked away at the same time, embarrassed.

"I think," he said, "that we should go see if we can help the ladies in the kitchen. A dry red wine would be nice," he said, ignoring the beer he'd left sweating on the fireplace.

Sara was stroking the cat. "Oh, Jean Paul," she said, as the cat arched his back, "you're so elegant."

"The cat from France," Hanson said. Helen gave him a look and he grinned at her.

"Cats are okay. I just don't trust anything from France. I was thinking the other day. You know that first 'dirty' song you learn as a kid?

"There's a place in France—Where the women wear no pants—And the men walk around—With their weenies hanging down.

"I've decided that about sums it up. That's all anybody really needs to know about France."

Hanson felt himself blush as he smiled at her, feeling stupid for singing the song. He let Helen pour him a glass of wine, then he saluted Sara with it. "I flunked French one-oh-one."

"I'm sorry," Helen said. "I should have introduced you two, but I thought you had to go, Sara."

She looked at her watch, then gulped half her wine. "I do have to go," she said.

"Where are you off to?" Hanson said, wishing he could taste the wine on her lips.

"I'm going to spend some time with my parents at Cape Cod, and visit my boyfriend in Baltimore. He's in law school at Johns Hopkins."

"Oh," Hanson said. "An attorney. Good. Very good. We *need* more attorneys. We don't have enough."

"Don't you like lawyers?"

"Just kidding," Hanson said. "I work with attorneys all the time." He put his hand to his head. "Just ignore me. I think I have a fever or something."

"Helen," she said, "I'd better go. Thanks for the wine. Dana, good to see you."

She set the wineglass down, walked over to Hanson and looked in his eyes. She pressed her cool hand against his forehead. "No. I don't think you have a fever."

Hanson smiled at her. "Have a good trip."

They ate supper out behind the house in the fenced-in brick patio. Dana barbecued steaks. It was a warm night, and clear. Hanson could lean back in his chair and see the stars. The stars always made him think of Vietnam. The nights on ambush when he watched the stars, perfect and indifferent to time and death, secure in their turning.

"Is North having that dog-hunt thing again this year?" Helen said.

"Yeah," Hanson said, finishing another beer. "It's already started."

"I can't believe they still allow that."

"The dogs are a problem . . ." Dana began.

"You two aren't *participating?*"

"Not yet," Dana said.

"I wish you were resigning tomorrow. There's no reason to wait till the first of the year. It's *stupid*. With the income from that property on the coast . . ."

"I said 'maybe,'" Dana said.

"I'm gonna get another beer," Hanson said, standing up, "anybody want anything from the kitchen? Okay. I'll return."

"There's some vicious dogs out there," Dana said as Hanson went into the kitchen where he got another Oly out of the refrigerator and took a sip of bourbon out of the bottle on the counter. The cat was on top of the refrigerator, watching him.

"Hiya, Jean Paul," Hanson said to him. "How's it hanging? Maybe we can take you on a ride-along some time. You can play with the night dogs."

The cat looked imperiously down at him.

Hanson gave him The Look. The cat held his eyes for a moment, then his head twitched as if he had heard some distant sound, and he looked away.

Hanson smiled and took another swallow of bourbon. He washed his hands at the kitchen sink, and went back outside after pausing for one more sip of bourbon.

"I've never killed one," Hanson said, looking up at the sky. "I kind of admire them for surviving, but Five Eighty's had a couple of attacks in the past month or so, an old man and a kid. They had to take that whole series of rabies shots.

"On the other hand," he said, looking at the palm of his left hand. He knew he was getting drunk but Dana was there, and nothing would get out of control. "The *other* hand. There's always another hand. Three hands or four hands. You can't blame 'em for being crazy or for getting rabies, or for eating each other. Can you?

"Sometimes it seems like, for all the good we do out there, we might as well take out our nightsticks and hit our*selves* in the head with them. Like that guy Fox busted the other night. For being dumb. That's what they *all* go to jail for. Watch the TV all day, get drunk and go rob somebody. Go to jail. Watch TV in jail. Get out and start over again.

"I can't hardly get angry at 'em anymore. Like that burglar Quentin Barr. I could shoot Quentin, but I can't blame him for anything. You know? I could walk up and shoot him in the fucking head and it wouldn't bother me a bit. I shouldn't say that, but it's true. Do him a favor and do the world a favor. Erase a mistake. Solve his problems."

Helen gave Dana a look, and Hanson saw it, but he didn't care. "The fuckin' liberals all say, 'Oh, everything will be okay if we're just *nice*. *I'm* not a racist, and if everybody was like me, gosh, things would be fine. I don't even notice if a person is black or white. It's the *bad* people out there causing all the trouble. We just need to *educate* people and they'll be decent and everything will be okay.'

"They've never even *talked* to a black person. I mean really *talked* to him. They're scared of 'em, and they're scared shitless to think that there's *evil* out there, and evil in their own little gutless liberal hearts too.

"I like the job. The adrenaline. I love it when some fucker decides he's gonna fight. Oh boy, you know? Bounce him off the hood of the patrol car a few times, kick his legs out from under him, slam him down on the street and handcuff him. Like, 'Whew, thanks. I needed that.' It's a good thing I'm a cop, or I'd probably be in prison."

"Consider yourself lucky," Dana said. "You've found your niche in life."

"I've found my *community*," Hanson said. "The Avenue. They hate me there, but that's okay, that's my job in the community. To be hated. I know where I stand. *Hate* me, motherfuckers."

"You need to slow down," Helen said. "You're going to wear your brain out."

"Yeah," Hanson said. He passed his hand across the front of his face. "There. All gone now. Frontal lobes *smooooooth*.

"Better get going. 'Out in the *country*,' " he sang.

"Why not stay here tonight?" Dana said. "You're pretty drunk for that drive."

"Gotta go. The dog will wonder where I am."

HE WAS ON the other side of town, almost to the freeway, when he gave in, and drove by Falcone's house. It was one of her days off, and he thought maybe he'd stop and talk to her. But her house was dark. He drove around the block twice, then parked down the street, knowing he was acting like some asshole jealous boyfriend. He looked at the house, remembering how she'd looked, thinking that maybe he should have taken her up on the "sport fuck." She probably thought he was a wimp, or maybe a fag. But fuck it. If that's what she thought, too bad. Best to forget her, and simplify his life.

He was about to leave, when a red Corvette pulled up in front of her house and turned off the headlights. He didn't want to drive past them, so he waited. The driver, a well-built guy wearing khaki trousers and an expensive-looking knit shirt, opened the door for Falcone, and the two of them walked to the house and went inside.

That's that, Hanson thought and didn't look at the house as he drove away. It was well after midnight, and Mr. Jones was talking. *". . . somebody had painted on a wall down there, 'The circle is not round,' but that's not true. The Bible tells us it is round. The Sioux Indians said, 'Even the seasons form a great circle in their changing, and always come back again to where they were.' It all comes around . . ."*

DAKOTA HAS OPENED the latest Knights of Columbus Bible test, after carrying it around for days.

    1. What is another word for sorrow?

After writing the answer "contrition" beneath question #1, Dakota opens a two-liter bottle of warm Pepsi, and it foams out of the bottle onto the desk and the blue test sheet. He bolts out of his chair, shaking the test sheet, looks around the room, and finally pulls his shirttail out to blot the mess up.

    2. Are we sorry for our sins if we are not deter-
       mined not to sin again?

" '. . . not determined *not* to . . .' " he mutters, the Pepsi drying beneath the desk lamp, brown and wrinkled, like a birthmark " 'not determined . . .' "

A door slams down the hall, and he hears the nigger queer, the transvestite, out in the hall.

"I need *money,* honey."

"My disability check should of been here . . ."

" 'Should' don't get it."

"Where you gonna go? It's late."

"I'm staying with a very dear friend."

"What if I want another date?"

"Just ask anybody at Van's Olympic Room. They all know Roxanne," she says, and Dakota listens to her high heels as she walks down the hall to the stairs.

3. What is hope?

Dakota walks to the window. Roxanne is waiting at the bus stop, beneath the streetlight, wearing a strap-back, shiny plastic bustier. Dakota watches the muscles in her back as she lights a cigarette.

Roxanne seems a little nervous. She looks both ways down the dark street. She looks at her watch. She brings the cigarette to her mouth, then turns and looks up at Dakota in the window.

"You must like what you see, staring at me like that," she says to him. "I guess we *both* know what you need."

When the bus turns the corner down the block, she drops the cigarette and crushes it, grinding it beneath the toe of her high heel as the bus pulls up, her eyes on Dakota.

"Call me sometime," she says.

The bus door opens with a hiss, and she gets on.

Dakota watches the bus drive away, then sits back down at the desk.

2. Are we sorry for our sins if we are not determined not to sin again?

He writes "ROXANNE" on the answer sheet, underlines it, then wads the test sheet up, reaches down and opens the unlocked bottom drawer. He takes out the quart of vodka and opens it, breaking the seal.

FOX WAS ON the computer downtown, back in the DOD files. Accessing Millon's files was easy, but there seemed to be no connection between him and Hanson.

SIXTEEN

IT WAS QUIET for a Friday night. After the usual rash of late-afternoon burglary reports and a false alarm at a bank, the radio was quiet, and Hanson was finishing the last of the backed-up crime reports, a typical burglary. The couple had come home from work and found their home violated.

Doing paperwork for the insurance company, part of the overall economy most people didn't know about, Hanson thought as he filled in the serial number of a stolen TV that would never be found. ⬥

The burglars sold the stuff to fences who re-sold it out of the trunks of their cars to people who couldn't afford to buy it in stores. The burglars bought their heroin with the money from the fence, and the heroin dealers put the money into cars and clothes, jewelry and TV sets. Some of what the dealers bought was stolen too, but they bought a lot of it from local stores who were glad to make the sales. Then the people who could afford insurance paid higher rates to finance the whole cycle. He looked out at a fire-gutted house, the windows boarded with plywood.

But most of the people in district Five Sixty Two couldn't afford insurance. They just lost what little they had. To *assholes*, he thought, signing his name on the report and putting his pen into his shirt pocket.

The radio silence was almost annoying, like a night without music. He liked the rhythm of a busy radio, keeping track of car-stops and radio calls in the surrounding districts. He fingered the mug shots in his breast pocket, the most current, the ones wanted for recent felonies. Sometimes, he thought that the photos were like mojos, like he had a grip on the souls of the people in the photos.

Dana swung the car south, to the boundary of the district, then east. A whore on the corner watched the car, her hands on her hips. "Let's say hello to Rita," Hanson said, and Dana pulled to the curb. She was wearing an orange vinyl miniskirt that matched her lipstick.

"Hey, Rita," Hanson called to her, "what's happening?"

She glared at him, tapping the rainbow-striped high heels that laced all the way up to her knees.

"Nothin' happinin', Hanson." She looked to her right, then to her left. "Nothing *gonna* happen either," she said, "with the police around. You know what I mean? What you want?"

"We're lonely."

"Everybody lonely," she said, looking at her watch.

"Okay," Hanson said, "see you later," as Dana pulled away.

"A *lot* later," she said.

Dana laughed. "You're a real charmer. Just like on TV. Even the whores are in love with you. Charmed her right out of her socks."

"She's trying to conceal her real feelings for me. That was just an act so you wouldn't know. Rita, oh *Ree*-tah," he sang, "come fly with me to Bra*zil!"*

They drove through the alleys, the hissing radio turned low, lights off, watching and listening. But all they heard was the crunch and pop of the tires over gravel and broken glass.

"Let's do a walk-through at the Texas Playhouse," Hanson said. "I'm falling asleep."

"Excellent suggestion," Dana said. "We haven't done one of those in a while."

They pulled out of the alley, scaring a junkie who was leaning against a building. He started to run, out of habit, then seemed to realize he wasn't doing anything illegal.

"What you *doin'*?" he said, shaking with fright. "Coming up on people with a police car like that."

"Sneakin' around," Hanson said. "Watching you. How come you're so nervous?"

"Don't have to scare people like that. I'm not nervous," he said, rubbing his arms.

"We never sleep," Hanson said, as Dana pulled the patrol car out into the street, picking up speed, a breeze coming through the windows. Two blocks behind them, a battered old police car, the insignia painted over with flat black paint, glided through the intersection like a bad omen, trailing smoke.

They parked a block away from the place, and around the corner. When Dana pulled the mike off the Radio, Hanson said, "Let's not bother Radio. I think we should just kinda handle it our *own* selves. More interesting that way, don't you think?"

Dana smiled at Hanson, hung up the mike, and they walked up the littered street.

"You're not really thinking about early retirement are you?" Hanson said, adjusting the heavy pistol belt and resnapping one of the brass-studded "keepers" that attached it to the wide leather belt running through the belt loops of his wool trousers.

"I promised Helen the first of the year. We're making more money than we can spend."

They could hear the music when they turned the corner. Two of the regulars were standing out in front of the Chicken Hut, drinking mickeys of wine out of paper bags that they discreetly set on the buckled sidewalk when the two cops walked past. The regular card game was just visible through the greasy, yellow and black checkerboard window. The alley behind the Chicken Hut was a place you could buy leather coats and TV sets out of automobile trunks.

"Gentlemen," Hanson said, holding up his hand in greeting as they walked past.

"Good evenin', officers," one of the men said while the other nodded his head in greeting.

"We're gonna go to the dance," Hanson said.

"I 'spect they'll be happy to see you," the man said.

Hanson turned around and they exchanged smiles. The man had been playing this game all his life.

They opened one of the big double doors and stepped inside. Three tiers of wide steps led up to the third-floor dance hall. The stairway smelled of liquor and marijuana and sweat and perfume. Music crashed and banged down on them from above, "Ain't no jivin', no conniving, *uh-huh,* we movin' now!"

It was a huge stairway with two big landings on the way to the top. The wide wooden steps were concave in the middle from decades of boots and shoes and high heels. Hanson wondered how many people had fallen or been knocked down the Texas Playhouse stairs over the years. How many had died of broken necks and fractured skulls, had bled to death there waiting for help. The steps were stained and gouged, scorched and splintered, rising and opening above them to the reinforced double doors.

Hanson was sweating slightly from the heat and the climb. He laughed and did a little move to the music. "Here we come, guys," he said, tapping his shirt pocket of mugshots, "got your *pictures* here, close to my heart."

He and Dana took out their nightsticks and held them upside down in their right hands so that the length of them ran along beneath their forearms, like heavy swagger sticks.

They opened the doors at the top of the landing and stepped into the noise and light, the only white people in the cavernous dance hall. The four sweating singers on the raised stage wore flowing white silk shirts and crimson pantaloons, sweating and dancing like a chorus line, backed up by guitars, keyboard, drums and three gleaming trumpets.

The music hit Hanson like a rush of speed and he grinned, his eyes mean now. He *liked* the music, a soundtrack for their walk-through of the dance.

The people nearest the door glared at them, then turned away, cursing. Word of their presence rippled through the crowd. One of the trumpets missed a note. The sound of the crowd seemed to recede, as if everyone was taking a breath at the same time, then it surged back, as the two cops stepped into the crowd. They were the center of attention, not the band, even though the music seemed louder now. It was like being on stage, Hanson thought, as he smiled into the angry eyes around him, the words "Pig" and "Motherfuckers" hissing beneath the music. Someone at the far edge of the crowd shouted "Honky peckerwoods," and Hanson laughed with excitement.

The dance floor reeked of sex and rage, and Hanson felt the music on his face and chest like a hot breeze. When he heard that kind of hard driving music he didn't want to dance, he wanted the world to stand up and fight. He wanted to kick ass.

The crowd parted for them, surly and slow, as they crossed the floor, pushing past tense shoulders and arms. A pair of muscular nineteen-year-olds pretended not to see Hanson, standing in his way. "Excuse me," Hanson said.

"Look out child. Look out child. Uh-huh. Get down," the band sang, trumpets keeping the rhythm, quick and clear.

"Excuse me," he said, tapping one of them on the shoulder with the finger of his left hand. The kid looked down at Hanson's finger on his shoulder.

"Excuse me," Hanson said, "I guess you didn't hear me over the music. Mind if I slip on by you guys?" He smiled, his eyes dancing, as the three trumpet players dipped and strutted, taking the song to the next chorus.

The kid looked at Hanson, held the look, then stepped, very deliberately, to one side. The others did the same.

Hanson gave them a little wave. "Thanks a lot," he said. "Good band, huh?" as he walked through them, brushing their chests as they looked stiffly down their noses at him. "I love those trumpets."

"What you want?" the kid said from behind him.

"Just looking around. That's our job, you know."

"Yeah. *I* know," the kid said, and Hanson laughed.

"Wanted to hear a little music too," Hanson said, turning to look at the kid, doing a little dance step. But the dance step involved a slight movement with the nightstick and Hanson's left arm so that it looked like a martial arts movement more than dance. "Know what I mean?" Hanson said.

"I been around. Get down. Uh-huh."

"Yeah," the kid said, almost smiling.

"Thanks a lot," Hanson said, and walked on, brushing past people, "Pardon me. Sorry. Excuse me," his lips in a tight little smile, his eyes open wide. He looked crazy, and he knew it. He had the *glow* going, the handle of the nightstick tight against his holster, tapping the inside of his arm slightly with the other end, in time to the music. Then he began to strut, just slightly, holding the nightstick as if it were a cane. Fred Astaire, he thought. Strutting through two hundred black people who hated him, he was ready to die. He wanted to die. Everyone in the hall sensed that, even if they couldn't explain what it was, and they were afraid of him.

Kill me, motherfuckers, he thought, Fred Astaire wants to die.

"Ever think that maybe you're pushing your luck?" Dana said from behind him.

Hanson laughed. "No, sir, not tonight. I got the glow, got that *aura* working for me. They'd have to drive a stake through my heart to kill me tonight. *Whoa*," he said, "listen to those trumpets."

"That looks like your girlfriend over there," Dana said, nodding towards the bandstand.

It was Asia, wearing a slinky yellow dress with a short skirt that showed off her muscular legs. The egg-yolk yellow material was cut in a low scoop neck, highlighting the brown cleavage and neck, her cheekbones and short black hair. She was surrounded by men. Hanson heard her laugh, bitter and vicious, picking it out over the music and noise. He stood and watched her, dappled with light from a mirrored ball that turned like a splintered planet above the dance floor. Then, as if she had just heard someone call her name, she turned and looked directly at him. She spoke to the men she was with, then walked through the crowd in her yellow dress towards him, the men following behind.

"I hope this turns out okay," Dana said. "There's an awful lot of people here who don't like us."

"You said it was an 'excellent suggestion.' "

"You're a bad influence on me. I'm too old for this shit. Helen's probably right."

"If you get killed can I have that new elk gun of yours?"

"Yeah, but I'm gonna *shoot* some people before I'm gonna let 'em kill me."

Asia stopped in front of them, the men behind glaring and posturing. She had a fresh black eye and a bruise around her neck, fingers and a thumb. The black eye against her brown skin was hypnotic. Somehow it made her even sexier.

Hanson smiled and gave Asia a little salute. "Enjoying the dance?" Still smiling, he looked at the men behind her. "Good evening, gentlemen," he said, making eye contact with all of them.

Asia slowly licked one red-nailed finger. "Umm," she said, "that looks like it hurts." Her pupils were pinpoints, and Hanson saw track marks inside her elbow when she reached out and traced the scab on Hanson's cheek with the fingernail, the scratch she'd put there when he arrested her.

She stepped closer and whispered in his ear.

". . . and tell Doc I'll laugh when he's dead. Come on," she said, turning to the men. "I didn't come here to talk to the *police*."

Hanson stood there like he'd forgotten where he was, the music and the crowd a faraway noise. Then the drums and trumpets took focus, most of the tension in the place gone now as they finished the walk-through.

"What was that about 'Doc'?" Dana said, his voice echoing as they went back down the high empty stairway.

"He dropped by the place to see me."

"Uh-huh," Dana said.

"He saved my life once. I wouldn't have come back without him."

"There's people who would like to see you get mixed up with something like that so they could nail you. Not everybody on the department likes you."

Hanson grinned. "He's gone back to L.A."

"What does he do down there?"

"I told him I didn't want to know what he did. He understands. We're the last two left," he said, looking at the scar below his thumb as they reached the bottom of the stairs.

"Just be careful."

"Don't worry, boss. Who knows when I'll see him again?"

They pushed the doors open and stepped into the fresh cool air of the street. The guys at the Chicken Hut put down their wine and watched them.

"How was that dance?" one of them asked.

"More fun than I thought it would be," Hanson said. "But we couldn't dance very good with all this stuff on," he said, holding his arms at his sides and jiggling the holster and nightstick, handcuffs, Mace, and packset. The guy laughed, the way he'd been laughing at cops all his life to flatter them and show that he was harmless so they'd leave him alone. A survival laugh.

"Good night," Dana said, as they walked past.

"Good night, officers," the man said.

At the corner they turned onto the dark side street where the streetlights had been out for years. A Corvette with two men in it was parked behind their patrol car.

Hanson began to turn sideways to the car, reaching for his pistol, looking for possible cover.

"What it *is*, gentlemen? What it is?" Fox said as he got out of the car and leaned across the roof, watching them. He was wearing a striped railroad cap, part of his narc costume. "How do you like the car? The DEA seized it in a drug deal. We've got it on loan."

"Been to the *dance?*" Peetey said from inside the car. "Radio was wondering where you were."

"Anything we should know about?" Fox said.

"Fuckheads," Hanson muttered.

Dana nudged him. "Play the game," he said. "Yeah," he called out to the two narcs. "We did a little walk-through but didn't see anybody who needed our attention."

Fox had the hat pulled down low over his eyes. Peetey sat with his feet up on the dashboard, snapping a switchblade knife open and closed. "Do you believe I took this off a *ten*-year-old?" he said.

"You have to call for a backup to do it?" Hanson asked.

Peetey looked up at him. "Now why you got to be that way? You got a lot of personal problems?"

"Yeah," Hanson said, "I'm plagued with personal problems."

"I think he's got one of those Vietnam Syndromes," Fox said. "Flashbacks. Nightmares."

"Let us know if he comes to work with photographs pinned to his uniform," Peetey told Dana.

A garbage can crashed in an alley off the street and they all turned towards the sound. A gray-brown possum, the size of a prehistoric rat, waddled out from the alley. Peetey turned his flashlight on the animal. Hissing through needle teeth, it raised up, smelling the air, graceful as a cobra now, and vanished into the alley.

"What can we do for you guys?" Dana asked them.

"We need to do a little deal down here," Fox said, "and we want to avoid any, you know, uniformed presence in the area for a while. We got some kind of new stuff showing up around here lately."

"Have at it," Dana said. "We're on our way."

"Appreciate it," Fox said. "Got something you might be interested in, Hanson," he said, handing him a folded computer printout. Hanson stuck it in his pocket without looking at it. As they got into their car, Peetey called, "Hey, Hanson. You ought to relax more."

"Yeah, yeah," Hanson said, waving his hand, his back to Fox, "have a nice night."

"What's *wrong* with him," Peetey said, watching them walk away. "Thinks he can fuck with *me*. My arm's as big as his goddamn leg. You know?"

"My *man*," Dana said when he and Hanson were back in the car. "I don't like 'em either, but they're pretty harmless. And if it wasn't them, it would be somebody else. What can you do? One of the things you have to learn in life is what to ignore," he said.

They drove past a biker bar, music pumping out the door into the street. Some of the bikers were sitting on their motorcycles out front, drinking beer, their arms around women in black T-shirts and halter tops. They cheered as the patrol car went past, giving them the finger.

"Like those guys," Dana said. "What are you gonna do? Beat 'em all up? Then what do you do? Go to the next bar and beat up all the assholes in that one? And the next one? You can't beat 'em *all* up."

Zurbo and Neal called them for a meet in the Mor-4-Les parking lot and told them about finding Roxanne, a black transvestite, cut up behind Van's Olympic Room.

"Somebody cut that poor faggot every which way but loose," Neal said. "Then fucked her. Yeah. *After*."

"Must of used a case cutter," Zurbo said. "Wasn't cut deep, but she was cut *large*. All over. They're gonna be sewing her up . . ."

"Jeezus," Neal said. "He was cut . . . I wouldn't wish that on *anybody*. I mean, I got no use for fags, but they got problems too, I guess."

"You turning liberal on us, Neal?" Zurbo said, laughing.

Zurbo and Neal got a call on a family fight, and Dana cleared from the meet.

Uh, Five Six Two . . . go to channel three. Five Seventy wants to talk to you over there.

"Going to three," Dana said, reaching down to change the frequency as Hanson unfolded the computer printout.

"Five Sixty Two," Dana said into the mike.

Yeah. Dana, Larkin said, *we need a CDK over here at the end of*

Lombard. Where it dead-ends at the Interstate. Could you guys swing by?

"CDK?" Dana asked Hanson.

"Dead dog," Hanson said. "Confirmed dog kill." He turned on the little goosenecked lamp on the dashboard and studied the printout.

"On our way," Dana told Larkin. He turned right at the next intersection. "What's it say?" he asked Hanson.

"Millon didn't win a Silver Star. He spent most of his time in-country locked up in a Long Binh jail for desertion, and for killing a Vietnamese policeman. They lost all the paperwork on it when he got back to the States. Dismissed the charges."

Larkin's patrol car had its parking lights on next to the boarded-up Mt. Zion Baptist Church where Lombard Street ended at a chain-link fence. The church was raised three feet off the ground on huge timbers. They planned to move it, to make way for a new on-ramp to the freeway, but it had been waiting like that for over two years. A length of gutter hung down over the front door like a broken arm, and a church bus, its windows broken out, rode low behind the church on slashed tires. The other patrol car had dug ruts across the churchyard, fishtailing through the grass.

"Up here," Larkin said, getting out of the car. He was a tall skinny guy from Texas who stuttered sometimes. His partner was sitting on the front fender, smoking a cigarette.

"Here he is," Larkin said, shining his flashlight down just in front of the car. It was medium size, with short hair, part Lab maybe, but it looked deformed. Its legs were too short and its ears too big, as if it had some basset or beagle blood.

The patrol car had broken its back just behind the front shoulders. Hanson shone his flashlight down at the animal. Its lips were drawn back, showing bloody teeth. It had mange, patches of raw red skin on its head and neck where fleas appeared and vanished each time Hanson blinked his eyes.

"A ghetto thu-thoroughbred," Larkin stuttered. "Fucker was trying to make it through the fence. Almost did, too," he said, shining the flashlight at the base of the chain-link fence where it had been pried up.

Down below, at the bottom of a steep, grassless hill, interstate traffic, gasoline-fueled rivers of light, silver and red, flowed north and south at sixty miles an hour.

Halfway to the PAA, Hanson took a freeway off-ramp that fun-
neled him back the way he'd come, onto the Avenue. He drove to
the apartment complex where Millon had lived, parked in the lot,
and killed the engine. Ten minutes later, he quietly closed the
door of his van and walked to Unit number seven, the tattooed
woman's apartment. Blue light from a TV showed in the windows. He listened at the door. Canned laughter, rising and falling
like a windstorm, was all he could hear. Finally, half-dizzy with
excitement and dread, he knocked.

"Bachelor number . . . *three!*" a woman on the TV said,
laughter whistling in the background. Hanson turned to leave,
then, after a moment, knocked again.

The locks snapped open, and a white man in his forties loomed
in the doorway, shirtless, unbuttoned white work pants hanging
below his huge belly.

"What do you want?" he said, his breath sweet with fortified
wine.

"Sorry to bother you so late," Hanson said, "but I heard the
TV . . ."

"Late?" He snorted and emptied a nickel bag of peanuts into his
mouth. "I'm real sorry," he said, chewing, "if the TV bothers you.
That's too bad. I like to stay up."

A woman about his age and size was passed out, propped up on
the cushions of an enormous curved sofa that almost filled up the
living room. The room smelled of cigarettes and burnt food.

He didn't know anything about a woman with tattoos, the man
said.

Hanson thanked him just as a teenage girl appeared in the bedroom hallway, watching him. She was wearing low-cut bell-bottom pants that were too tight and too short, and a T-shirt, cut off
just beneath her tiny breasts. She looked around the doorway, at
the woman passed out on the sofa, and vanished back down the
dark hallway.

"She moved out just before Christmas," the landlord told Hanson.
He was watching *The Dating Game* too.

"That guy she was living with stayed a couple more months.
Drinking pretty heavy. Then he skipped out owing two months'
rent and the cleaning deposit. That's about all . . . except, I
heard he was in a motorcycle wreck. Paralyzed from the neck

down, somebody said. Or brain damage, maybe. Name was 'Scott'
or, uh . . .''

"Steve."

"Well, shit. I'da had it in a second. Steve. A real asshole, that
one. I almost felt sorry for him, though, when that woman left. He
didn't know whether to shit or go blind, to put it in plain language. You a friend of his?"

"Thanks for the information," Hanson said.

The girl was waiting for him, hunched down below the window
in the passenger seat, hugging her knees to her chest.

"You're a cop, right?" she said.

"Why would you think that?"

"I've seen you."

She was about sixteen, Hanson thought, seductive, exotic and
pathetic, all at the same time.

"Get in," she said. "I won't bite."

"Yes, *ma'am*," he said, feeling foolish, "whatever you say,"
banging his knee when he got in, trying not to show how much it
hurt. When he closed the door, she hooked her foot under the seat
back and lowered herself beneath the dashboard, like an assistant
in a high-wire act, Hanson thought. Yellow light flared under the
dash when she lit a cigarette. She looked up at him, smoking. The
black eye was almost gone, a banana yellow, but the split lip was
less than a day old. She had to know he could see her breasts, he
thought. The ribs below them looked bruised too. He looked out
the windshield at Unit number seven. The TV was off and it was
dark.

"I need some legal advice," she said.

"I'm not . . ."

"I can pay for it. Okay?"

She smelled like sour milk. Like a baby who needed a bath.
Like the kids he saw every day in filthy cribs or tottering around
in dirty diapers, the soles of their bare feet black and patterned
with ringworm.

The tip of the cigarette glowed. "Okay?"

Fifteen, he thought. More like fifteen.

"What's the problem?"

"I've got this friend whose father comes in every night after her
mother's passed out drunk and fucks her. Is she within . . ."

"Tell her to report him to the police."

"Is she within her legal rights to kill him?"

"It depends . . ." he said, looking at her tiny breasts again, the bruised ribs expanding when she inhaled.

"Depends on *what?*"

"The jury, her attorney, how the crime report is written up, the way she comes off when she testifies . . ."

"Thanks for nothing," she grunted, pulling herself up, sitting with her back against the passenger door, legs crossed Indian style.

"Was she afraid for her life?" Hanson said. "That's what they'll want to know."

The cigarette between her lips, she reached behind her back, rolling the window open. She took a last drag on the cigarette, her eyes meeting Hanson's, and tossed it out the window.

"She's afraid for her life."

Gripping the window crank, she leaned in close, then back, then close, rolling the window up, a half turn at a time.

Hanson touched his thumb to the cut on her lip, holding it rigid as she pushed against it, pressing it against her teeth until it began to bleed.

"Gotta go," Hanson said, pulling his thumb away. He started the van, and reached past her to open her door. "I'm late."

"Right," she said, swinging her legs out and dropping to the asphalt.

"Tell your friend to report it to the police."

"I don't think she wants to do it that way."

She slammed the door, and walked towards the dark unit where she lived. Hanson drove up alongside her, the van shuddering, about to stall, as he rolled the window back down. "Tell your friend . . ."

She kept walking, looking straight ahead.

". . . if she goes through with it, to be *sure* he's *dead.* That way he can't testify against her, or ever get custody again."

He hit the curb, killing the engine, while she stepped over it and kept walking. When he turned on his headlights, he saw the tattoo snaking out of the collar of her shirt, up into her hair.

SEVENTEEN

HANSON OPENED HIS EYES, the sun touching his neck and cheek, glowing on the sawmill-plank wall behind him, filling the bedroom with light and the clean smell of trees cut down and dragged from the forest eighty years before. He walked naked to the window, motes of dust tumbling in the light around him. A pair of Steller's jays, bright blue and big as pigeons, chased each other through the apple trees, white blossoms exploding off the gnarled branches.

Hanson spotted Truman wandering off towards the barn.

"Hey," he called to him. "What's happenin' in the world of old blind . . ." stopping in mid-sentence, listening. He cocked his head, his unfocused eyes listening too, then he reached up for the short-barreled shotgun behind the molding above the window. Holding the heavy twelve-gauge in one hand, he waited, the windowsill against his belly.

"If anybody comes all the way out here to find me," he'd told Dana, "it's probably something serious."

The yellow Firebird flickered through the trees that screened the gravel road, going slow, as if the driver might be lost. Hanson smiled, the sun warm on his chest and stomach, watching the car turn into the drive and stop by the porch.

Falcone got out, wearing white tennis shoes, cut-off white jeans, and a white T-shirt. She looked brand new. And a little uncomfortable—cops don't like trespassing when they're not in uniform. They've seen too many people with gunshot wounds in backyards, shot by some frightened old man, or a kid, or maybe an out-of-work husband who'd been drinking late at night in the kitchen—"I didn't mean to . . ." he'd say, dry-mouthed and bewildered, as if he didn't recognize his own yard, littered now with discarded bandages stiff with black blood, the gauze ties fluttering in the moonlight, looking again at the bullet hole in the screen door, at the bloody patch of grass and the gurney tracks snaking away. "I just wanted to scare him."

Hanson enjoyed watching her move, remembering how she'd looked with her clothes off, as he had done scores of times since that night, several times every day and during the nights. He stepped back for a better look, into a faint breeze out of the west, from Stormbreaker. The air was still cool, smelling of apple blossoms and blackberries. A sexy woman who moved like a cop, he thought.

"Hello?" she called, walking around the porch. "I'm sorry to . . . bother you," she said, looking at the front of Hanson's van, pulled around to the other side of the house.

"No bother," Hanson called down, "not at all, ma'am. I'll put on some pants and be right down."

He pulled on a pair of jeans, picked a faded olive-drab T-shirt off the floor, and looked for his shoes.

"All mine," Hanson said, spreading his arms to take in the farmhouse and the sagging barn in a sea of blackberry bushes. He was barefoot.

"New construction?" she asked, nodding towards a plot of freshly turned earth, marked off with wooden stakes and twine.

"The garden."

She narrowed her eyes, as if he might be putting her on.

"Come and look," he said, striding through the grass, turning to look at her, walking sideways, backwards, then, "God *damn*," he said hopping on one foot as she came up behind him. He put his

arm over her shoulder and pulled his foot up. Twisting and hopping on the other leg, he looked at the bottom of his foot and saw
the spiked little sandspur in the tender hollow of the arch. She
pinched it between her thumb and forefinger. "You should wear
shoes out here," she said.

"I always . . . *do*," he said, as she pulled it out, "but to*day*
. . . you're absolutely right," he said, leaning closer, smelling her
hair.

"Come on," he said, limping the rest of the way. "Look. Swiss
chard and beets over there. Some spinach. Cucumbers. Pumpkins,
just for fun.

"It doesn't take much time. Put seeds in the ground, a little
fertilizer, water it once a day, and vegetables pop up."

She was smiling at him.

"Considering how things are out there in the world," he said,
jabbing his thumb towards the road, "that's pretty, it's reassuring.
Beans," he said, pointing at the rows of heart-shaped leaves.

"Fred," he said, reaching into his hip pocket, "the guy at the
seed store, threw these in for free." He spread the seed packets
like a hand of poker. "We got zinnias here, we got spiky dahlias.
Mixed pansies, the guys with little faces. That's right, yes,
ma'am," he said when she laughed, trying not to look at her
breasts. She wasn't wearing a bra under the T-shirt.

"Don't go away," he said.

"I'd better get . . ."

"Be *right* back," he said over his shoulder, limping and hopping
towards the house.

"I thought you'd be able to see the mountain from here," she
said when he came back.

"You can see it from my room up there."

She looked at her watch.

"Give me your hand," he said, tearing open the seed packet
he'd brought from the house. "It'll just take a second. Okay?"

He took her wrist and turned her palm up. "Crackerjack marigolds."

The seeds looked like tiny boulders piled in her cupped hand.

"Okay, now," he said, kneeling by the new plot, digging a line
across it with his finger, "it says on the package to plant them a
quarter inch deep. This looks about right." She knelt next to him
and, taking the seeds out of her open hand, began dropping them

into the earth. Hanson reached over and took a few out of her palm, pinching them out with his thumb and forefinger. He paused, touching her there, for just a moment, while she looked at him.

When the seeds were all in, Hanson swept the loamy soil over them with the edge of his hand, smoothed the ground, and stood up. "Come and see the house," he said, brushing the dirt off his hands. Behind her, Truman appeared from out of the blackberries, walking towards them.

"Better not," she said. "I just stopped by to apologize for the other night. Really."

"Nothing to apologize for," he said, giving up.

Truman brushed against her leg and looked up at her.

"Who's this?" she said.

"Truman," Hanson said. "My roommate."

"You must have had him a long time," she said, kneeling down to scratch his ears, something he seemed to enjoy.

"Just a couple of months," he said.

She looked up at him.

"I kind of inherited him. Everybody says I should have him put to sleep, as old as he is. Probably they're right, but . . ."

"They are *not*. Look at him," she said, running her hands over his shoulders and hips, down his legs, checking his teeth, all the while whispering to him. "He's a little stiff with arthritis, but other than that . . ."

"And blind."

"He's *used* to it."

Truman walked towards the house.

"Come on and look at the house. As long as you're all the way out here."

"A quick tour, then I *have* to go."

"You really think he's okay for now?"

"He's fine."

Hanson smiled at her. "That's good to hear. Every other motherfucker—except Dana—says 'put him to sleep.' But I've gotten, well, real fond of him. I like having him around. But I don't want to be selfish, you know?"

Two hours later, Falcone came back out of the house, followed by Hanson. "No," she said, not looking back. "This was a big mistake," she said, walking towards the Firebird. "I'll be gone in less than a month. I've simplified my life—for *once*—and I don't need this . . ."

Hanson stepped around in front of her, reached to put his hand on her neck, and she stepped back and glared at him. "I *mean* it. This was my fault, and I'm sorry, but I don't want to see you again. I'm *not* getting involved with a cop, not even you. *Especially* you. Wondering which night you'll get killed by some asshole who's not worth anything to anybody. Some junkie street nigger or grunt-dumb white trash. For nothing. Cool. My hero."

"I'm a good cop," Hanson said. "If people like me don't do it, they'll . . ."

"Who cares? They can do whatever they want to when I'm gone. They're gonna do it *any*way. And you go ahead and commit suicide if that's what you want. Do it. I've *already* forgotten about you. And if I see that van of yours parked near my house again, I'll call the police. Now get out of my way."

Her perfume was mixed with the smell of the garden, and the blackberry vines, and Hanson's own sweat. The cotton T-shirt clung to the curve of her shoulder and breast.

She got in the car and slammed the door.

"I'll let you know how the marigolds do," he said.

She ignored him, backed the car around, started to drive off, then stopped. "You take care of Truman," she said. "Don't you *listen* to those other people. They don't know . . . they don't . . . you *better*."

She floored the Firebird, fishtailing and throwing gravel, vanishing in a cloud of dust, her tires squealing when she got to the main road.

Hanson went back up to his bedroom and sat on the edge of the bed. All the sheets were on the floor. Out the window, to the east, thunderheads were piling up behind Stormbreaker.

EIGHTEEN

2. Are we sorry for our sins if we are not
   determined not to sin again?

NO.

Dakota has smoothed out the wadded-up blue answer sheet,
though it is still wrinkled, and printed with the bloody loops and
whorls of his fingerprints.

3. What is hope?

He takes a drink of vodka, and copies the answer to question
number three from the dog-eared *Knights of Columbus Study
Guide.*

HOPE IS DIVINE VIRTUE BY WHICH WE TRUST IN GOD.

He studies what he's written, puts the answer sheet in the
folder marked Top Pryority—Classifide, and locks it away in the
desk drawer with his Motel Six Gideon Bible.

Dakota walks around his room, drinking from the bottle, kicking his mojos across the floor.

"They just make that shit up," he says aloud, tearing the pictures of Gunther and the big cats off the walls. "They don't know the answers either."

On his desk, the police scanner is turned low.

. . . *'monsters,' that's what she said, Five Sixty Two* . . .

"Okee-doke, we'll go . . ."

Dakota stops, fists full of wadded-up pictures, tiny flakes of dried glue fluttering into his hair and face and scarified chest. He stops at the sound of Hanson's voice, on the scanner, turns his head without moving his body, grimacing now, but still straining, the flakes of glue on him and around him like gnats. His feet braced, shoulders rigid, he twists his head, veins in his neck swelling. Ignoring the *pop* behind his ear that will leave his neck stiff for a week, he strains, glue-gnats pumping in and out of his nose, his watery, dilated eyes on the scanner.

. . . *we'll go take a look,* Hanson said, his voice lost now in the rushing static from the monitor in Fox's office. Fox took another bite of his Big Mac, threw the rest into his wastebasket, and went back to his computer.

"**HOW SHOULD I KNOW?** He said it was 'monsters,' " the woman told them. The little boy stood in the doorway next to her, looking up at the two cops. He had a cold, snot on his face, breathing loudly through his stuffed-up nose. Both the woman and the boy smelled bad. The woman was fat and pale, probably not yet thirty, but already old. Her plaid shorts were too tight, and Hanson wondered how she'd gotten the black bruises on the backs of her dimpled thighs. She took the cigarette out of her mouth. "If I knew what the hell it was," she said, "I wouldn't of called the police." The TV was on in the living room, a rerun of *I Dream of Jeannie,* canned laughter in the background, like freeway traffic. "Try to be a good goddamn citizen, and all you get is a hard time."

"No, ma'am, we're glad you called," Hanson said. "We just like to know as much as possible before we go into a house."

"Well, I don't appreciate your attitude," the woman said. The little boy grinned and, fast as a snake, grabbed her bare leg and bit it, then ran into the house.

"You little *fucker*," the woman screamed, going after him, slamming the door behind her.

Hanson put his notebook in his pocket. "Charming," he said, and they both laughed all the way across the yard to the neighboring house. "A nigger, with a white woman and a little girl," the woman had told them. They'd moved out during the night, only a couple of weeks before. Already half the windows were broken out. The little boy had heard "monsters" inside the house. Probably winos, or junkies using the place to shoot dope.

"*Mon*-stirs," Hanson said, imitating the little boy, as they walked around to the back of the house. Bicycle parts and shopping carts were scattered about the backyard and a washing machine was laying on its side. They had to watch where they walked to avoid stepping into the dogshit half-hidden in the dead and dying grass. The screen door hung from one hinge.

"You could probably get a good deal on this place. An excellent deal," Dana said. "Another fixer-upper like that shack you live in."

Hanson laughed. "Wonderful neighbors too. I'll talk to my accountant."

The backdoor was locked, but it had been kicked in and repaired more than once. "A little *nudge*," Dana said, throwing his hip into the door, "should do it." The door bucked, then swung open the second time he hit it. The kitchen was filthy, plates of rotting food on the table and stove. Boxes of household junk were stacked against one wall, covered with grimy bedsheets. "Police," Hanson called, "po-*lice* officers."

"A nice little fixer-upper," Dana said, stepping around black plastic bags of garbage. He opened the refrigerator a crack, then slammed it shut. "They better arc weld this shut and bury it at sea," he said.

"I wish I'd had the franchise for these," Hanson said, looking at a Martin Luther King–Robert Kennedy memorial plate over the door. "I'd be retired in Hawaii now."

The living room was furnished with broken and stained furniture. Dogshit, baked by the heat, littered the floor. Dana pointed at a bent spoon and a pile of blackened match heads on the arm of a plastic sofa, part of the works for shooting up heroin or speed or crumbled Percodan tablets or aspirin or whatever they could find.

A child's watercolor was taped to the wall above the sofa, crude but brilliant in green and blue and yellow—a little girl in a blue sky, arms extended, her skirt billowing like a parachute. She's flying. Amazed. Her huge smile is full of amazement, and yet, Hanson thought, there is a suggestion in her smile that she has been hoping for this, half-expecting she could fly. The two dogs rising with her smile too, tipped like balloons, one tethered to each of her hands, both look up at her, their eyes full of love. A short-legged brown dog with floppy ears, like a bassett hound and a big white one with long fur, the names BOBBIE and ALETHA printed beneath them.

"Who *are* these people," Hanson said, "who just move and leave everything behind? 'Come on. Get in the car. We're leaving.' Where do they go? Where do they come from? What do they *do* except shoot up heroin and . . ."

"Did you hear that?" Dana said.

"Yeah," Hanson said, looking down the hallway.

"Mon-stir," Dana said.

Hanson pulled out his nightstick. "Probably rats," he said. "Police," he called down the hallway. They walked to the closed bathroom door at the end of the hall. The toilet was running.

Flies and white plaster dust rolled out the door when Hanson pushed it open. The basset hound was dead. The white Afghan looked up at him where she lay, starved almost to death, on the floor. Too weak to stand and drink from the toilet now. Her head huge in comparison to her emaciated body, like those African children you see on the six-thirty news, dying of starvation, with flies crawling on their faces, beyond saving. The bathroom door was raked and splintered and gnawed, Sheetrock on the walls gouged down to the studs, the floor covered with a layer of plaster dust that rose beneath their feet and powdered their blue wool pants.

"Aletha?" Hanson said. She twitched her tail at the sound of her name. Hanson knelt down to touch her, and she tried to lick his hand with a swollen, dust-covered tongue, looking at him for help like a wounded civilian, Hanson thought, because Hanson was all she had.

"I'll go out to the car and call Animal Control," he said. In the living room he looked again at the watercolor of the flying girl. Carefully, he pulled it loose and rolled it up as he walked out of the house.

He leaned in the open door of the patrol car, called for an animal control unit, and put the picture in his briefcase. Just as he slammed the door, the snot-faced kid from next door jumped out from behind a tree and ran past him, shouting *bam bam*, pointing his finger like a gun. He stopped halfway across the yard and grinned back at Hanson.

"Blew your brains out. *Po*-lice," he shouted through his stuffed-up nose, then sprinted away, tripped over a scarred tree root and fell on his face. He pushed himself up on his knees, surprised, watching Hanson, then gingerly cupped his mouth and bloody nose, the bony hand covering his horselike lower face like a surgeon's mask.

He took the filthy hand away, slowly lowering his eyes to look at it, and Hanson thought how much he'd like to shoot him. The kid saw blood on his hand and lurched to his feet, screaming, blowing blood and snot, "Mom! The cop. Hit me!"

Hanson brushed the plaster dust off his pants legs and looked up at the house. Last year's "MERRY CHRISTMAS" was still painted in one front window. The other windows had been broken out and replaced with plastic sheeting that moved with the breeze, sucking in and out like lungs.

NINETEEN

IT **WAS JUST** after nine, on Hanson's day off, when Truman went into the kitchen and stood looking out the door. He'd been acting a little odd since the sun went down, as if he was worried about something. A few minutes later the lights of a car turned off the main road and swept through the trees towards the house. A gold Trans Am, rumbling with torque, a black eagle design across the hood, pulled up behind the house.

"Where's the Porsche?" Hanson said.

"More trouble than it was worth," Doc said. "Always *some* fuckin' . . . imagine you're me, limping into the Santa Monica Porsche dealership, trying to get some peckerwood mechanic to look at your car.

"That's right," he said while Hanson laughed.

"Scary eyes, and a limp," Hanson said.

"Trans Am is stronger and faster. A brother . . ."

"Say *what?*" Hanson said.

". . . did two tours with the 173rd—I *liked* the man—whole-saled it to me through a garage in Compton."

He looked exhausted, Hanson thought. Like the time he'd come back to camp after a week-long patrol when he lost half his 'Yards to booby traps.

"Business problems down in L.A.," he said, looking around the kitchen.

"Truman was expecting you . . ."

"Any of that cognac left?"

They went into the other room, and Hanson handed him the bottle. "How's that girlfriend of yours?"

Doc drank from the bottle and handed it back. "*White* boys have 'girlfriends,' " he said.

"Asia," Hanson said.

"*She* got to be more trouble than she was worth." He took a glass vial from his pocket and tapped it on his knuckle. "You got something I can chop this stuff up on? A mirror?"

"General Sherman," Hanson said, taking a framed photo of the Civil War general from the bookcase, laying it flat on the footlocker he used as a coffee table.

"The one that burned Atlanta," Doc said. He tapped a mound of the white crystal on the glass, reached behind his neck, and came out with a pearl-handled straight razor on a breakaway nylon cord, opening it as he brought it down to the picture. He chopped the cocaine on Sherman's chest, and divided it into four lines. He looked up at Hanson and closed the razor.

"Trick I learned when I was a kid. Wear it around your neck on a cord, hanging down your back. Cops won't find it if they pat you down."

Hanson nodded. "Pretty dramatic."

"I fuckin' guess *so*," Doc said, and they both laughed.

"Here," he said, handing Hanson a piece of a candy-striped plastic straw, "have some."

"In the movies they use rolled-up hundred-dollar bills," Hanson said.

"McDonald's milkshake straw works better. It's free and you can find 'em wherever you go."

Hanson took the straw and snorted two of the lines off the picture. The cocaine tasted cold, icy on the backs of his eyes as he watched Truman walk in from the kitchen. He knew his way around the house now.

"William Tecumseh Sherman," Hanson said.

Sherman, craggy-faced, his hair sticking up in back, stood with his arms crossed, looking into the distance at Lincoln's funeral, a black cloth of mourning tied on his left arm. "A good general," Hanson said. "Did his job. Even when people called him a monster.

"Hey, bud," he said to the dog. "Getting used to this place?"

Doc bent down as if he were examining the photo. "Best not to get too close . . ." he said, snorting a line, "to *any*thing. *You* know that."

He snorted the other line, wiped the last of the coke off the glass with two fingers, and rubbed it on his gums. "Let's go for a ride."

They took the bottle and the cocaine with them after Hanson made sure the dog had water and food.

"He's gonna die," Doc said.

"I'll take care of him until then," Hanson said, pulling the door shut. "That's the deal. Sometimes at night I hear him moving around down here, blind and in the dark, just like me."

"You say shit like that to the other cops?"

Hanson laughed. "Most of 'em just ignore it now. I'm a good cop."

"Same as 'Nam. Quinn would tell people, 'Hanson's weird, but don't let it bother you. He kills a lot of gooks.' "

"Fuckin' Quinn . . ." The night air smelled of apples and blackberries. Hanson tipped his head back and drank the sweet, hot cognac from the bottle. The stars were brighter than he had ever seen them. Like pinholes in the fabric of the night sky, he thought, protecting them from a fiery universe.

They drove through the little town of Douglas, past the post office, the general store and gas station, past the whining lumber mill working the night shift, clouds of smoke and ash reflecting the glow of the sawdust burner, across the railroad tracks by the Douglas Tavern where an Indian with shoulder-length hair, standing under the streetlight, watched them pass.

"Where we going?" Doc said, shifting the powerful car into third gear, taking the on-ramp to the freeway.

"I don't know," Hanson said.

Doc shifted again, and Hanson watched the speedometer climb to sixty, seventy, eighty. The interior of the car glowed a faint green from the bank of instrument panel lights. They swept past a tractor-trailer truck, the chrome hubs of its wheels flashing in the amber running lights around the wheel well.

Hanson settled into the bucket seat as the headlights of the truck faded and vanished behind them. It was like riding in a spaceship.

"Got any more of that cocaine?" Hanson said.

Doc handed him the vial. "Get one of those little spoons out of the glove box."

"McSpoons," Hanson said, when he took one out. Little plastic coffee-stirrers from McDonald's, tiny golden arches at one end. Still holding the bottle in his left hand, Hanson pushed one side of his nose shut and snorted the icy powder. The lights on the dashboard brightened. "Ah," he said, "having fun."

He leaned back in the seat and listened to the engine, the cocaine smoothing him out, feeling relaxed and alert at the same time. "Remember that afternoon when the two companies of Nungs, Mike Force they sent up from Da Nang, said they'd kill all the Vietnamese and Americans in the camp if we didn't hand over the Vietnamese camp commander?"

"Gave us one hour," Doc said. "I looked at my watch. Three seventeen. Those Nungs," he said, as if remembering a favorite uncle, the one who takes you fishing, and treats you like a man instead of a kid, "they were some *bad* motherfuckers."

"Silver had artillery plotted on top of us, air bursts, on-*call*. 'Firecracker rounds.' I remember thinking they'd be red, white and blue, like Fourth of July bunting. We were gonna *immolate* the place. Kill ourselves and everybody else. I was *happy*, man, sitting in front of the TOC with that old 3.5 recoilless, on a box of fléchette rounds, the tube in my lap, singing . . ."

Hanson began to sing, his voice soft and sweet as a child's, " 'Daisy, *Daisy*, give me your answer, *do*, I'm half *cra*-zee, all for the *love* of yooouuu . . .' Ready to start killing people, a *lot* of 'em. That was the happiest hour of my life. Until the Nungs changed their minds."

"Life's full of disappointments," Doc said.

At eighty miles an hour the engine rumbled effortlessly, and he wished that they could just keep driving down dark highways, the white center lines snapping beneath the headlights.

"Good to see," Doc said, "you're not one of those, you know, 'troubled' veterans I hear about."

"Not me. I'll be in the grocery store and some fat doofus will bump into me and just go on, selecting his favorite brand of potato chips. 'Doo-doo-doo.' I just *remind* myself, 'Act nice, or go to prison . . .' "

"I had that difficulty all my life," Doc said.

" 'Hi!' " Hanson continued, in someone else's voice, " 'How *are* you? It's a pleasure to meet you. Isn't this a tasty dip? Oh no, please excuse *me.*' "

They were coming up on three trucks rolling along in a convoy. Doc downshifted, punched the gas, and they passed all three at ninety miles an hour—Bekins—PIE—and a truck full of cattle that smelled like fear and shit and death, on their way to be slaughtered. Hanson looked for their eyes through the slats in the truck as the car boomed past.

Doc pulled back into the right lane. "If I go into a store, they're scared. Nobody looks at me, but I can hear them all thinking, 'nigger.' Like a bunch of bugs, crickets. 'Nigger. Nigger-nigger-nigger. Niggernigger.' I go up to the pretty cashier and she smiles at me. Like she's saying, 'Hi.' " Doc raised his voice and spoke very precisely, in a "white" voice, " 'Hi. *I'm* not prejudiced. I *like* black people. Please don't hurt me.' "

A blue shield with a glowing number "5" in the middle, rose above the horizon, turning slowly against the sky.

"I gotta piss," Doc said. "Let's pull in here. Get a drink, too."

They took the off-ramp and drove into the big I-5 truck stop parking lot. The truck-wash bays at one end glowed massive and white, like hangars for spaceships. Rows of trucks filled the lot, their engines idling, the cabs turned left and right like huge, searching heads, the trailers outlined in amber and blue lights.

They parked away from the light and did more cocaine, then ambled, laughing, across the lot, the huge trucks looming over them like dinosaurs—reefers packed with frozen meat, their generators sobbing, airbrakes hissing, starters whistling. A woman wearing tight shorts and high heels swung down from the cab of a reeking livestock truck and lit a cigarette, watching them pass as the big I-5 truck stop sign turned like a red and blue planet above them.

The entire wall was covered in plastic and glass and chrome. Every mirror, light, wire bundle, or chrome accessory you might want for a truck was displayed in a pattern like an exploded diagram, a truck autopsy. Convex mirrors, round, oval and rectangular. Bullet, hexagonal and round lug nut covers, silver and brass license plate frames. Running lights—round, oval, bullet-shaped in red, yellow, blue and white.

"God *damn*," Hanson said, "makes me want a truck just so I can put some of that shit on it. Jesus," he said, delighted, walking up to a silver hub cover and looking at his reflection, moving his head so that his grinning face distorted and slid over the concave cover as if it were dissolving in mercury. "I wonder if I could put some of this stuff on my van?" he said, stepping back. "I need some running lights, a couple of those big turn-arrows, and red reflectors all around."

As they walked past the dining room, the cashier and a trucker with swept-back blond hair, sideburns, and a Fu Manchu mustache stopped talking and watched them. The bathroom doors said Bucks and Does, the men's logo an antlered head, the women's a white-tailed rump. A big man in a silver satin jacket walked out the "Bucks" door just as they were going in.

Bright neon lights buzzed and flickered inside the men's room, the green walls cold as a morgue. Hanson stood at one of the urinals, reading the graffiti as he urinated. "Looks like these truck drivers are big on blowjobs," he said. A toilet flushed across the room, and the man who came out of the stall was wearing a cowboy hat covered with badges and buttons. He walked to the sink and washed his hands, watching Hanson and Doc in the stainless steel mirror over the sinks. He dried his hands, took one more long look, and walked out, the heavy door closing with a thud.

"Taking a shit in a cowboy hat," Hanson said.

"Reminds me of Fayetteville. Bars like the Circus Lounge, where you don't go to the bathroom unless you go in a group and carry weapons," Doc said.

They walked through the restaurant towards the country and western music, "Oh Ruuu-bee, don't take your love to town . . ."

The Mountain Cowboy Saloon opened out into a room twice as big as the restaurant, and twice as crowded, red candles glowing on the tables in the cigarette smoke around the dance floor. A redneck band, guys with dirty blond ponytails and baseball caps, played as couples danced the two-step, circling around the dance floor.

". . . wasn't me who started . . ."

Hanson and Doc sat at the bar, the front end of a Freightliner truck etched into the mirror behind the bar.

". . . that ole crazy Asian war . . ."

Covered wagons rolled west on a Budweiser sign, yellow popcorn bubbled out of a stainless steel bucket, and sweating Polish sausages turned on a spit. The handles on the beer taps were shaped like cattle horns.

". . . patriotic chore . . ."

The bartender was washing glasses, his back to them. Hanson turned on his stool and watched the dancers—plaid shirts, rodeo belt buckles, American eagles, names tooled around the backs of their belts, bouffant hairdos and satin trucker jackets.

He turned back around, picked up a pair of red and yellow squeeze-bottles, catsup and mustard, and moved them around on the bar as if they were dancing together. "They call it the Texas one-way two-step," he said.

Down near the other end of the bar, the bartender was talking to a woman with frizzy hair, tight jeans and a satin jacket with stylized palm trees and the words "ALOHA FREIGHTWAYS," on the back.

Hanson thought he heard somebody say, "Nigger."

"Uh-huh," Doc said.

"I'm *half* cuh-*ray*-zee, all for the love of youuuu," Hanson sang to himself. "Say bartender. Hey. Excuse me," he called, "could we have two beers and a couple shots of tequila. Please, sir?"

"That your sidekick there?" he asked Hanson, nodding at Doc as he set the drinks down. "Doesn't talk much, huh?"

Hanson looked at Doc, shook his head, and smiled. The two of them held their tequila up in a toast and drank it down. Hanson felt the cocaine, cool behind his eyeballs, burn the liquor away. "Let's have *one* more of these," he said.

"You boys aren't gonna get crazy on us now, are you?" the bartender said, and winked at two couples sitting at the table behind them.

"No, sir, boss," Doc said, putting a hundred-dollar bill on the bar. "Let's have a couple more."

The bartender looked at the bill like Doc had blown his nose on it.

"You boys from around here?" one of the men at the table said. Hanson and Doc turned on the chrome and red Naugahyde barstools, and looked at him. "You all are drinking that ta-kill-ya like a couple of cowboys," he said.

He was wearing a baseball cap with a patch that read, "VIET-NAM VETERAN AND *DAMN* PROUD OF IT."

The other one, younger, had on a leather cowboy hat. The women with them smiled, silver eye shadow glittering when they blinked.

"Nawsir," Doc said, "we're not cowboys. Just passing through. Nice place," he said, looking around.

The woman with the vet snorted smoke from her nose and took the cigarette out of her mouth, lipstick on her teeth, grinning at him. "You behave now, Duane," she said.

"Say," Doc said, pointing to the hat. "Couldn't help but notice that hat, Duane. Are you gentlemens Vietnam veterans?"

Everyone at the table lost their smiles.

"That's right," Duane said.

"I'd of been there too, except for a heart murmur," the other one said.

Hanson nodded. "I can see that."

"See a lot of combat?" Doc said.

"You *know* he did," Hanson said.

"More than I like to remember," Duane said. "Lost a lot of good friends over there."

The woman stroked his hair.

"A lot of *good* friends, huh?" Hanson said.

"You got it, buddy."

"What unit were you with?"

"Special Forces. Long Range Recon."

"Well, suck my black dick. Green Berets," Doc said, looking at Hanson.

Duane wasn't *sure* if he'd been insulted.

" 'Fighting soldiers from the sky,' they call 'em," Hanson told Doc, then looked back at Duane. "That must of been the biggest unit in the army. I keep running into you guys. Every bar I go into. What was your MOS?"

"What the hell do you . . ." the younger one said.

Duane held up his hand. "I'm talking to them, Bob."

"Nothing, sir," Hanson said. "Sorry if we brought up painful memories."

"You think it was worth it, going to Vietnam?" Doc said.

"Sure as hell was."

"God bless America," Hanson said.

"Toe to toe with the bad old Communists," Doc said. "Fighting for that fat whore and a place in the trailer court."

The bartender was reaching under the bar when Hanson raised up and sidearmed the shot glass down, in a silver fan of tequila, into the back of his head, dropping him to his knees on the rubber duckboards behind the bar. Out on the dance floor, under pink and gold spotlights, the band launched into "Tie a Yellow Ribbon Round the Old Oak Tree."

Bob was still trying to get out from behind the table when Hanson rolled off the bar stool and hit him with an awkward but effective left hand, breaking his nose and knocking the leather hat off. Hanson felt Bob's nose *snap* and smelled his woman's perfume as she tried to stand and fell backwards into her chair.

Duane was still in his chair and Doc was hitting him at will, each punch spraying blood and sweat. He looked at Hanson, a light coat of sweat on his brown skin, stumbled on his bad leg, caught himself, and hit Duane in the neck, breaking his collar bone and toppling him to the floor.

"Time to go," Hanson said. One of three men at a table near the door started to stand and Hanson *looked* at him. The man shook his head and sat back down.

The two of them went through the swinging doors into the brighter lights of the restaurant, striding through the gauntlet of red Naugahyde booths. A man wearing a Peterbilt hat stood halfway up, and Hanson gripped his face like a basketball, shoving him back in the booth without losing a step.

A huge, moonfaced man wearing a black shirt with "SECURITY" across the front in yellow letters came out of the kitchen and blocked the aisle, a billy club in his hand. Hanson and Doc kept walking, shoulder to shoulder, and he stepped aside. At the double glass doors, the two of them turned and looked back at the booths of startled people, then pushed through the doors into the warm, humid air that smelled of diesel fumes and livestock.

They walked through the rows of idling, growling trucks towards the Trans Am, almost reaching it, when the sound of running feet stopped them, six men, two of them with tire irons. Doc pulled a pistol from the shoulder holster and held it down beside his leg. "Come on, you cracker motherfuckers," he shouted, limping towards them. "*Use* those tire irons."

"Let's go, Doc," Hanson said to him. "We did as good as we're gonna *do* here."

"Come *on*, you fat white motherfuckers."

"We been lucky up to now. Time to cut and run," Hanson said.

Doc seemed to relax. He looked at Hanson and smiled. "Let's kill 'em," he said.

"I'm *asking* you, let's go."

"Shit."

"Let's go," Hanson said.

"Let's *do* it."

"Not now. I'm *asking* you, man."

Doc shook his head.

They backed the rest of the way to the Trans Am and drove slowly out of the parking lot.

They'd gone only a few miles on the interstate when a pair of state police cars passed them, blue and red lights silently flashing, going the other way. "Yes," Hanson said, as Doc took the next off-ramp, "a *quieter* road would be good."

"How about taking over?" Doc said. "I need to close my eyes for a little while."

"You sure? This new car?"

Doc grunted, searching the road, out beyond the headlights, for a place to pull over.

They drove west, towards the coast, Doc asleep in the passenger seat, his bad leg propped on the transmission hump.

Hanson didn't feel the exhilaration he might have expected from the fight. It had been too easy, almost like a day at work. He'd been wrong to do it. It could get him fired and put in prison.

He sucked his bloody knuckles and looked out at the edge of a suburb they were passing. The houses seemed to be of three basic styles, alternating along the cul-de-sac streets like a wallpaper design. The streetlights were orange, each one circled by a delicate nimbus of fog. The suburb looked more like an idea than a place where real people lived, someone's concept of heaven. Everyone asleep, their new cars safe and shining in well-lit driveways. As the road climbed towards the coast mountains, Hanson could see glowing 7-Elevens and gas station logos scattered across the development like clues. Rows of half-finished houses, in the same alternating designs, stood between the suburb and the rolling fields beyond. They were skeletal and raw, piles of roofing stacked neatly and identically on top of each one. They had no lawns or streetlights yet, no sidewalks or little trees.

They all thought they were safe, he supposed, and expected to live a long time. Maybe that was the big difference. Whenever he drove through one of those suburbs wearing a gun, he felt like an outlaw, a threat, the kind of person they were trying to keep out. He couldn't blame them for that.

Why did they *want* to live a long time, Hanson thought, if it would only be more of the same. Less. Their bodies would start to let them down and they would have to give up their secret dreams. Modest dreams at that, but dreams that nonetheless helped them at first to get up in the mornings and drive to their jobs. To tell themselves that it was only temporary. If it was boring, at least it was safe. But then when they had to admit that it *wasn't* temporary? That they would do it until they retired and died. Why would they want to live a long time?

They left the suburbs and finally even their glow on the horizon behind, passing farms and collapsing barns and huge rolls of hay. The big engine of the car pulled them along easily. Across the fields the yard lights of farmhouses shone like ships at sea. They passed boarded-up restaurants and the concrete slabs of abandoned service stations. Failed dreams of independence and success.

Hanson downshifted as the road got even steeper, dropping off on one side to a river valley. He reached over and shook Doc by the shoulder.

"I *know* this road," he said. "I was on it a couple of years ago. There's something coming up that you have to see."

A few miles farther on, he saw it, rising up in the distance, blocking out the sky. The only surviving grove of virgin Douglas fir trees in the Tillamook burn. It was a ways off, and they had to drive through miles and miles of charred monster trees, prehistoric giants burned to death thirty years before. The smell of the old fire made Doc edgy. Hanson could sense it.

The temperature dropped as they entered the grove, and the moonlight turned green, then black. Moss and pine needles softened the contours of the earth as the car's headlights threw black and silver shadows across them. Hanson downshifted, and again, feeling the engine pull the car down. He came to a stop, turned off the headlights, and cut the engine. "Get out of the car," he said.

The interior light came on, Doc's eyes hard and alert, the fatigue gone when he got out and looked across the roof of the car at Hanson.

"Close the door," Hanson said, and Doc pushed the door shut with a solid *click*, darkness swallowing him up.

Hanson tilted his head back as if he were smelling the air. "Listen," he said.

It was absolutely quiet. Not even the whisper of a breeze in the tops of the enormous trees, just the *tic tic tic* of the car's engine cooling off, and the hiss of Doc's pistol coming out of the holster.

Something ruffled the air above them, a bat, or maybe an owl hunting the road in the dark.

"You think I was setting you up? Gonna shoot you? I just wanted you to hear this. Silence. Don't you *know* me?"

Doc's holster clapped softly, taking the pistol.

"I haven't slept in three days," he said.

"It was quiet like this across the border in Laos," Hanson said. "As soon as the insertion choppers were gone."

"Move and listen," Doc said. "Listen and move."

Hanson couldn't see Doc, but he spoke towards the sound of his voice. "I never wanted to come back."

Some tiny thing, a mouse or a falling pine cone, way back in the trees somewhere, moved in the pine needles.

"What do you think happens," Hanson asked him finally, "after you die?"

"Dead meat."

"Sometimes I think, maybe, if you're brave, and keep your word, you know? Do what you say you'll do, don't complain, and don't kiss any more asses than you absolutely have to . . ."

Doc snorted.

"Maybe something *happens*, after you die."

Doc smiled at him through the heat rising from the eagle on the hood of the Trans Am, his eyes and teeth and cheekbones catching a hint of starlight falling through the shadow of the ancient trees, light that had traveled thousands of years to illuminate that moment. It was a smile with no hope or mercy in it. A smile that spoke the one thing most people try to deny all their lives. The light was so faint that Hanson had to look beyond Doc, into the woods, to see his eyes, and then he felt his own face taking on the smile.

"Dead meat's not so bad," Doc said. "I don't mind that."

The muffled rush of wings passed over them again, faster this time, diving, and whatever had moved the pine needles squealed, its cries rising towards the stars as it was carried away, muffled by the tops of trees, then gone.

"Anything 'happens,' " Doc said, "it's just another hell. Worse than this one. They keep getting worse."

"Let's drive on out to the coast," Hanson said.

The big engine took them through the rest of the woods, headlights flickering through the trees at every curve, the smell of pine needles and night air purling through the open windows.

Out of the woods now, the road began to climb, but the big engine took them effortlessly on up, and they drove west until they came to a T-intersection and Hanson turned to the right. Below them, beyond the cliff-edge road, the ocean caught the light of the new moon. The ocean, rising and falling as if it was a breathing creature, as far as they could see.

TWENTY

AT ROLL CALL Sgt. Bendix read a memo from the chief's office urging all officers to work towards improving their image as professionals serving the community, and soften the "us versus them" mentality that had developed in some districts.

"Which districts," Zurbo said, "might those *be*, I wonder?"

Hanson suggested that the Narcotics and Vice division give all the heroin in the evidence locker to North Precinct. "Hair-on," as it was called on the street, was usually packaged in balloons, the long thin kind. A "dime," ten dollars' worth of dope, was dumped in the balloon which was then knotted tightly and cut off above the knot. The bottom of the remaining length of balloon was knotted and the next dime was dropped in, knotted, and cut. Four or five little marble-size packets could be made from one kid's balloon. You could carry them in your mouth, and if the cops grabbed you, swallow them. If you didn't go to jail, you could vomit them up, or if it was too late for that, shit them out, good as new.

"Give us an hour's overtime," Hanson said, "and we could

package the loose stuff. Each district car could carry a little box of balloons, their own trademark color. Or we could mix 'em up, primary colors, pastels, that Day-Glo stuff, and toss 'em out the window as we drive through the district. Like throwing candy kisses from parade floats on the Fourth of July. Instead of destroying all that hair-on, we could use it to soften that 'us vs. them' mentality. People in the street would *like* to see us drive by. Smiling, on the nod, no more crime."

"I don't think the chief will go for it," Sgt. Bendix said, trying to smile.

"I've got a few more items, but we're running a little late. Try to familiarize yourselves with them at the end of the shift," Sgt. Bendix said, putting the bulletins and announcements on the long, scarred table.

"Be sure and take a look at this interagency memo from Tillamook County," he said, holding up a composite drawing of Hanson and Doc, stapled to a teletype which he read. "The suspects initially assaulted and battered two individuals, seriously injuring both of them, for no apparent reason. Possibly high on drugs. They assaulted a number of other subjects on the way out of the truck stop, and after exiting the facility, the black suspect menaced several individuals with a handgun. They were last seen westbound from the scene in a gold Trans Am, possibly with California plates. Consider them armed and dangerous."

"Salt-and-pepper f-faggots," Larkin stuttered, "from down in the land of . . . fruits and nuts."

"That one looks like Hanson."

"I've said it all along. All Green Berets have the extra male chromosome. Violence queers," Zurbo said.

"Come on, Hanson. Who's your friend?"

Sgt. Bendix walked through the parking lot with his clipboard as they checked out their patrol cars. Zurbo and Neal waited until he was one car over before they each cupped their hands around their nose and mouth and bent over the ozone generator, inhaling vigorously.

Bendix stopped, watching them sob and gasp for air, then tapped on the closed window. He tapped again. Zurbo threw his head back, swelling his chest with deep breaths, then "noticed" Bendix and rolled the window down.

"Are you two okay?" Bendix said.

"Sure, Sarge," Zurbo said, panting. "We had this . . ."

"This idea," Neal said, out of breath, "about the, the chief's memo."

"We thought if," Zurbo said, "we sucked up a whole bunch, of this ozone, at the beginning of the shift—"

"It'd mellow us out," Neal finished.

"I don't think the units are designed to be used in that manner," Bendix said. "Normal respiration during the day should maximize the benefits."

Just off their district, on Fremont Street, Fox's van pulled out of the Hollywood Palms Motel, a place used mostly by prostitutes and their pimps. Peetey was laughing until he saw the patrol car, but Fox, not even smiling, never changed expression, his eyes on Hanson as they passed going the other way. One of the whores, wearing black leather shorts and a string halter top, was just opening the door to one of the second-floor units. As she stepped inside, she turned to glance at the patrol car. It was Asia.

It wasn't until they were on the Avenue that Dana said, "That composite really *did* look like you and your friend."

"Yeah. Spooky, huh?"

Dana nodded.

They drove by the Pathfinder Socialist Bookstore, an African National Flag in a grimy window webbed with BB gun holes.

A white guy with skin the color of cold bacon grease scratched his chest in front of the American Plasma Donor Center, turning away when he saw the patrol car.

They passed a burned-out house, plywood over the windows pale against the charred siding where plaster lath showed through in spots like ribs. The stink of wet, charred wood and burned food filled the car, then slowly went away, sucked out the windows.

"On his thirty-day leave, before his second tour, Doc killed a guy who was flashing an unloaded pistol. Doc knew it was unloaded. Killed him just for fun." Anyone looking at Hanson's eyes would have thought he was recalling a happy childhood. "Doc said they couldn't *prove* he knew it was unloaded. 'And *besides*,' he'd say, 'I'm a motherfuckin' *war* hero, on my way back to fight the bad ole Communists some more.' "

"I don't know about you, my man," Dana said. "No wonder people look at you funny sometimes."

"It was a hard world over there."

A gaunt, tiger-striped cat, hunting the tall grass of a vacant lot, watched them drive past.

"And simple. That's why I liked it. 'Good' was staying alive. 'Evil' was everything else. Sounds, smells, movement. Hesitation. Pity. Anyone you didn't know, or trust, you killed. Doc and a few others were the only ones I trusted, out of all the millions of people in the world. The others are dead—just me and Doc now. I haven't figured it out to explain it, but we're stuck with each other, and neither one of us is happy about it.

"I've never told this to anyone, not even myself. I didn't know it until just this minute . . .

"If one of us dies, the other will be alone in a way . . . I can't explain *that* either. Forever. *That's* what I'm so scared of. Doc, too, and he's not afraid of anything . . ."

The faint smell of smoke from the burnt house, still clinging to Hanson's uniform shirt, stopped him.

"He's afraid of fire. Of getting burned real bad."

Hanson turned north on Union, into the *boom* and feedback-shriek of tent revival loudspeakers, the evangelist's voice lost in the noise at first. Three intersections later, a red light caught them half a block from the blue-and-white-striped open-sided canopy. The street was deserted, as if the huge, dented loudspeakers, drooping where they were bolted together, blowing the evangelist's voice into shreds, had scoured the street of people.

". . . when you *hear* it, or see it there on the *printed page* of your *hymn*-nal . . ."

The rows of folding metal chairs under the tent were mostly empty, barely a dozen people, all of them black and over fifty, sitting near the front. The evangelist looked down at them from a podium on a raised stage, a microphone in one hand and a white handkerchief in the other.

Hanson rolled his window up against the gale of sound, filtering out some of the static, so the evangelist's voice came through.

". . . it appears to be a single word, a joyful, two-syllable, *one*-word definition of faith. But break that same word, *Christ*ian, into its individual, component parts, and you'll see that it is much more than that.

"The first part of the word 'Christian,' what a scholar of language at *Harvard* University would call the *root* word, is *Christ*, praise God! But what about the *rest* of this word, this apparently *simple* word that connects us with *God*, those last three letters, I. A. N?"

Up the block, Pharaoh pushed his cart across the empty intersection, disappearing behind a boarded-up record store.

The loudspeakers buzzed and droned while the evangelist wiped his face, then wiped the microphone, twisting the wire-mesh head into his handkerchief, the amplified hiss like a steam locomotive leaving the station.

"Now *some* of you—the gentleman there in the fine-looking suit, or perhaps this young woman down in front," he said, wiping his face, indicating a lady with gray hair, "are *think*ing, 'Preacher, what you talkin' about? Preacher, I don't believe even *you* can preach your way out of this, 'cause I *know* that I. A. N. don't mean nothin'.' "

The light turned green, and Hanson drove on, past the tent.

"You're right. One *hundred* percent right. Right as *rain*," he shouted, his laughter out of the speakers like sonic booms. " 'Cause I. A. N. is short for, *I. Ain't. Nothin'. I . . . Ain't . . . Nothin'.* Amen to that. Without *Christ*, don't you see, *we ain't nothing.*"

Five Six Two—Can you go?

"Five Six Two," Hanson said.

Check for an ambulance. Three seventeen North Wygant. A juvenile with a dog bite. We're trying to kick a code-three loose. Everything on this side of the river is tied up with that multiple fatality on I-80.

"On the way," Hanson said, accelerating through the next intersection, picking up speed as he thought ahead, working out the fastest route, the preacher's voice behind them now, fading back into the noise, gone.

Hanson had seen him before. A tow truck driver. "I told her a hundred goddamned times," he said, " 'don't fuck with King.' "

The little girl was two years old, lying on a grimy sofa, staring at the ceiling.

"Five Six Two," Dana said into his packset, "we *need* that code-three . . ."

Car calling?

Dana looked at the packset. "I'll use the car radio. And get a blanket and first aid kit," he said, slamming out the screen door.

Hanson walked over to the sofa, casually, smiling as if it was a routine call.

One gash came out of her hair, ragged, tearing across her forehead through the eyebrow, peeling wider, to pearly-blue bone, down her temple to the torn ear. The other one opened her cheek.

"What's her name?" Hanson said.

He leaned down for a better look at something deep in the wound, beneath the smooth skin, popcorn gouts of baby fat, torn jaw muscles and clotting blood. Teeth. Tiny white molars.

"Her name?"

"It's, uh, my girlfriend's kid, you know, uh . . . *Marcy. She* should have been watching her. I can't do every goddamn thing."

"Hi Marcy," Hanson said, his smiling eyes a lie. "You're okay, now. We'll take care of you."

He touched her and she began screaming, the clotted blood crumbling, opening the wound, fresh blood seeping out.

"You got a real bedside manner there, champ," the tow truck driver said, stepping out of his way when Dana came through the door. Hanson helped Dana wrap her in the cheap wool blanket, pulling it tight over her arms and legs so she couldn't move and make the bleeding even worse.

The dog, locked in the closet, threw himself tirelessly against the door, the barking muffled, like somebody coughing.

"I had his vocal cords taken out," the tow truck driver said. "I want a dog who doesn't bark. Just attacks."

"We got an ambulance yet?" Dana asked Radio, the packset working now.

Coming from the West Side.

Marcy began choking on the blood, fighting the blanket, until Dana and Hanson wrestled her into a sitting position, so she could swallow. Through the window, Hanson saw a rusting old Pontiac skid over the curb and stop in the yard. The woman driving jumped out, fell, pulled off the broken high heel shoe, limping and hopping towards the house. She was pretty, maybe twenty-five years old, but putting on weight.

"Marcy!" she screamed, coming through the door. "Baby."

"Give her to me," she yelled, pushing Dana, then hitting him to get to the little girl. He took the blows, holding the little girl upright to slow the bleeding.

"Ma'am," Dana said, "we're trying to . . ."

"I'm her mother," she screamed.

"Let the cops do their jobs, goddammit," the tow truck driver yelled.

Hanson stepped in between them. "Ma'am, *look* at me," he said, blocking her with his body, his arms at his sides. "*Look* at me." But her eyes had gone blind with panic, and she clawed past him, getting a handful of Dana's hair, the little girl's screams as loud as hers now.

"You do what I *tell* you to do, goddammit," the tow truck driver shouted. He took her arm and jerked her away, threw her against the wall. "You *hear* me? You give me any more *shit* and I'm *gone.* We're through."

Sobbing, she reached out to him, and he slapped her hands away.

"I told you a hundred fuckin' times, don't let her near King. How stupid *are* you? Huh? Huh?"

"Fuck the ambulance," Dana said, picking the little girl up. "Let's take her to Good Sam."

Hanson followed him out the door, telling Radio where they were going. ". . . and send Animal Control out here for the dog," he said.

"Hey. Hey!" the tow truck driver shouted, following him down the sidewalk. "It wasn't *King's* fault. He's trained to do a job, man. The kid *provoked* him."

Hanson turned, slamming into him, almost knocking him down, walking him backwards towards the porch, yelling in his face, "It's *your* fault, motherfucker," butting him with his chest, "*your* fault . . ."

"Come on," Dana yelled, his shirt torn, blood speckling his glasses, the little girl kicking and screaming in his arms, bloody and mad with fear, her mother screaming on the porch as Dana struggled to open the door and get her in the car.

She fought them as they belted her legs to the table with the leather restraints, forced her arms into a little blue straitjacket and buckled it across her chest. When they strapped her head down and began injecting her torn face with novocaine, Hanson left the room.

It was early afternoon, and the emergency room wasn't crowded yet. There were only a few patients behind the cotton screens, waiting to see bleary-eyed interns on 24-hour shifts. Hanson was usually happy for a trip to the emergency room or the psychiatric ward. It meant at least an hour off the street to get some coffee, catch up on paperwork, and make phone calls.

In a few hours the gurneys would be banging through the double doors, rumbling down the halls on their little rubber wheels, IV bottles swinging above them like lanterns, ferrying gunshot wounds, stabbings, heart attacks, bloody drunk drivers who had gone through the windshields of their four-hundred-dollar Buicks, gray-faced and distant from blood loss and shock, or bucking with convulsions, vomiting, talking in tongues.

In the early afternoon, though, it was quiet, almost peaceful, as Hanson stood at one of the wire-reinforced, barred windows, looking out past the interstate and the warehouse district, beyond the fringes of the city and the suburbs, the distant trees and foothills, to the horizon, where Stormbreaker loomed through the haze and shimmering heat like doom.

Dana and Hanson were finishing up the paperwork when the doctor came into the office he'd let them use, and told them that she had severe nerve damage. They'd do what they could to minimize the scars, but she'd never have any feeling or movement in the left side of her face.

Hanson imagined her going to school, scarred, her face sagging, drooling, ashamed.

"It'll be a while yet before we're done," he told them, "but I wanted to catch you before you left. We need to call the Child Protective Agency on this one," he said, opening his notebook to a sexual abuse report form with the simple, almost crude drawings of a naked man and woman, frontal, back, left side, right side. The more detailed drawings of genitalia below, which he had marked with a felt-tip pen, looked almost like something you might see on a toilet stall in a public bathroom.

"These lacerations on her genitalia, and around her anus," he said, pointing them out, "are consistent with long-term sexual abuse. The burns, here, and here, were probably done with cigarettes. That's usually how they do it."

HANSON COULDN'T SLEEP, even after finishing the bottle of cognac. The house was dark except for a lamp in the living room where Hanson sat, the blued-steel 9mm in his hand. The pistol gleamed as he turned his wrist and looked down the rifled barrel to the sullen, copper-jacketed slug he'd chambered. He lowered the heavy pistol and tipped it side to side, feeling the balance, then thumbed the hammer back to full cock with a *click*. When he looked up again from the pistol, he saw Truman standing just outside the cone of light, watching him.

"But hey, if anything happens to you," Fox had called after him, *"we'll be sure to send Animal Control out to take care of that dog."*

He turned the gun towards the wall, lowered the hammer, and laid it on the table.

"How you doin', bud?" he said. "Couldn't you sleep either? Come on, I'll split a beer with you out on the porch."

When they came back inside, Hanson picked up the book *Steam* and thumbed through it until he came to page fifty-five:

TABLE OF COMBUSTIBLES

Combustible	Temperatures of Combustion
Hydrogen	5750
Petroleum	5050
Charcoal	
Carbon—Coke	4850
Anthracite Coal	
Coal—Cumberland	4900
Coking Bituminous	5140
Cannel	4850
Lignite	4600
Peat—Kiln Dried	4470
Air Dried (25% water)	4000
Wood—Hickory, Shellbark	4469
Red Heart	3705
White Oak	3821

And on through Spruce, New Jersey Pine, Hard Maple, and down the page, finally to White Pine, then back up to Hydrogen again. He looked over at Truman.

"Mister Thorgaard, did *he* ever . . . ?"

He put his hand on Truman's shoulder, and went back to the

book, searching through the columns of combustibles, tempera-
tures and thermal values for a pattern, some kind of logic hidden
in the words and numbers, maybe something he'd never thought
of, reading under the lamp until he fell asleep, with Truman next
to him, on the lopsided sofa.

TWENTY-ONE

IT WAS HANSON'S day off, but he'd come in to testify to the Grand Jury about the tow truck driver and the two-year-old. Since he'd driven all the way to town, he treated himself to a prime rib dinner at one of the expensive new places in "Old Town." He wore jeans, rough-out cowboy boots, a light blue shirt with a dark blue tie, and a khaki safari jacket he'd just gotten in the mail from L.L. Bean. He thought the jacket was a little pretentious, and he didn't like the shoulder holster he had to wear with it.

At his table by the window he had three brandies for dessert, watching the winos out on the street and, reflected in the window, a pretty young woman at the bar. She was pale, with short black hair and dark lipstick, wearing a black dress with spaghetti straps. She smoked her cigarette gracefully and elaborately, gesturing with it and blowing smoke out of the side of her mouth.

After his third brandy, the fresh gash on the bridge of his nose stopped throbbing.

The meal cost half a day's pay, but was worth it, he thought, when he paid the bill. Taking a last look at the woman, he left the restaurant and decided to walk the eight or ten blocks to the Blue Dolphin before going home. It was a nice night.

Just up the street, Champ shuffled out of the foyer of the Nordic Seas Hotel, a flophouse where residents hung their clothes from the chicken-wire ceilings. As a rookie, Hanson had gotten a call there once on a dead body that turned out to be a natural death.

"Hey, Champ. How's it going," Hanson said.

Champ cocked his head and looked at him, the strap on his football helmet dangling loose.

"Knock 'em down, shove 'em around," Hanson said.

"Think ya can pull a *Sullivan* on Champ? Ya son of a *bitch*," he said, making fists and raising his arms.

"I'm *Hanson.*"

"I'll knock your dick stiff," Champ snarled, fists up on either side of his head, spit running down his chin, the sour stink of wine and urine on him.

"Hanson. Out of uniform. See?"

"You better fuckin' believe it," Champ said, shuffling closer as Hanson backed away, holding his open hands up.

A huge Indian with shoulder-length hair, his chin and cheekbone freshly scabbed over, came out of the hotel.

"Wha's up, ole buddy?" he asked Champ, slurring his words. He put his arm around Champ. "Ole Champ," he said.

"Speeding Bear," Hanson said, "you know me, right?"

"Right?" Speeding Bear said. "Right what?"

"Tried to pull a Sullivan," Champ said.

Speeding Bear's eyes were black as stones as he looked Hanson up and down. "Do you live here?"

"Remember . . ." Hanson began.

"Go back where you belong."

Hanson nodded, and walked up the street, past the Rescue Mission, the Union Clothing Store, and across the street.

He smelled books even before he walked through the open doorway of the Blue Dolphin, a bookstore covering an entire city block. A blue neon dolphin flickered in the window, like something out of an old detective movie.

As usual, he stopped in the front room to look over the "New Arrivals." From one of the rooms way in back, a woman was shouting tirelessly. Her words weren't clear, but she sounded like an evangelist whose *joy* is in *spreading* God's word. After a minute, he worked his way through the store towards the sound. A poetry reading.

The rows of folding chairs were full, with more people standing against the walls or sitting cross-legged on the floor. The chanting woman stood on a raised stage, her arms out, the full sleeves of her purple dress like wings. She was pale, the heavy purple eye shadow giving her a death's-head look.

She smiled at the audience. "The war *they* say has . . . ended, the men who peer down at us. From boardrooms. From private jets too high to be heard. From . . . oval offices."

Hanson watched the audience, imagining them in a jury, wondering how he could win them over to his side. The younger women wore jeans with T-shirts, tank tops, or Mexican blouses. The men wore beards, workshirts, and logger's boots, the kind of guys, Hanson thought, who drove pickups with bumper stickers that said "Rugby players eat their dead," or "Go climb a rock."

Many in the audience listened with bowed heads, their eyes closed in order, Hanson supposed, to *concentrate* on the words.

"*They* say it is. They want us to believe the war is over but it goes on and on at night in the backs of my . . . eyes. Yesss," she hissed.

Young couples wore children slung over their shoulders like backpacks. Older women, many of them handsome and obviously wealthy, looked like Russian exiles, in high boots, long dresses, and shawls. They were earnest listeners, leaning forwards in their metal chairs.

"Like a movie I can't turn off. Playing nightly. And the killers pass me on the street every day in their three-piece suits and corporate ties. Yesss."

He leaned farther into the doorway, off balance, looking around at the back of the room, and almost fell when he locked eyes with the redhead he'd tracked in the rifle scope that night at Dana's—Sara. He gave her a little salute and, feeling stupid, walked back to the general fiction section to look for a detective novel Zurbo had recommended, by James Crumley. He moved down the stacks—Crawford, Crews, and over to the next row where a tall guy in a bicycle-riding outfit stood in front of the rest of the Cs, reading a book. He was a couple years older than Hanson, wearing an Italian cap, a knit shirt advertising some sort of bicycle, knee-length tights, and funny-looking square-toed shoes.

Hanson couldn't see over his shoulder. He stepped to one side, trying to look around him, as he cracked the spine of the book, folding it open to a grainy photo covering both pages. Dead villagers in a ditch.

Maybe he's just involved in the book, Hanson thought, and doesn't know I'm back here. He stepped to the other side, throwing a shadow on the open book. The cyclist turned to an index at the back of the book, then opened it to the photo again.

You can come back later, Hanson told himself, studying the cyclist. He was big, and in good shape, but he'd probably never been in a fight except for a junior high school shoving match, and thought that ditches full of dead people only happened in books.

When he licked his finger to turn the page, Hanson imagined breaking the finger, but quickly put that out of his mind. Don't be stupid, he told himself. You've got *liquor* on your breath, and you don't need any more trouble.

The cyclist turned his head slightly, showing his profile.

A *"patrician"* nose, Hanson thought. Long and thin. Easy to break. A bloody and pretty spectacular beginning. Or, he could just choke him out and dump him, unconscious, on the floor, as he often did to people who resisted arrest and were too big for him to subdue any other way. They'd usually exhale the last of the air in their lungs, struggling to get loose, and panic. Sometimes they'd try to scream, before they lost consciousness, wet their pants, and hit the sidewalk, but with most of their air gone, and their windpipes compressed, the sound they produced was more of a high whistle, like a wounded rabbit. Tough, two-hundred-and-fifty-pound black men, squealing like gutshot rabbits. It was weird, Hanson thought, staring at the cyclist's throat.

Hurting people was a regular part of his job, *normal,* as long as he was a cop. This guy in the spandex shorts wouldn't know what to do, Hanson thought, if he spun him around and started hitting him. He'd waste time thinking, Why is he doing this? Did I do something *wrong?* while Hanson hit him some more. Then he'd try to *defend* himself rather than *fight,* and by then it would be all over.

If he surprised Hanson, and gave him any trouble, Hanson could knee him in the balls or stick a thumb in his eye, or punch him in the throat, which, of course, might kill him.

What would he tell the homicide people?

He was standing in my way so I killed him.

Why didn't you ask him to move?

The cyclist turned another page and Hanson wondered if he could hit him hard enough, just once, in the kidneys, to make him fall. Instead, he stared at his ear, giving him The Look. He concentrated, focused, looking at the ear.

The cyclist slowly looked around. "What's your problem?"

"I don't know," Hanson said. He laughed, and the cyclist backed away, turned and walked quickly down the stacks, the book still in his hand.

"A friend of yours?"

Hanson turned around. It was the redhead, Sara.

"Nope," he said. "He probably thinks I'm crazy."

"Why would he think that?"

"Watch this," Hanson said. He walked in a tight circle, there between the shelves of books, his head down, taking tiny shuffling steps. "Say what, boss? My problem? I dunno. Can't be sure, but sometime it seem like it's a hellhound on my trail. Out there in the dark. Trackin' me down. Uh-huh. That's right."

He looked up at her, smiled. "See?"

"Want to go to a party?" she said.

"Aren't you afraid I'm crazy?"

"I enjoy a certain amount of tension in my personal life," she said, smiling back, tilting her head so the carotid artery showed blue through the pale skin, just beneath her jaw.

Hanson reached out and put two fingers against it, feeling her pulse.

"I forgot your name," he said, still touching her throat.

"Sara," she said, and he felt her voice on his fingertips.

They took her black VW bug. Her skin was luminous in the dark car. The party was up in the West Hills, and it was cooler up there. The air smelled of grass and Douglas fir trees.

"How did you like the reading?" she asked, pushing in the clutch and shifting to second gear.

"I just looked in to see what the chanting was about."

"You're not a poet then?"

Hanson laughed. "Are you?"

"No."

"Glad to hear *that*," Hanson said. "Have you got anything to drink in here?"

"Try the glove box."

He found a pint of vodka, and held up the flat, silver bottle.

"Help yourself."

He took a swallow, started to put the top back on, then took another. "Ah, thank you very much."

"I probably should have some of that," she said, and Hanson gave her the bottle. The liquor had felt good burning down his throat, and so did the heat he felt in the car between the two of them. He took another swallow when she handed the bottle back, before putting it in the glove box. He knew he should take it slower, but he felt good, the best he'd felt in a long time. He relaxed and leaned back in the seat. "If you're not a poet, what are you?" he said, watching the muscles in her leg flex as she shifted gears.

"I paint," she said, her eyes on the road.

"What kind of paintings?" Hanson asked her, watching the way her hands gripped the steering wheel.

She looked at him and smiled. "You'll have to see them. Maybe I'll paint *you*. And what is it *you* do?"

Hanson inhaled, smelling her perfume with a hint of sweat, hot engine oil, the sweet, fruity vodka, and fir trees. "I . . ." he said, closing his eyes, leaning his head back on the headrest. She shifted gears again and the little car shuddered. "I work for the city."

"Yuk," she said. "You don't *look* like you work for the city. What do you do for them?"

"Oh, it's pretty interesting. I work out of the DA's office. Kind of a liaison agent with the ACLU."

He looked over at her, his head pillowed against the headrest, and smiled, the same smile he used in court when he looked at the jury and wanted the women to like him. At the police bar he called it his "nice liberal smile."

"I'm kind of a trouble-shooter," he said. "They call me a 'regional representative.' "

"What kind of trouble do you shoot?" she asked, and Hanson laughed.

"I, uh, check into claims of judicial prejudice in indigent cases, investigate claims of police brutality in the black community. The cops. Try to keep *those* guys in line. Keep 'em on the up-an'-up," he said, laughing again, feeling the vodka.

"What happened to your nose?" she said.

"I fell off my bicycle."

It was a big, ranch-style house overlooking the city. Hanson had worked the district up in the hills for a little while when he was at

Central Precinct. Sometimes it was hard to find addresses in the curving streets and cul-de-sacs, but it was an easy district, mostly burglary reports to write when the doctors and lawyers, business-men, media consultants, and stockbrokers came home in the late afternoons. They were usually patronizing, treating him like an insurance company flunky, which he was in a way.

His good mood began to darken when they walked into the house. It was loud and crowded and smoky. He didn't mind crowds when he was working. He *enjoyed* them when he was in charge, the adrenaline sweat on him. When he told someone to move, turn around, *put your hands on your head,* they did it. Watching peo-ple's faces and hands, the way they reacted when he made eye contact, his own eyes radiating threat, making the rules abso-lutely clear. *"Do what I say."*

But at a party like this, the same instincts were working, and he had to suppress them because no one knew the rules. "I don't really want to stay for long," Hanson told Sara.

"Neither do I," she said. She nodded towards one of the women dressed like a Russian countess. "I have to talk to her for a min-ute. You go on. I'll find you," she said, touching his arm.

He walked carefully through the room, returning the smiles of a couple of college girls on his way to the kitchen. He supposed there would be some beer in there, and it gave him something specific to do. "Excuse me," he said, "excuse me," pushing through the crowd in the living room, conscious of the pistol he was wearing in a shoulder holster, feeling the vodka.

It was a big kitchen with black and white tile, a stove and counter area set in the center like an island. Dull silver kitchen knives, blunt cleavers, and heavy, copper-plated pans hung on hooks from a rack suspended above the island. At family fights the kitchen is the most dangerous room in the house. The check-erboard pattern of tile made him dizzy for a moment.

The refrigerator was full of imported beer, and Hanson took one, then went through drawers of kitchen utensils, drawing blood on one of those two-pronged corn-on-the-cob holders, until he found a bottle opener.

The famous poet, the one whose picture had been on the flyers in the bookstore, sat in a kitchen chair against the back wall, cornered by people who wanted his attention. A girl in an African-print dress, her blond hair pulled back in a ponytail, knelt in front of him, searching his eyes. "Does that make any sense?" she asked him.

Hanson watched from the refrigerator, the pulse on the inside of his left arm throbbing against the 9mm. If he *had* to, he wondered, would he be able to kill the seven or eight people in the room with the nine rounds in the pistol? Probably not. No. He'd have to score with head-shots on most of them, and they'd be running around. The best way—he'd have to lock the kitchen door somehow—would be to pull the gun and make them all lie face-down on the floor with their hands on top of their heads. Chances were that none of them would fight as he shot them one by one, each of them pretending that it wasn't really happening, that they couldn't die like that.

Hanson stepped away from the refrigerator, and the poet smiled politely at him, looking for some excuse to break the relentless eye contact of the girl. In the safari jacket, with his troubled eyes, Hanson could have passed for a poet himself. The fact that he was carrying a gun and was thinking, however theoretically, about shooting these people meant that they were in real danger, and none of them even suspected it. The people who lived on the Avenue knew that guns were on the street and in the room with them all the time. These people in the kitchen were living in a dream world.

"It's that summer I want to write about," the girl in the African-print dress told the poet, "the summer with Head Start. The summer in the ghetto, trying to help," she said. "To show them that not *all* white people are racists."

"You ought to do it," the poet said.

Hanson stepped back so he could hear better, his ears ringing a little now, and stumbled against a guy wearing little round glasses and a red beret.

"Sorry," Hanson said, the guy frowning at him, blowing cigarette smoke out of the corner of his mouth. Hanson took another sip of beer and wondered if Dana ever thought about things like shooting people at a party.

The girl shuffled a little closer to the poet's knees, assaulting him with her sincerity. "The fact that you were the only woman working there would give it even more resonance," the poet said.

Hanson tried not to, but he couldn't help imagining them all dead, the tile red with blood, gun smoke in the air and his ears ringing from the shots. Then what would he do? Too late to do anything then. He should never have allowed himself to think about it. Hell, his ears were ringing now. "Artillery ears," he'd heard them called once, though small-arms fire and the helicopters caused it too.

The guy in the beret exhaled cigarette smoke that drifted into Hanson's hair and eyes and up his nose.

"I think so, too," the girl said, "but I need to fill some empty spaces in my life—does that make sense?—before I'll be ready to write about it."

The poet looked at his watch.

The ringing got more insistent and the lights in the room seemed to dim. Going slowly, one careful step at a time, Hanson walked out of the kitchen.

The open front door looked tiny and far away, the distant end of a tunnel he was in, and Hanson kept losing sight of it in the darkened room. He had to focus directly on it as he worked through the crowd, their voices almost lost in the ringing now.

"Excuse me," he said, trying to keep his voice calm.

Someone took his arm. "Help us out here," a man said, laughing. "We're taking a poll . . ."

Hanson removed the hand, smiled like a blind man in the direction of the voice, and said, "Thanks. Good luck."

"Lewis doesn't work," someone said as Hanson made the door. "He's not a protagonist, he's a symbol."

He smiled at the people in the front yard, fighting the urge to run, and once he got to the street, away from the light, he began to feel better. It would be a long walk back to town, but that was okay. For a while there, he'd thought he wouldn't make the door, afraid he was going to lose all control of his body and fall, *float* to the floor, unable to move or talk. People would look down at him, asking what was wrong, and he'd try to smile from the floor. "I'm okay. I'm fine. No need to pay any attention to me."

He took a deep breath. The asphalt was solid beneath his feet. It was a nice night. "God *damn*," he said aloud, the tension going. "Boy howdy," getting his stride now, looking up at the stars. He could march all night if he had to. He'd have to tell Truman about it when he got home.

A quarter mile down the hill, he heard the VW shifting through the curves, then headlights bloomed behind him, throwing his shadow down the street. It pulled alongside and he looked in the window.

"Why didn't you tell me you wanted to leave? You said you wanted to go to a party," she said.

"Sorry. That was a mistake."

"Do you want a ride?" she said.

Neither spoke all the way down the hill, then she said, "You *are* a little strange. If I hadn't met you at Helen's, I don't know if I'd have picked you up back there at the bookstore."

"It must have been that vodka. I'm okay now," he said, watching the light from streetlights wash over her face. "You're the prettiest thing I've seen all day."

She looked at him, then shifted gears through an intersection.

"You would like to see my paintings? *Yesss?*" she said, imitating the poet at the bookstore.

It was a decaying Victorian house in the northwest part of town, a neighborhood that could go either way, become gentrified or turn into a slum. College students, retirees, and working people lived there, but also white dopers and at least one biker gang.

"I worked in this area for a few months," Hanson said as they pulled up to the house. "I enjoyed it."

You didn't have to be so careful with *white* dopers. If you knocked them on their ass, they couldn't accuse you of racism. You could use street justice on *white* assholes, save time and eliminate paperwork.

The house was falling apart, the ground beneath it humping up with tree roots, overwhelming the foundation. The elaborately carved door was warped, the stained glass peacock sagging in its lead seams so that it bowed out when Sara pushed the door open. Big, high-ceilinged rooms opened on either side of the entry hall. The room on the right was dark.

A TV lit the other one, lazy tendrils of marijuana smoke uncoiling in the blue light. Humphrey Bogart was on the screen, sitting with his feet on his desk, listening to a woman who stood in front of him wringing her hands.

A shirtless man looked at them from an overstuffed sofa in front of the TV. He was painfully thin, hair halfway down his back, his lips purple in the TV light. "Well, well," he said, "what have we brought back to our lair?"

"This is Mister Hanson," she said.

" 'Hanson' will do."

"Oh yeah?" the man said, in a Humphrey Bogart voice, "Hanson, eh? Just Hanson. No first names for tough guys. Is that it?"

"The cheaper the hood, the tougher the patter," Hanson said, a line from the movie, *The Maltese Falcon*, on TV.

The man laughed, then sucked on a joint. "I'm Timothy," he said, holding in the smoke, "a pleasure, *Hanson*. The movie's just starting. Let's have a triple date."

"Good night, Timothy," Sara said, pulling Hanson by the arm.

Bogart looked at the woman, exhaled, and watched the smoke drift away. When he spoke, both Hanson and Timothy said the words, "When somebody kills your partner, you're supposed to do something about it."

Timothy shrieked with laughter as Hanson and Sara went upstairs. "I think I'm going to like this one, Sweet Sara," he called after them.

As they turned at the landing, Hanson thought he saw someone else asleep on the sofa.

The walls in the small bedroom were almost completely covered with paintings—miniatures, the size of postcards, ten-by-twelve, bigger, a few the size of windows, framed and unframed, some not finished, all of them fitted together like parts of a puzzle.

Lizards and snakes and armored insects, part animal and part machine, done in a pointillist style, purple and turquoise, orange and yellow, black and bloodred. Reptiles in dripping green jungles, fighting, eating or mating, difficult to tell one activity from another, all fangs, gear-teeth and forked red tongues, their eyes droop-lidded and evil.

"How do you like them?" she asked.

He nodded, working his way to the end of the wall. "Who was the other guy down there?"

"Probably Lojeck," she said.

Hanson glanced at her.

"Timothy's current lover—an unemployed attorney," she said, smiling.

Hanson nodded, thinking she was the prettiest woman he'd ever come home with. Smart and rich, too.

"I did that one," she said, pointing, "last year when I was doing a lot of acid." It was a self-portrait, clearly her face, but she had the body of a Gila monster.

"Are you shocked?" she said, sitting on the bedspread, a quilt patterned with pentagrams. "Sometimes they shock people," she said as she took off her shoes. Her pale legs glowed through the pearly black stockings.

"Nothing shocks me anymore," Hanson said. "Nothing lately, anyway. I've decided that the weirdest thing I can imagine, there's a thousand people out there doing it right now.

"I'm not really with the ACLU," he told her, still a little drunk, his mouth dry.

She crossed her legs, slipped off one shoe, then recrossed them, the stockings hissing, like a long-fingered woman, Hanson thought, soaping her hands.

"I didn't think so," she said, opening the top button on her blouse.

"I *do* work for the city. That was true." He licked his lips. "Don't you ever worry, when you take somebody home like this, that he might be a maniac?"

"What do you do for the city?" she said, looking up at him, undoing the next two buttons. A siren wailed in the distance, and for a moment Hanson wasn't sure he wanted to be in this woman's bedroom. He might be happier at work.

"I'm a cop. Which is why," he said, slipping off the safari jacket and laying it across a chair next to the bed, "I'm wearing this gun."

"Wonderful." She smiled, her teeth flawless, as she stood up and slipped out of her skirt.

"You don't see garter belts very often. These days. Anymore," Hanson said, his voice almost a whisper.

She finished unbuttoning her blouse and it draped over the inner curves of her breasts, a few freckles showing in the cleavage. Light reflecting off the fabric gave her pale skin a green tint.

Hanson felt an enormous pressure on his chest, as if the shoulder holster was tightening up on him.

"You don't see shoulder holsters very much either," she said. "It's very sexy. The leather straps between your shoulders and your chest like that." She put her arms around him, her breasts touching his chest, her crotch against his, and ran her hands down his back, over the straps, to his waist. She smelled of perfume and cigarette smoke, sweat and vodka.

"What's that?" she said.

"Handcuffs."

"Oh, even better," she said, pulling them out of his belt. "Handcuffs at a poetry reading."

She held one of the silver cuffs and swung the other on the end of the short chain. Then she pushed the toothed jaw clicking through the ratchet until it dropped open. "What's this?" she said, holding the cuff in the light, rust-brown flakes in the teeth.

"Uh," Hanson said, "a couple days ago we had to arrest a guy who didn't want to go to jail. He got a little bloody before he decided to let us handcuff him. I've been meaning to clean them."

She put the open cuff over her left wrist and slowly closed it, one tooth at a time, *tic, tic, tic.* "I hope you have a key," she said, smiling and slipping off the blouse, working the cuffs through the sleeve and draping it on top of his jacket. "You ought to take off that heavy gun," she said, undoing the buttons of his shirt. Her breasts were milky white, blue veins deep inside. Hanson cupped one with his hand and kissed it. "Good idea," he said, hoarsely, slipping the straps off his shoulders like suspenders. "It's hot up here." He laid the holster and heavy gun on a chest of drawers behind him and slipped off his shirt and T-shirt.

She tugged his belt open, then stepped into him, her chest against his, and reached back behind him, lifting the holster. "What kind of a gun is it?"

"Do you know anything about guns?" he said.

"Just what I see on TV."

"Everything's TV."

"What does that mean?" she said.

"Nothing.

"I'll show it to you, but then we put it away. Then we forget about it."

"Show me."

When he turned and took the pistol out of the holster, she reached around his waist and cupped his crotch in her hands, the handcuff draped along the inside of his thigh.

"Smith and Wesson Model Thirty-nine," he said as he pushed the magazine release, dropped the clip out of the grip, and laid it on the dresser. "Holds nine rounds, eight in the magazine and one in the chamber."

He tilted the pistol, thumbed the safety down, and jacked the slide back. A glittering brass cartridge arced out of the receiver and Hanson caught it with his left hand.

"Let me see it," she said, kissing his ear.

"Nine-millimeter parabellum," he said, dropping it into her hand. "A good round. Half-jacketed hollow points. They come out of the gun at about eleven hundred feet per second. They're supposed to expand when they hit tissue, but," he said, tipping his hand side to side, "don't depend on it. Still a good round, though. Hundred and fifteen grain. A good gun."

"Can I hold it?" she said.

"Okay," he said, pulling the slide back once more, checking the empty chamber. "It won't fire unless this safety is *off,*" he said, putting the clip back in the grip. "Here," he said, handing it to her. "Point it at the wall and pull the trigger."

"It's *heavy,*" she said, taking a wide stance as she brought the brutal gun up. The muscles in her shoulder and arm stood out as she aimed at a painting of a blue lizard and pulled the trigger.

Click.

Still holding the pistol at arm's length, she smiled at him, shiny with sweat.

"Okay," Hanson said, taking the pistol from her hand, returning it to the holster. "Maybe we'll go shooting sometime."

She ran her hands down the sides of his chest to his waist, then unbuttoned his jeans. "You're a rough lover, aren't you?" she said. "It's okay. I kind of like that. I kind of like to fool around that way," she said, holding up her handcuffed wrist.

"I don't, uh . . ."

She took his wrist, gently, then tighter, pulling his hand to her chest, awkwardly mauling her breast with it.

"I don't think so," he said, pulling his hand away.

She dug her nails into his arm and lunged for the hand, catching the webbing between the thumb and forefinger with her teeth. She smiled up at him as she bit down.

He gripped her wrist and squeezed until her fingers lost their strength and opened.

"Okay," she said, "okay," laughing, "you're too strong."

"What really happened to your nose?" she said, touching the fresh scab on the bridge.

"The guy who didn't want to get handcuffed. He shoved me into a car door."

She smiled, then hit the bridge of his nose with the knuckles of her first two fingers.

"Is it tender?" she said, as it began to bleed.

"Come on," she said, unzipping his jeans. "I like it." She took his hand again and patted it against her breast.

"*Do* it," she said, looking into his eyes as she slipped her hand into his pants.

Hanson patted one breast with the palm of his hand, then again with the back of his hand.

"Harder," she said, removing her hand. "Don't *pat* it like some scared little guy. *Slap,*" she said, slapping his face.

She lowered her hand, and as she looked at him, Hanson could feel the blood run down the side of his nose.

"Okay?" she said.

She gasped when he hit her, then smiled.

"Give me your other wrist," she said, and snapped the handcuff on it.

TWENTY-TWO

FRIDAY AFTERNOON WAS hot and humid, and traffic was heavy on the Avenue, where greasy rainbows flared in the carbon monoxide. Hanson was hung over, patrolling the district in patterns where he could avoid driving west into the sun. The tent revival in the parking lot of the fire-gutted JC Penney's was already going strong, the loudspeakers squealing with feedback, and Hanson rolled his window up against the noise, muffling the evangelist's voice, ". . . say, 'Preacher, gimme another chance. Preacher, give me *one more chance.*' So I say, come back to the church. I believe a man can *redeem* himself. But it's gonna come a time. I *say*, it's gonna come a *time*. When it ain't gonna *be* no more chances . . ."

Dana was in court, so he'd be working alone for the first couple hours of the shift. He was supposed to team up with a temporary partner, a rookie or one of the guys in a wild car, but that was too much trouble for just a couple hours.

As he passed the liquor store next to the Mor-4-Les, an old man in a baggy suit stepped off the curb and yelled at him, waving his arm. Hanson flipped on his overhead lights to stop traffic, made a U-turn, and double-parked in front of the liquor store.

"Officer," the man said, pointing at the front end of a green Pontiac, "look here. I want you to write in your report that this damage is fresh." The car was ten years old, but it had been well taken care of. It had fender skirts and mud flaps, plastic-tipped curb feelers, purple running lights and a windshield visor. The interior was spotless.

"He backed into it, and I want satisfaction," he said, pointing to the old police car, painted black and primer gray, parked in front of the Pontiac. "I want it fixed. I wasn't even in the car."

His headlight had been broken, and the front quarter panel showed a streak of black paint transfer.

"Right there, officer. That's him," he said, pointing at Dakota as he came out of the liquor store, dressed all in black, carrying a half-gallon jug of vodka. A big poster in the liquor-store window showed Jerry Lewis, smiling, holding a little girl whose legs were wrapped in steel braces.

"Howdy," Hanson said, remembering him, staying an arm's length away, frisking him with his eyes. "This gentleman says that you backed into his car. Is that what happened?"

His eyes were bloodshot, but he didn't seem drunk. He looked at the broken headlight, then at the old man.

"Is that what he said?"

"Yessir. That's right."

Traffic behind Hanson had to slow down, the double-parked police car with flashing overhead lights creating a bottleneck.

Dakota turned from the old man and looked at Hanson, breathing through his mouth, like he'd forgotten what he was going to say. Maybe he *was* drunk, Hanson thought, but he hoped not. A DWI arrest would take up the rest of the afternoon.

"I must have done it then."

"Okay," Hanson said, "good. Simple enough. Could I see your driver's license, please?"

He pulled out a hand-laced leather wallet, the kind kids make in summer camp, and turned back a flap to show Hanson the cheap, mail-order badge, shielding it with his hand so no one else could see it. When Hanson ignored it, he tilted it to catch the light.

"Just your driver's license," Hanson said.

Dakota opened the wallet and thumbed through it with dirty

hands, his fingernails bitten to the quick, one fingertip crusty with dried blood, and removed a wrinkled California license.

"What about him?"

"Got it right here," Hanson said, holding up the old man's license.

Dakota partially blocked the door to the liquor store, and two young black men, bagged quart bottles in their hands, looked him up and down.

"Couple of gentlemen need to get by you there, looks like," Hanson said.

Dakota looked around at them, stepped a little farther out of the way, and they strutted past, one of them deliberately brushing Dakota's shoulder. They moved well down the sidewalk then, knowing better than to get between a cop and someone he might be arresting.

Hanson stepped up and took the license. "California, huh?" he said, smiling. "What part?"

"Vacaville. It's on the license."

Hanson leaned in to smell his breath when he spoke. No liquor. It smelled like burnt popcorn. What a job, Hanson thought, where you *try* to smell a person's breath, noticing for the first time how bad Dakota's teeth were.

"I'm on a case," Dakota whispered.

"Good," Hanson said. "Let me run a couple of checks, you two exchange information, and we can all be on our way."

The Muslims pulled up and parked just down the block, on the other side of the street. Four of them got out of the car, in their suits and bow ties and sunglasses, and stood on the sidewalk, watching. Hanson gave them a long "fuck you" look as he reached in the window of the patrol car for the radio mike, then heard Dakota speak to the two men who had been in the liquor store.

"What're *you* lookin' at, nigger? That's right. I'm talking to you, Sambo."

"Are you crazy?" Hanson asked him over the roof of the car, throwing the mike in the seat as the two men walked towards Dakota. "Just stay *there*, and don't say anything. Okay?"

Hanson walked around the back of the car, rolling his eyes. "I don't know," he said, his arms out, intercepting the two men. "Lemme talk to you, okay? Come on over here for a second," he said, herding them towards the Mor-4-Les while they shot looks over their shoulders at Dakota.

"I don't know *what* his problem is," Hanson said. *"Look* at me, okay? Would you do me a favor and ignore him? I just want to settle this accident. Get him out of here. Back wherever he came from, and be on my way. I'd appreciate it.

"Okay?" he said, looking at one, then the other, nodding as he backed away. "Thanks.

"C'mere," Hanson said to Dakota, gesturing as he walked back around the car. He spoke into his packset, running Dakota's name for warrants. ". . . and you might have another car slide by here if you got one available," he added, looking down the street at the impassive Muslims.

"What's wrong with you, man?" he asked Dakota, his voice low, the two men watching from the Mor-4-Les parking lot. "Look around. How many other white boys do you see? None. Zero. We got the Muslims down the street *lookin'* for trouble. If you start a race riot down here, we're at a big disadvantage. So be *cool.* All right?

"Sir," he said to the old man, "come on and look at the damage, if you would. We'll write this up so everybody will be satisfied, and we're gone."

They were kneeling down at the broken headlight when Dakota said, "You got something you want to say, *boy?"*

Hanson stood up and looked over at the two men, shaking his head, *no.* He opened the rear door of the patrol car. People were coming out of the Mor-4-Les to see what was going on.

"Why don't you get in here and sit down until we're through, okay?" he told Dakota. "We're already drawing a crowd."

"I was right about you," Dakota said. "You just don't *get* it."

"Please. Get in the car," Hanson said. "I don't need a riot this afternoon. I gotta *work* down here every day, okay? Get in there, sit down, we'll take care of the broken headlight, then we're gone, *adios,* no problem."

Dakota seemed not to hear him, watching the Muslims stroll up the sidewalk.

"Get in."

The jug of vodka burst on the street, and pain burned up Hanson's neck and exploded in his eyes, filling them for a moment with blackness and red sparklers.

The subject's license is valid and he has no outstanding warrants, the tinny voice on the packset said, far away.

Dakota had grabbed a fistful of Hanson's hair with one hand, snapping his head back, while pulling his pistol from the front-break holster with the other.

"I've got your gun, nigger lover."

The muzzle ground into his ribs, in the four-inch gap between the sides of his protective vest, the little *click click click* of the trigger muffled in his uniform shirt, racing through his chest like a heart attack.

Other car calling? the dispatcher asked from the packset as Hanson sidearmed it into Dakota's head.

Other car with traffic? as he drew back and drove it down again, aiming for his eye.

The stoplight down at the intersection changed from green to yellow.

It's gonna hurt, Hanson thought, when he finds the safety. The *click* would trigger a *boom* blossoming in his ribs, and it would hurt. He would taste powder and the copper slug as it burned into him.

The stoplight turned red as the packset bounced off Dakota's head, out of Hanson's hand, and as both of them fell into traffic noise, vodka and broken glass, grunting as they hit the street, Hanson watched an airliner high overhead until it disappeared in the shadow of a blue sedan as big as an ocean liner, rolling past on huge black tires. The bolt-studded transmission, the gas tank, the muffler and tailpipe floated over, like a space station in a movie. He threw himself on top of Dakota, both hands on his gun arm, pushing the pistol away from his face as Dakota snapped the hammer with his thumb.

Someone in overalls and brogans, his bare black feet showing through splits in the leather, walked through the traffic as Hanson fought for the gun, and then a thick black hand pressed the muzzle of a long-barreled old Webley .45 against Dakota's temple.

"I'll blow your head off," Pharaoh said. He jammed the muzzle into his ear, and Dakota rolled his eyes to look at it.

"That's right, cap'n," Pharaoh said. "I'll blow those blue-devil eyes clean off your face."

Dakota dropped the gun, and Hanson turned him onto his stomach and handcuffed him. He picked up the gun, holstered it, and stood Dakota up.

. . . uh, Five Eighty, we have a report of a possible rape, complainant . . .

Hanson picked up the packset and put it in the holder on his belt, turning the volume down as he walked Dakota to the still-open door of his patrol car. "Get in," he said, twisting the handcuffs, forcing him into a crouch, pushing him into the car and slamming the door. He leaned against the hot roof of the car, panting, as Pharaoh, his yellow hard hat catching the afternoon sun, pushed his shopping cart around the corner and out of sight.

A traffic car pulled up behind Hanson's car and its overhead lights came on. Fuller eased himself out the door and looked around at the crowd. He was a traffic cop who doubled his salary with court overtime.

"What you got?"

"This guy," Hanson said, nodding at Dakota, "tried to shoot me. Would you keep an eye on him while I get some witnesses' names?"

"Oh yeah? Sure. I'll watch the son of a bitch."

Hanson got the names and phone numbers and addresses from half a dozen people who'd seen the fight.

"What kind of a gun did he have?" Fuller said.

"Smith and Wesson Model 39," Hanson said, holding up his 9mm.

"You oughta be more careful, those . . ."

"I think I've already said that to myself. A couple of times."

"It's those front-break holsters you hotdogs wear, the gun butt sticking out. Just *invites* somebody to grab it. That's why I wear one of these old flap holsters," he said, slapping it.

"Thanks for swinging by," Hanson said. "Got all the names I need. I'll take this guy down to jail, then talk to detectives."

"What about me?" he said, rubbing his hand through his gray, crew-cut hair. "I'm the first officer on the scene."

"I'll put your name in the report."

"Thanks. I need all the overtime I can get."

Hanson got in the car, made a U-turn, flipped off the overheads, and almost ran a red light at the first intersection.

When the light turned green, he glanced at Dakota in the rear-view mirror. "Okay," he said, looking back at the road. "You have the right to remain silent. Anything you say can and will be held against you in a court of law . . ."

"Anything *you* say, white nigger, traitor, will be held against *you* in a *higher* court," Dakota said, just as they passed the Fred Meyer store where Hanson had made his first arrest, the first day they let him work alone as a rookie. He'd been pretty eager then, and had volunteered to take the call off his district.

"So you'd better figure out a way for me to escape."

A crowd had cornered him in the appliance department, Hanson remembered, a two-hundred-and-fifty-pound, retarded man the crowd said was a "child molester." He was crying, his nose running as Hanson walked him out to the parking lot, telling the crowd to ". . . stay back. I *mean* it. He's in *my* custody now." He'd put him in the back of the patrol car and then, making sure no one was watching, had wiped the handcuffed man's eyes and nose.

"You *hear* me?" Dakota shouted.

"Why should I do that?"

"I'll *tell* you why, white nigger. I might do some time, but I'll be out again. I'll find you."

Up ahead was the gas station where they'd found the kid with the "smile" button, dead on the toilet. They'd kicked in the locked door, which pissed off the owner. The kid had shit himself, of course, and was covered with vomit.

"You'd be a *dead* nigger now if there'd been a round in the chamber of that pistol," Dakota said. "The *real* police would be drawing chalk lines around your body right now."

Something called *The Harder They Come* was playing at the Pussycat Theatre. There were never more than a dozen people in the place at a time. It was a money-laundering operation, but no one had been able to prove it.

"Hey! I'm talking to *you*," Dakota shouted.

He and Dana had gone on a stabbing in the Pussycat once. The victim was in the men's room, moaning and bleeding on the dirty tile floor in one of the stalls, his pants down around his ankles. He was the projectionist. No one knew how to turn off the projector, so they listened to the movie while they waited for the ambulance, the soundtrack a combination of cheap porno music and moaning. It was pretty funny, the way the guy on the floor was moaning too.

"You have a family? *Do* you?" Dakota demanded.

Hanson wondered if Truman was okay.

"When you're home some night, and your family is asleep—you can hear them breathing and you go in to look at your wife asleep, or your little boy. I'll be out there in the dark. I like little boys. I like to make them obey me."

Hanson wondered if there were some way he could jerk Dakota out of the car and shoot him in the head. But it was too late now. The glass-and-steel high-rises were right up ahead. He should have thought of it sooner.

"You better let me *escape*."

Hanson turned right at a red light and drove two blocks to the twelve-story Justice Center.

"Hey," Dakota shouted, and the car shuddered. He'd slumped down in the seat and was kicking the cage with both feet. Hanson parked in front of the jail, the car shaking with each kick.

"Five Sixty Two," he said into the mike.

Five Six Two.

"I'm out in front of the jail with a prisoner . . ."

BANG. The heavy Plexiglas cage snapped against its hinges.

". . . and I think I'm going to need some help getting him upstairs."

BANG.

I can hear it. We'll have the jail send somebody down to give you a hand.

"Thanks. If I try to take him up myself I'd probably have to hurt him. And that's what I'd like to do."

Dakota had stopped kicking the cage. He'd scooted up on the backseat, his mouth against the cage.

"Don't you under*stand?* I won't *ever* forget. Every push-up I do in my cell, I'll imagine your little boy watching his momma suck my big, purple cock. I'll picture his face and what I'm gonna do to it after I fuck his ass."

A bus took on passengers up the block, mostly black people and old white people.

A patrol car from Central Precinct drove past, and Hanson waved to the driver, a guy he'd gone through the academy with.

The jailers came through the glass doors of the Justice Center, and Hanson got out of the car. They were both big guys with beer bellies, one white, one black.

Each of them had the last name of Miller. Everyone called the white guy "Miller Lite."

"Hey, Hanson," Miller Lite said, "what you got for us?" looking in the window at Dakota.

"This guy tried to shoot me with my own gun. He's been kicking the cage and threatening my family. If I put my hands on him, I might hurt him a little."

Miller bent down and looked through the window. "We'll handle it," he said. He opened the backdoor and said, "Come on outta
there, man. You gonna give us any trouble?"

"I'm not gonna give *you* any trouble, nigger. *He's* the . . ."

"Shut the fuck up," Miller said, jerking his arms up.

Hanson followed as they walked him into the building and back
to the wire-mesh jail elevator. They got in the elevator and closed
the door.

"Face the back of the elevator," Miller said.

"Fuck you, boy," Dakota said.

Miller smiled at Hanson, then jerked Dakota's arms back and
up, lifting him to his toes.

"Take care," Miller Lite told Hanson, as he pushed the UP
button. The elevator jerked and began to rise as Miller pulled out a
short blackjack.

Hanson listened to them until he couldn't hear anymore, then
he called North and asked if he could have the rest of the day off.

Hanson was wearing jeans, tennis shoes and a khaki workshirt
when he walked into the district attorney's office. The green can-
vas bag slung from his shoulder contained his pistol and handcuffs, a pen and a small notebook, a copy of the crime report on
Dakota, and a copy of *The Killer Angels*, a Civil War novel that
had just come out in paperback.

The room smelled of fresh paint and new carpets. The woman
behind the counter was typing, and Hanson waited for her to notice him. Finally he said, "Excuse me."

"Yes?"

"Hi, I'm Officer Hanson from North Precinct. I'd like to see DA
Werner."

"What is it regarding, please?"

"I think I've got an appointment."

"Hanson?" she said, looking down at her calendar. "No. I'm
sorry."

Hanson pulled out the Arrest Report and showed her the pink
appointment slip clipped to it.

She sighed. "We've had some scheduling problems since we
moved to the new building. I'll see if he can fit you in. What was it
concerning?"

"A guy who tried to shoot me on Friday."

She dialed the phone. "There's an Officer Hanson here who would like to see you."

She looked up. "From North Precinct?"

"Right," Hanson said.

"Yes. All right."

She hung up the phone. "Have a seat, please. He'll be out in a few minutes."

Hanson sat down on a mauve sofa beneath a stylized print of a cute little girl holding a cluster of balloons. He looked at the clock, then pulled the novel out of his bag and opened it to the map of Gettysburg facing page one. Black arrows snaked north, and white arrows arced down from the northwest, converging on the fields where thousands of men would die. Most of them veterans by then, Hanson thought, who would know how to stand up and die. Good soldiers.

He was on page fifteen when two men in suits came into the room. They laughed as they shook hands. The one in the gray three-piece said, "A shoot-out, then. One on one." He pretended he was shooting a basketball.

"Take no prisoners. You tell him I said so."

The other man said, "I will," and went out the door.

"Officer Hanson?" the man in the three-piece said.

"Right," Hanson said, standing up.

"I'm Bill Werner," he said, shaking hands. He was a handsome man, a few years older than Hanson. "How you doin'? Come on back."

They went through the door and down a hall lined with offices. "Sorry about the appointment mix-up," he said over his shoulder. "But you're pulling in that double overtime, right?

"Come on in. Have a seat," he said. "I've got an eleven-thirty appointment, but I think we've got time to get things rolling."

Hanson picked up the basketball that was on the chair.

"Sorry 'bout that. Just put it on the floor."

He sat behind his desk, picked up a manila folder and rapped it on his desk. "Good report. Lemme tell you, I read a *lot* of crime reports, and this one is really well written. That must have been some experience, though. I'll bet you had a couple of drinks after you got off work. Am I right?"

"Right," Hanson said, trying to smile but failing.

He glanced at his watch. "I'll get right to it. I can't file for attempted murder. For attempted murder I need holes and blood. Two, maybe *three* holes. I'm going to charge him with recklessly endangering. We can convict on that."

"Recklessly endangering," Hanson said, "is a misdemeanor."

"It carries a maximum penalty of nine months. We can get the max."

Hanson stood up, then sat back down. "Recklessly endangering is like," he said, thinking, "like a guy gets drunk. He walks out in the backyard on New Year's Eve and shoots off a rifle to celebrate, and the shot goes through a neighbor's window."

"Sure, but your case is *much* more serious."

Hanson stood up and drew his foot back to kick the basketball, but didn't. He walked to the window and looked down at the traffic below.

"Yeah, it was more serious." He turned and looked at the DA "The fuckin' guy tried to *kill* me. He stuck the gun in my side and pulled the trigger. Repeatedly. He pulled the trigger repeatedly. Then in the car he said, 'If there had been a round in the chamber you'd be a *dead* nigger.' "

"Why would he call you a nigger?"

"I guess he's crazy."

"Another potential problem if . . ."

"I've got six witnesses. Good witnesses. Willing to testify."

"Look. I know how you must feel. If it had been *me*, I'd want to see him in the electric chair. But we're dealing with the realities of the courtroom. That's *my* beat, and a jury is going to need more than we've got for attempted murder. We've got to have *serious injury*. Don't you see that there's no point in charging him with something we can't convict him of? He'll *walk*."

"I'll tell you what . . . Bill. If you're not going to charge him with attempted murder, don't charge him with anything," Hanson said. "*Let* him walk."

"Maybe we can look at 'assaulting a police officer.' Lemme look at that."

"Look up your ass," Hanson said, walking out the door, knowing what he'd just said sounded stupid.

"You're upset. I understand. Call me tomorrow," the DA said, following him out into the hall.

"Fuck you," Hanson said, almost walking into a woman in a tailored suit who looked at him like he was a criminal.

———

He'd had to park blocks away, in the small "Chinatown" section of the city. A number of Vietnamese had opened shops and were doing well, hard workers with strong family loyalties and a respect for the wisdom of their old people. Hanson had been meaning to pick up one of the cheap little cleavers all the shops carried, made of high-carbon steel that took a very sharp edge. He picked a shop at random, the New Vietnam Grocery, and went inside. The stink of Vietnamese cigarettes and *nuoc mam,* the cluck and whine of spoken Vietnamese like the ringing in his ears, surprised him, took him back, for just an instant, to *all* the war's smells and sounds, the old instincts soaring through him like a rush of speed.

But he resisted, like he always did, returning, a little light-headed, to where he was now. A Vietnamese grocery store. Not the sort of place where attorneys' wives shopped for ethnic dinner parties, though. Hanson was the only non-Vietnamese there, attracting attention that didn't seem friendly, but he tried to ignore it as he walked down the aisles of exotic goods. At first, he thought the soft hiss and thump was just his ears, anxiety, but it was a dishpan full of turtles, covered with a cage of chicken wire. One of them was on his back, tirelessly paddling his thick legs, trying to rock himself upright.

He walked past them, up another aisle, but couldn't ignore the sound. He walked back to the dishpan, looked to see that no one was watching, and knelt down. He couldn't reach the upside-down turtle through the wire with his fingers. The turtle was hard-eyed, like a hawk stripped of its wings and trapped—who knows why—in the dead weight of that shell, uncomplaining, heroic, Hanson thought.

He looked around again before trying to tip him over with a ballpoint pen, worried that someone would think he was trying to torment the creature.

He was about to give up when a pair of deformed feet wearing shower sandals stopped at the cage.

"You want turle?"

Hanson smiled up at him, still a little light-headed, the words making no sense.

"Turle. You want?"

Hanson nodded as if he understood, standing up. Then it came to him. *"Turtle.* Right. I'll take that one," he said, pointing to the one on its back. "I'll get it in a minute," he said. "Be right back."

Hell, he thought, walking up the aisle, I can put him out in the backyard. He smiled, wondering what Truman would think of a turtle.

When he took the cleaver to the cash register, the Vietnamese clerk put a package wrapped in butcher paper on the counter. "Turle. Okay. Very good."

Hanson thanked him, paid him, and dropped the package of turtle meat in a garbage can down the street.

DOC CALLED THREE nights later from a pay phone somewhere.

" 'Must be some *other* Hanson,' I said. 'The one I know wouldn't let some crazy person take his gun away.' But I was wrong. And the DA lettin' him off? That's some outfit you're working for. If it was me . . ."

The roar of a jetliner landing or taking off drowned out his voice for a few seconds.

". . . threw him over, or an accident . . ."

The roar became a whisper, lost in the long-distance static, ". . . three stories to the concrete floor and only broke a few bones. They say maybe he jumped over the railing 'cause he was ashamed of hisself. Lettin' those niggers fuck him in the ass the way he did."

The operator broke in asking for more money, and Hanson listened to the jingle and gong of coins.

"You be more careful."

"I'll try."

"Is that old dog still alive?"

"Yeah, he's . . ." The drone of the dial tone interrupted him as something broke the connection.

TWENTY-THREE

LIKES WHAT?'' Sara said.

"Ducks," Hanson said. "She likes ducks. Not real ducks. The *idea* of ducks. Duck designs. Duck themes. Duck, pardon my French, *motifs*. All over the house."

"How do you *relate* to these people?"

"Zurbo's a good cop," Hanson said, changing lanes to pass a pickup loaded down with firewood. "He's real smart."

Hanson felt pretty good, considering it was only nine in the morning. He smiled at Sara, reading her eyes. She didn't believe that a cop, in a working-class suburb, could be "smart." She almost said so.

He looked back at the freeway and slowly inhaled, her smell as distinct and recognizable as the way she looked. He closed his eyes and pretended he was blind.

"Sounds like a racist to me," Sara said.

"Because he says 'nigger'?"

"That's a pretty good indication."

He opened his eyes and checked the rearview mirror.

"Isn't it?" she said.

"The police are an army of occupation," he said, pulling back into the right lane. "There's combat every night. We're white and they're black. Sometimes we call them niggers, and sometimes they call us pigs, honkies, and white peckerwood motherfuckers." He laughed.

"In Vietnam, black guys, 'bloods,' called the Vietnamese gooks, slopes, and dinks. The Vietnamese called the Montagnards *moi*, 'savages,' and the Montagnards called them *dook braak*—'shit-eating monkeys.' That's just the way it is with people. It doesn't mean you're a racist."

"What?"

The van droned up a long hill, trucks passing on the left, the van shuddering.

"It's impossible to explain," Hanson finally said.

She leaned over and licked his neck, her breast against his shoulder. "How did you get this?" she said, touching the scabbed-over cut above his eye.

Hanson smiled, shook his head. "I got a little careless, and a guy named Eddie Delbert Moore hit me with a catsup bottle."

"Why?" she whispered in his ear, tracing the cut across his eyebrow with her finger.

"He didn't want leftover fish for supper, so he broke his wife's arm. One of her kids called the police."

"What happened after he hit you?" she said, pressing harder, the tip of her finger turning white.

"Dana got in a little stick-time on him," Hanson said, as though she wasn't hurting him, enjoying the game. "He's in the hospital now . . . *ow*."

She sucked the blood off her finger, her eyes on his, the van drifting over the center line into the path of an oncoming log truck. Hanson jerked the wheel, the chain-strapped logs rocketing past. Sara laughed. She took the finger from her lips and used it to stroke his erection through his Levi's.

He glanced at the back of the van where he had blankets and a sleeping bag. A PIE double trailer overtook and passed them, the cab and two trailers flexing like a snake, blowing the van towards the shoulder of the freeway.

"There's no place to pull over, between here and his house," Hanson said.

"Keep driving," she said, unzipping his jeans, and ducking her head under his arm.

"If he's so hot for machine guns, why didn't *he* join the army?" Sara asked as they walked to the door.

"He sure wanted to," Hanson said, ringing the doorbell, "but he'd just gotten married, and then their little girl, Alice, was born, and . . ."

Zurbo answered the door with a fat aluminum disk in his left hand and another one tucked under each arm. He looked Sara over quickly, politely. She was wearing tight jeans, soft leather boots, and a creme-yellow T-shirt with no bra.

"Hiya," Zurbo said, shaking her hand. "Dehumidifier units," he said, nodding his head at the disks, "gonna cook 'em while we're gone."

Ducks were everywhere, duck wallpaper, duck doormats, framed duck prints, duck coatracks, duck designs in the carpet, a cast-iron duck over the door that said, WELCOME TO OUR HOME.

They followed him to the oven where he added the disks to the others on the oven racks like metal cakes. He closed the oven door and turned on the gas with an open-ended wrench where the knob was missing. "Low heat for about eight hours dries 'em right out," he said, bending down like a housewife in a commercial to peer at the disks through the window in the oven door, a pistol stuck in his belt at the small of his back.

Zurbo used the dehumidifier disks in his "bunker," the reinforced garage with its steel shutters, counterbalanced 300-pound door, and perimeter alarms, where he kept his guns and ammo. He had .22s and .45s, 9 millimeters and .44 Magnums, heavy revolvers and sleek automatics. Colt, Smith & Wesson, Walther, HK, and Browning. He had riot guns and a seven-hundred-dollar sniper's rifle. He had four machine guns. Two of them with silencers. All legal. The ATF forms signed by the county sheriff, a friend of Zurbo's.

"You remember that guy up the street?" he asked Hanson, putting the wrench in his pocket. "The Mormon who borrows tools from everybody in the neighborhood and forgets to give 'em back?"

Hanson nodded.

"I was over there the other day, to get my big pry bar and this wrench back, and he shows me all the food he's got stored in the garage. 'A two-year supply,' he says. Now I *know* that the fuckin' Mormons do that. It's a good idea, I'll give 'em that, but I say, 'Oh. Is that part of your religious beliefs?' And he says, 'Yeah,' and I ask him, 'Do you have any guns?' He says, 'No.' And I look at all this food, like I'm *thinking* about it, and I say, 'You've got all this food and no guns, and I've got a lot of guns and no food. That's something, huh?' I hear he's putting his place up for sale.

"All set," he said, taking another look in the oven. "Honey," he called, "would you keep an eye on the oven while I'm gone?"

"I thought that case of nine millimeter was just for *emergencies*," his wife yelled from somewhere back in the house. "It's half gone already."

"Come *on*," Zurbo said, "I used a few boxes . . ."

"*More* than half gone. You've been into the case of forty-fives too. Those automatic weapons just burn it up."

"I'll look forwards to discussing it *later*, okay?" Zurbo shouted.

"What's to discuss? We're overdrawn again because you like to play with . . ."

"I collect guns, you collect ducks," Zurbo shouted. "If the fuckin' *economy* collapses, like I know it will, and the niggers are out takin' whatever they want, you gonna defend the place with ducks?

"My wife," Zurbo told Sara. "We were having a little disagreement before you got here."

"I'm not worried about niggers," she yelled. "That piece-of-shit stove is gonna kill us first."

"There's *nothing* wrong with . . ."

"We'll all wake up dead some morning."

"Let's go out to the bunker," Zurbo said, raising his voice, "*where we can have a normal fucking discussion.*

"*Willkommen,*" he said, unlocking the fireproof door to the garage, "*en meinen Bunker.*"

Stacked on his filing cabinet, broken-down sofa, and the gerbil cages were old issues of *The National Rifleman* and *Shotgun News.* Zurbo liked to say, "The only newspaper I read anymore is the *Shotgun News.*" His old Pontiac sagged in the rear from the weight of guns and ammo.

"If that oven *did* start a fire, which it won't, and if it burned through that door, which it wouldn't, we'd *make* the six-thirty news. Even with all the stuff I'm taking, there's enough shit in here to flatten the whole neighborhood. Surprise, surprise," he said, laughing to himself, "a smoking crater and no more suburb." He looked out the window, across the street, at a man watering his yard. "If it ever *does* go," he said, pointing out the window, "I hope *that* guy and his dog *Bruno* are walking past. *Bruno.* The dog shits on my yard. I've asked the guy, you know, in a nice way, 'How about not letting Bruno defecate on my yard. I'd appreciate it.' He gets huffy. 'It's not Bruno,' he says. Right," Zurbo said, throwing up his arms. "There's one other dog around here, a little poodle some lady owns. He's not dropping turds the size of sweet potatoes in my yard.

"Maybe the niggers are *busing* their dogs in from the Avenue, to shit on white people's suburbs. I just now thought of it. Fine. They were slaves for two hundred years and we owe them. Tyrone is bringing his Dobermans to shit in my yard."

"Who's . . . Ty-rone?" Alice asked, rolling through the door in her electric wheelchair, her head twitching, sunlight flashing off her thick glasses.

"You know who Tyrone is," Zurbo said.

"Yeah," she said. "Just givin' . . . givin' ya," she said, "a hard. Time. How you doin' . . . Hanson?"

"Pretty good, Alice. This is my friend, Sara."

She smiled shyly at Sara, tried to say something, then rolled the wheelchair over to the gerbil cage, the little wheel squeaking with a running gerbil, others streaking from one pile of cedar chips to another, thousands of rounds of ammunition stacked in green steel boxes behind the cage.

Zurbo pushed a button that opened the heavy garage door. "Hey," he said, when the chain drive stopped clanking, "you in the wheelchair. When you get tired of watching those *rats*, be sure and arm the motion detectors, okay?"

"Try not to . . . shoot yourself . . . in the foot," she said.

Zurbo smiled at her humped back, his eyes shining. "I'll try not to," he said. Then he turned, ramrod straight, thrust his right hand out towards the open garage door, and barked, *"Zum front!"*

They'd been on a potholed, two-lane road for half an hour, wind blowing through the windows of the car, when Zurbo put his hand to his ear. *"Raus."*

It was another quarter mile before Hanson heard it. The crackle of submachine guns, assault rifles, and the pounding of a larger gun.

"Achtung!" Zurbo said. "Many automatic weapons . . . the boss thirty-cal honking in the background."

It doesn't sound like a firefight, Hanson thought, trying to relax. Too many different guns, firing long bursts at random, without regard for one another. It was not the sound of two units trying to kill each other. They took the dirt road towards the firing, past the hinged sign, Master Blasters MG Meet.

The Big Pine gun range was a bullet-torn swath of bare dirt bordered by low banks of scrub pine and brush. A little roofed grandstand, weathered and sagging, fronted the firing line. Two teenage girls had set up a lemonade stand at one end, and they waved at Zurbo as he drove through the gate.

"Sisters," Zurbo said. "Their folks own that dairy farm we passed. They never miss a meet."

Zurbo pulled in next to a VW thing painted to look like a German staff car. "Keep an eye on our stuff," he said. "I gotta check with the range master."

He walked away just as the .30 caliber was drowned out by a pile-driver booming that snapped Hanson's head around. Sergeant Becker's .50 caliber, the size of an Oldsmobile transmission. Becker had paid four thousand dollars for it, and the six-inch bullets cost two dollars apiece.

It didn't sound like a *rational* firefight, Hanson decided. He tried not to look nervous, fighting his instinct to dive under the car, keeping track of every shooter over Sara's shoulder. He smiled at her, gun smoke in his nose like some bad drug he'd survived and almost forgotten. "A few months ago," he told her, "I asked Sergeant Becker *why* he wanted a .50 caliber. *Why* he wanted one," Hanson shouted over the guns, his eyes cutting away from hers.

"He's a *cop?*" she shouted.

"Yeah. Works downtown. He *said* . . . 'It'll kill *anything.* Three miles *away.*'"

She didn't smile, and Hanson realized it wasn't a joke for everyone. Maybe, he hoped, she just hadn't heard him over the shooting. He shook his head, as if saying, "Pretty crazy," feeling the half-assed smile on his face, wishing he was at home instead of standing in this baked-dirt field, the crackle and *boom* of the guns touching his scalp and the back of his neck like the first stirring of bad weather to come. The fifty-five-gallon drums danced in the dust, ricochets droning away, and downrange white scars broke through the trunks of the big trees. Gunshot wounds.

"Some fun, huh?" he shouted at Sara, just as the range master, sitting behind his .30 caliber in a plastic lawn chair, shouted something through a bullhorn and the firing slowed. In the growing quiet, Hanson heard only thousands of shrieking birds in his ears, trying to read Sara's lips. He nodded, as if he knew what she was saying, happy to see Zurbo coming back. Zurbo laughed at something Sara said, and she put her arms around his neck and kissed him. ". . . shoot," he said, coming closer. "She wants to shoot."

The range master, a pale, heavy man, wearing long sleeves, sunglasses, and a cowboy hat glittering with dozens of badges and stickpins, pulled on a huge pair of asbestos gloves. He squared his shoulders and picked up the heavy gun by the grip and the perforated barrel jacket, the belt of finger-long bullets draping down onto his cowboy boots. He stumbled, got his balance back, and pulled the trigger, leaning into the gun like it was a fire hose, advancing, John Wayne style. He held the trigger down, the belt of ammo snaking up through the receiver of the smoking gun, spent brass glittering out the other side.

Hanson thought that he'd have been assigned to a year of KP for shooting like that, burning out the barrel, instead of using three-round bursts.

The range master heaved the butt of the gun onto his hip, turned towards the applause and tipped his hat through the silver-blue heat waves rising from the gun. "Cease fire," he shouted, looking left, then right, shifting the gun into a more recognizable *Sands of Iwo Jima* swagger. "Clear on the left! Clear on the right!

"All clear," he shouted, and two twelve-year-old boys ran from the bleachers with a four-by-eight piece of plywood, the red CEASE FIRE bleeding dried paint. Once the sign was up, more kids swarmed down range to autopsy the lacy fifty-five-gallon drums, shaking the blue-green propane bottles—looking for flattened bullets—then propping them back up like exploded bowling pins. Local boys and farmers in overalls watched from the sidelines.

Sara got in line for the Porta-Potty, while Zurbo and Hanson unloaded the trunk, stacking the ammo boxes behind the car. Hanson was leaning into the trunk, about to lift two more ammo

cans out, when, through the chirping in his ears, he heard Zurbo
say, "Your truck-stop buddy's girlfriend . . . ?"

He froze for a moment, gripping the handles of the cans, then
heaved them out and stacked them on the others. He nodded,
"Uh-huh," reaching farther back in the trunk for the tarp Zurbo
used to catch spent brass. "Asia?"

"Right. His ex-girlfriend now . . ." Zurbo said, tapping an AK
47 magazine into his palm to align the rounds ". . . is turning
tricks out of the Palms Motel. And guess who's got her on his
snitch payroll? I hear she signed a complaint against your pal,
and Fox got a warrant for Assault Two, but he's keepin' it in
reserve. Terry, the janitor downtown," he said, leaning into the
trunk, "tells me Fox has been working real late, all night sometimes."

They laid the tarp on the cans, and Zurbo slammed the trunk.

"I guess I'm fucked," Hanson said. "Seems like everybody in
the department knows it was me at the truck stop."

"Naw. Half a dozen." He smiled. "Maybe ten or twenty *think* it
was you, but most of 'em don't give a fuck. So don't panic," Zurbo
said, picking up a can in each hand. "Peetey is stupid, but Fox
isn't, and he'll break the rules if he has to, when he's really after
somebody.

"Damn," he said, "whenever you get a new haircut, you look
like you're about twelve years old. I bet you get carded when you
buy beer."

"Sometimes," Hanson said, picking up a pair of cans. "What
about Internal Affairs?"

"Rivas and McCarthy think you're okay. Did you know that
McCarthy had a kid who got killed over there? Hundred and First
Airborne. Three weeks after he got in-country, his first patrol,
some dipshit tripped or something and shot him in the back of the
head.

"Took it real hard. On the sauce all the time after it happened.
Everybody tried to cut him some slack for a while, even the brass.
Then he fucked up—real bad—on a situation, something they
wouldn't have been able to ignore, but I happened to be in the
right place at the right time, and made it go away."

They walked together towards the bleachers and the "ammo
point," taking deliberate, slow steps, leaning left, then right with
the weight of the ammunition.

"Those two," Zurbo said, "Rivas and McCarthy, know where

most of the bodies are buried. They keep an eye on Narcotics and Vice.

"Dope and buy-money," Zurbo said, "*will* lead a person astray. Then there's the whores. Some of them are pretty good-looking, for a while. I hear Fox might have something going with this 'Asia.'"

"Fox?"

"That's what I hear."

"He *hates* whores," Hanson said, "and I've never seen him out with a woman, period. For a while I thought he might be a little queer."

They set the cans down behind a yellow ribbon marking the ammo point. Zurbo put his hands on his hips and leaned backwards, rolling his head across his shoulders.

"Everybody's a little queer," he said, "one way or another. Some just hide it better than others."

"Hi, Officer Zurbo," one of the girls at the lemonade stand called.

"Shane and Blaine, the lemonade ladies," Zurbo said. "You two are better-looking every time I see you."

"Could you possibly sell us a couple of lemonades? Great. Hey, I want you to meet my buddy, Hanson. He was in Special Forces over in Vietnam."

Hanson smiled sheepishly at Shane and Blaine, waved "Hi," and leaned closer to Zurbo. "Gimme a break."

"What?"

"You know 'what.'"

Zurbo grinned. "I'm proud of you. You did a good job over there."

"That was a long time ago."

"Come on," Zurbo said, "let's get us some lemonade and look at automatic weapons.

"Before I forget, though, I was talking to a guy who works for Tillamook County, outta the sheriff's office, a deputy I used to go hunting with. That incident at the truck stop happened to come up. He says all those interagency memos disappeared, and now they can't even find the original paperwork on it. Gone."

Hanson looked at him.

"That's what I hear. Yeah. But nobody's too upset, 'cause both those guys who went to the hospital are well-known assholes out there.

"This deputy's kid got in a jam with a whore and a gun, over on Five Ninety's district a while back. His old *man's* gun, and it went off. The kid had a pocketful of Seconals too.

"Make that *three* lemonades," Zurbo said, when he saw Sara on her way across the lot.

"Nobody got shot, though," Zurbo went on, watching Sara over Hanson's shoulder. "The gun got back to the . . . county, the pills disappeared, and the whore's pimp thought she should go work down in California for a while.

"She looks like a real firecracker," he said, smiling at Sara. "Master Blaster lemonades, all around," he called to her, putting his arm around Hanson's shoulders.

"Try not to step on your dick anymore," he told him. "At least for a while."

They drank their lemonades and strolled over towards the guns. Sgt. Becker's .50 caliber had drawn the largest crowd, the kind of people you might see at the auto show around a finely tuned hemi-head .427 V-8.

A smaller, quieter group was examining a WWII German machine pistol, the MP .38, one of the finest weapons of that war. Displayed in a panzer-gray, felt-lined case, it had the patina of old pewter, and they might have been admiring a piece of Tiffany glass or a silver flute. When the owner saw Sara, he asked her to pose with it.

"Seconal," Zurbo said, shaking his head, watching Sara tuck the evil-looking gun against her breast. "I wish it had been amphetamines or codeine, something useful. Seconal just makes you dumb."

Sara was the sexiest woman at the meet, a slumming aristocrat with a machine gun, erotic and dangerous-looking, posing for the middle-aged men drifting over to snap her picture with fifty-dollar instant cameras.

"Tanya!" one of them called to Sara. "Patty Hearst." "Sling it with the assault strap," a man in a lime-green orlon shirt called, pushing past his wife for a better angle.

It was like any other gathering of collectors or enthusiasts, Hanson thought—the Corvair club, Audubon Society birdhouse carvers, Civil War buffs, people you'd expect to see at the Elks Club, or convoying across Arizona to the Wally Bynum Airstream

Trailer Annual Splendorama. People who have one thing in common, who get together on Sunday afternoons and feel like they belong.

But there were some you *wouldn't* see at those other get-togethers, loners who never smile and rarely talk, wearing fatigues and jump boots, their eyes hidden behind aviator sunglasses.

The MP .38's owner snapped a leather strap on the gun, and helped Sara sling it over her head and across her chest.

"Come on," Zurbo said. "Let's look at the real stuff." Hanson waved to Sara, and they walked on to the rows of blanket-covered card tables displaying weapons. The collectors, milling around or sitting behind the tables, stopped smiling when they first saw Hanson. It was his shirt. He'd worn the "ANOTHER MOTHER FOR PEACE" T-shirt he'd found at the jail after one of the anti-war demonstrations, other people who wanted to "belong." Zurbo had smiled at the shirt and said, "These folks aren't big on irony." And because he was with Zurbo, they nodded when Hanson asked permission to pick up a weapon, and soon they were smiling and nodding in approval.

The weapons were beautiful, and Hanson enjoyed handling them, cocking and locking them open, feeling their weight and balance in his hands. He was accepted by the others because of his obvious skill and familiarity with the guns, and his pleasure in handling them.

Submachine guns—little stamped-steel MAC 10s in .45 and 9mm; Car-15s; a solid, dependable Thompson; crude Sten guns and M-3s; a rare Stirling, its 30-round magazine side-mounted; sexy, expensive HKs; little selective-fire M-1 carbines; Uzis; and Swedish Ks—designed to kill small groups up close, in trenches, restaurants, hallways, people in living rooms, kitchens, or behind the wheel of a car.

The assault rifles were effective at longer range, AKs, FNs, Galils, M-16s, SIGs and AUGs, 308s, 223s, the Communist 762x39s; Hanson knew them all, handling them, *moving* with them like a professional athlete on a team sponsored by the local tavern. He didn't notice the people wandering over to look at him until Zurbo announced, "He was in Special Forces in Vietnam," then grinned at the look Hanson gave him.

"Is that right?" said a heavy man in black trousers, a light blue shirt draping over his belly.

"Yes, sir," Hanson said quietly, putting down the exotic, scoped SIG, looking for a way out of the crowd as Sara came up behind him.

"I was with the First Air Cav."

Hanson looked up, smiled politely, nodded.

"Long Range Recon," he added, his tone a challenge, wearing baggy fatigue pants and a T-shirt with a grinning skull beneath the words, "DEATH FROM ABOVE." He had long hair and a full beard, like a biker, obviously the group's resident Vietnam veteran. His wife, or girlfriend, dressed in tight jeans with a rodeo buckle, tight western shirt, cowboy boots and hat, looked Sara over.

"Down there in War Zone C?" Hanson said.

"Highlands," he said. "Cambodian border."

"Right," Hanson said, trying to be pleasant. "You guys did a great job down there."

He nodded, his hair shaking on his shoulders, looking at Hanson, who tried to avoid eye contact, because his eyes would *not* be pleasant, and he didn't want trouble here with Zurbo's friends.

"Better go get our stuff," Hanson said, putting his arm around Sara, "burn up some ammo."

"What was *that* all about?" Sara asked him. "I thought all you guys were 'buddies.' "

Hanson smiled, walking towards Zurbo's car. "Do I *look* like the kind of guy who would be buddies with him? I wasn't *buddies* with most of the guys in Vietnam. I wasn't buddies with a lot of guys in Special Forces. I don't even know if that guy with the hair over there was really *in* Vietnam. He might have been a truck driver, or a cook, or a motor-pool mechanic. I *do* know he wasn't with any 'Long Range Recon' unit."

"How do you know?"

"The same way you'd know if his girlfriend said she was a debutante from the Baltimore Cotillion."

"When do I get to shoot?" she said.

The kids set the propane bottles up like bowling pins, took down the CEASE FIRE sign, and the ragged assault line of hobbyists blasted away. A fat lady firing a Thompson raised her hand. "Honey, it jammed on me again," she crooned. Her boyfriend cleared the weapon, put in a new magazine, and stepped back as she ripped it off in one long burst, the muzzle rising, spraying heavy brass-jacketed .45s into the splintered dying trees down-range, her breasts and heavy arms rippling with recoil.

"I hope they don't ever come in here to do any logging," someone shouted through the firing.

The veteran in the "DEATH FROM ABOVE" T-shirt stood behind his girlfriend, helping her hold an AK 47 as if it was a bat at a softball game. She fired a burst, shouting, "I love this gun. I just *love* this damn gun."

Zurbo smiled at Sara, screwing a fat, black suppressor onto the stubby barrel of his MAC 10 machine pistol. Hanson took it from him, locked in a 32-round magazine and walked Sara to the nearest gap in the firing line, between the fat woman with the Thompson and the veteran. He ignored Hanson's nod, staring at him through mirrored sunglasses while his girl emptied the assault rifle, its distinctive, flat rate of fire taking Hanson back to ambushes and firefights, red mud, leeches, medevac choppers, the wounded arching their backs and bucking in pain, bodies wrapped in ponchos.

Hanson smiled back at him, holding the slab-sided MAC in one hand, pointed at the sky. He stepped in behind Sara and brought the gun down, his arms around her.

"Take the grip," he said, his lips on her ear so she could hear him over the noise. "And hold it *here*," he said, placing her other hand on top of the suppressor, covering it with his own, and she pressed back into his crotch. A fine oil of sweat, dust, and perfume glistened on her neck.

"Keep the barrel down. Pull the trigger and release. Bursts of three and four."

The muzzle jumped up against his hand on hers, like it was trying to take flight, spitting hot brass out the side.

She laughed, recovering from her surprise. "I've got it now," she said, emptying the clip in quick, muffled bursts. Hanson replaced it with a full clip, cupped her breast, and whispered, "Try it this way."

She arched her neck against his jaw, looking back at him, and he could *feel* her laughing as she fired. She took a wider stance, the muscles in her thighs flexing through the soft denim of her jeans, shuddering into Hanson.

Finally, the range master called for a "mad minute," all four .30 caliber Brownings, the M-60, and Becker's .50 caliber firing at once, from tripods. Their muzzle blasts raised dust devils, caustic with gunpowder, blowing back on the husband and wife in matching camouflage fatigues, who stalked back and forth behind them, the husband filming with a super-8 movie camera, his wife with a tape recorder over her shoulder, holding a parabolic microphone out towards the guns.

"That war you went to," Zurbo shouted in Hanson's ear. "Was there really an *enemy* over there?"

"I think so," Hanson said, "but they were always dead by the time I got a look at 'em."

"I talk to guys I knew back in high school," Zurbo said. "They all went. We'll get drunk together and after all the war stories are used up, I'll start to, *interrogate* them, in a way. None of 'em remember seeing whoever was killing them over there. Guys just took a wrong step and blew up, or fell down dead with a bullet from nowhere, or got bombed by their own airplanes, or committed suicide . . ."

HANSON TOOK SARA HOME. The creaking Victorian was empty, his voice echoing when he asked her, "Where's Tiny Tim?" He followed her up the stairs, his legs aching, taking a fistful of her hair, stopping her at the landing, turning her face to his and kissing her opened mouth before they climbed the rest of the way to her bedroom.

They pulled off their clothes, sunburned and exhausted, filling the room with the smell of gunpowder. He gripped her sunburned shoulder, watching her smile with pain the harder he squeezed, leaving a white print of his hand in the sunburn, an oily silt of sweat and dust between her breasts. Her lipstick flaking off, her lips cracked from the sun, salty when he kissed her.

"Wait," she said, and walked naked to the little refrigerator in the corner of the room. Later, Hanson would remember that it was exactly like the one Doc had in Da Nang when he was there doing courier work for Sergeant Major, the bungalow paid for with C.I.A. cash.

She opened the door, the light inside throwing a nimbus around her damp hair and sweaty arms in the shadowy room, then turned, holding a purple vibrator in one hand, and something else in the other.

"I like it when they're cold," she said.

It was late when he got home, sober for a change, and checked the pebble under the door, expecting to hear Truman coming through the blackberry bushes behind him. He looked out towards the barn, rolling the pebble around in his hand.

"Hey. Truman. Where you at, buddy?"

He kneeled and pressed his hand on Truman's favorite spot on the porch. It felt warm.

"Out there in the studio audience. You in the dog costume. Come on *down*."

He closed his hand over the pebble, shook it a few times, then went inside. He tapped the spiderweb, and the spider appeared at the quivering rim of the web, looking for food.

It climbed towards the center in quick zigzags, stopped, and looked at Hanson.

"Where's Truman?" Hanson said.

The spider leaped free and dropped away, riding a single strand of silk into the shadows.

Hanson took a beer out to the porch where he opened it with a hiss, holding it at arm's length, out towards the barn.

"Hear that? Truman?"

He drank the beer, waiting, called Truman once more, then went inside. He came back out with a flashlight in one hand and his pistol in the other, just as Truman crashed through the brush, panting and limping, into the clearing by the gardens.

"What you been . . ."

The dog's ears went up and he turned, growling. Hanson swept the flashlight through the high grass, the blackberries, to the barn and beyond, then turned it off and listened.

Truman stopped growling, limped up onto the porch and lay down on his spot, head up, watching the yard. His fur was wet, and blackberry thorns had scratched his muzzle. He ignored the bowl of beer Hanson set next to him.

"What'd you find out there, buddy?" Hanson said, wiping him down with a towel. "A snake? I was worried about you, man."

Truman refused to go into the house, and Hanson propped the door open for him, wide-awake himself now. He treated himself to a shot of cognac, then another, looking through a copy of the *Shotgun News*. But he couldn't keep his mind on it.

"Thought I'd stay out here with you," Hanson told Truman, throwing a sleeping bag down, a shotgun in his hand.

"If there *is* anything out there," he yelled, "this buckshot should take care of it," cocking the shotgun, *clack-clack*.

"Wake me up if you need me," he told Truman, and fell asleep telling him about perimeter guard duty, listening posts, two hours on, two hours off, after the camp had been overrun, NVA sappers in the wire every night.

In the morning, Hanson remembered seeing a fire during the night, out in the blackberries, way beyond the barn. But he couldn't be sure it wasn't just a dream. Holding the shotgun close to his body, he worked his way through the blackberries, stopping to listen when he smelled gasoline and charred wood. He heard crickets, a high-flying jetliner, the birds in his ears, and kept going until he found the campfire. The ashes were warm. One person had been there, and Hanson followed his footprints until he lost them on the sunbaked dirt road along the irrigation canal.

The phone was ringing when he got back to the house.

"Hanson?"

It was Miller, the black one, down at the jail.

"I thought I should let you know, he escaped from the hospital sometime last night. The recruit they assigned to guard him just got out of surgery. What I hear, they were able to save one of his eyes."

Truman squeezed through the screen door and lay down in a patch of sunlight.

"The motherfucker can't get far, the way he was fucked up from the fall. Half the day shift's looking for him.

"Hanson?"

"I'm here."

"He sure did have a hate for you," Miller said. "The word is, though, he's gonna die resisting arrest. This time. Or maybe commit suicide with a gun he found somewhere. That recruit was a nice kid."

"Thanks for calling, man."

TWENTY-FOUR

THOUGHT IT MIGHT be worth checking by," Rivas said. "Hope I didn't interrupt anything."

"Wish I could tell you I found something," Fox said.

McCarthy waited impatiently by the door, ignoring Peetey, who was looking through a stack of Field Contact Report Cards on his desk, the July issue of *Police* magazine open facedown in front of him. "Can we get some lunch, then?" McCarthy said.

"Thanks again," Rivas said, ignoring McCarthy. "Let us know if there's ever anything we can help you guys with."

"No problem," Fox said. "I'll let you know if I turn anything up."

Down the hall, Rivas said, "Hey, I hope you'll forgive me for allowing police work to delay your lunch."

"If you'll make an effort to avoid it in the future," McCarthy said, pushing the DOWN button on the elevator.

"That grease is gonna kill you."

"One of the dangers of police work," McCarthy said, looking down the hall towards Fox's office. "The fucker's lying to us."

"Yeah," Rivas said.

"Come *on*, goddammit," McCarthy said, punching the button with his thumb.

The doors opened and they got in.

"I don't *like* the fuckin' guy," McCarthy said. "No sense of humor. And I don't trust anybody, with more than five years on, who's still that serious about 'fighting crime,'" he said, as the doors closed.

Back in the Narcotics and Vice office, Fox dug the composite drawing of Hanson and Doc out of the wastebasket where he'd dropped it when Rivas came in and continued his name search.

Peetey turned the *Police* magazine faceup. Miss July was twirling a pair of silver handcuffs on her finger, a police badge and a nickel-plated .25 automatic wedged into her black garter belt. The calendar inset above her naked shoulder asked, "DO YOU HAVE COURT TODAY?"

Peetey opened the bottom drawer of the metal desk and reached inside, his eyes on Miss July. He pulled the drawer out farther, digging through old paperwork and report forms. Finally, he leaned down and looked, kicked the drawer shut, and went through the other drawers, one by one, slamming them closed.

Fox turned in his chair.

"Mother*fucker*," Peetey said, opening his equipment bag, digging through the report forms, penal codes, disposable plastic handcuffs, leg shackles, sap gloves, extra ammo.

"What?" Fox said.

"That Nazi .45."

"The throwdown gun?"

"It's gone."

"It's probably in the van somewhere."

"No, it's not," Peetey said, opening the bottom drawer again.

"We'll *check*."

"I *know* it's not in . . ." He sat up and looked at Fox.

"Ira . . . Asshole . . . Foresman. He was sitting here last night. When we were out of the room to sign for that snitch money."

"He's not *that* stupid," Fox said.

Peetey just looked at him.

"We'll talk to him," Fox said, looking from the composite drawing to the computer screen. "I'm *on*to something here, but, *shit.* I've gotta crank up the teletype to get it from this hick southern department."

"Well, *gosh*, Andy, think we can catch the varmint?" Peetey said, trying for some kind of southern accent.

Ignoring him, Fox went into the teletype room and typed his information into a gray steel contraption the size of a two-door Studebaker, then went back to his computer. Fifteen minutes later, the office shuddered as the teletype began printing out the response to his query.

DD WAG JU 16:51 Wednesday 23 JUNE 75 KBZ 01 # 12 ENTER: 345090 FROM #12 00516 S/14 GAFFNEY, S.C. ATTN ALL UNITS—SUSPECT INFO ON MURDER SUSP, THIS LOCATION 15 FEBRUARY 74. SHOT VICTIM RANDALL "JUNIOR" LOTT MW 3/5/46 NUMEROUS TIMES WITH 9MM HAND GUN AT "RANDY'S FILLUP" 7-ELEVEN. ROBBERY APPARENTLY NOT A MOTIVE. SUSPECT APPARENTLY RECOVERED EXPENDED BRASS, POSSIBLY TO PREVENT COMPARISON ID. ROUNDS RECOVERED FROM VICTIM TOO DISTORTED FOR RELIABLE COMPARISON. NO VEHICLE SEEN. FOLLOWING ACU-KIT COMPOSITE BASED ON INFORMATION FROM POSSIBLE WITNESS.

CAUTION—SUSPECT SHOULD BE CONSIDERED ARMED AND DANGEROUS

The machine hesitated, changed gears and slowly printed out a grainy composite that could have been any black male in America between the ages of fifteen and sixty.

"Go to lunch," Fox told Peetey. "I've got a lot of work to do."

"Want me to bring you something back?" Peetey said, his feelings hurt.

"Yeah. A Diet Coke and some potato chips. Barbecue potato chips."

"You got it," Peetey said.

"Diet Coke."

''**Y O U ' L L   D O U B L E   Y O U R** money in three years," Dana said.

Hanson crumpled up the bag containing leftover french fries and what was left of a Big Mac, peeled the top off his coffee, and set it on the grimy dashboard of the patrol car.

"It's up to you," Dana said, taking a sip of his coffee, "but why give all that money to the IRS when you don't have to."

"It's simple. The city gives me my check, I put it in the bank. The IRS takes what they want, fine. I don't have to worry about it."

"What I'm saying, though . . ."

Five Sixty Two . . .

"We're still at lunch," Hanson said, talking to the face of the radio.

. . . incomplete call for the police. Four ten North Cook. A woman screaming in the background. We don't have any other cars available.

"Shit."

The steaming cups of coffee went out the windows as Hanson snatched up the mike and Dana started the car.

"Five Sixty Two's got it," Hanson said, as Dana turned on the overhead lights and pulled out into traffic.

"Yeah, yeah," Hanson said, jamming the mike back down on the radio. "Screaming in the background. Barking dog complaint, screaming in the background. Stolen bike report, screaming in the background. Somebody *always* be screaming in the background."

Dana laughed, slowed at the intersection, checked both directions and ran the red light.

. . . and Five Sixty Two, when you clear that call, we have a couple more backed up on the district.

It was Dana's call, a duplex with a row of dead shrubbery across the front. He rapped on the door with his nightstick. "Police. Police officers." He cocked his head, listening, while Hanson looked up the street, watched the windows and kept an eye on both corners of the building.

Dana tapped again, harder, "Police officers," then tried the doorknob and looked at Hanson. Hanson shrugged, and Dana pushed the door open.

"Police."

"Police officers."

Dana swung the door around until it touched the wall as they stepped into the living room and the familiar smell of sweat and cigarette smoke, spoiled food and urine.

A pink princess phone was on the floor, its coiled cord tied in knots, the other cord ripped from the wall. The glass coffee table was broken, the purple carpet beneath it soggy with wine that smelled like rotten fruit. Dana looked towards the kitchen; someone barely breathing. Hanson pulled his nightstick.

"Police officers."

The kitchen sink was full of catfish, many of them still alive, swelling and shrinking as their mouths worked open and closed, their hard little eyes fixed in concentration through each seizure. Sightless fish heads and iridescent ropes of intestine were strewn across the drainboard and onto the floor below where a filleting knife, its narrow blade snapped off at the handle, lay in a puddle of thick blood. Bloody bare footprints on the dirty linoleum led to the backdoor, down the two concrete steps then faded away on the sidewalk.

They pulled their guns and checked the bedroom, slamming the door open, looking in the closet behind the hanging clothes, and beneath the unmade bed where they found an empty Black Velvet bottle, a car radio, pieces of fried chicken and a used Tampax. The bathroom was empty.

Hanson went next door, rang the bell, and a small dog began barking inside. A woman cracked the door open as far as the night latch, kicking the Chihuahua back each time it lunged for the door.

"What you want?" she said. The room behind her was dark, the shades pulled, and it was hard to tell her age. "Get back," she said, kicking the frog-eyed barking dog.

"The people next door," Hanson said, "we . . ."

"They already gone. You too late. You *way* too late," she said, and slammed the door.

Hanson wrote the address and the time in his notebook, and the words "way too late," when he heard the rattle of a shopping cart down the sidewalk and Pharaoh singing ". . . open our *eyes,* sweet Lord. So come on, *come* on, and open our eyes . . ."

"Pharaoh," Hanson called.

"Yes, *sir,* young captain. How you makin' out today?"

"Hey, I want to *thank* you. You saved my *life* the other day. Then you disappeared . . ."

Pharaoh waved, "Awright," and kept pushing his cart.

"Pharaoh," Hanson said, catching up to him, "I need to get a statement from you . . ."

"I'm not gonna tell you a lie, young captain," Pharaoh said. "I *could* say that wasn't me, but I rather just ask you—*respect*fully— ask you to forget I was there."

Bees swarmed around Pharaoh and the shopping cart of empty beer and pop cans. The sun was setting behind him.

"I'm just an old man, captain. Trying to get along."

"Okay," Hanson said. "Sure."

Pharaoh nodded. He pushed the cart a few feet, then stopped and looked back at Hanson. "Young captain, we know you done the best you *can*. So don't you be so hard on yourself. Just keep on," he said, and pushed his cart up the street, singing, "*Lean*-ing, *lean*-ing, leaning in the . . ."

THE GLOWING RED BEAD, bubbling cheerfully across the face of the police scanner, hesitated . . .

Five Sixty Two . . .

then cycled away, running the frequencies again, firing in sequence down the channels like a neon arrow, then stopped, burning sullenly, when Hanson keyed the mike.

"It's your dime."

Five Sixty Two, we've got a man down at Thirty-nine and Hawthorne. There are no East Precinct units available. Can you check that on your way in?

"Police cruiser Five Sixty Two is always happy to assist East Precinct when they can't handle their own problems."

Hanson laughed at the clatter from the radio, East Precinct cars clicking their mikes, saying "Fuck you."

At . . . eleven forty-three.

"It *is* a little late in the shift to be processing winos for East Precinct," Dana said.

Hanson propped his feet against the dash. "Not your *preferred* overtime. I'll take it. You're way behind in your paperwork."

"You're a fine officer and a wonderful person," Dana said, turning left and accelerating up the Avenue. The reflection of the patrol car shuddered across the dark storefronts at what seemed like an incredible speed, leaping from window to window across doors and intersections, past the Mor-4-Les store and the window of the Hollywood Market as Hanson watched it, trying for a couple of blocks to spot his face in the exploding mirror image.

The Hollywood Market had been padlocked since just before Christmas, when Aaron Allen shot the owner in the head with an old army .45 he'd taken in a burglary. He and the others pistol-whipped and raped his seventy-two-year-old wife, then went over to Lincoln High and shot some baskets.

In the emergency room, she looked at her hands when the detectives told her she could "take these animals off the street so they never do this to anyone else."

But since Aaron and his partners were children, the police didn't have any mug shots to show her, and they gave up after a few days and left her alone. When she finally got out of the hospital, she rode home in the back of a cab, the first she'd ever been in, and found that her house had been burglarized.

A few nights later Aaron had to ditch the army "four-five" in the park across the street from the Foursquare Gospel Church when Hanson and Dana pulled him over and arrested him for DWI. The next day he looked for the pistol, but it was gone. He bought another gun, a .38 Special revolver, from Quentin Barr for eight dollars, but he'd really liked that old .45 with the swastikas on the grips.

"Motherfuckin' *Hanson*," he said, loading the cylinder of the .38 Special, spinning it and snapping it closed like they did on TV. "I'm gonna blow his motherfuckin' *head* off next time he *fucks* with me," he said, aiming the pistol out the window of the Cadillac at an old lady waiting for the bus. "That was my *Hitler* four-five."

Twelve-year-old Doogie asked him who Hitler was.

"Fool!" Aaron said, ignoring him until they pulled into the alley behind Volume Shoes. "My man Hitler," Aaron said, "was the motherfuckin' *pres-i-dent* back in the olden days, killin' *all* the Jews till the *po*-lice *shot* his ass."

The December calendar, on the wall behind the checkout counter in the Hollywood Market, was covered with dust now, a photo of the pope blessing thousands in some third world slum. Hard to tell in the dark which country or continent it might be.

Dakota was lying behind the counter on a bed of crushed cardboard boxes, staring at the ceiling with his left eye. The other eye was swollen shut above the cracked cheekbone, the side of his face purple and bloated. He wore orange prison pants and a white hospital gown patterned with tiny blue pine trees. The left leg of his pants was slit to accommodate the cast they put on before he escaped from the hospital. He'd strapped his swollen and discolored arm across his chest with a roll of duct tape he found in the back of the market, passing out only once, briefly, from the pain.

He sat up and looked at the case of sardines on the shelf beneath the cash register, Product of Finland stamped on the cardboard. He'd managed to tear it open with his teeth and good hand. All the other food in the store had been stolen long ago. A pile of empty cans, their tops peeled open, lay against the far wall.

He lowered himself back down, spent some time trying to get comfortable, then lay still. A car went by, throwing shadows through bells and wreaths, illuminating the three wise men on the front window for a moment. When the car was past, a fly began bumping against the window.

He bolted up, punching the taped arm, grunting with the effort.

Twenty minutes later he was sitting beneath the front window, his legs spread flat on the floor, looking at a year-old newspaper in the light from the street. The paper was folded to an ad for the movie *The Man With the Golden Gun.* Blond Britt Ekland, pressing a sexy little PPK/S to her cleavage, pouted from the page. Her hip was cocked, one high heel propped on a stack of ammo boxes, the tight skirt hiked to her crotch. She was covered with oily thumb prints.

He studied the picture, working a headless silver fish out of the can on the floor, eating it in two bites, then passing his hand across his mouth and wiping it on his crotch before getting the next one. He didn't break his rhythm when the pile of empty sardine cans began to rattle and scrape the floor behind him, and the lights of patrol car Five Sixty Two flashed through the window as Dana drove north on the Avenue.

THE ''MAN DOWN'' was unconscious, spread-eagled on his back, two teenage couples standing over him. One of them, a wiry shirtless kid, his shoulder-length hair pulled back with a leather strap, had a radio the size of a suitcase on his shoulder, electric guitars screeching and sobbing from the cracked speakers as Hanson shone his flashlight down at the man.

"Turn it off," he said. The kid grinned at the others, put his hand to his ear and shouted, "Say *what?*"

Hanson reached over and turned off the radio. "Do you know what happened to this guy?" he asked them.

They shrugged and shook their heads. "Whatever it was, man," the kid with the radio said, "it was some bad shit."

A beefy middle-aged couple on a motorcycle, wearing matching satin tavern jackets, stopped by the police car and rode the bike onto the sidewalk to have a look. The driver revved his engine, and the yellow headlight, shining down on the man, brightened and dimmed.

"I wouldn't fuck him for a *million* dollars," one of the teenage girls said.

"I'll call a code-three," Dana said.

The man didn't have a nose, just two ragged holes in the middle of what once was a face. He seemed to be grimacing because he had no lips to cover his teeth, only clusters of tiny blisters along the gum line. The skin stretched over his forehead and cheekbones and down his neck was shiny and stiff, like pink plastic. Tufts of black hair hung from between welts of scar tissue on his scalp, and the top of his head throbbed gently in and out, beating like a heart.

"Motherfucker missed his bus for the fifth dimension, man," the kid with the radio said, and the others laughed.

Hanson jabbed his finger at them. "Why don't you get the fuck out of here right now," he said.

"Okay," the kid said. "Take it easy."

"Don't tell me to *take it easy*, motherfucker. I'll put your ass in the hospital."

"Okay. Fine. Okay."

"And you," Hanson said, pointing at the couple on the motorcycle, "get outta here."

They waddled the motorcycle backwards, the headlight bobbing. Holding the big flashlight on his shoulder like a club, Hanson looked down at the man with no face.

His eyes were closed, the lids melted shut, but there were slits in the eyelids that he must have been able to see through. One of the eyes was magnified and distorted by the thick lens of the eyeglasses hooked over one of the ear stumps.

Down the street, the radio began to shriek and thump again. ". . . fuckin' *monster*," the girl squealed.

Hanson had blinked it away the night Doc mentioned the bunker they'd found on that operation south of the river, the bodies all in one corner where they had huddled against the fire. It had been a long time since Hanson had allowed himself to remember how they'd looked, joined at their arms and chests and faces like Siamese twins, the way napalm melted flesh like it was wax. There had been a joke about it up in I Corps, a variation on the "peace sign," he remembered as he knelt to look for fresh wounds.

There were none, and the man was breathing, the nose-holes fluttering open and closed like sea creatures. Just beyond one outthrown arm was a box with "Winchell Donuts" printed in cheery yellow letters. Donuts had rolled across the grass and onto the sidewalk.

In the distance a siren warbled, working its way through the blocks.

Hanson had read that disfigured people often begin to feel that they are invisible. No one looks at them, acting as if they don't exist. Hanson imagined himself, a monster, walking into a donut shop.

The ambulance turned up the street behind him, throwing light through the treetops, cutting the lights and siren as it pulled to the curb. A rose painted on the side of the white van opened, then closed, red and black, as emergency flashers clicked on and off in the quiet street.

"I don't know," Hanson told them. "He's breathing. No fresh wounds I could see."

One of the attendants knelt down by the man. He had a rose patch on the shoulder of his uniform. "Jesus," he said, "some scary shit out here on the streets after dark."

"I'll meet you at the hospital then," Hanson said. "You going to Good Sam?"

"Right."

Dana parked close to the big double doors of the emergency room so he'd have enough light to work on his reports.

"This shouldn't take long," Hanson said. "We can type the rest of those up back at the precinct."

After they'd rolled the man with no face into an OR and were folding up the ends of their gurney, Hanson asked the EMS guys if they knew his name. The blue blanket with the rose design looked warm and out of place in the chilly green corridor as the attendant folded it on the gurney and clicked the aluminum-tube sides closed.

"Radmer? No," he said. "We've carried him before." He took a ballpoint pen out of his pocket and clicked it open and closed. "Epileptic. He usually wears a football helmet. Radke? Yeah, that's it. Radke."

"Got an address on him?"

"We got his address, Ron?" he asked the other attendant.

Ron thumbed through his notebook. "Somewhere off Hawthorne, I think. Group home."

"Same thing last time. Didn't take his medication and crashed on the sidewalk," the other attendant said.

"Don't have it," Ron said. "It's that group home on Hawthorne. They have that freak parade to the park every day to eat lunch. Nothing covering that hole in his head but skin. Needs a plate in there."

"The story *we* got," the attendant said, "when he was a baby his mother wrapped him in a blanket and put him in the oven. To keep him warm. Low heat. Baby setting." He clicked the pen twice. "She was drunk. Forgot about him and the blanket caught fire. Good old mom."

"There it is," Ron said. "We'd better hit the street if you're through with us. They got us working a twelve hour shift this month. Two more hours," he said, looking at his watch. "Things are beginning to get strange. Street monsters."

"Rose City Ambulance," the attendant said, in a voice like a radio commercial, "Twenty-four hours a day. We haul your dead and dying meat. Whoa," he said, slapping his own cheek, "wake up now. Later. Gotta go."

As they rolled the gurney down the corridor, the attendant did a little dance step.

"He's conscious," the doctor said behind him, "if you need to ask him any questions. Another seizure. He hasn't been taking his Dilantin.

"Name's Arthur," the doctor said as Hanson followed him into the OR.

"How do you feel, Arthur? This police officer wants to talk to you," the doctor said, taking the transparent green oxygen mask off his mouth and nose-holes. The sound of his breathing filled the pale green room where glass cabinets along one wall displayed clamps and silver probes, scalpels and forceps, syringes, drills, steel collars and blunt chrome speculums.

Arthur's pupils rolled beneath his eyelids towards Hanson.

"Where do you live, Arthur?"

His stiff pink throat flexed, the nose-holes fluttered, "Aughoo," he said, the lip blisters trying to form the word.

"Hawthorne, Arthur?" Hanson asked. The sweet smell of alcohol and disinfectant was strong in the room.

Spittle rolled over the blisters and slid down Arthur's neck. "*Aughoo*," he said, louder.

"Where on Hawthorne, Arthur? Do you know the cross street?"

"*Aughoo*."

"Okay, Arthur," the doctor said, the pager on his belt beeping, "take it easy.

"I have to go," the doctor said, looking at his pager. "You're welcome to ask him a few more questions."

Arthur looked at Hanson's pistol, choking on a word that had been trapped, sealed inside his throat all the years since the night he lay inside the oven, on fire, black smoke boiling above him in the glowing electric coils. So young, Hanson imagined, he must have thought the blistering heat was normal, no worse than the pain of his birth.

"*Another hell, worse than this one,*" Doc had said. "*They keep getting worse.*"

Hanson saw it struggling in his shiny throat, beneath the steel tracheotomy plug, the voice of whatever took possession of him all those years ago. A voice Hanson had heard before.

"Oonth," Arthur grunted, looking at the pistol again, then glaring at Hanson through the lesions in his eyelids. His eyes, behind the melted lids, were like Kraang-the-Hawk's eyes had been that day out in the wire and burning grass. "Oonth." He raised his head, his eyes fixing Hanson's. "Oonth," he said once more, so Hanson could never deny it.

"I can't, Arthur," Hanson said. "Forgive me." He turned away and walked towards the double steel doors, trying not to run, because if he started to run he wouldn't be able to stop until he collapsed three, or five, or ten miles away.

"*All you know is how to kill something,*" the woman had screamed at him.

He stopped and willed himself to turn around. Closing his notebook, he looked at the back of Arthur's ruined head shuddering with thought.

"Good night Arthur," he said. "I'm sorry."

———

Down the hall, a blond nurse with dark red lipstick was walking his way. Jim Bell, an East Precinct patrolman, called after her. "In an hour, then."

She met Hanson's eyes, holding them as they walked towards each other. She read his name tag and smiled. "Have a nice night, *Hanson*," she said as they passed.

"Boy howdy," Bell said. "Finally. I been working on *that* one ever since she started working in the emergency room. Some fag took a screwdriver to his boyfriend tonight, and I had three hours to romance her while I waited to see if the guy was gonna die. That did the trick."

After work, Hanson went to the police club bar. They were having a "Christmas in July" party, and he had to buy tickets at the door that were good for drinks and a drawing for door prizes. Some of the girls from Records and Radio had gotten together and rented sexy little elf costumes. Sgt. Farmer was dressed as Santa Claus. Jim Bell, who was there with his nurse, won an aluminum Christmas tree. Hanson went through a lot of tickets, but none of them were winners.

When he got up to leave, Hanson gave Zurbo and Neal and the others a two-fingered salute, the first two fingers of his right hand pressed together so hard it hurt. "Be advised, people," he said, "napalm gets it together."

When the door of the club closed behind him, he brought his hand up to his face, feeling his nose and lips, gently touching his eyes. He was glad it was late. He didn't want to see anyone on the way to his car.

He'd just crossed Fremont Street into North Precinct when he looked to the right and saw Fox and Peetey parked at the curb. Asia was leaning down, talking to them through the window.

TWENTY-FIVE

IT WAS ALMOST ten o'clock when they managed to break into the heavy radio traffic to clear from the forgery call, and Radio sent them to see a complainant about a "suspicious noise." The report was a couple of hours old, Radio said, they'd been backed up with more urgent calls.

"How about some supper after that?" Hanson said.

You're next on the list, Five Six Two, Radio said.

"Okee doke. Thank you very much."

At . . . nine forty three.

"About *time* God cut me a little slack on these fucking calls tonight," he told Dana.

"Luck of the draw," Dana said. "I might be a nice guy and write up that second burglary for you. If you promise to treat me with more respect around the other officers."

Hanson laughed. "We'll kiss this one off, then it's code-three to dinner. 'And how suspicious *were* these noises, ma'am. Would you say they were *very* suspicious, or only somewhat suspicious?' "

They alternated calls during the shift, and so far Dana had gotten a woman who was drunk and angry at her ex-boyfriend, telling them that he was a dope dealer, a family fight where the husband agreed to leave for the night, and a man with a gun call that turned out to be a loud music complaint. The complainant had mentioned a gun so the cops would get there in a hurry. They were all calls that could be written up in a few lines on a miscellaneous report form.

Hanson had gotten two burglaries and then a prostitute trying to pass a forged check for her pimp at a Safeway. Just that one call had involved a crime report, an arrest report, statements from employees at the Safeway, a property report for the check, and a complicated form called a "Worthless Document Report." They had to take the prostitute to jail and the check to the property room. They'd been going from call to call since the beginning of the shift.

Hanson rang the bell at the address on Mississippi Street. Light showed through the peephole in the heavy front door that looked as if it had been recently installed. He shifted his weight from foot to foot on the porch, playing a nervous rhythm on a squeaking board. Suddenly, he stopped.

"Shit," he said, "it's too late to slip over on Five Fifty's district for Chinese. Where do you want to eat?"

"French's closes the kitchen at ten. That's about it. After that, it's McDonald's or spaghetti at the Town Square."

Hanson rapped on the door with his flashlight. "Come on," he said.

The peephole dimmed and someone began working through a combination of locks, sliding and snapping them open with mechanical efficiency. A heavyset black woman, wearing only a slip and a waist-length red wig, opened the door a few inches.

"Hi," Hanson said. "What's the problem?"

The woman cocked her head to the left, then cut her eyes that way, as theatrical as a Kabuki dancer. She looked back at Hanson, and when he didn't respond, she did it again, the Dynel wig parting over her shoulder.

"You're gonna have to *tell* me, ma'am. I'm not allowed to take non-verbal reports."

She opened the door and leaned out, the red hair framing her face and breasts. "It was over in the garage," she whispered, liquor on her breath. "But it stopped."

"Honey?" a man called from another room. "Who is it?"

"It stopped now," she whispered to Hanson.

"Some people at the wrong address," she shouted, closing the door.

Hanson shone his flashlight on the sagging garage next to a fire-gutted house one lot over, as the woman reset the series of locks and deadbolts and night chains.

"Dogs," Hanson said. "Probably night dogs. Let's eat."

He stopped halfway to the car. "I'd better take a look, just so I can say I did in the report. We've still got time." He thumbed his cast-aluminum flashlight on and swung it over his shoulder like a bat, sweeping the ground ahead. When it dimmed, he smacked it into the palm of his hand, and it brightened.

He dragged one of the double doors partway open and worked the flashlight beam through the garage, across the charred and water-stained sofas and mattresses piled against one wall, over blistered table tops, piles of scorched clothes, liquor boxes heaped with dishes and shoes and books.

"Fucking for-shit Korean flashlight batteries they give us," Hanson whispered.

"You want me to lend you a couple of dollars so you can buy your own?"

Hanson snorted. "I think the city should 'Buy American.' Why'd they send me over there to kill all those gooks if they aren't gonna Buy American?"

Dana laughed.

"That's right," Hanson said.

Soot hung in the air, drifting through the beam of light as it picked out a birdcage, a melted coffee maker, and flared back at Hanson from a smoky TV screen. Something moaned and Hanson slashed the light through the black fog, striking at the sound until he saw her through the broken furniture, the bloody face and matted blond hair, her eyes. She looked up at him from her hands and knees, her breasts and bare shoulders and arching naked back a pasty gray.

"Five Six Two," Dana spoke into his packset. "Five Six Two." He banged it with the heel of his hand. "Five Six Two. Shit. I'll use the car radio. Get us a code-three and a couple of cover cars. The guy might still be in the area."

As Hanson worked his way through the junk, she stood up and began to scream, sucking air in and screaming it out.

A bedspring caught Hanson's pants and he kept walking, holding her in the light, dragging the springs until they wedged to a stop. Her cheeks and chin were slashed to pearly bone, her upper lip split from the nose down. One ear hung from a strip of skin, a blue glass earring dangling from it. A unicorn, turning one direction, then the other, blinking in the faint light. An electrical cord, knotted around her neck, ran down between her breasts to a shattered ceramic lamp hanging against her pale belly.

He kicked back at the springs. "It's okay," he shouted, slamming his hip into the springs. Something cut into his thigh. "It's okay," he said. He'd need a tetanus shot.

"It's okay."

For a moment her swollen, bloody face looked familiar. He lunged towards her, ripping his pants free, kicking a chair out of his way. She threw her arms up to shield her face, and Hanson saw the crude tattoo, Billy, on her left breast.

It was Brandy, Marcus Johnson's whore. When he needed money, Marcus sent her out on the street to turn tricks. The last time he'd seen her was on the third floor of the Sunset Hotel, after he'd told three Mexicans to pay the rent or get out. The bathroom was at the end of the hall, the door open as Hanson walked past it to the stairs.

Marcus, black and muscular, was naked, standing with his legs apart, his hands braced on the wall above the toilet where Brandy knelt, holding his black cock as he pissed, the jailhouse tattoo peeking above her halter top.

Faraway, their eyes dreamy with heroin, they had looked at Hanson in his uniform and leather and pistol, the packset chirping on his belt, looked at him as if he was some frightened white bureaucrat's foolish idea of "justice," too insignificant to deserve even their contempt.

He'd turned away and walked down the stairs.

"It's okay, Brandy," he said, slipping the flashlight under his arm. "You're *safe* now," he said, cupping the broken bloody lamp, trying to pull the cord loose.

"Is this what he hit you with?" he said, knowing he was covering the lamp with his own bloody fingerprints.

She screamed and jerked away, the lamp gashing the tender ball of Hanson's thumb as the cord pulled free.

"God *damn*," he yelled at her, smashing the lamp on the floor. "You're *safe* now."

She began coughing, choking on her own blood. She lowered her head, looking up at Hanson as the blood spooled from her split lips. The other earring had been torn from her earlobe.

"Brandy, can you tell me who did it?"

"Duk tabe."

When she tried to speak he saw, in the yellow light, that her teeth had been broken off in clusters of two or three, hanging from her gums like chunks of stew meat.

"Was he black or white?"

"Duc tape."

She sounded like she was talking while she was eating, with a mouthful of food.

"Duk tabe."

"Black or *white?*"

Catching her breath, she began screaming again.

"White or *black?"* he yelled.

The call was two hours old. Why had *he* gotten it?

"White or black? How fucking hard is that?"

He took both her wrists in one hand and pulled her arms down, shining the flashlight in his own face.

"Look at me, goddammit," he said. "Look. You *know* me."

The light was hot on his face, blinding him. He closed his eyes and it glowed red through his eyelids.

She stopped screaming.

"Hahn. Hahnthun," she said, and he took the light from his face. Hanson knew the sound of his own name.

She came to him out of the dark and his arms opened against his will, like a gesture in a nightmare, pulling her to him. Her blood tickled his cheek and he tried to remember if he had cut himself shaving. Syphilis, gonorrhea, hepatitis. Who knew what else she might have. He could go back to the precinct as soon as the ambulance came and take a long shower, flush the blood away, but he'd never get the blood out of his uniform. A hundred and eighty-five dollars to replace it.

Her broken jaw grated as she sobbed in his ear, stinking of urine and feces and charred wood. He stroked her hair. It was oily beneath his hand and smelled like sardines.

"It's okay, Brandy," he said. Hating her for being the kind of irresponsible—didn't she know that life has *consequences*—nigger-fucking white trash she was. For forcing him to deal with all this pain. Her pain, not his. Who said that was part of the job?

"I've got you now. It's okay."

What did he have to do with her fucked-up life that was only going to get worse but she didn't know it yet and he *did* and what the fuck was *he* supposed to do? Too late to change anything now except maybe shoot her and put her out of her worthless, useless, miserable fucking life, goddammit, and end it now and save her from all the years ahead.

"You're okay now, Brandy," he said, hating himself, hating her for making him lie and tell her it was okay.

That she was safe.

TWENTY-SIX

IT STARTED EARLY in the shift, the *pop* of firecrackers, random and sporadic at first, like the beginning of an insurrection crackling through the district, then more of them, faster, quick stuttering bursts of ten or twelve, of twenty, overlapping, too many to count.

Hanson tasted burnt powder in the air as he drove past dying elm trees in Woodlawn Park.

"We give them parks, ladies and gentlemen," Hanson said, "verdant refuge from summer's heat, where neighborhood children dream in the dappled shade of mighty elms."

It looked more like a landfill than a park since it had been erased from the city budget, the black bags of garbage torn open by dogs, abandoned sofas and TVs and shopping carts, winos passed out in the weeds like ambush victims.

"What are those little gangsters up to?" Dana said.

They were gathered around something in the middle of the street, beneath the stone arch at the entrance to the park, first or second graders, some younger, wearing shorts or cut-off pants and oversize high-top tennis shoes.

"Probably torturing a cat," Hanson said, taking his foot off the gas, the kids keeping track of the patrol car over their shoulders. "Torture is just a form of curiosity here in the, uh-ruh, black community."

"That's our man Russell the Muscle in the tiger-stripe shirt," Dana said.

Hanson smiled. " 'Call me Russell the Muscle, *po*-lice,' " he said, imitating the little boy's rap. He tapped the brakes. "Come on, guys."

They huddled closer, heads down, eyes quick as sparrows. The smaller kids danced from toe to toe, pushing into the circle as the patrol car rolled closer.

Dana picked up the mike and spoke over the PA system. "We're sorry to bother you young men, but . . ."

They bolted, tripping over each other as they broke and ran shrieking past the patrol car, their eyes bright with fear and excitement.

Watching them in the rearview mirror, Hanson pulled to the stop sign just as the fuse flared into the trash-covered pack of Black Cat torpedos beneath the patrol car. The kids watched from the far side of a garbage-filled fishpond, poised to run again, as the first string of firecrackers cooked off in erratic yellow bursts, twitching and writhing in a cloud of shredded paper.

Five Six Two.

"Five Sixty Two," Dana said, rolling the window up against the noise. The kids leaped in their tennis shoes, slapping high fives as they turned in the air. They cakewalked the edge of the pond, bowlegged, their shoulders back as the explosions rang off the muffler and gas tank.

Check for an ambulance. Somewhere in the three hundred block of Monroe Street. Unknown problem.

"We're close," Dana said, the explosions sputtering out. "You got a better address?"

Both hands on the steering wheel, Hanson stared through the dirty windshield, blinking at each sporadic *pang.* In the parking lot down the street, a black transvestite with the legs of a running back leaned down to the driver's window of a blue '69 Mercury, exposing garter belt straps and the tops of his mesh stockings. He pouted into the window, smoothing the leather miniskirt over his hips.

That's the best we could do before she hung up.

" 'Screaming in the background,' " Hanson said, speaking in the dispatcher's monotone as he turned right, angling back towards Monroe. " 'Machine guns possibly involved.' "

An M-80 boomed like a mortar round in a Dumpster behind them.

"A bit tense, are we?" Dana said.

Hanson turned left through a yellow light, dodging a shopping cart in the street.

"A little nervous today?"

Hanson clenched his teeth and looked at Dana. "Nerwous?" he said, not moving his lips. "Whutaya mean?" he said, bugging his eyes out. "Whut makesyew say that?"

"Police training."

Hanson laughed. "I got nervous in the service."

'' . . . **HOLD MY HAND,** make me *under*stand, I wake up, *uh-uh-uh uh,* inacold sweat."

They heard the radios two blocks away, James Brown gasping for air across the backyards and garbage-choked alleys of the district.

"Mister James Brown," Hanson said, rapping like Wardell the DJ, "the hardest-working man in show business."

The band slowed, faltered, only drums and one saxophone keeping the beat. Hanson slowed for a stoplight, flipped the overhead lights on and drove into the sobbing that filled the air.

"I can see him," Hanson said, turning down Mason Street, "on stage. Slumped over the microphone in exhaustion, sweat dripping from his nose. Is he through? Can he go on?"

Five Eighty. Check for an unwanted son with a gun. Sixteen fourteen Killingsworth. Cover . . . ?

Uh, we're familiar with the problem. We don't need a cover car.

"But listen," Hanson said, cupping his ear as the band picked up the beat again. "More saxophones. James Brown begins to move with the music, raises his head, kind of *remembers* where he is . . ."

" . . . need a little *help* now, y'all! Huh! Yeow!"

". . . and explodes into the spotlights, spraying sweat as he throws back his hair and *bares* those white teeth. Yes," Hanson said, shouting now, the music just up the block, "he *snatches* the mike, strutting to the sound of a thousand trumpets. He's okay, ladies and gentlemen. He's got the *power* again."

"This must be the place," Dana said.

It was a Fourth of July party, people crowded around barbecue grills, filling their paper plates from platters of ribs and chicken and hamburgers on card tables in the tiny front yard. Radios on the front steps, on the card tables, on top of the old Ford farm truck parked in front of the house, all tuned to the same station.

". . . I just wanta, huh! tell ya 'bout your dos an' don'ts . . ."

"Mister James Brown, ladies and gentlemen," Hanson said, pulling to the curb behind the farm truck and putting the car in PARK. "A living legend in his own time *live* from the Apollo Theatre. James Brown!" Hanson said as he turned off the ignition. He and Dana got out of the car, their eyes on the crowd.

"Yeow! Huuh! Ow!"

"He's a lover. A preacher. A gangster and a prophet. A gun-fighter . . . and a man of peace," Hanson said, pulling his night-stick from the holder inside the door, doing a little dance step as he dropped it through the ring on his pistol belt.

"The man we call," he said, slamming the door, "the godfather of *soul.*"

". . . when you miss me, ho-oh-old me tight . . ."

The men in the yard held quarts of Colt .45 and Black Cat Ale by the neck, like weapons. They kept their eyes on the cops, watching them over the bottles as they drank, each swallow a challenge.

The women turned away, hips cocked, watching the cops over their shoulders, taking long, angry drags on their cigarettes. Dana pulled out his packset. "Five Six Two."

Go ahead Five Six Two.

"We might want another car down here at Three twenty Monroe. We'll let you know."

Hanson glanced at Dana and walked up to a three-hundred pounder with long ratty hair, Delbert Mack, "the ugliest nigger in the West." The biggest man in the yard, he wore bib overalls, one broken strap peeled away from a huge hairy chest. His left eye-brow pulled from old suture scars over a blind eye. The end of his nose had been bitten off in a fight over a doe-eyed Jamaican boy,

and the prison doctor had reattached it without anesthetic while
Delbert fought the restraints on an oak slant board.

"Delbert. What it is?" Hanson said, talking loud over the music. "What's the problem?"

He looked down at him with his good eye. Blinked. "I'm looking at the problem."

Hanson laughed. "Hey," he said, smiling as he stepped a little
closer. "I hear you been carrying a sawed-off shotgun."

Delbert worked his tongue up into his cheek, then jammed his
finger back there and probed. One of the radios went silent.

"Under the seat of that old farm truck of yours."

Delbert pulled his finger out and looked at it.

"Is that true?"

Another radio went silent.

"You stepped in *what?*" Delbert said.

"I hope it's not there when I pull you over for those expired
plates."

Hanson turned towards the sound of crying, then back to Delbert. "Don't forget now. If you ever decide to sell that truck, let
me know. I need a farm truck."

"Your money as good as anybody's. But the way things are, you
understand, you might have to pay a premium."

"You see how it's done, then," Hanson told Dana as they
walked away. "I drive a hard bargain with these people."

Dana was still laughing when they worked their way through
the crowd towards the crying and were confronted by a wiry
woman with light-brown skin and red hair, wearing high-waisted
satin pants and a halter top. Her arms were crossed under her
breasts, a cigarette smoking between the long red fingernails of
one hand. Behind her, a little boy writhed in the dirt and dogshit
and knobs of dead grass, screaming in his two-year-old voice, one
of his feet caked with bloody dirt. Dee Brazzle squatted drunkenly
next to him. When he reached out to him, the little boy slapped
his hand away.

The woman watched Hanson, smoke curling from her nostrils,
as Dana called for an ambulance on his packset.

"What happened?" Hanson asked the woman.

"Step on a cherry bomb," she said. She had full lips, wearing
lipstick the color of primer paint. Purple birthmarks splotched her
cheek and neck like clouds. Her eyes on Hanson, she brought the

cigarette to her mouth and took a long drag, filling her lungs, her breasts lifting.

"They're trying to break loose an ambulance," Dana said. "All the emergency rooms in town are swamped. Good Sam's setting up cots in the lobby."

"Holiday casualties," Hanson said, still making eye contact with the woman.

"I'll get the first aid kit," Dana said.

"Excuse me," Hanson said.

"We didn't call the motherfuckin' *po*-lice," the woman said, as Hanson squeezed past, inhaling her smoke and perfume. "Why they always send the police when black folks need a *ambulance?*"

Dee was wearing pea-green bell-bottom pants and no shirt, a dark puckered scar just above his hip, where his girlfriend had shot him two years before.

"What's his name?" Hanson said, kneeling next to Dee, wondering if it was the little boy or Dee who had shit his pants.

"I *told* you, get your ass . . ." Dee looked at him, the whites of his eyes creamy yellow and bloodshot, too drunk to recognize him. "I'm this baby's uncle," he said, losing his balance, falling on his butt.

"Where's this baby's momma?" Dee shouted, to no one in particular, trying not to look drunk. "Where's his *whore* momma?"

"Come on, kid," Hanson said, half-standing, reaching for him. Suddenly, the little boy threw both arms around his neck, and Hanson fought to keep his balance, struggling to his feet. The kid tightened his grip, screaming again and kicking Hanson with the bloody foot. It was the kid who had shit his pants.

"Why *me?*" Hanson asked him, looking down at him. "Why not Uncle Dee?

"Hey, buddy. Hey, my man," he said, his lips close to the crying boy's ear. "Look at me.

"Up *here*," he said, taking the kid's head in both hands, turning it until they were face-to-face.

His lips and chin were shiny with tears and dried snot, his eyes dull, retarded. Hanson wasn't surprised by that, he realized; he'd expected it.

Dumb as dogshit, he thought, looking down at him. Not a chance in the world. They should just kill him now and get it over with.

"If it was a *white* baby, if that baby was *white,* don't you know, ambulance would of been here and on the way to the hospital," a man yelled. He sported a little goatee and wore his hair in corn-rows. It was too hot for the long-sleeved, white turtleneck, and Hanson guessed that he wore it to cover needle marks.

"That's right," he said, looking at Hanson through tinted avia-tor glasses. "I'm talking to you."

"What's his name?" Hanson asked the woman with the birth-marks.

She cupped her left breast and adjusted the strap on her halter top. Parting her lips, burnished lipstick showing like blood on her white teeth, she took a drag on her cigarette. "His name Ali."

A cherry bomb *boomed.* Hanson crouched and spun towards the noise, poised to run, the screaming child hanging from his neck like a voodoo curse. Dee staggered, laughing, through the cloud of white smoke drifting across the yard. "Just a little bitty *cherry* bomb," he shouted.

"Hey. Ali." Hanson said, gripping his shoulder. "Ali. Look at me," he said, looking into his wet eyes, unfocused with pain. It was like trying to see through muddy water. "Look at me. Right in here," Hanson said, pointing at his own eye.

"But they take their time if it's black folks," the guy with the goatee went on. "Am I *lying?* Uh-uh. I ain't telling no lie. Little *black* baby, they takes their time."

"Come on, partner," Hanson said to the kid. "Little Ali. Right *here.* Yeah. *Now* you see me," he said, rubbing Ali's muscular little back as he sobbed soundlessly for air.

"Can't *talk* to that, can you, 'cause you *know* it's true."

"Give me the pain," Hanson told Ali. "Look right *here,* in my eye, and give it to me. That's it. Come on. Good. I got it. I got it. It's mine now," he crooned as the kid's breathing slowed.

"Gimme my baby."

Hanson smelled sour sweat and semen when she came up from behind, slurring her words in his ear, her arms coming around him—a zombie embrace—reaching for the little boy, her breath rank with decay and Night Train tokay. The filthy gauze dressings on her slashed wrists were frayed and unraveling, the wounds puckered with infection, tearing loose from the emergency room sutures. Pressing into him, reaching, the emaciated arms burned, scarred, marbled purple and black with abscessed needle tracks weeping pus.

"Gimme my *baby*."

Ali began screaming again, tightening his grip around Hanson's neck, strong as a boa constrictor, choking him.

"Ma'am," Hanson said, "ma'am," turning to face her with open arms, proof that he wasn't trying to keep Ali from her, the little boy holding on by himself. "He's all *yours*. Just *wait* a second." But she was pulling at Ali's arms, and when that didn't work, she took a handful of his hair.

"That's his *momma*," the woman with the birthmarks yelled. "Don't you *hurt* that little baby."

"Ma'am. Look at me," Hanson shouted, his arms still open, while she pulled the little boy's hair.

"Look," Hanson grunted, stepping back, finally grabbing her bleeding wrist. It felt like a piece of wood, dead as a mummy's arm from too many injections of heroin, black market methadone, stolen Ritalin and Demerol, codeine, sometimes even Midol or aspirin, powdered and cooked in a bent spoon, or plain water, when she couldn't find anybody who'd fuck her in exchange for dope.

"You gonna let the police *torture* that little boy," the guy with the goatee yelled. "Tryin' to *kill* that little baby . . ."

Ali screamed in pain when his mother stumbled backwards, tearing a tuft of his hair out, and fell backwards into the crowd.

". . . an' his momma. What's wrong with you people? *Get* 'em. Be proud. Kill the po-lice motherfuckers!"

Hanson saw Dana trying to get through the crowd, but they blocked his way, pushing him back. Hanson knew the shoves would quickly turn into punches and worse unless one of them could get a packset out, hope it worked, and call a code-zero, but it might already be too late for that.

Ali's mother pushed up off the ground, alive now, strong with pure, mindless rage. She took one of Ali's ankles in both hands like a baseball bat, yanking Hanson towards her, off balance with the weight of the little boy around his neck, teetering on the tips of his toes. He lurched back to stay on his feet, and a fist hit him in the back of the head.

Someone pulled at his holstered pistol and he knocked the hand away. In a few more seconds, he knew, he'd have to start shooting people, or let them take his gun.

Then he heard Delbert Mack, three hundred pounds of the ugliest nigger in the West, louder than all the curses and screams,

"Get outta my way. God *damn,* you *better* move, nigger." Heard
the huge hands slapping heads, thumps and grunts as Delbert
straight-armed them out of his way, parting the crowd, coming
closer. "Move. I said, *move.* I'll tear *your* nappy damn *head* off,
boy."

He pushed past Hanson, the crowd backing away, to Ali's
mother, and peeled her hands off the boy's ankle.

"Somebody take care of this woman," he boomed, and they
took her. Then Delbert Mack turned and nodded at the little boy
still hanging from Hanson's neck.

"You bet," Hanson said, up on his toes, chest out, his arms and
head back as if he was offering himself to God. "Take him."

Ali released his grip and stopped crying the moment he felt
Delbert's enormous hands around him.

"Come on, poor little baby. Delbert's got you now."

He pointed at the guy with the goatee. "Come here," he said.

"Clarence," he told him, "I'm gonna kick your ass one of these
times."

"Kick my ass? All I did was . . ."

"Shut up."

"I'm just sayin' . . ."

"What'd I say?"

"But . . ."

"I'm not telling you again."

Clarence nodded and looked away.

"What 'all you *did'* was almost get some people shot, and I ain't
talkin' about no *police* getting shot. They the ones gonna do the
shooting. That mouth of yours . . ." Delbert said. "Get outta
here."

Hanson watched the ambulance drive away, taking Ali and his
weeping, gibbering, junkie mother.

"Thank you, Delbert," he said.

Delbert Mack looked at him, shook his head, and walked away.

Hanson pulled away from the curb and drove down the street,
watching the dispersing crowd in the rearview mirror.

"Wow," he said, "that perked me right up," his eyes on the
road, "but those near-death angry-mob deals always do that."

"Delbert was right," Dana said. "I thought I was gonna have to
shoot some people back there."

"He can *keep* the sawed-off shotgun," Hanson said, "as far as *I'm* concerned."

"And we've only just started our day," Dana said.

"We need to freshen up a little," Hanson said, looking down at his shit-stained shirt.

He picked up the mike, cleared, and asked permission to return to the precinct.

Negative at this time, Five Sixty Two. Five Forty's requesting a cover car at Union and Dekum, and you're all I've got right now.

"Okee-doke . . ." Hanson said.

Dana turned on the overhead lights.

". . . we're on our way."

Five Fifty's close to that location. We can take the cover.

Five Fifty's got the cover. Five Sixty Two's clear and headed back to North.

"Thank you, Five Fifty," Dana said into the mike.

"Jesus," Hanson said, looking at himself in the rearview mirror. "I'm gonna take a shower."

He turned onto Failing Street, past the Black Muslim temple on the corner where four Muslims stood shoulder to shoulder, military style, in front of the red brick building. Their hair was close-cropped, and they wore dark suits, white shirts and black bow ties. Tall and slim, unsmiling, their eyes hidden behind sunglasses, they seemed to be looking through the buildings across the street into some spartan and fundamental truth.

When Hanson turned to stare into their sunglasses, a long-haired mongrel dog came howling out of nowhere, a string of ladyfingers wired to his tail. Hanson hit the brakes as the dog ran in front of the patrol car, past the temple, into Haight Street. The little firecrackers snarled and snapped, blinking tiny orange flames, trailing a cloud of shredded paper as the dog ran in circles, trying to bite the copper wire braided into his tail. When that didn't work, he tried to get away from the firecrackers by squeezing beneath a car parked across the street on four flat tires.

The Muslims turned their heads slightly when Five Fifty, the cover car, came over the hill up Haight Street, running code-two with overhead lights. One of them smiled when the dog bolted from beneath the parked car, into the path of the speeding patrol car.

The dog made a metallic *bang* against the bumper and was

sucked under the car where it bucked and twisted its way from the radiator to the transmission to the muffler and into the frame, hung up between the gas tank and the rear axle, its broken legs kicking sideways until it bounced into the wheel well and was thrown free, pursuing the police car in bloody cartwheels until a pothole threw it, twisting in midair, over the curb into a blue mailbox.

That wouldn't have happened, Hanson thought, the *boom* of the mailbox echoing up the street, if I hadn't had to change my shirt. If the kid hadn't grabbed my neck. If Dee fucking Brazzle hadn't been throwing cherry bombs around.

He put the car in reverse and backed up to the Muslims who looked over the roof of the patrol car, arms folded, as if the police were too insignificant to consider.

"Fourth of July," Hanson said to them. "Some fun, huh?"

The afternoon sun glinted off their mirrored glasses as they seemed to listen to a distant, angry voice.

"Makes you proud to be an American, doesn't it."

A firecracker popped in the next block. Another.

"Let that be a lesson to you," Hanson said, pointing up the street at the mailbox, a bloody starburst dripping down the side. "Don't jump in front of police cars."

"What was that all about?" Dana said after they'd driven a few blocks.

"Fuck those guys and their *we be bad* act. If they're so fucking bad, then come *on*, let's . . ."

"You're the guy who *likes* the Muslims. 'They're disciplined. They take care of their own. They don't beg.' "

Five Fifty.

Go ahead Five Fifty.

Uh, yeah, after we clear could we get a meet with somebody for a CDK at Haight and Failing? We just nailed our fourth *dog of the season on the way to cover Five Forty.*

Five Eighty can do it. Give us a call on channel three when you're ready for the meet.

"How about driving the rest of the shift," Hanson said. "I'll make it up to you."

"Five Sixty Two, clear," Hanson said into the radio, the Burgerville USA sign groaning above them as they pulled out of the parking lot. "Headed back to the district."

"God," he said, hanging up the mike and settling into the passenger seat. "Ugh. The shit I eat on this job. Grease. Grease runs through my veins. I may look good on the outside. I may *appear* to be a handsome young officer, but inside? I'm a walking grease trap. I feel like drinking Drano. You know that commercial where they have the transparent sink drain full of grease and . . . *hair?* Hair! There's probably cow hair in those burgers. Drano. Officer Drano. When I eat shit like that, you know what I think?"

"I wouldn't want to guess," Dana said.

"I think, 'Please God, don't let me get shot in the stomach until I've digested this stuff.' I've gotta start bringing my lunch. Lettuce and whole grain bread. Sprouts. Healthy fruits and berries.

"Hey," Hanson said, "how about lending me ten bucks?"

"First you want me to drive, and now it's ten bucks?"

"I got a date with that Sara after work tonight, and I forgot to bring any money."

"Helen told me you were going out with her. She says you two don't seem compatible."

Hanson laughed. "No one is what they seem. How about that ten bucks? I'll pay you back tomorrow."

"I'm not worried about it," Dana said. "Here's twenty. I don't have a ten."

"Maybe you *should* be worried," Hanson said, snatching the bill from his fingers. "Fuckin' *possession*," he said, taking out his wallet, "is nine tenths of the law."

"That's what I hear."

"I'm tucking it into my secret, big-money compartment here, just in case I need it," Hanson said. "Thanks."

It was almost dark when they got back to the district. The city's big fireworks display, up in the hills, would begin soon. As they drove past Jefferson Junior High, a preliminary pair of aerial bombs lit the sky, throwing shadows through the chain-link fence surrounding the school, flickering in the bundles of razor wire coiling along the top. The dull explosions rolled through the district, echos following like aftershocks as the last light faded.

Five Eighty.

"Five Eighty, go . . ."

Uh, Five Eighty, check on a drunk and disorderly customer at the Artistic Hair Haven . . .

"Five Eighty, copy."

There weren't many streetlights in the district, and half of them had been shot out or smashed with rocks. There was no moon. Only a few stars glowed through the haze—supernovas, violent suns exploding towards them from some distant past or future, feeding on time itself, centuries, light-years, burning history into black holes.

The patrol car parted clouds of acrid smoke as it rolled deeper into the district, lurching over broken pavement, through children running the streets waving silver sparklers, illuminating their cheekbones and hollowing their eyes as they swung them in roaring circles.

"*Po*-lice. *Po*-lice," they screamed, running alongside the car, shrieking with excitement and terror and, in their world of neighborhood shootings and jail time, dead fathers, bad drugs, and the drone of TV sets left on day and night, something like joy. The screams Hanson remembered from monster movies on Saturday afternoon, when the beast's claw thrusts out of the dark towards the hero's throat. And misses. "Everything looks okay to me," the hero says, lighting a cigarette, his back to the shadows. "Just some old superstition."

Hanson had learned that terror and rage grew from the same source, and it occurred to him now that perhaps joy came from there too. Maybe even love, he thought, watching parked cars, doorways, fire escapes and open windows, glancing at the rearview mirror.

The sparklers burned a red afterglow in the backs of his eyes, bundles of loops and arcs like ribbed tunnels fading into another dimension.

Five Seventy, a car stop at Mississippi and Grant. A red, uh, red-over-white Pontiac Adam Mary King, seven three seven. No cover needed.

Copy the car stop, Five Seventy.

Roman candles coughed and threw balls of light over junked cars, over broken curbs where cardboard tubes spewed fountains of sparks. Batteries of bottle rockets whistled into the haze, and flaming propellers exploded out of vacant lots, hovered, then corkscrewed away.

Two-hundred-pound women floated through the smoke and strobing light. Young girls laughed, their eyes glittering, as they danced away in a kind of fast-slow motion, and children on bicycles looked as if they might pedal into the sky.

Hanson smiled and the big fireworks display in the hills began in earnest. Double and triple star-clusters blossomed, the stuttering reports booming through the neighborhood seconds later.

A silver sun flashed over the hills, swelling to a fragile sphere, flickering points of light. Just as it seemed about to vanish, everyone silent now, watching from the street, backyards and porches, a red star-cluster flared inside it, opened like a heart, and a collective sigh swept through the district.

Five Sixty Two.

"Five Six Two," Hanson said, "out here in the smoke and fire."

Okay, Five Sixty Two. Since you're out there, check on a possible mental. We've gotten some complaints down around Mississippi and Fremont on a white male creating a disturbance.

"What's he doing?"

Walking through backyards. Yelling racial slurs.

"Okay," Hanson said, "we'll go speak to him."

They drove slowly through the blocks, wide-eyed kids darting across the streets, lighting firecrackers then running, heads down and arms pumping, paying no attention to traffic.

"Racial slurs?" Dana said. "Is that a felony?"

"Not yet. It's very naughty though, and I'm deeply offended."

Five Six Two, we got another call on this guy. He exposed himself to some children. Uh, for what it's worth, one of the complainants said he looked like "a mummy."

"A mummy? Like . . . *Curse of the Mummy?*"

That's what the man said.

"Okee-doke. Five Six Two meets the mummy."

Up in the hills, huge star-clusters burst silver and green, majestic as they opened, arcing up, fanning out into thousands of tiny stars that swarmed towards the district like a plague, gaining speed, then, one by one, blinking out.

"I'm the one that called," he said as they pulled to the curb. "Some kind of child molester running around. He was gone by the time they told me about it."

He was a big guy in black can't-bust-'em jeans and a blue workshirt. A little boy and girl, nicely dressed, stood next to him on the sidewalk.

When they got out of the patrol car, the two children hid behind the man.

"Now get on back here," he said, taking them by the arm. "It's the police. You tell 'em what you told me."

They stood on either side of the man, looking up at the cops.

"Hi," Hanson said, kneeling down. "Was he a white guy?"

"Tell him what the man said to you."

Another aerial bomb flashed, and they grabbed their father's leg. The little girl started to cry.

"Go on back into the house then," the man said. "Go on."

"A crazy white guy?" Hanson said, as they ran to the house.

"If he'd of touched her, I wouldn't have called you. Look there," the man said, pointing at the sidewalk.

Dana shined his flashlight on the cracked concrete.

"There."

The flashlight reflected off a puddle of urine, the smell suddenly strong.

"Stood right there and pissed in front of my little girl. She said he 'talked bad' to her."

"Let me get your daughter's name and date of birth," Hanson said, pulling a notebook from his hip pocket, "and I'll get you to sign a complaint."

"I've signed complaints before. Never did a bit of good. If he comes around here again, I'll take care of it myself."

"You don't want to do something that might put you in jail," Hanson said. "If I can just get your name . . ."

"I called you once," he said.

Hanson watched him walk back to his house, wrote "comp. uncoop." in his notebook and put it back in his pocket. When he turned to walk back to the patrol car, he stepped in the urine.

"Went right through my backyard," an old man in overalls told them. "Yelling 'nigger' this and that." His face was shiny black, eyes yellow with age. "I got, *got* something for him if I see him again," he said, trembling with anger as he fumbled in the deep pocket of his overalls. "I'll be on him like white on rice," he said, looking back at his house as he pulled a big pocketknife. He opened it and held it down by his leg.

"Sir," Hanson said, stepping back. "Sir. Put the knife away."

He continued to look at his house as if the cops weren't there, bringing the knife up, the blade ground to a hawkbill point.

"Sir," Hanson said.

The sound of Hanson's nightstick sliding from the ring on his belt turned the old man around, and for a moment Hanson was afraid he might have to break his hand, or worse.

"Levi! What's wrong with you?" a gray-haired woman shouted from the porch. "Come on back in the house."

The old man's eyes seemed to focus, and he looked at the knife as if he'd forgotten it was there.

"Levi!"

He closed it, dropped it in his pocket and smiled at Hanson. "That's the boss," he said. "I better get back inside. One of our programs is on the TV."

He took a few steps towards the house, then turned and looked back at them. "Thank you, officers. We sure do thank you. God bless you," he said, bowing slightly as he spoke, his eyes on Hanson's knees. The woman watched from beneath the porch light, her eyes hard as iron.

They hadn't gone more than a block when a woman and two teenage boys waved them down. "*We* the ones that called," the woman said. "About that *crazy* man."

"Look like a motherfuckin' *mummy,*" one of the boys said, blue curlers in his hair.

"*Watch* your mouth," his mother said, slapping him on the back of the head, knocking a curler off.

"Duck tape wrap all around up here. Leg in a cast," the other boy said, laughing at his brother. "He be laughin' and talking like this." He held one arm against his chest and limped down the sidewalk, looking up at the sky. "He go, 'I know it would be beautiful.' "

"He got any weapons?" Dana said, leaning across the seat of the car.

"Naw."

"He don't have shit."

"I *told* you," his mother said. He dodged her slap this time and pointed up the street.

As they drove through the smoke and hard-edged silver shadows of the fireworks, more people called to them and flagged them down. People in the neighborhood were arming themselves with baseball bats and rakes.

A pair of blue star-clusters with purple centers burst over the hills and swarmed towards the district.

"*That* way," a woman with a hatchet yelled at them. "I saw him lookin' in my *window.*"

"You don't need that hatchet, ma'am," Hanson said. "He's not gonna hurt anybody."

"Not as long as I got my *hatchet*," she said.

"Jesus," Hanson said to Dana as they rolled on, "they're gonna kill the guy if we don't find him first." He laughed.

Five Sixty Two, would you check on a possible burglary. The complainant sounds a little flaky.

"Right," Dana said, when Radio gave them the address.

"Ira Foreskin," Hanson said. "My favorite white puke."

Complainant's name is Ira Foresman.

Ira was a burglar and crank addict they'd arrested in a Safeway that was closed for Thanksgiving the year before. He was standing in the doorway when they drove up, waiting for them in a tank top and bell-bottom jeans that bunched up at his ankles and completely covered his feet. He tensed up when he recognized them, as if he might run, then seemed to remember that he was the complainant this time.

"How you guys doin'?" he said, smoking a cigarette and chewing gum. He was a little drunk.

"Doin' okay, Ira. What's the problem?" Dana said.

"I'll tell you, man," he said, flicking his cigarette away, then smoothing back his long red hair with both hands.

"Somebody's been fucking with my shit, man."

Hanson absently thumbed his flashlight on and off several times, doing what he called the "dildo light." Dana bit his lip to keep from smiling.

"How's that?" Dana said.

"Come on in, man. I'll show you."

The house smelled like spoiled food and cigarette smoke, stuffy and humid. The windows were all nailed and painted shut.

"Check it out, man," he said, nodding through the open door of the bedroom. The sheets on the unmade bed had turned gray, and the floor was littered with beer cans, fast food boxes and piles of clothes. A big black puppy crawled out from under the bed, frightened of the cops, looking for a way out of the room.

"Some fucking watchdog *you* are," Ira snarled. The dog hunched down and squirted piss on the floor, then ran for the door. Ira kicked at him as he went past, and almost fell down.

"So what's the problem?" Dana asked.

"Check it out, man," he said. "Look at that closet. And here," he said, walking to a dresser with a cracked mirror. The drawers of the dresser were open, and Ira scooped up a handful of socks and T-shirts.

"Somebody's been fucking with my shit, man, and I've got a good idea who it was."

"And who would that be?" Dana said.

"My fucking ex-old lady. I want her fuckin' put in jail. This isn't the first time she's tried to rip me off, man."

"What's she after?"

"What do you think?" Ira said, slamming the drawer. He looked at them in the cracked mirror. "Uh, money, you know. She might *think* I had some drugs, but I don't fuck with that shit anymore, man. Hey, let's go in the other room. I want to show you something else," he said, walking towards the door as Dana opened another drawer and looked into it with distaste.

"Out here, man," Ira said.

"What about this?" Dana said, holding up a box of .45 shells.

"I don't know where those came from. Uh, I *used* to have a gun, but I got rid of it. I'm an ex-con, and that means no guns. I'm scared of guns, man. Look at this," he said, walking down the hall.

"I don't need the arrest bad enough to go through those drawers," Dana told Hanson.

"Hey," Ira said, "I want to tell you. Excellent response time. I got home. Called nine one one. And you were *here*, man. Excellent."

"Maybe you could write a commendation letter to our captain," Hanson said.

"Sure, man," Ira said. "Excuse the kitchen," he said as he turned and hit his head on the edge of an opened cabinet door.

"God *damn*," he yelled, slamming the door. The puppy raced out of the kitchen.

He pulled open a curtain to a little room off the kitchen. "Check it out, man."

A soundless TV threw shadows across the room. The drawers of a small chest had all been dumped, and clothing spilled out of a partly open closet door. Hanson felt the dog brush the back of his leg.

"Hey, puppy. Come on, Spade. Come on, now," Ira called in a high voice, squatting down and duckwalking towards the dog.

"C'mere," he said, grabbing the dog's collar.

"I really love this dog," Ira said, the dog's nails scraping the floor as Ira pulled him. "He doesn't *judge* you, you know what I mean? No matter what you do, he still loves you, man."

Ira twisted the dog's collar and pulled him closer. "Isn't that right, Spade?"

"You mind taking this one for me?" Hanson asked Dana. "I'll go back to the car and work on the report on that kid. Then I owe you one."

Dana nodded. "Ira," he said, "you want me to take a crime report on this, or what? What's missing?"

"Yeah. A crime report. We need to check for fingerprints too, man."

When Hanson walked out the door, a green and silver rocket burst in the sky behind him, the reflection sliding over the trunk and roof of the patrol car. A firecracker flashed up the street as he got in the car. He pulled the little hooded lamp on the dashboard down and turned it on, filling the patrol car with dim red light.

Five Fifty will be jackpot with one adult male.

Copy, Five Fifty jackpot.

A blue starburst lit the sky for a moment, then faded as the clustered points of light blossomed, their reflection flickering on the patrol car windshield, reminding Hanson of the last time he'd gotten a concussion. He clamped a Miscellaneous Report Form onto his clipboard.

He blinked when a cherry bomb went off up the street, pulling the notebook out of his hip pocket. It was damp with sweat, warped to the curve of his hip. Some of the entries in black ink were smeared, and the stitching was unraveling. He'd start a new notebook next week.

A firecracker popped just behind Ira's house, then another, as Hanson thumbed through the notebook, a diary of his days, past the names of victims and suspects, heights, weights, dates of birth, license plate numbers, statements, threats, complaints, phone numbers, addresses, dates and arrival times, drawings of intersections and crime scenes, mug shots, folded arrest warrants.

A kid pedaled his bicycle past the patrol car, holding clusters of hissing sparklers above his head in both hands.

Five Eighty Two. Traffic stop at Eighth and Killingsworth. White T-bird. California plate David Edward Young Four Three Two. No cover needed.

Copy, Five Eighty Two. Other car calling?

He looked down at a quote from a man they'd arrested earlier in the month. He'd been sitting on the sidewalk eating ants. "We dead stand undefended everywhere," he'd told them.

The smoke from the kid's sparklers drifted through the car, and Hanson looked out the window as if he was trying to remember something.

Other car calling?

Hanson thumbed to the last entry and began filling in the report form. His fingers threw shadows in the red light, and he moved them like finger puppets in front of the form. He looked at the house again and reached for the mike just as another radio broke the rushing static, someone keying their microphone without speaking.

Car calling?

Hanson tapped his pen on the report form.

Go ahead with your transmission.

A strange gurgling noise answered the dispatcher, reminding Hanson of something he'd heard before, something unpleasant. He tried to wave the memory away, submerge it, lose it again before it had time to take shape. It was a trick he was getting better at, turning away from the memory, looking off at something else and pretending not to hear as it groaned or shrieked or called his name, until it gave up and went away. He watched a pair of rockets in the rearview mirror as they sank below the hills and the sound came over the radio again. He held his hands under the red light, palms up, the fingers curved, turning them in, then out, throwing symmetrical shadows like Rorschach blots, insect heads, on the report form.

The memory wasn't giving up this time. To keep ignoring it would be like ignoring a screaming wino following you down the street. After a block or so you have to turn around and say, "Okay, goddammit. What *is* it?" Hanson looked up and let the memory into his eyes.

The Viet Cong in black pajamas was on his knees, his elbows lashed so tightly behind him that his scrawny chest stuck out, his shoulders almost dislocated. The Vietnamese lieutenant smiled at Hanson and gave him a thumbs-up. He spoke to his men and they pushed the prisoner backwards to the ground. One of them grabbed his throat and squeezed, yelling into his face until he opened his mouth. Another soldier stuffed a towel into his mouth and began pouring canteen cups of muddy water down the towel, slowly drowning him, laughing as he gagged and bucked.

Hanson had walked away, trying not to listen. It wasn't his prisoner. There was absolutely nothing he could have done.

He closed the notebook and looked down the street. He tapped the notebook. Then he was out the door, gun in hand, running for Ira's house.

The TV was still on, throwing shadows into the open closet door where Ira lay on his back, his hands over his stomach.

"Ambulance," he said, looking at the ceiling. When he vomited through his mouth and nose, he didn't even turn his head, trying not to move. But he gagged on it, choked, and vomited again.

Car calling?

Hanson looked towards the sound of the radio. Dana had left a thick swath of blood across the floor dragging himself to the wall where he could sit up and elevate the wound. He sat in a puddle of blood, legs straight out, holding the packset in his lap.

"Five Sixty Two, emergency," Hanson said into his packset. "I need a code-three ambulance at this location. We have a citizen and a police officer badly wounded." His voice came from Dana's packset like an echo, whining with feedback. He put his own back on his belt, while Dana's continued to transmit.

Copy, Five Six Two. All units stay off this frequency. Keep this channel open.

Dana's eyes were wide, his face freckled with blood that pulsed through the fingers of the hand he had cupped over his throat. His uniform shirt looked slimy black in the blue light from the TV. It was full of blood, ballooning out over his belt like a beer belly.

Five Seventy's on the way.

Five Eighty's going.

Hanson picked up a T-shirt from a chair and knelt in front of Dana, the blood warm as it soaked through the knees of his pants. He pulled Dana's hand away and pressed the T-shirt over the ragged hole where cartilage and tendons quivered, could feel them working against his palm as the blood soaked through the T-shirt and down his arm. With his other hand he turned off Dana's hissing packset, his fingers slipping on the little chrome knob, greasy with blood.

"You can still make it," Hanson said. Dana stared over his shoulder at the TV as if he hadn't heard, his eyes absolutely calm.

Five Six Two?

"Just hang on," Hanson said.

Dana nodded, his eyelids flickering like he was fighting sleep, then he closed his eyes and slumped forwards, the blood-filled shirt pulling loose and spilling onto his lap.

Hanson stood up, slipping in the blood, and looked down at Ira. "Who did it?"

Ira didn't move, his hands tight on his stomach.

"Can't talk," Ira whined.

Five Six Two.

Hanson turned down his packset and kicked Ira in the thigh. "Who did it?"

Ira choked, turned his head and retched.

"I'll kick you to death," Hanson said, drawing his foot back.

"Crazy guy." He gagged, tightened his lips, fought it back down. The smell of shit rose from him and filled the room.

"The guy who burglarized the place? Hiding in the closet?"

"Yuh."

Hanson looked over his shoulder at Dana slumped in his own blood like some monster stillborn fetus.

"He did this with your gun, didn't he? That he stole out of the bedroom. Didn't he?"

"Yuh."

"What kind of gun?"

"Four five."

The planes of Ira's pale face shifted as the light from the TV dimmed and brightened. His pasty skin was covered with a fine down of blond hair around his mouth and nose. Angry pimples studded his chin, and his teeth were bad. He looked up at Hanson, his eyes filling with tears.

"How many rounds in it?"

"Seben.

"Please," he sobbed, snot bubbling out of his nose and over his lips. He held his stomach, grunting with pain, and the shit smell got stronger. "Help me."

Hanson turned and walked from the room, leaving bloody footprints down the hall and out the door as sirens warbled in the distance.

He was easy to follow. People in the neighborhood pointed the way, looking at Hanson as if *he* was a monster.

"You all right, man?" one of them asked. "You look like you been in a wreck or something."

His pants and the front of his shirt had stiffened as the blood dried. His face, reflected in the window of a parked car, looked like it was mottled with dark birthmarks. The volume of his packset was turned so low that the radio traffic was an urgent mur-

muring, like voices around the bed of a dying man, calling Hanson as they deployed around Ira's house. Hanson ignored them. This wasn't about the law, and the rules didn't apply. Maybe he'd been wrong about that all along, thinking that the badge and the laws written down in a book made it possible to understand and judge the world, that it was okay, even honorable, to carry a gun and risk his life because he was *helping* people. Doc was right to have laughed at that, Hanson thought, as a kid on a bike pointed down the street.

"You *after* him, huh? Knew *some*body be after him, but didn't know it was the *po*-lice."

When he ran beneath an unbroken streetlight, a woman in her yard looked at the blood-soaked cop and snatched her little boy up, holding him as Hanson ran back into the dark.

He hadn't gone three blocks when he saw Dakota running across the street, towards the lights of a laundromat and a corner grocery store. Ignoring the boom and flash of star-clusters, people washed their clothes, smoking and watching the tumbling dryers as if they were TV sets. They were framed in the plateglass window that fronted the building, behind the words Betty's Wash House, and an amateurish painting of a smiling black woman wearing a red turban.

Dakota looked up as another rocket burst in the hills and loomed over the district, his face bluish-white in the light, as if lit from inside. The silver duct tape banding his chest gleamed like scales, then flickered with the dying starburst and faded to a dull gray. He stopped in front of the laundromat window, pointed a pistol at his head, and shouted, "I'm laughing inside. *Laughing.*"

A few of the customers noticed him, then, one by one, the others turned to look.

"*All* angels are pure spirits. Good *or* wicked," Dakota shouted. "The answer is *true.*"

By now everyone in the laundromat was looking out the window, not quite sure what was going on, as Dakota turned the pistol and fired. The window shuddered, and Betty's right eye opened as if she'd just been startled out of a long sleep. He fired yellow flame again and another hole appeared just below her nose.

The people inside froze, crouched, trying to sort it out, as cracks appeared around the bullet holes and spiderwebbed across the window. When the window collapsed, they dove onto the floor or ran for the doors behind the falling curtain of green-edged glass.

Dakota walked up the sidewalk holding the gun loosely at his side, as if he'd forgotten it was there. He stopped, looked over his shoulder at Hanson, then turned down an alley past dull silver garbage cans and out of sight.

Hanson unsnapped his safety strap and pulled the pistol free from the grip of the front-break holster. He thumbed the safety off and ran across the street, glass grinding beneath his boots, people in the laundromat screaming, into the mouth of the alley that smelled of rotten vegetables, grease, and the hot exhaust of clothes dryers. He dodged garbage cans and a Dumpster the size of an APC, then slipped on a half-eaten cheeseburger, his head catching the edge of a fire escape.

Black stars and smoke exploded in his eyes, but he glared past them and kept moving, tasting the pain in his nose. He ran through an open gate into someone's backyard as the stars faded and flickered out and the smoke drifted away. He crouched next to an overturned shopping cart, the packset whispering at his belt. He turned off the packset. Something was rustling bushes in the shadows of the house just ahead.

Hanson stared into the dark, above the sound, then past it, wide-eyed and dreamy as a blind man, trying to pick up a shadow or flutter of movement. He stepped closer, his eyes unfocused, passive. He stopped. Listened. Opened his mouth and inhaled, tasting the air. Sirens wailed in the distance.

A light went on in a window where a man walked to the refrigerator, took out a quart of beer, then walked back out of sight. The light went off, but it had been on long enough for Hanson to see the shrubbery on the far side of the house where the noise had come from. He started across the yard, then froze when the light came on again. The man looked up at the ceiling, then carefully opened a cabinet, lifted out a fifth of vodka and took a sip. Another. He started to screw the top back on the bottle, then took one more sip before he slid the bottle back and closed the cabinet. The light went out.

A step at a time, stopping to smell the air, listen, cocking his head to look out of the corner of his eyes and use his night vision, Hanson worked his way to the other side of the house and edged along a chain-link fence. He was sweating now, his underarms and stomach and crotch sticky where sweat moistened the dry blood on his uniform, its sweet metallic stink hanging on him like death.

Aaron Allen's Cadillac cruised down the street in front of the house, pumping out a bass line from its radio, and Hanson used the noise to cover his own footsteps. When the car passed, he stopped to listen. A faint scent of honeysuckle rode the air.

Hanson heard the snarl an instant before the fence hit him. The dog hooked a tooth in his shirt, then lunged and got a better bite through the fence as Hanson fought to keep his balance. The dog's breath was hot against the small of Hanson's back as he was jerked back into the fence. Hanson rode the shuddering fence, holding his gun arm across his chest, stumbling as he tried to line up a shot at the dog and not hit himself.

Dakota, just a shadow, stepped around the corner of the house, the gun glinting, and Hanson instinctively threw his left hand up to shield himself. Dakota appeared, vanished, strobed in and out of the dark, his head like a jack-o'-lantern, like magic, in the yellow muzzle flash of a single shot. Hanson felt the heat of the muzzle blast on his hand, heard the slug *snap* past, just as the dog yelped behind him and his shirt tore free. Dakota appeared again and Hanson stumbled forwards, hitting his head on a window box before falling on a lawn mower, his ribs flaring with pain, losing his pistol.

Six shots, he thought, grunting as he rolled off the lawn mower, the wounded dog whining and thrashing somewhere behind him. He pulled himself to his knees, then his feet. His head roared, turning the world red as he tried not to throw up and hurt the ribs even more. He walked to the corner of the house very slowly, breathing shallowly, his vision coming back, pulse by pulse, risking a look around the house.

He's got one more, he thought, watching Dakota hop and stagger across the street, chunks of plaster breaking off the cast. He tripped on the curb, screaming with pain and rage as he fell.

Hanson fumbled the little keychain flashlight out of his pocket and flicked it on in one-second bursts, looking for his gun. Across the street Dakota talked to himself, the words garbled, hurrying through long sentences that stopped in mid-phrase, the rhythm of an auctioneer.

Hanson found the pistol, looped the flashlight around his left wrist, and got to his feet.

"Good," Dakota yelled to no one in particular. "Hit me," as he ran on, lurching and screaming each time his bad leg hit the ground, vanishing between two houses.

Hanson went after him, grunting, the cracked ribs sawing against each other. He tried to ignore the pain, leave it behind, but it wouldn't go away. He stopped in the middle of the street, breathing, getting ready, then *took* the pain and made it his, sucking it up and using it to get him across the street, walking, then jogging, screaming out each breath as he began to run. Thorns snagged his shirt and pants, slapped his face as he stumbled and fell through blackberry vines as thick as bullwhips into another backyard.

Dakota half-turned, still running, and swung the gun around. A clothesline caught him in the throat, slamming him down, the gun throwing yellow flame past Hanson's ear, blinding him for a moment.

Click. Click.

Dakota sat with his back against the clothesline pole, pointing the gun at Hanson's face. It clicked and snapped, slide locked open, like a broken machine as he continued to pull the trigger. Hanson shone the little flashlight on him and he grinned, showing Thorazine-rotted teeth, one side of his face swollen, lopsided as a rotten pumpkin, an earring driven like a fishhook beneath the closed eye, the little blue unicorn dangling like a spider. He dropped the gun and held out his good arm. "Put on. The cuffs."

Hanson smelled him. His burnt popcorn psychotic sweat almost overpowering the gunpowder and honeysuckle.

"Too late," Hanson said, "for that."

"I surrender," Dakota said.

Hanson fired twice, knocking Dakota back into the clothesline pole, punching two holes in the duct tape around his chest.

". . . your prisoner."

Hanson fired again into the tape. Again. Gun smoke burned his eyes and his ears rang.

"You're in. Big. Trouble now," Dakota said, looking up into the weakening yellow flashlight. "Eeeeee. Eeeeee," he keened, grinning, his rotten teeth black and pink now with blood.

He choked on a laugh, grunted, snorted, waggling his tongue. "Eeeee. Eeeeee."

He leaned back against the clothesline pole and closed his eye, his breathing wet and ragged. When Hanson bent down for a closer look, the eye opened, meeting Hanson's.

"I know something . . ."

The sirens much closer now, blue and red lights fanning the yards, the blue unicorn crawling on his face.

". . . you want to know."

Hanson leaned closer, poised to jump back, the pistol close to his side. "What?" he whispered.

Dakota smiled, the eye drawing Hanson closer. He pursed his lips as if he were going to kiss Hanson, the eye shining, and spit hot blood in his eyes and mouth.

"Some night," Dakota croaked, breathing through his mouth, "in the dark . . ."

Hanson blinked blood out of his eyes, and shot him through his open mouth, the high-velocity, hollow-point slug blowing out the back of his skull, shrieking into the dark.

Dakota's shaved head gonged off the clothesline pole, vomiting blood. His bad leg twitched, kicked, danced heel-and-toe, then he toppled over the army .45 with swastika grips.

TWENTY-SEVEN

IT WAS LATE AFTERNOON, and Hanson was already a little drunk. The medical examiner's building looked like a dentist's office, one-story stucco with a blond wood door. When he rang the bell, an electronic reproduction of a woman's voice spoke one word from the corroded aluminum gills of the intercom set in the door. "Yes?"

Hanson identified himself and the door buzzed open.

It looked like a dentist's office inside too. The receptionist sat at a desk on the other side of a counter, talking on the phone. The nameplate on the desk said, TAMMY—how may I help?

"I did not," she said into the phone. "No. I said, 'I *might.*'"

Little potted cacti bristled at either end of the counter and a small aquarium glowed in the center. Xeroxed cartoons and slogans, those little signs you see in most offices, were Scotch taped to the counter. Things like, You Don't Have to Be Crazy to Work Here, But it Helps. Or, You Want it *When?* A water-stained "Happy Face" said, Smile—It's Contagious.

The receptionist had long straight blond hair, nice lips, and a perfect little nose.

A California girl, Hanson thought, *with a nose job.* She gave him a quick smile and said, "Be right with you," showing off her breasts as she turned in her chair.

Hanson smiled too and said, "Okee-doke." He folded his arms across his chest and watched the fish glide past each other, turn at the glass, and pass again going the other way.

"Weh-ell, the East Coast girls are hip, I real-ly dig those styles they wear-eh-ear," he sang softly, leaning down for a closer look, moving his shoulders to the beat of the Beach Boys' "California Girls."

"And the southern girls, wi-ith the way they . . . talk, they knockmeout when I'm downthere . . ."

"I have to go," the girl said to the phone. "I've got a customer waiting." She listened, smiled, and said, "Don't you? Well, okay then. I thought you did. Um-hum . . ." She glanced at Hanson. "I don't care if they hear us," she said, lowering her voice. "I can't help it. Anyway, it's your fault. Yes. Me too," she said, and hung up.

She turned her smile to Hanson. "How may I help you, officer?"

"Do I have time to get my teeth cleaned?"

"I'm sorry?"

"Just kidding. This place looks like a dentist's office."

She glanced around the room and Hanson laughed. "At last, painless dentistry. For the dead."

"Excuse me?"

"How come you keep the door locked like that? Do people wander in and shoplift bodies?"

"You'd be surprised at some of the people who try to get in here."

"Oh yeah? Not normal?" Hanson said.

"Do you have some ID?" she asked him.

"Yes, ma'am," Hanson said, taking out his wallet and holding his police ID card out towards her. "I'm a normal guy. I know who I am, and what I represent."

The girl looked at the ID, then at Hanson. "Yes?"

"The ME said I could pick up an envelope. Some old evidence. Maybe in that box there?"

The girl swiveled her chair around and thumbed through a cardboard box full of envelopes. "Hanson?"

"That's it."

She pulled an envelope out and laid it on the counter. "You'll have to sign for it," she said, sliding an appointment book over to him.

Hanson signed the book and picked up the envelope. Stamped in red, across the flap, were the words: INACTIVE—DISCARD. He shook it. The paper rattled.

"Okee-doke," he said. "Thank you very much and *muchas gracias.*" She watched him as he walked to the door. "And," Hanson said, turning around, "you be sure and have a nice day."

He walked out the door into the sullen afternoon sun. "I know, Truman, I know," he said, opening the door of the van, "I better straighten up."

"Truman?" he said, looking at the empty passenger seat. "Truman?" his voice tinny in the empty van, panic filling his chest until the dog crawled out from beneath the seat.

"Hey. Hey, bud. You had me worried there for a second." He reached back for a ragged wool blanket stuffed in the wheel well, spread it on the passenger seat and lifted Truman onto it. "I'm sorry, man," he said. "I know you don't like riding in this van, but I didn't want to drive out here alone today. We'll be home in no time."

Traffic was heavy on the freeway, commuters and vacation traffic. Family cars with luggage racks and tied-down trunks. Four-wheel drive trucks. Vans with bubble windows, metal-flake paint, and airbrushed murals of mountain sunsets. Elk on the ridgeline. Muscular, big-breasted women in steel bikinis, swinging enormous swords, fighting off wolves.

He pulled out to pass a Winnebago Apache camper with a trail bike strapped to the front, another to the rear, towing a boat. The driver looked down at him, squinting through the smoke from a cigarette in his mouth, accelerating. Hanson dropped back as he pulled away. The eight lanes of asphalt stretched on and on like a pair of skid marks, silver clouds of heat and gas fumes boiling from them. Keeping his eyes on the road, Hanson reached over and scratched Truman's ears. "Almost home," he told him.

Once he turned off the freeway to the two-lane blacktop, the temperature dropped fifteen degrees. It began to smell more like berry fields and pine trees than hot oil. Stormbreaker dominated the eastern horizon, snow still heavy on the peak. It killed a few skiers every year. Solid stone, the mountain was serene and indifferent as time, the hate and sorrow and stink of the ghetto no more than a season of bad weather that would pass, Dana's death as insignificant as a pheasant shotgunned in a cornfield.

Hanson sat in the garage-sale easy chair, in the pool of light from a gooseneck lamp, looking at the fingernails of his right hand. A small blue glass full of Scotch on the side table caught the light. Something dark was wedged under his thumbnail. It couldn't be blood. He'd showered and scrubbed two and three times a day after that night. Dana had been in the ground for almost two weeks.

The book *Steam* lay open on his leg. He'd read the paragraph on page nine so many times, it had become gibberish.

    A cubic foot of heated water under a pressure of
    60 to 70 pounds per square inch has the same en-
    ergy as one pound of gunpowder. At low, red heat,
    it has forty times this amount of energy, in a
    form to be so expended.

Too drunk to read now, the Model 39 stuck between his right thigh and the arm of the overstuffed chair, he listened to bluegrass banjo and mandolin on his stereo. He liked the melodramatic mandolin, and when the banjo and fiddle came in, they were funny and sad at the same time.

He put the book on the table and stood up, took a drink of the Scotch and walked over to the woodstove. A photo of Falcone in uniform, cut from the group academy portrait, was propped on a shelf above the stove, where the yellow envelope was still sealed, circular EVIDENCE stamps along the edge of the taped flap. He took it back to his chair, ripped it open, and dumped the seven lumps of lead into the palm of his left hand. The slugs taken out of Dakota's body. Half-jacketed hollow points. One hundred and fifteen grains each. Unfired, they were pretty. Conical lead slugs, a hole drilled down the center, set in a scalloped brass jacket. But these were distorted, the gray lead cores peeled back like wax over the brass jacket from the impact with muscle and bone. The one that had gone through Dakota's head was flared like a mushroom.

They were heavy in his hand as he held his palm up to his nose and inhaled. They stunk of bad breath, sweat, fear and shit. Rotting meat and corruption. The smell of death.

Bits of muscle tissue and flesh and shiny flakes of black blood were trapped in the ridges and folds of lead. Hanson inhaled again and smiled, picked up the mushroomed slug and pressed it against his own forehead. He dumped the handful of slugs on the table and set them up on their bases. They leaned sideways like brutal little trolls, drunken, swaggering chessmen in a game where the rules kept changing, and losing quickly was the best anyone could hope for. He lined them up like a rifle squad and, forearms on his knees, studied them, giving each one the name of a dead soldier he had known. When he'd named them all he dropped them, one by one, into a small deerskin pouch he'd bought earlier that day at one of the head shops that sold bongs and pipes and incense. They'd called it a "stash bag," for carrying dope, but now, he thought, hanging the bag around his neck by a leather cord, it was a *katha*, a kind of amulet the Montagnards wore on combat operations.

Hanson sipped the last of the smoky scotch, listening to the Dobro and harmonica come in on "Soldier's Joy" until it ended and the needle hissed in circles around the center of the record.

He pulled the pistol out, tilted it slightly side-to-side so it caught the light, thinking about the Fourth of July yard party, little Ali and his junkie mother. He should have let them *take* his gun, but whenever he was threatened something took over and he fought to survive. The ones who *wanted* to live all died.

He'd field-stripped the pistol and cleaned it twice—with Hoppe's #9, a copper bore-brush, cotton patches and an old toothbrush—after Internal Affairs returned it to him the week before. He pulled the slide back just far enough to see the half-jacketed round in the chamber, then dropped the loaded clip out, tapped it against the heel of his hand to align the rounds, and slid it back into the grip where it locked with a *click*.

A good gun, he thought, thumbing off the safety that had saved his life when Dakota had taken it away.

He'd told the shrink what he wanted to hear, and the department had given him two weeks off with pay. A better deal than the three days' vacation he'd gotten for killing Millon.

He tested the play in the trigger, then pulled it back just far enough to lift the hammer a tiny fraction of an inch. A pretty good gun, but he didn't like the alloy frame either. Doc was right, he thought, raising the hammer another fraction, and another, holding the trigger against the spring-tension halfway between the firing pin and full-cock, when he felt Truman brush his leg. He looked down at him, past the muzzle of the pistol. "How you doin', bud? I didn't hear you come in," he said, putting the gun down.

Truman lowered himself until his stiff legs gave way, sat with a *thump,* and found a comfortable position against Hanson's leg. "I'm okay," Hanson told him. "Just thinking."

A FEW DAYS LATER, Doc came by just after dark. They went driving in the Trans Am, a "road trip," and it was almost dawn when they got back. Truman was waiting. Doc asked Hanson if he could leave something for safekeeping.

"Don't do it if you don't want to," Doc said.

"I'll take care of it for you."

"It's not what you think it is," Doc said.

"I don't know what it is, and I don't want to know."

Doc opened the trunk of his car and took it out from behind the spare tire, a cardboard box, not much bigger than an unabridged dictionary, wrapped in duct tape.

"Watch your back," Doc said. "Don't trust anybody."

"I trust you," Hanson said. "I always did."

Doc looked at Truman, and for a moment, Hanson thought he was going to say something to the dog, maybe even pet him, but he turned and walked away without looking back.

Hanson took the box inside and turned on the light. The words "PRODUCT OF VIETNAM" were half covered by the tape. Above them, in larger, orange letters, the words "GOLDEN TUR-TLE BRAND" and a turtle with the serene eyes of a Buddha, rising phoenixlike from boiling clouds of flame. Truman sniffed it, then backed away, snorting.

"Chili powder," Hanson said. His eyes and nose were burning too. He pulled away a baseboard in the kitchen, over the half-finished new foundation where a section of floor was cut away, and slid the box up behind the wall, wedging it in with a short piece of two-by-four. By the time he finished, the fresh timbers around the foundation glowed with the first gunmetal light of dawn.

———

He was making coffee that afternoon before going to work, when he noticed the new spiderweb, spun while he'd been asleep, spreading like a hand over the cutaway section of floor and wall where he'd hidden the box. It had already entangled a fuzzy, tiger-striped bumblebee.

Hanson sat on his heels by the open floor, drinking his coffee and watching the fat bee buzz and quiver itself deeper into the web. He sensed Truman behind him, or maybe he'd heard him breathing, or smelled him. He picked up a sixteen-penny nail, rolled it in his fingers as if he might use it to tear the bee loose, then dropped it on the floor and stood up. "Nature's hard core," he said. "There's no changing that." Truman followed him out the backdoor.

He wanted to plant some more Swiss chard and beets for the fall, and put in more of the sturdy Crackerjack marigolds. The ones he'd planted with Falcone were two feet high, orange and yellow blossoms the size of snowballs, bobbing in a breeze so faint he could barely feel it on his cheek.

The tomato plants looked good, pale green tomatoes the size of marbles hanging from the dark green leaves. Some of the peppers were already big enough to slice up into salads. The cucumber plants showed yellow blossoms and even a few tiny cucumbers that seemed to double in size every day. He watered them all down, using his thumb to vary the spray from the hose, hung the hose on the side of the house, and hands in his pockets, looked back at the marigolds, thinking about Falcone while the phone rang in the kitchen.

"Okay, okay," he said. He snatched the phone up in mid-ring and brought it to his ear just as the connection vanished into the dial tone.

He found the nail and knelt down by the spiderweb, his eyes adjusting to the shadows until he saw the bumblebee, its black eyes bulging beneath the dirty white cocoon in which it was wrapped. The bottom of the web quivered, the spider appeared, then glided away, up into the flooring, like a witch on a broom. Too late.

WHEN HANSON WENT to work the next afternoon, he was assigned to work the district with Duncan. At roll call, Bendix read an FBI report on the two unidentified Asians found dead out near the airport, their wallets full of phony ID, both of them shot in the head and chest with a 9mm. They had been identified as Vietnamese working with the DEA, one of them a police captain with the South Vietnamese National Police, both shot with the same gun that killed LaVonne Berry.

TWENTY-EIGHT

DON'T YOU GET tired of nothing but, you know, blacks every day? I don't mind working down here once in a while, it's pretty interesting, but all the time? No thanks," Duncan said, as they drove south on the Avenue.

Pharaoh was picking up cans in the parking lot of the Top Hat, a nightclub whose entrance opened through a painted plywood facade of a huge top hat. Hanson clicked the PA button on the radio, the speaker atop the car clattering.

"Hey, Pharaoh," he shouted out the open window.

"All right," Pharaoh growled, not looking up from his work.

"The Avenue," Hanson said. "My hometown."

Down at the end of the block, Dee Brazzle stood in the doorway of the Bon Ton Billiards, arms folded across his chest, glaring at them.

"Oh, yeah?" Hanson said, meeting Dee's eyes through the dirty windshield. "You some kind of badass today, Dee?"

Duncan glanced at Hanson, smiled, and shook his head.

"You want to *look* at me?" Hanson said, slowing the patrol car.

"You wanna look," he said, angling the car across the street towards the Bon Ton. Duncan's patronizing smile faded. Dee turned *slowly* and stepped inside.

"That's right, Dee," Hanson said to the empty doorway. "That's right," he said, drifting back over to the right side of the street, "maybe you need to go to jail before long."

"Who *cares?*" Duncan said. "Nothing will ever change down here. It's just a game."

"Everything's a game," Hanson said.

"Not for me. I plan to get some rank and get off the street. The only way to do that is go by the book."

"Uh-huh," Hanson said.

"Isn't that the way it works?"

"Yep," Hanson said, "trouble is . . ." He waved at a man wearing a bloody apron in front of Gilbert's Country Kitchen. He looked at Hanson, took the cigar out of his mouth, and nodded back. "Maurice there shot an asshole who deserved it. He'd be doing ten to twenty years if I'd gone by the book. He hates cops. It *kills* him to nod back like that, but he knows I kept him out of jail." Hanson laughed. "What a world."

A new red Monte Carlo was pulled up to the curb in the next block, a dark-skinned woman wearing pink satin short shorts and a tiny matching halter leaning in the window on her four-inch, stacked-heel shoes. She was one of the three prostitutes in the district whose name was "Candy." The mug shot Hanson had of her in the shoebox showed a swollen ridge beneath one eye, stitched with bright beads of blood.

When Candy saw the patrol car, she straightened up and strutted down the sidewalk, her silver-pink Dynel wig glowing in the sun. The driver of the Chevy, a white guy in a shirt and tie, leaned across the seat and shouted out the window after her.

"Get me the registration on that Monte Carlo," Hanson said as they drove past, "and I'll show you a new game."

There wasn't much they could do about the whores in the district. Every summer some citizens' group complained and the cops had to harass them more than usual, but that only drove them to a different block or another part of town for a week, then they came back.

But there was an etiquette the cops and whores went by. One of the rules was that they couldn't pick up tricks in front of the cops. If they broke the rules, they'd get cited for jaywalking, littering, hitchhiking, or obstructing traffic, and their names run for warrants. If their attitude was bad, they'd be driven out to the stockyards where they'd have to walk at least a mile before they could find a pay phone to call their pimp. That was a long walk in the kind of shoes they wore. Dana and Hanson had exerted the same discretion with the illegal gambling and liquor in the pool halls and cafes. It was a game that kept things from getting out of hand.

As they drove around the block, Radio came back with the registration . . . *a nineteen seventy-five Chevrolet—two-door—in the name of Caspar J. Edwards of five oh one North Price Place, Oxford, Washington. Also registered to Betty C. Edwards, same address.*

They found the red Chevy cruising slowly up Fremont Street. "This guy was hanging around here last week looking for whores. He's gonna end up getting rolled," Hanson said, "and I'll have to do all the paperwork. And he'll tell me, 'Gee, officer. I was stopped at a stoplight and this . . .'—he'll kind of hesitate here, deciding if he should say 'nigger'—'. . . this *nigger* jumped in the car, showed me a gun, and took all my money.'

"I'll ask him what he's doing in this part of town, and he'll tell me he took the wrong freeway ramp and got lost."

Hanson turned on the overheads. The driver of the Chevy looked in his rearview mirror and pulled to the curb.

"We'll be out at Williams and Fremont for a minute," Hanson told Radio, "talking to a citizen.

"Don't say anything," he told Duncan. "Just *look* at him, like you're about ready to kick his ass."

Hanson walked to the driver's window and looked down at the driver, a big guy who was starting to get fat. He still had freckles across his nose, and wore a pencil-thin mustache. He looked up at Hanson with a salesman's smile. Hanson didn't change expression, and Caspar looked over at Duncan. Hanson's packset hissed. He looked back at Hanson.

"What's the problem?"

Hanson took out his notebook and pulled a pen from his shirt pocket. He looked down at Caspar, tapped the notebook with his pen.

"What's this about?" Caspar said, sitting straighter, trying to bluff it out.

"You're asking for trouble when you come down here to pick up whores," Hanson said.

"What?" he said, trying to sound outraged. "Whores? Are you kidding me?" Then, "Oh. That girl back there? I was just asking her for directions. I took the wrong damn freeway exit."

Hanson tapped the pen, looked over the roof at Duncan.

"I got *lost*, okay?"

"Caspar, does Betty know you're down here picking up whores?"

He barely hesitated. "I *told* you what I was doing."

Not bad, Hanson thought.

"Don't *lie* to me, Caspar," he said. "Maybe Betty should know about this . . . *activity* you're engaging in, before you give her syphilis. If you haven't already."

"What's your badge number?" His forehead was damp, and a drop of sweat rolled down his temple.

Hanson smiled at him.

"I *want* your *badge* number. My wife and our marital relations are none . . ."

"I *was* gonna cut you some slack, Cas-*per*. I wasn't going to arrest you for 'engaging in prostitution,' take you to jail, and im-pound your car. But you had to lie to me. I guess you think I'm stupid, but . . ."

"Not at all. I just . . ."

". . . but *worse* than that—and don't interrupt me again, Cas-par—you thought you could *threaten* me. Maybe you don't care what it's gonna do to your reputation up there in Oxford when they find out you've been picking up black whores. Oral sex in the front seat of the car. Nigger blowjobs right where Betty sits when *she* drives the car. She'll like that, won't she?

"And you're gonna lie to me because you think I'm some kind of dumb fucking cop," Hanson said, clicking his pen and writing in his citation book.

"No, sir, officer, I never thought you were, you know, and I would *not* threaten a police officer. I'm sorry, if I said something that sounded like that. And I apologize."

Hanson clicked the pen. He looked at Duncan who was trying not to smile. He clicked the pen again, put it in his pocket, leaned down and looked at Caspar. "I'd better not see you around here again. Pick up your whores somewhere else, okay?"

"Yes, sir. Thank you," he said, putting the car in gear. He sig- naled, checked his mirror, and carefully pulled out into the street.

"Great," Duncan said.

"Only problem is, if the registration isn't current, you call him somebody else's name and look stupid. But with a new car like that, from a little town in Washington, I figure it's probably okay." He laughed. "Unless he's a little crazy, or drunk or strung out on cocaine and gets so scared he shoots me. Then the joke's on me."

Hanson could see it was trouble a block away, people clustered around the door of the Dekum Tavern, a white, working-class bar. Across the street, on the other corner, black people spilled out the door of Soul Train, a concrete-block bar painted in a checkerboard of red, black and green, the colors of the Black Liberation flag.

"Only about half the people in those two bars carry guns," Hanson said.

Duncan reached for the mike.

"Wait on that," Hanson said. "We don't need a backup *yet*. Just tell 'em we'll be doing a bar check."

Hanson and Dana had made regular walk-throughs at both bars, and got along with the owners and bartenders. Everybody in both bars knew that if any trouble started, it would get *serious* in a hurry. Whites and blacks were usually polite to each other when they passed on the sidewalk, walking to their cars.

An armed society is a polite society, Hanson thought.

When Duncan told Radio about the bar check, Sgt. Bendix came on the air, *I'm just off the freeway from that location. I need a quick meet with Five Sixty Two. Put me at that location as well.*

"Shit," Hanson said.

The problem was at the Dekum Tavern. The customers at the Soul Train were just watching. So far. Hanson pulled up in front of the Soul Train and got out of the car. "How's it going, Arthur?" he asked the owner, who was leaning against a parking sign, an unlit, half-smoked cigar in his mouth.

"Going fine. On this side of the street."

"What's happening over there?"

He shrugged.

"Lonnie, how you doin'?" Hanson asked the bartender who was wearing a red and green dashiki, watching the Dekum Tavern through big, wraparound sunglasses. Lonnie ignored him.

Hanson cocked his head and squinted at him. "Those sunglasses. You know, they make you look like a . . . some kind of *insect*. You know that, Lonnie?"

Arthur laughed. "That's exactly what I said. Looks like a bug." He nodded across the street. "You know the kid who drives that old 'Lock Doctor' truck?"

"Dewey Davis?"

"I don't know his name, but some motherfucker I never seen before whuppin' him bad out in front a minute ago. And his *friends* just watching it," he said, shaking his head.

"Trouble with you people," Lonnie said, "is you don't stand together against the common foe. That's the thing gonna be your downfall."

"You may be right, Lonnie."

"You want me to take it?" Duncan said.

"Sure. White people. Your specialty," Hanson said, as Sgt. Bendix pulled up across the street. Hanson got to the car just as Bendix reached for the radio to call for cover.

"It's okay, Sarge. No big problem."

"Are you sure?" he said, looking at the crowd in front of the Soul Train. "Looks pretty explosive to me."

"The problem's in the Dekum Tavern. Those guys are just watching. They want to see the police abuse a *white* guy. Duncan's got the call."

Dewey was just inside the doorway, out of the sun, saying something to a guy in greasy coveralls. His face was bloody, broken glasses hanging from one ear.

"Are you okay, sir?" Duncan said. "Should I call an ambulance?"

"Ah'b okay," he said, breathing through his mouth, blood bubbling from his broken nose.

"Are you sure you don't want an ambulance?" Bendix said.

Dewey nodded.

"What happened, sir?"

"Nothing."

"Sir," Duncan said, "obviously *something* happened."

Dewey shook his head, turning to go.

"Dewey," Hanson said, blocking his way. "Look at me."

"I'm *okay,*" he said, the white of one eye completely red. "Can I go?"

Hanson nodded. "Okay."

Someone in the bar said, "Called the cops, huh?" He had a New York accent, and he was loud.

"Now why do I think that's our guy?" Hanson said.

"Where's your hat?" Bendix asked Hanson.

Hanson looked down at the sidewalk, then turned to Bendix. "Right."

He jogged across the street and pulled the hat out from behind the driver's headrest. "You better watch out *now*, Lonnie," he said, slamming the door. He leaned over the hood, looking at him. "I'm wearing my special, no-slack, law-enforcement hat," he said, jamming it down on his head so his ears stuck out.

"Watch out, my ass," Lonnie said, never turning his head.

Duncan and Bendix were talking to a stocky guy in a yellow shirt over by the pool tables. Hanson stood with his back against the bar, watching. Darla, the barmaid, came over, taking the cigarette from her mouth, and leaned on the bar with her forearms. She wore tight jeans, a belt with a western buckle, and a low-necked gray T-shirt with no bra.

"That's the kind of chickenshit dump this is," the guy in the yellow shirt announced. "People who can't take care of their own problems. Gotta call the fuckin' cops."

"A real asshole," Darla hissed in Hanson's ear. "He beat the shit out of Dewey. For 'looking at him,' he said."

"You willing to sign a complaint?" Hanson said, leaning back on his elbows, remembering the perfume she wore.

"What's the charge?" the guy said. "What's the fuckin' *chaage?*"

She took a drag on the cigarette. "Dewey's a sweet kid, but it's up to him. I don't have time to be going to court. I just want the asshole to leave and go back to New York or wherever the fuck he's from."

"Is *everybody* afraid of him?" Hanson asked, looking at her over his shoulder.

"*Look* at him. And," she said, leaning closer, the neck of her shirt sagging open, looking Hanson in the eyes, "he said something about a gun in his car."

She blew smoke out of the corner of her mouth. "Red GTO. New York plates. Up the street."

Hanson smiled. "Okee-doke."

"It's good to see you," she said. "I guess you know Frank's back in the joint?"

"Yeah," he said, looking back towards the pool table. "Sorry to hear that."

"Come by some time."

"If you got no *chaage*," the guy said, "I got better things to do."

"I still think about you. You know?"

Bendix said, "We're trying to determine exactly what . . ."

"Make a *decision*, fa' chrissake," he said. Duncan looked at Hanson, shrugged his shoulders.

"I better get over there," Hanson said, standing up. He looked back at Darla. "I think about you, too."

"Whaddaya talkin' about?" the man asked Duncan as Hanson walked up and, by the look in Bendix's eyes, realized that his hat was still jammed down on his head. He left it that way.

"I come in here for a beer, and right away some guy wants to suck my cock. Ask *him* for ID."

"Yes, sir, but . . ."

"*Another* one?" he said, looking past Duncan to Hanson. "Where's the fuckin' SWAT team?"

Hanson smiled at him.

"You got something to charge me with, then *say* so," he said, picking up a glass of beer and drinking it down, " 'cause if you don't, I'm out of this faggot gin mill. I know my fuckin' rights.

"Anybody got a problem with that?" he said, looking around the bar. "Okay?" he asked Duncan. He set the glass on the pool table, and walked past him to the door.

"Excuse me, sir," Hanson said, following him outside, moving to keep the sun at his back.

Across the street, Arthur grinned. Lonnie watched like a green and red bug-eyed lizard.

"Okay, *what?*" the man said, turning around. His shirt was dark with sweat at the armpits, hanging loose at the waist, just above his pants pockets. He didn't move like he was drunk.

"*Hanson*, huh?" he said, squinting at his name tag. "*Officer* Hanson. What do *you* want?" he said, looking him slowly up and down with a kind of theatrical exaggeration. He had big forearms and a face that had taken some damage over the years.

"I really would like to see some ID, sir."

"Is that right?" he said, beginning to smile. "What the fuck for, Hanson?"

"Well . . . gosh, it's just that I need your name for my report.

So I won't get in trouble with my sergeant," Hanson said, smiling pleasantly, a public servant, his ears sticking out beneath his hat.

"Gosh?" the man said. *"Gosh?"* He laughed. "For your report, huh?"

"Yes, sir," Hanson said, laughing with him, his chest swelling with happiness, the best he'd felt in days.

The man walked up to Hanson, almost into him, but stopped just before their chests touched, staring into his eyes, breathing in quick snorts like a bull.

"Sure," he said, stepping back, "I'll show you some ID. Why not?" He opened his left hand, then slowly made a fist and thrust it up between their faces, turning it to show Hanson the watch he was wearing, the crystal freshly broken. The silver ring on his hand, a lion's head with ruby eyes, glowed in the light.

"Here. How's that for ID?"

"A driver's license would be better. A *picture* ID of some kind would be, that would be *perfect,* I think."

"Will that make you happy?" he said, pulling out a packet of credit cards and ID, held together with rubber bands, his driver's license on top.

"Yes, sir."

"Well *enjoy* yourself then," he said, holding the packet up.

"Great," Hanson said, looking at him over the top of the license as he read the name, "Morris Martin Murphy."

"You got it, Jack."

When Hanson reached for the license, Murphy pulled it away and put it back in his pocket. "You seen it long enough."

"New York, huh, Mister Murphy?"

"Fuckin' A, right. I'm goin' *back* there too. This is the shits out heah."

"You must be of Irish extraction, I guess," Hanson said.

"Is the fuckin' pope Catholic?"

"Yes, sir."

"You're not too bright, are you?"

Hanson grinned and shook his head.

The man looked over at all the people in front of the Soul Train. "What the fuck *you* lookin' at?" he yelled.

"You got enough niggahs out here," he said to Hanson, still looking across the street. "Looks like fuckin' Newark around here, for chrissake."

"I read once," Hanson said, stepping close, his voice low, "that the Irish were the niggers in New York until the other niggers moved up there. What a world."

Murphy looked at him.

"So I guess your grandmother was a nigger."

"You think I'm that stupid? Fuck you," he said, stepping off the curb.

"Mister Murphy," Hanson said, louder now. "Please, for your own safety, would you please step back on the curb until the light turns green?"

"Fuck you."

The stoplight shone from its yellow hood like a happy idea, glowing through the busy lightning bolt pattern of the glass, as Hanson stepped out and reached for Murphy, feeling like a dancer who has found his place in the music, almost watching himself now from where he had been standing a moment before, knowing that the next few seconds belonged to him.

"Here, Mister Murphy. Please," he heard himself say, as he cupped Murphy's elbow, a harmless gesture to anyone watching.

Pain flared in Murphy's eyes as Hanson, still smiling, ground his thumb through the soft pocket of tendons in Murphy's elbow to the tiny bundle of nerves that controlled the joint, mashing it against the bone.

"You should have seen it," he told Zurbo the next day, "I looked like a movie star. You know how those fucking pressure points don't work half the time? You jam your thumb in there, and nothing happens. You push harder and the guy just *looks* at you, like maybe you're queer and you're trying to feel him up or something. Not *this* time, Your Honor. Fucker straightened up like I'd hit him with a ninety-watt cattle prod."

Hanson felt Murphy shift his weight to throw the punch, and ducked beneath it, stepping behind him. He jammed Murphy's elbow up behind his back and, using Murphy's own momentum, ran him headfirst into the brick wall of the Dekum Tavern. He bounced him off the wall, kicked his legs out from under him, and slammed him face-first into the sidewalk. He dropped down on him, driving one knee into the small of his back, and handcuffed him, then jumped to his feet and threw his arms up like a bulldogger going for time. Applause came from the doorway of the Dekum Tavern, and Hanson thought about taking a little bow, but decided he'd better not carry it too far. He looked up at Sgt. Bendix and said, "I wonder what made him go *off* like that?"

Duncan leaned down to help Murphy, but Hanson said, "That's okay. I've got him.

"Here, Mister Murphy," Hanson said, taking the handcuff chain in one hand, "let me help you up." He pulled his arms back and up, twisting the shoulders painfully away from their sockets. "I'm afraid I'm going to have to arrest you for assaulting a police officer, Mister Murphy."

Murphy got to his knees, snarling. "Fuck ya, Hanson. Fuck ya, you motherfucker."

"Take it easy now, Mister Murphy," Hanson said, bringing more pressure to bear on the cuffs. "Can you get to your *feet* okay?" he said, jerking the cuffs, levering him up.

"Fuck ya," he yelled, twisting to spit at him, but Hanson pulled the cuffs higher, raising him to tiptoe, bent at the waist like a diver about to go off the board, and pushed his head into the wall.

"Better pat you down, Mister Murphy," Hanson said, kicking his legs back so his weight was on his forehead.

"Mister Murphy, could you spread those *legs*," he said, kicking them apart, "just a little. For everyone's safety and convenience?" He found the keys in his pocket and gave them to Duncan.

"We'll probably have to tow his car, so I need you to inventory it . . ."

Murphy tried to stand up, and Hanson pushed him back into the wall.

"Red GTO up the street. New York plates. Look it over good."

He finished patting Murphy down, and walked him, stiff-legged, on tiptoe, across the street and put him in the car.

"Good work," Bendix said. He smiled at the crowd in front of the Soul Train. "How are you gentlemen today?"

No one answered.

Bendix nodded, trying to hold the smile. "Good."

"I'd better get back on the street," he told Hanson. "We'll have that meet another time."

"Fuck ya," Murphy yelled at a pair of black teenagers who were staring at him through the window. "You fuckin' niggers." They laughed and pressed their faces against the window, distorting their noses and cheeks, mugging and grunting at him like he was an animal in a cage.

Murphy twisted towards the window, pulling against the handcuffs as if he could break the chain. "Uughhhh," he groaned, pulling on the cuffs, his face red and contorted.

"Ya fuckin' niggahs," he yelled, spitting at them until his mouth went dry, spittle running down his chin. "Fuck ya," he shouted, raising up, "fuck ya." He launched himself, headfirst, towards the laughing teenagers, splitting his scalp against the spit-streaked window, smearing it with blood.

"Crazy motherfucker going to break his own neck," Arthur said.

Hanson got in the patrol car and looked up at Murphy's face in the rearview mirror. "You ought to watch that temper, Mister Murphy."

"Fuck ya," he said, throwing his legs onto the seat, twisting and wrenching himself like a berserk paraplegic as Duncan crossed the street, smiling and holding up a snub-nosed Chief's Special .38 in one hand and a vial of white powder in the other.

"Gosh, Mister Murphy," Hanson said, "looks to me like that's *two* felonies."

"Uughhhh," Murphy groaned, like a scream caught in his chest, as he twisted and hopped into a crouch on the backseat. "Fuck you," he yelled as Duncan got in the car, then lunged headfirst into the Plexiglas shield, rocking the car.

Thud.

"I'm afraid he's going to *injure* himself," Hanson said, loud enough so witnesses could confirm he said it if the case went to court. "And I'm *responsible* for his safety."

"I'll *kill* ya."

Thud.

"I *hate* to Mace a handcuffed prisoner," Hanson announced, "but it's all I can think of to calm him down."

"In the car?" Duncan said.

"We'll hit the freeway and open our windows," Hanson said quietly, pulling the Mace canister off his belt, "blow it all back on asshole there."

"Internal Affairs is gonna . . ."

"Fuck them," Hanson said, getting out of the car, shaking the Mace so it would spray better. He leaned down to look at Murphy, holding the Mace behind his back, then raised his voice, "Just a *tiny* bit."

Thud.

He opened the door, soaked the front of Murphy's shirt down and slammed the door shut before he could jump out.

When he pulled away from the curb, Hanson opened the wing window so it blew air across his face, but already his own eyes were beginning to water as the hot-pepper sting of Mace seeped around the sides of the cage into the front seat.

"You're not any *better* than me," Murphy screamed, crouched like a gargoyle in the backseat, blood running down his face.

Hanson glanced in the mirror and met Murphy's bloodshot eyes, his livid, bloody face. "That's right," Murphy sobbed, weeping with rage, snot bubbling from his nose with each exhausted breath.

Hanson looked back at the road, his own face burning, the stinging oily breath of Mace seeping up his nose into the back of his throat, clinging to his uniform, burning his underarms and crotch.

"You *think* you're better, but you're *not.*"

Hanson knew Murphy was right, but he didn't care.

At the end of the shift he drove to Sara's, still in his uniform. Tiny Tim answered the door. "Oh, dear God," he said, when he realized it was Hanson. "It's *you.* I love your uniform. Do we have time for some police brutality?"

"We might," Hanson said.

Tiny Tim's smirk twitched, turning into a forced, shit-eating grin. "I'll get her," he said.

Hanson heard her high heels crossing the huge, gloomy living room. "I didn't expect to see *you* again," she said. A moment later she emerged from the shadows, wearing one of her sexy, expensive "business" outfits, and hesitated when she saw Hanson in the uniform. She came closer, studying his face. "But I'm glad," she said. "You look different. And it's not just the uniform."

Just as they took the stairs, somewhere beyond the living room, behind the heavy sliding doors, a light flickered and grew brighter with the clatter of a small movie projector.

Upstairs, in her small, stuffy room, she reached up to kiss him. "No," he said. He grabbed her wrists. "Not yet."

"What happened to you?" she said.

He released her wrists. "Don't move," he said, in the voice he used with armed suspects. She obeyed him, watching his face as he undressed her, the hot smell of Mace coming off him like gasoline fumes. She gasped when he pulled her to him, the dried

Mace in his uniform mixing with her sweat, burning her. Then she smiled, pushing closer into the wool trousers, up against his thighs and the heavy gun belt, pulled his tie off and unbuttoned his shirt.

And later, the red imprint of his belt buckle and ammo pouch snaps on her belly, he straddled her, naked except for the *katha* around his neck. Their thighs and stomachs and breasts on fire, she smiled up at him, flushed and weeping from the Mace, her eyes glittering.

"Now," she said. "Now."

TWENTY-NINE

THEY CLEARED AND headed towards the precinct. It was still a little early to start back, so instead of taking the freeway they angled north through the district.

Hanson heard Aaron Allen's Cadillac before he saw it, heard Wardell the DJ from the stolen, cracked, hissing speakers, raving like an evangelist predicting the end of the world ". . . *that's right, uh-huh! We down here at Fred's Total Detail—the detail shop that does it all! An' we talkin' to Fred hisself, Detail Fred, my main man here on the Ava*-new. *I take* my *ride to Fred, knowin' he gonna treat me right, an' I leave with my ride lookin'* good, *looking* right, *impress some young laa-aay*-aidees *to-night* . . ."

Hanson gave Radio their location as he pulled in behind him. He bleeped the siren, but Aaron didn't even glance up in his rear-view mirror.

"How about hitting the overheads," Hanson said, watching Aaron's head and shoulders.

"If this goes to court," Duncan said, "what's your probable cause for the stop?"

"He's weaving . . ."

"I didn't see it."

Hanson looked at him and almost rear-ended the Caddy. Duncan turned on the overheads, but the huge, rust-scabbed red car rolled on like a boat in choppy water, shocks destroyed, tires almost flat, the diamond-shaped rear window awash in blue and red light, Wardell yelling over the radio ". . . *Fred, tell all those people out there listnin' to* Wardell *about your Roun' the Worl' Detail Special you offerin' this week.*"

"*Wardell, we offerin' a . . .*"

"He was weaving," Hanson said.

Each time the Caddy hit a pothole, loose wiring in the radio speakers shorted out, cutting Wardell off for a moment.

"*How much you chargin' for that Roun' the Worl', Fred?*"

Hanson was about to tell radio that they had an "attempt-to-elude," though the Cadillac hadn't increased its speed, when it pulled into a dark parking lot in the shadow of an abandoned warehouse.

"*Wardell, for one week only, we gonna . . .*"

"Twenty *dollars for everything. Right, Fred?*"

"*Well, uh-huh, that's . . .*"

"*All* right! *Thank you, Fred. Now let's go to the B.T. Express an'* 'I'll Take You There.' "

The doors of the Caddy flew open and five or maybe six kids bolted into the dark while it was still rolling. Aaron sat behind the wheel, illuminated by the strobing overhead lights of the patrol car, the radio booming out bass.

"Get out of the car," Hanson said, opening the door, keeping the beam of his flashlight in Aaron's eyes. Duncan stood just back from the open rear door, hand on his holstered pistol.

The car was full of Twinkies, hundreds of them, some loose and others still in boxes of twenty on the seats and floor, along with half a case of Annie Greensprings wine. The smell of marijuana was strong.

Aaron stared out the windshield as if he was alone in deep space, his dilated pupils black and cold as a crippled hawk's.

"Out of the car."

He didn't seem to notice Hanson until he reached in to turn off the ignition.

"Don't touch my shit, man," he said, shoving Hanson's hand away.

Hanson jerked him out of the car in mid-sentence, bounced him off the door and slammed him facedown on the trunk.

"You touch me again," Hanson grunted, bouncing him off the trunk, "you little fuck," kicking his legs apart, "and I'll break your hand."

Duncan handcuffed him and put him in the back of the patrol car. Five Eighty, Zurbo and Neal, drove up as Hanson was running a record check. They looked in the Cadillac and turned off the ignition, killing the radio. Zurbo jingled the ring of keys he'd taken from the Cadillac as they walked back to Hanson's car.

"Twinkies and Annie Greensprings," Zurbo said. "I think that covers all the major food groups. Is he fucked up?"

"He doesn't even know what town he's in," Hanson said. "Hey, we'll be happy to give you the DWI arrest."

Zurbo laughed. "No, thank *you.*"

"Two hours of paperwork," Neal said, leaning down to shine his flashlight at Aaron, "for nothing."

"Besides, it's time to go to the club," Zurbo said. "Maybe we'll see you there later. It shouldn't take you more than a couple of hours to inventory all those stolen Twinkies and log 'em in down at the property room."

"Twinkies? What Twinkies?"

"Let's get a picture and go home," Zurbo said when he'd stopped laughing. "I don't have one of Aaron." They turned off all the lights and Hanson took Aaron out of the patrol car.

"What kind of pills you been taking tonight, Aaron?" Neal asked as Hanson walked Aaron to the front of the Caddy.

"I don't take no dope."

"You're free to go," Hanson said, taking off the handcuffs, "as soon as we get a picture."

Aaron turned and looked at him, summoning up the will he needed to fight the dope in his system. "Suck my dick, *Han*son. You can take me to jail if you got a charge, but you can't have a picture of me until I'm eighteen," Aaron said, eyes gleaming in the dark parking lot, as Zurbo put his camera down and walked to the Caddy. "By then I be pimpin' whores in L.A.," he said, grabbing his crotch, "white bitches sucking my black cock while I drink Chivas Regal and you still here in the rain writing parking tickets, motherfucker."

"What's this for?" Zurbo said, pulling a tire iron from under the seat.

"For changing tires, my man."

Zurbo put it on the roof.

"You want to be careful of the paint job? My man?"

When Zurbo raked the sharp end of the tire iron along the roof of the Caddy, Aaron pushed past Hanson.

"Don't you raise your hands to *me*," Hanson said, grabbing him by the throat. Aaron's eyes fluttered, his throat throbbing in Hanson's grip. He squeezed harder, working his fingers around the windpipe. Aaron swung at him, then Zurbo and Neal were on him, quick and professional. A few moments later Aaron was vomiting on his pants and shoes.

"Come here," Zurbo told him, taking the tire iron off the roof. He shone the flashlight into his face where undigested bits of red capsules were mixed with the vomit dripping from his nose and down his chin. The sour stink mixed with something else.

"I believe you shit your pants, Aaron," Neal said.

"Wipe your face off," Zurbo told him, "with your shirt.

"We're gonna take your picture, you little motherfucker. I could *shoot* your ass and say you tried to hit me with *this*," he said, hitting the roof of the car with the tire iron. "If you *want*," he said, driving the sharp end of the tire iron through the roof.

"Now *stand* there."

The flash caught him, his shirt in his hand.

"One more," Zurbo said. The flash went off, the image of Aaron smiling, his hand at his crotch. What he must have *thought* was a smile. Aaron never smiled. No one had taught him how to brush his teeth, or ever taken him to a dentist, and he tried to hide his decaying teeth.

Zurbo threw the car keys over the roof of the warehouse, then, looking at Aaron, pulled the tire iron rasping out of the roof of the car.

"Get the fuck out of here," he said. When Aaron didn't move, he smashed in the back window. "The windshield's next," he said. Aaron began walking, still trying to strut on his shaky legs. "Hunting the Negro with gun and camera," Zurbo said, putting the lens cap back on. "I'll give you a copy. Let's go get a beer."

Hanson took his citation book off the dash of the patrol car. "Might as well get a couple of movers out of the deal," he said.

"Street justice," Zurbo shouted, driving off.

Hanson walked back to the Caddy, watching Aaron pass beneath the street's only unbroken streetlight and disappear into the night.

"Didn't see him weaving?" Hanson asked, glancing back at Duncan. "How about . . . defective taillight . . ." he said, smashing it out with his flashlight, ". . . for 'probable cause'?"

He wrote a speeding ticket and a "failure to yield" by the flashlight tucked under his arm, and tossed them onto the driver's seat, big as a sofa, stained and coming apart at the seams. Rust was eating the wheel wells of the enormous old Cadillac, bleeding through the red paint, and chunks of bondo were sloughing off the dented fenders, but the expensive, stolen wire wheels gleamed.

Hanson turned off the flashlight. He tilted his head, listening. Across the lot, something rattled like a cage.

"Pharaoh?" he called.

"All of us in the dark tonight," Pharaoh's voice boomed, "but I know you there anyway. Hanson . . ."

Hanson smiled, the rattle of Pharaoh's shopping cart fading away. When he slammed the Cadillac door, the radio came on again, Wardell talking as if he'd never even paused for a breath.

". . . *talking to DeRoin, in the ninth grade at Lincoln,*" Wardell said, as Hanson walked away. "*How long you been checkin' out the show, DeRoin? Say what? Get the phone away from your radio so I can hear. . . . You want to know what Mister Jones is like?*"

Hanson stopped.

"*I've never actually met the man,*" Wardell said, "*personally. The brothers who have met him, well, say his name with great respect. You know what I'm sayin', DeRoin? Seem like he works all the time. A hard man to get an appointment with. A very powerful individual, they say. But he'll know you asked about him . . . here's that new hit single by the Commodores you requested . . .*"

Hanson walked on to the patrol car, Aaron's radio pounding behind him. "Zurbo's right. If it wasn't for street justice, there wouldn't *be* any justice. They're not scared of the courts. They have to be scared of us."

"Who cares? Jeopardize my career over a worthless piece of dogshit like him? I didn't see *any* of that. If they ask me why not, I was back looking for a property receipt in the trunk. Okay?"

Hanson nodded. "Five Sixty Two's clear," he told Radio. "Heading for the precinct if there're no calls waiting."

Nothing that can't wait for the graveyard shift. Five Sixty Two on the way in at . . . eleven fifty seven.

"I hope you won't take this the wrong way," Duncan said, "but I asked Sergeant Bendix if I can work some of the other districts. There's absolutely no negative reflection on you about it."

Hanson drank quick shots of Bushmills with his beer at the club after work, watching the clock. He'd dreaded the idea of facing Helen after Dana's death, putting it off until tonight. As he was leaving, he met a couple of the late relief guys coming up the stairs, laughing. Someone, they told him, had set Aaron Allen's car on fire. "Stole those wire wheels and torched the motherfucker."

The lights were all on when he drove by Dana's house. He circled the block twice, trying to think of what he should say to Helen.

"Hi," he said, when she came to the door. She stood, looking at him through the screen. "You're drunk," she said. People talked and laughed back in the living room. Classical music was playing.

"It was nice of you to stop by, but there's nothing to say. Dana was very fond of you, but he's gone now. Good night."

At least, Hanson thought, she waited until he was down the stairs before she closed the door.

THIRTY

IT WAS THREE A.M. when he pulled up and parked next to his house, having managed to get through his third week back on the street, assigned to a Wild Car now, working alone.

He turned off the engine and slumped back, exhausted, Sara's scent rising from his shirt and pants. He was sure she'd been fucking Tiny Tim, but he couldn't make himself stay away, or even confront her about it.

When he found the pebble gone from the threshold, he pulled his pistol, backed off the porch into the moon's shadow, and listened.

They could have ambushed him when he drove up, or killed him when he was sitting in the van, he thought. Shot him from the window or porch. He *deserved* to be killed. He lowered himself onto his chest, laid his head on the ground, and looked across the driveway where he could see fresh tire tracks shadowed by moonlight. Tracks coming and going, and a single set of footprints, one leg dragging slightly. Doc.

He crawled to the window, raised up to look over, and Truman, who he'd left on the porch that afternoon, stood at the window, looking back at him.

Hanson went inside, still careful, checking the house room by room, stopping to listen at each doorway. No one there but Truman. He found nothing disturbed until he went back to the kitchen.

The spider was working on a new web. Hanson reached carefully past him, into the foundation. The box was gone.

Doc showed up just before dawn, looking bad. He didn't complain, but Hanson could see that his legs were hurting him. "I need a place to disappear for a couple of days. Two days, max, but if you don't want to . . ."

"We better hide the car," Hanson said.

They pulled it back into the barn, and Hanson raked the Johnson grass back up, covering the tracks. He didn't ask him what was going on, because he didn't want to know. He didn't even ask Doc how he'd found the box.

Doc slept most of the day, getting up about the time Hanson went to work. At night, after he'd gone to bed, Hanson could hear him limping around downstairs, looking through the bookcases and talking to Truman.

He smelled burned matches, and knew Doc was cooking some kind of dope. Probably heroin, for the pain.

The third morning, when Hanson got up, Doc was gone. He'd left an ounce of cocaine with the note, "Had to go. Thought you might be able to use this." Beneath that, he'd hesitated, tapping the pen a couple of times before writing, "Take care of the dog."

HANSON HAD BEEN so hung over when he got to work he knew he'd made a mistake not to call in sick. Sitting through roll call he tried not to look as bad as he felt while he copied down suspect information and license plate numbers. Sweating, and trying to smile, he checked out his shotgun and avoided Sgt. Bendix on the way out to his patrol car.

But the street was worse. The late afternoon sun seemed to scream at him through the bug-smeared windshield, boiling off the asphalt like kerosene. The hot patrol car smelled of cigarette smoke, vomit, and blood. He stopped at a gas station bathroom and forced himself to throw up in the filthy toilet. He splashed some water on his face and looked at himself in the cracked and peeling mirror over the sink, his faint reflection trapped deep in the dirty glass.

"Hey! How's it goin', officer?" the teenage attendant said as Hanson came out of the bathroom.

"Pretty good," Hanson said, "pretty good," heading towards the sanctuary of the patrol car.

The kid walked alongside. "How do you like the new Chevys?" he said.

"Okay," Hanson said. "I wish they'd clean 'em up once in a while."

"They're pretty hot little cars though, aren't they?" the kid said. He was chewing gum and smoking a cigarette, the smoke blowing into Hanson's face like sewer gas.

"Yeah," Hanson said, getting into the car, "better than the Fords."

"I'm planning to take the test for the police department the day I turn twenty-one," the kid said. "I've wanted to be a cop ever since I was a kid."

"Oh yeah?" Hanson said, starting the car. "I've got a call waiting for me. Better get going. Good luck on that test. See you later," he said, and drove off, the kid still bent down to talk to him through the window.

Hanson bumped over the curb, fumbling for his sunglasses, and a car he hadn't noticed had to swerve to the far lane to avoid the patrol car.

Great, Hanson thought, *a real inspiration to the future crimefighter back there.*

He should have been nicer to the kid, he thought. He'd never pass the written test and the interview, but why not let him have his cheap dream until the assholes and his own stupidity took it away from him? *I'm* an asshole, he thought, but there was something wrong with a person who'd wanted to be a cop ever since he was a kid. What kind of fucked-up ideas did he have? He probably had a police scanner in his car, one of those guys who show up at traffic accidents in a station wagon with an amber light bar on top, wanting to "help."

Up ahead, an Al's Haul-it rental truck full of collapsible wheelchairs was weaving in and out of the right lane. Hanson pulled around to pass and the truck lurched into his lane, forcing him into oncoming traffic, the wheelchairs rocking and clattering above him like some language of dread. He managed to pass, then took the next left, into the sun, hoping the truck wouldn't follow him. He didn't want to spend the next two hours processing a drunk driver with a load of wheelchairs.

He drove past littered yards and sagging porches where old black men spent the days watching traffic and drinking from bottles in paper bags. Then, way up the street, a runner took shape in the glare, coming out of the sun, down the street towards him, shimmering like a wraith. It was Aaron Allen, a concrete block in each hand, his bare chest sweating as he pumped the heavy blocks, dodging traffic and parked cars.

He sprinted through the intersection straight at the patrol car, looking at Hanson with perfect hate. He kept coming until Hanson hit the brakes, but Aaron pivoted away and past. Hanson looked for him in the mirror, but he was gone, vanished like the Spirit of Will-In-The-Ghetto.

Maybe hate could save him, Hanson thought. Maybe hate was the only way anyone could escape. Probably it would only get him killed, but that was a way to escape too.

Five Sixty Two.

"Five Sixty Two," Hanson said.

Uh, Five Six Two, we've got a complaint from Tri-Met. The driver says that one of the passengers is creating, Radio said, "creating" being shorthand for "creating a disturbance."

The driver says that the subject has created before.

"Very creative fellow," Hanson said. "Gimme the location and I'll go talk to him."

The Tri-Met bus was pulled to the curb in front of a green bus-stop bench, the engine idling, belching diesel fumes. Hanson parked in front of it and walked back to the accordion doors of the bus.

The woman driver was standing at the top of the aluminum steps arguing with a man in a filthy suit. His brown skin was dry and scaly. A metal eyelet studded his throat. Whenever he spoke, he covered the hole with his finger and belched the words out.

The driver was one of those handsome, tough black women who seemed to drive half the buses in town. She was wearing a tailored gray Tri-Met uniform, her ticket puncher in a little black holster.

Hanson's head throbbed and he felt like he could drink a gallon of ice water.

"Well, call the bus company then," she was saying to the man.

"They the ones that own this whole mess." Her lipstick and fingernails were the same dark shade of red.

"Everybody want something," the driver said. "I want to be
sittin' at home instead of on that *bus* seat. What makes *you* any
different?"

Hanson walked to the top of the stairs, the passengers' eyes on
him, waiting to see what he'd do.

"I'm not leaving the bus," the man said, looking at the driver
and then at Hanson, "until I get a receipt."

The driver glanced at Hanson, then looked back at the man.
"Now that the police are here I'm goin' ask you once more. You
want a receipt for sixty *cents?* For a bus ride? What kind of company you work for? They awful cheap seems like to me. You could
take a *cab.* Sixty *cents?* Be real."

The man began to chant, belching out the words like a frog, "I
want a re*ceipt,* I *want* a re*ceipt* . . ."

"I'm *already* late," a heavy woman in a sleeveless sweatshirt
shouted from the back of the bus. "This fool holding us all up."

"I got to get to *work,* man," a kid in a Dairy Queen uniform
said. "Last time I was late, he done *told* me, 'you come in late
again . . .' "

"Okay," Hanson said, holding up his hand. "Wait . . ."

". . . *want* a re*ceipt,* I . . ."

"Hey!" Hanson said to the man with the hole in his throat,
"Please? I've got a headache."

The man stopped chanting. "Officer," he croaked, "I'll do whatever I have to to get my rights."

"Rights?" the driver said. "Rights? What rights are you *talking*
about? Right to be a fool? Right to be a pain in the butt?"

"Ma'am," Hanson said. "Ma'am. Look at me a minute."

"I'm lookin'."

"Why," Hanson said, "can't he have a receipt?"

" 'Cause he got on the bus with a *transfer.* That's why he can't
have a receipt. A transfer ain't *nothin'.* He could of found it on the
street. I can't *give* a receipt for a transfer. A *ticket,* now, *is* a
receipt. He didn't have no ticket . . ."

"I *want* a re*ceipt* . . ."

"No!" Hanson said, jabbing his finger at the man.

"I got *rules* to follow . . ." the driver said.

"I got an appointment," someone on the bus yelled.

"I'm tired of this," the driver said. "I want you to *arrest* him."

"Wait," Hanson said, reaching for his notebook. "Look," he told the man, *"I'll* write you a receipt, okay?"

"You can't write no bus company receipt," the driver said.

"Yes, I can," Hanson said, looking at the driver with bloodshot eyes, *"watch* me. It's *my* responsibility. Okay?" His stomach was churning. He wished he could lie down somewhere dark and cool and quiet. A place no one knew about. Somewhere safe. A cave in a riverbank, he thought, where he could listen to the river.

"What's your badge number?" she said, and Hanson turned so she could see his badge.

"Okay," she said, "we'll *see* about this," walking to the front of the bus and sitting down. She began to write in a notebook.

"Okay," Hanson said to the man, "what's your name?"

"Why you gotta have my *name?"* the man said. "I ain't done anything *wrong. She's* the one that's wrong."

"I need your name to put on the receipt," Hanson said.

"Duane Thomas. That's D. U. A. N. E."

"Thank you," Hanson said. He wrote: "RECEIPT—ONE BUS TRIP FOR DUANE THOMAS @ SIXTY CENTS." And he put the time and date, his badge number and name, and the phone number of North Precinct. "Okay?" he said. "If you have a problem with your boss or your wife. The IRS. Anybody. Have them call me at that number. Okay?"

Duane looked at the receipt.

"Okay?" Hanson said.

"It doesn't look very official," Duane said.

"It's official," Hanson said. "It's fine. Is this your stop?"

"Yeah . . ."

"Okay, good-bye. There's your receipt. Got all your stuff?" he said, handing the man a bag from the seat beside him.

"But . . ."

"Fine, good-bye. Let's let the rest of these people be on their way," he said, herding Duane out the backdoor. "Good-bye, Duane, thank you," he said, noticing his distorted face in the concave mirror over the exit, thinking that was how he *felt.*

"I can't see how the police can write a *bus* receipt," the driver said as Hanson walked back to the front of the bus. "You don't work for Tri-Met."

Hanson dropped two quarters and a dime in the fare box, watching the moonlike faces of the dead presidents tumble, *ding ding,* down the little series of slides and chutes and hit the bottom of the box as if the fall had killed them. "You're probably right," he said. "There's sixty cents for Duane's fare and his receipt. Gotta go," he said, walking down the steps, "thanks a lot."

ONCE THE SUN went down and he managed to eat a Big Mac and a milkshake, he began to feel a little better. Traffic had thinned out, all the angry people on their way home from jobs they hated were off the street. The sun was out of his face, and he could quit crisscrossing the city from north to south and spend more time on the east-west streets. There was even a little pine-scented breeze from the hills. It was a weeknight, and things were slow.

He drifted off the district down to the river where they were loading a seagoing bulk carrier with wheat, pumping the golden wheat out of silos into the ship's holds. The grain arced out of huge hoses, spreading beneath the floodlights on its way into the holds, almost the color of Falcone's hair, Hanson thought. He looked upriver, hoping to see her house, but the hills had gone dark.

Tugboats and barges passed on the river, their red and green running lights gliding through the dark, patient and sure of their direction, moving with purpose. Hanson imagined driving to the coast, leaving his uniform and equipment on the beach and swimming out to one of the ships. "Take me on," he'd say, and they would. And in the morning they'd pull the anchor, turn out to sea, and hose the garbage and filth of the land off the decks with sea water, blue and foaming, out of high-pressure hoses. He'd watch the dark shadow of land recede and disappear. And he'd begin a regular shift four hours on and eight hours off, chipping and painting during the day, steering the ship and standing lookout on the bow during the night as they sailed west away from everyone who ever knew him and away from everything he'd ever done or been, and before long no one would even remember his name.

Five Sixty Two. The little green light on the radio glowed and dimmed with each syllable.

Hanson picked up the mike and keyed it. "Five Six Two."

Yeah, Five Six Two . . . uh, we've got some kind of ongoing neighborhood problem over in Five Eighty's district. They're out on a call and . . .

"I can go. What's the address?"

———

ON THE WAY back to the precinct at the end of the shift, he got
a call to cover the state police on an accident on the freeway. It
was a fatal, they said. He was glad to see the flares and state police
cars and ambulances as he came down the on-ramp. He would
hate to get stuck with the paperwork on a fatal, especially this late
at night.

Traffic was backed up, people trying to get a look. He drove
along the shoulder of the freeway, lights silently flashing, into the
hissing funnel of flares. The overhead lights, he thought, sounded
sad. They moaned as they slowly turned, grinding on the roof
above him, *Row-Raw, Row-Raw.*

He pulled up behind a state police car and got out, putting on
his hat. There'd probably be a sergeant or lieutenant by on this
one, and they'd chew him out if he wasn't wearing his hat.

One of the state cops, wearing his wide-brim Smokey the Bear
hat was leaning against the car, watching a wrecker hook up to a
demolished pickup truck. The patterns of hissing red flares sent
up an acrid, eye-stinging smoke that hung over the freeway,
catching the yellow beams of headlights as it drifted into the
dark. His uniform, Hanson thought, would still stink of it in the
morning.

"Looks like you guys have got it under control," Hanson said to
the state cop. Out in the smoke another cop in a Smokey the Bear
hat was pacing down the freeway, pushing his wheeled measuring
device like some kid's toy. A technician was taking flash pictures
of the scene. Each time the light strobe on his camera flared, it
highlighted the boiling patterns of smoke and seemed to stop time
for an instant.

"Yeah," the cop said, "I'll be doing paperwork on this all night.
Thanks for swinging by though," he said. The state cops and the
city cops didn't really like each other very much, but most of the
time they tried to be courteous. You never knew when you might
need help fast.

"Migrant workers," the cop said, gesturing towards three lumps
covered with gray blankets, one of them smaller than the other
two. "Mexicans. Pickup full of them. Probably on their way north
to pick apples."

Paramedics were lifting a woman on a stretcher into the back of
an ambulance van. *"Alicia,"* she moaned, *"Alicia. Pobrecita."*

"Shit," the cop said, "probably none of 'em speak English either. I'll be all day *tomorrow* trying to get statements. And they're probably illegals. We'll have to fuck around with the INS too." He laughed. "Poor me. Life's a bitch and then you die. Guess I better quit whining and get to work."

"Nothing I can do?" Hanson said, as a formality.

"Naw. Thanks, though. Take care," he said, walking off through the smoke and headlights towards the ambulance, a clipboard in his hand. He seemed like a good guy, Hanson thought, for a state cop.

An eighteen wheeler hissed and groaned as it downshifted, inching along, a white convertible behind it blushing pink from the truck's brake lights. Four girls in the convertible were trying to see around the truck, to get a look at the wreck. They were all blond. College girls, Hanson thought, on their way home from a party. They were excited, talking and straining for a look. The passenger in the front seat was standing up, holding on to the top of the windshield. Hanson turned to walk to his patrol car, then stopped and looked back at the girls in the convertible. All four of them were beautiful.

Hanson got in the patrol car and, overhead lights streaking the ground cover and trash along the shoulder of the freeway—red and blue, red and blue—rolled past the wreck and back out onto the highway. He thought about going north to pick apples. He imagined the weather would be warm, but cooler in the apple orchards, fragrant, sounds muffled by the leaves and branches like they are in a silent snow. Voices calling out in soft Spanish from the trees as if the trees were talking to each other.

He realized that his overheads were still on, traffic pulling over to give him room. He speeded up and took the next exit ramp so he'd look like he knew what he was doing.

He took one of the main streets through the ghetto. He was already on overtime, and the streets were empty. The barred and boarded-up windows of shops were dark, half of them out of business. Miz T's Love Wigs, Living Art Tattoo Parlor, Flint's Ribs, Billy Cee's Detail Shop, broken down-gas stations with Out of Order signs on the pumps, handwritten on pieces of cardboard. Hanson imagined the celebration, the hope of the people who opened the businesses and how it must have faded just like the paint on the storefronts. Maybe it was better not to have had any hope at all than to feel it die. The wind was blowing from the freeway, bringing with it the sour stink of the huge Holsum Bakery on the edge of the district.

It was at about the point where the shops thinned out and the street became residential that Hanson saw the dogs. For a moment he thought it was shadows on the street, light coming through the scrawny trees. But it was dogs, a pack of twenty-five or thirty of them, walking up the middle of the street as if they owned it. Like a flock of sheep out in the eastern part of the state, clogging a country road as they are herded to winter pastures.

Hanson slowed and pulled behind them, big dogs and little ones, mongrels and purebreds, cute and ugly. Some wore collars while others were obviously wild, feral, abandoned, their fur tangled and matted like a wino's hair. Like a gang of thugs, leaders and lieutenants and hangers-on, some running ahead like point men, the leaders walking steadily as if they were on their way to a confrontation. Hanson honked his horn and flicked his headlights bright and dim. One or two of them looked back at the car, but they all stayed in the middle of the street, walking, as if they knew Hanson wouldn't run them down, that they held the power out there.

Whenever they passed a fenced-in dog, a half-dozen of them charged the fence, spraddle-legged. They snarled and slathered, bounced on stiff front legs, their snouts piglike, distended, lips flared over teeth and purple gums, striking like snakes at the fence. Then, as if on some signal, they turned away and trotted back to rejoin the pack.

Hanson accelerated slightly, into the pack of dogs. It was like taking a lifeboat through a school of sharks, like one of those encyclopedia illustrations where all the species of shark are swimming in the same small patch of ocean—great white, crescent-tailed thresher, mako, mongrel dog shark, tiger, mustached nurse shark, a hammerhead with stemmed eyes. The dogs slowly parted for the patrol car as if it was a minor annoyance, one of many in their brutal night-shift existence. A cocky Welsh terrier looked up as Hanson rolled past, then snapped at a mangy cocker spaniel who yelped and ran under the patrol car. Hanson jerked to a stop and honked the horn. He tapped the siren, then stuck his head out the window.

"Come on, god *dammit*. I'll run your asses *over*," he yelled, fear in his voice. "I'll squash you, motherfuckers, then I'll call for a confirmed dog kill . . ."

A half-breed Doberman leaped up, snarling, his claws raking the door of the car, and Hanson jerked his head back. The Doberman was missing an ear, the side of his head scarred and furless. He dropped back to the street where he cocked his damaged head and regarded Hanson with something that looked like a smile.

Hanson rolled through the dogs until he was ahead of them, watching his rearview mirror until they were gone.

The parking lot at North was quiet, graveyard shift already out on the street. He unloaded his shotgun and wondered if he'd really seen the dogs.

Even if he hurried, the police club bar would be closed before he got there, Debbie Deets and the other girls from Records or Radio gone home with someone else. After the last time, he'd promised himself he wouldn't call Sara again, but he didn't want to sleep alone tonight.

When he dialed Sara's number, a man answered and Hanson asked him if she was there. Sara sounded surprised, but happy to hear from him. She told him to "wait half an hour" before he came over.

He began using the cocaine to sober up for the drive home after the police club closed. The nights he didn't go to Sara's house, he sat up until dawn, studying the tables in *Steam*, or reading books about the war, cross-indexing conflicting accounts of enemy offensives and firebase sieges, hoping to find some agreed-upon "truth." Truman watched from across the room, listening, smelling the air.

He tried to stay away from Sara, but up in her little room, lizards watching them from the walls, he was able to forget the chirping in his ears, the knot in his stomach. The stairs creaked when he tried to slip out afterwards, past Tiny Tim's friends sleeping on the couch or floor, the stale air heavy with marijuana smoke. Too many people knew he was a cop.

When he woke up after three or four hours of fitful sleep, groggy and hung over, he'd snort more cocaine and go to work, resisting, for a while, the temptation to take a little with him for later in the day.

He watched himself more and more carefully as the days passed, but on the street, that was dangerous. Second-guessing himself, questioning his decisions, could cause him to hesitate when he couldn't afford to.

THIRTY-ONE

HE WAS IN a hurry, on his way back to North. Sara had told him to come over earlier than usual for "something special." He'd arranged to take off the last two hours of the shift on comp time, but a barking dog complaint had turned into a stabbing, and he was late. He'd have been working into overtime on the paperwork if Zurbo hadn't taken the call for him. EMS said the victim was stable. A sucking chest wound, one lung collapsed.

Please don't die, Hanson thought, turning onto Shaver Street. He'd be in shit for kissing the call off if the dumb motherfucker died.

A red light at Mississippi stopped him. "God *damn,*" he said, his ears whining and ringing. "Come on." He'd brought the cocaine to work, finally. It was in his pocket, but he didn't have time to find a safe dark spot to snort it.

Dee Brazzle watched him from the doorway of the Bon Ton, openly drinking from a quart bottle of Colt .45, which Hanson pretended not to see. He didn't have time to write a citation, and if it turned into an arrest he'd be stuck for at least an hour. The light turned green and he drove on. "Next time, motherfucker," he hissed, exhausted and tense, his hand cramping on the steering wheel.

Five Eighty jackpot, Duncan told Radio, working with Zurbo while Neal was on vacation. *We'll be out at Good Sam Hospital after we clear the jail.*

Duncan was probably right, he thought. What difference *did* any of it make? Stabbing somebody over a goddamn barking *dog. Fuck* these people, and *fuck* . . . he glanced down Mason Street, about to blow the red light, and saw the dog, its back to him, tearing at a flap of fur and dead meat, trying to peel it off the street. Hanson looked at his watch, killed the headlights, and turned down Mason, grinding his teeth.

"Left," he decided.

They'd developed a theory at North. The best way to get a Night Dog with your car was to guess which way he'd run to get out of the street, then accelerate that way an instant before the dog bolted. For some reason, the dogs never changed directions once they'd committed themselves, so you had a fifty-fifty chance of hitting them if your timing was right. By turning on the overhead lights and the PA feedback squeal as you accelerated, you could cost the dog an instant's hesitation.

The four-barrel carburetor droned, snapping the blue and white Nova into a skid that Hanson steered out of with one hand. With the other hand he flipped on the overhead lights, twisted the PA "gain," and turned on the headlights, holding dead for a spot to the left of the dog, the roof-mounted loudspeaker shrieking through the quiet street.

The dog looked up, into the headlights, eyes boiling red and silver, then bolted left and vanished with a *bang* beneath the car. Hanson grunted like he'd taken a punch.

The dog dragged her hips and broken back from beneath the patrol car, trailing intestines. Coiled and gleaming, they seemed to move with a life of their own, Hanson thought, turning his flashlight on them.

Stillborn pups, tiny and perfect. Two of them, three, the dying mother pulling for the shadows. Another one. More.

Hanson didn't remember getting out of the car, but he would always remember straddling her, shuffling like a hobbled convict above her, swinging his flashlight two-handed, the *clop* of the aluminum on bone, trying to kill the pain he'd made, until the bulb broke, still clubbing her in the dark behind the patrol car. Something began to howl back there, beneath the spokes of light, turning blue and red from the roof of the car, slapping abandoned and boarded-up houses, junked cars and graffiti, blue and red, tire-less, beyond anger or satisfaction, a blue and red wheel of pain and punishment and howling endless nights.

His two extra hours had vanished by the time he parked in front of the crumbling Victorian set back from the street. It was dark, all but hidden by diseased, hundred-year-old hemlock trees. A pale gray light from Sara's window, high up, washed through the bug-infested crowns of the hemlocks. Hanson went upstairs and opened the door to Sara's room.

A clattering little movie projector blinks and burns a silent nightmare on the wall opposite the bed—a pudgy white woman, naked and blindfolded, bucks and strains against the ropes lashing her to a heavy wooden chair. The ropes flatten and crease her breasts, wooden clothespins clamped to the nipples. Her open, raised legs are lashed over the arms of the chair, and a rubber ball gag fills her mouth, bulging her cheeks, held in place by a buckled leather strap. She is covered with bruises, burns and the puckered impressions of teeth. Ductwork sprouts from an old furnace in the background, dust riding the air. A basement somewhere.

"I didn't think you were coming," Sara said.

"All the other fun-lovers have gone home," Tiny Tim said, "but it's never too late."

Nails where paintings had hung studded the wall behind and within the movie, a faint checkerboard of squares and rectangles, lighter than the rest of the dirty wallpaper, like an X ray of their positions. Beyond the square of shifting light, lizards crawled the walls, strobing in and out of shadow.

"Hell-*ooooh*," Sara cooed.

"I be*lieve*," Tiny Tim said, "your police-boy digs it. This is what he likes."

The lighting glares and fades as the little projector chatters relentlessly on, a bad memory taking shape now behind Hanson's eyes.

A shadow falls on the bound woman then slides away as some-one out of the frame steps through the light.

"I hope you brought your handcuffs," Tiny Tim said.

The woman strains against the ropes, lifting the front legs of the chair and banging them back down. She does it again, as if being instructed to, and Hanson looked away from her, turned away from the memory forming like the shadow in the basement.

Sara and Tiny Tim were sitting on the bed, pillows propped up against the wall behind them, each wearing a pair of Sara's silk panties.

"What about the nightstick?" Tiny Tim asked him, rolling his eyes and grinning at Sara.

"Get out," Hanson told him.

"Ohhh," Tiny Tim moaned, wiggling against the mattress, "I love that command voice. Won't you join us?" he said, sliding over, patting the bunched-up sheets.

Hanson could smell them in the stuffy room. He could taste the hot film, oil and electricity radiating from the projector. He felt hot. It was hard to breathe.

"You better leave." This time Hanson saw, not fear yet, doubt, in Tim's eyes, the possibility that he might be making a bad mistake.

"Don't be such a silly little jealous boy," Sara said, raising up on her elbows, her breasts shifting as she scooted back into the pillows, settling into a more comfortable position. She was beautiful. In spite of everything. He couldn't deny that. Her panties gleamed like pewter over the mound of pubic hair that curled out into the hollows of her thighs.

"We didn't," she said, working her shoulders deeper into the pillows, *"do* anything . . ."

The light on the wall brightened, and Hanson glanced that way, a defensive reflex, the camera zooming in on the woman's bound and clamped breasts.

". . . we were just fooling around."

Closer, out of focus, but clear enough to see it wasn't a bruise or birthmark he'd noticed beneath the ropes, but a crude tattoo.

"Did you hear me?"

A shooting star, or the initial "W," or a flower. Maybe a rose. And the memory he'd been trying to ignore was *on* him—*the stink of wet, charred wood in the garage where Brandy crouched naked in his flashlight beam, the lamp cord wrapped around her neck and down between her breasts and the crude tattoo. The sound of his name when she spoke it through a mouthful of broken teeth.*

"It's just an act," Sara said. "She *likes* it."

The weight of her breasts against him when he put his arms around her.

"*He* likes it, too," Tiny Tim said, when a skinny little guy with a mustache and bad skin walks into the movie and stands over the woman. He takes the long, thin cigar from his mouth and speaks to her, laughing silently on the wall when she bucks, tosses her head, rocks the chair side-to-side. He blows on the glowing ash of the cigar, turning it in his fingers.

His own wooden voice telling her she'd be okay, his revulsion and disgust, his contempt, ashamed of himself for feeling that way, hating himself most of all, not the rapist or the pimp or the pathetic whore in his arms.

Tiny Tim's laughter stopped when Hanson turned off the projector and the room went dark.

Hanson crossed the room in two strides, the final image of the movie still playing on the backs of his eyes, but fading. Tiny Tim howled when Hanson pulled him from the bed and threw him into the wall. His shoulders and arms and thighs swelling with adrenaline, Hanson effortlessly continued slamming him against the wall until even his grunts stopped, and he went limp. He dragged him by the wrist out of the room, and closed the door.

"So *what?*" Sara said.

She managed to slap him once before he got both her wrists in his hands. He flipped her onto her stomach, tore the panties off, and forced her legs apart with his knees.

"No," she shouted, clawing back at him, when he pushed her face into the mattress, using his other hand to guide himself into her.

"No." He took her wrists again and held her, spread-eagled against the mattress, his lips at her ear.

"No? It's too late now." He closed his eyes and saw Brandy, screaming again in the burned-out garage, Dana bleeding to death on Ira's floor, fading in and out of the blue TV light. Sara's moans and the thumping bed carried him back to the little girl with the torn face, the dog hitting the closet door, his coughing bark.

Arching his back, groaning, he rode the memory of Arthur's blistered lips, Christmas in July and the stink of napalmed bodies. "Napalm gets it together." Dog lab. Millon's gluey dead eyes. Hanadon swimming in white fire. Gunships. Air strikes. The dead and wounded twitching as you walked among them making sure they were dead. Smiling death.

So he was a monster. Fine. Perfect. Everybody is.

Sara cried out, sweat-slick, bucking beneath him like Kraang-the-Hawk keening in the bloody poncho, begging for release . . .

Hanson opened his eyes.

She was laughing.

"Yes," she said, twisting under him, the muscles in her neck straining, her mouth on his now, her tongue inside him.

It was after three when Hanson skidded the van to a stop in the gravel behind the house. He opened the door and stepped out while it was still in gear. The van bucked and lurched forwards, throwing him out, before it finally choked to a stop in a ragged hedge of blackberries, the headlights glowing. Hanson got to his knees, then his feet, and staggered to the porch where the broken screen door hung open, the main door ajar.

Rats scurried across the kitchen floor, and when he found the light switch, cockroaches dropped off the walls and counters, fanned out and vanished into the floorboards. The place was filthy, dirty dishes, garbage, liquor bottles. He opened drawers and cabinet doors, hoping he'd find some of the cocaine he'd hidden and forgotten about, looked in canisters, old coffee cans, under the filthy stove. He found a wad of tinfoil in the refrigerator and opened it carefully on the table, his hands shaking, almost retching at the stink of rotten meat inside.

He knew Truman was watching him while he searched the living room, staggering in front of the bookcase, trying to read the titles on the spines, picking one book, then another, holding it upside down and riffling the pages, dropping it and pulling out another. The floor was covered with books when he found a Baggie with a residue of cocaine inside a copy of *The Green Berets*. He slit it open, scraped a tiny pile of white powder up, snorted what he could, then licked the Baggie.

"What do you know about it? What do you know about anything," he said, turning to face Truman. "It's a tough fucking world out there. All shit and bad luck. All I did was save those fuckin' dogs a world of misery. They're *lucky*.

"You're nothin'. A pain in the ass," he yelled.

Truman's ears went up, but he didn't move, his pearly eyes on Hanson.

"I should of let Animal Control have *your* gimpy old ass too. Get it the fuck over with. Simplify my fuckin' life.

"Get the fuck out," he shouted, walking towards him, waving his arm. "Get," he said, choking back a bubble of vomit, his head throbbing. When he slapped him on the rump, Truman got to his feet, walked through the kitchen and out the door as the phone rang, and kept ringing until Hanson found it behind the sofa.

"Hello. Yeah," he said, wiping blood off his cheek where he'd fallen out of the van onto the gravel. He held the phone to his ear and studied his bloody fingertips as if he was reading a message in the loops and whorls. A jetliner on its way to Los Angeles passed over the house at thirty-five thousand feet, leaving a pair of moonlit contrails behind.

"What time . . ."

General Sherman glowered up at him from the floor, through the shattered glass of the picture frame.

"Right. I don't know," he said, and hung up.

He lay on the bed for an hour or two hours, looking at the ceiling, trying to leave his body, to float away from the cocaine and liquor hangover. Finally, he went down to the kitchen. The dog's food and water bowls were empty and filthy, and he managed, through his nausea and throbbing head, to wash and fill them up. When he tried to make himself vomit into the sink, nothing would come up.

He pushed the sagging screen door out of the way and set the bowls on the porch.

"Truman. Come on back. I'm sorry, man."

He woke up with the sun in his face, lying next to the untouched food and water bowls. The first thing he saw when he opened his eyes, up through the branches of an apple tree, was Stormbreaker, then Truman, walking towards him through the grass.

"Hi, pal. I'm gonna try and get straight. At least that cocaine is *gone,*" he said, sitting up. "Last thing I remember about last night . . ." He looked at his hands, the knuckles skinned, gravel driven into his palms. He touched the scrapes on his face.

"I must look like a wino." He pulled himself to his feet using one of the porch supports and looked at the bus in the blackberry bushes.

"I'll just drink beer for a while. Lay off that hard stuff."

When Truman came inside, Hanson put down the garbage bag he was filling up.

"I murdered her. The puppies too. I tried to tell myself, 'If not me, it would of been somebody else,' but that's just bullshit. I'm sorry. More than sorry. I don't know who else to apologize to."

He kneeled down to get an empty beer bottle wedged under the refrigerator.

"It could have been you."

He was picking up books in the living room when he accidentally kicked the phone, freezing at the clang of the ringer, suddenly remembering the call he'd gotten the night before.

He sat on the floor and looked at the phone for five minutes before he dialed North, remembering what Norman had told him the night before while Sgt. Doan told him again.

Zurbo and Duncan were dead, killed by a drunk driver, an oral surgeon fucked up on Russian vodka and his own pharmaceutical cocaine. He blew a red light doing at least sixty and center-punched the patrol car.

"Killed Duncan outright," Doan said.

So much for his long-range career plans, Hanson thought, his head pounding.

Zurbo managed to pull himself out of the wreckage and drag what was left of his hips and legs—both femoral arteries severed—to the dentist's Mercedes before he bled to death.

"You could see the blood trail from the patrol car to the asshole's Mercedes," Doan said. "Pulled himself up to the window. As far as the ME could tell, the fuckin' dentist came through the wreck with only a couple of cracked ribs and a broken nose. Before Zurbo shot him in the head."

Later that afternoon, he and Truman walked out to the road to check his mail for the first time in over a week. Log trucks thundering by, he kneeled and kept his hand on Truman's shoulder, reaching up to pull the mail from the box. On the way back to the house, he folded the few envelopes inside the current *Shotgun News.*

"You *know* not to go near the road without me, don't you?" he asked Truman.

He sat on the porch to look through the mail—an electric bill, a tax statement, something from the VA, advertising flyers, a knife catalogue, and a postcard.

"From Montana," he told Truman, showing it to him—an Indian mask of carved and painted wood, hammered copper, and translucent green seashells.

"It's three masks in one," he told him. "Looks like a fish, but when you pull these strings," he said, pointing them out, "the jaws open and reveal a raven—see the bill and the face? The *bill* opens, see, and inside *that* it's a man."

He scratched the dog's ears. "Sometimes I think *you* might be like that."

He turned the card over. It was from Falcone.

"You remember her?"

He started to say that Falcone was about the only person he knew who didn't think he should put Truman to sleep, but changed his mind. "She really liked you, buddy.

"She says, 'It snowed last night, up in the mountains . . .'" Hanson looked up at Stormbreaker, the peak still white with last year's snow. "'. . . Everything was glowing and the silence was endless. I watched the snow fall, and found myself thinking about you, wishing you could see it. Be careful, and take care of yourself—Your ex-cop friend. PS—Say hello to Truman.'"

"Well," Hanson said, looking at the card, then up at Stormbreaker. He smiled, stood up and put the card in his shirt pocket. He tapped it with his fingertips.

"Let's get something to eat."

They ate out on the porch, watching Stormbreaker turn pink when the sun set.

THIRTY-TWO

HANSON LOGGED IN a stolen, hacksawed Italian skeet gun at the property room, and took his reports up to Detectives. On the way back downstairs the elevator stopped at the second floor. Fox got in and pushed the button for the parking garage.

"I hear you're falling apart," Fox said, his back to Hanson. "If I were you, I'd cut my losses and get out now. Come in and talk to me, while you still can," he said, the elevator dropping. "Tell me what you know about your black buddy, 'Doc,' and *maybe* you won't go to prison."

Hanson got off at the first floor.

"He's not your friend," Fox said, before the elevator doors closed.

He was unlocking his patrol car when Bishop, the lesbian, spoke his name.

"I don't know what's in these printouts," she said, slipping Hanson a manila envelope, "but you might want to take a look."

"I appreciate it."

"I'm not doing it for you."

"How's Falcone?"

"Fuck you," she said, walking away.

In another twenty minutes he could clear from the district and head back to the precinct. Radio had been slow since eleven, and Hanson wanted to finish his last two reports before heading in. He could kiss off the family fight where he'd talked the husband into leaving the house. He'd be back when the bars closed, but the guys on graveyard could arrest him. They had more time to do the paperwork.

The burglary report left over from early in the shift would take longer, describing the point of entry and exit, the path the burglars had taken through the house, stopping in the kitchen where they drank three of the victim's beers and ate a can of chili, leaving with a TV: "RCA 19 WITH WOODGRAIN PLASTIC CABINET." And tape deck: "MAKE UNKNOWN. BLACK PLASTIC WITH SILVER TRIM—VOLUME KNOB MISSING—VALUE—$49.95."

He parked the patrol car under a streetlight across from Unthank Park. A victim of budget cuts, the park's basketball courts were crumbling and littered with garbage, used mostly for drug dealing and an occasional rape.

As he wrote, Hanson glanced up, out the windshield and open windows of the patrol car, checked the side mirror, the rearview mirror—"like a sparrow in a parking lot," he'd once described it to Dana—listening to the darkness and radio calls.

He clicked his pen shut. Something moving on the far side of the park. A big guy, coming through the scrubby bushes, a duffle bag over his shoulder and a radio in the other hand. It was too late to be fucking around with an arrest, an hour's overtime at least, but he put the pen in his pocket and picked up the microphone.

"Five Sixty Two," he said, "looks like I've got a burglar on the east side of Unthank Park. Could you have another car swing by?"

A traffic car, Fuller and his trainee out looking for drunk drivers, broke in, *Three Sixty can cover that.*

Copy. Three Sixty will be out with Five Sixty Two at Unthank Park.

"I'm gonna go ahead and talk to this guy," Hanson said. "Male Negro, about six-two, one-ninety. He's wearing a white T-shirt and black . . . looks like can't-bust 'em jeans."

He got out of the car, taking his nightstick out of its holder on the door, holding it tucked against the inside of his left arm.

"Hey. You," he shouted across the street. "You," he shouted, pointing the butt of the nightstick at him. "Put that stuff down, and *keep* your *hands* where I can see them," Hanson said, walking towards him.

"I *said*," Hanson told him, "to put that stuff *down*."

As he set the radio and duffle bag down, Hanson saw that he was muscular, maybe twenty-two years old. Nobody to fuck around with. As he walked, Hanson pictured where he would hit him, two-handed, with the nightstick.

"Okay," Hanson shouted as he got closer, "turn around. Turn *around*, goddammit. Put your hands on top of your head."

The guy turned around and held his hands up in the air.

"On *top* of your *head*. Get 'em up there. Interlace your fingers."

He put his hands on his head, and Hanson stepped up behind him.

"Okay," Hanson said, "spread your legs. *Wider*," he said, kicking one leg farther out, stepping back, the nightstick in both hands, ready to drive it into his kidneys.

"Yes, sir. I'm sorry."

Hanson slipped his nightstick in his belt, reached up and gripped the guy's interlaced hands and stepped back, keeping the guy off balance, ready to pull him backwards and kick his legs out from under him. He smelled bad, and his hands were crusty.

"You carrying any guns or knives?" Hanson demanded. "You better fucking *tell* me if you are," he said as he reached around to pat him down.

"No, sir," the guy said, "I don't have nothing like that."

"You fuckin' *better* not," Hanson said as he ran his hand over the guy's chest, around his waistband, and down his groin and thighs to his ankles.

"Okay," Hanson said, stepping back, "keep your hands up there, and turn around."

In the few lights around the basketball court that had not been broken out, Hanson looked into his eyes.

"What's your name?" Hanson asked him.

"James," he said, "James Morton, officer. What did I do wrong?"

In the quiet night, Hanson could hear Three Sixty's engine winding up, two or three blocks away, slowing for a corner, then winding up again as Fuller held the gas to the floor.

"What's in the bag, James?"

"It's *my* stuff," he said, taking his hands off his head, then quickly putting them back. "I can show you," he said.

Hanson heard Three Sixty pull up behind his car. Without looking back at them, he raised his hand to signal that everything seemed okay.

"You got any weapons in there?"

"No, sir, just my clothes and stuff."

Three Sixty's doors slammed and Hanson listened to footsteps coming up behind him.

"Go ahead, then," Hanson told him. "Open it."

He took out a basketball, tucked it under his arm, and dumped the rest out on the cracked concrete—dirty clothes, shoes, shaving gear, an old *Playboy* magazine.

"What are you *doing* out here?" Fuller said.

James looked at Fuller over Hanson's shoulder and tried to smile. "I'm good at basketball." He held the ball with both hands and looked at Hanson. "And I take care of business."

"What the fuck does *that* mean?" Fuller said.

"Well, it's like, if you good at *one* thing, then . . ."

"The park closes at ten."

James nodded, looked at Hanson. "I was gonna stay at the mission. I gone down there, but they already given out all the tickets. I should of gone earlier but I was shootin' some hoops over at Jefferson an' I forgot till they didn't have any beds left."

"And?" Fuller said.

James bounced the ball. "I thought I could, you know, shoot some baskets. Kill some time and stay warm. I *take* care of business. I can leave if that's what I should do. Go back to Jefferson. No problem. Somebody stole my ball last winter, so I just walked all night. But I got this ball now, so if . . ."

"It's all yours, James," Hanson said, gesturing at the buckled, trash-strewn court. "Sorry I bothered you. Good night," he said, walking away.

Fuller glared at James, and Hanson said, "Come on. What's the guy gonna do?"

"It's your district," Fuller said.

"Thanks for the cover."

He watched them drive off, and got back in his car. Radio traffic was beginning to pick up. The bars would be closing soon and the drunks would be out. He needed a continuation page to finish listing the stolen items from the burglary, and when he took one out of his briefcase, he glanced at the envelope Bishop had given him. He'd read some of the printouts inside. Fox knew everything about him. It was all true. *Guilty as charged, Your Honor,* he thought.

The sound of the basketball was steady as James dribbled from one basket to the other, interrupted by a metallic *bong* each time he shot a basket. He sidestepped the fast-food trash and the shards of green and brown liquor bottles. He saw Hanson watching him, smiled and waved, then drove in hard and leaped up for a hook shot. He made it and Hanson was glad he did.

Hanson went back to his report, watching James out of the corner of his eye so as not to make him self-conscious. It was going to be a chilly night. Already ground fog was rising from the grass. Hanson thought of James, dribbling and shooting, through the night, patient and uncomplaining, as the stars turned and the moon rose and set and the sun moved slowly around to another dawn.

It was time to head in. He could finish the report at the precinct. Starting the car, he looked over at James going up for another shot. He wouldn't be able to sleep tonight, he thought, knowing James was out there in the park while he was in bed. Not unless he got real drunk.

He looked in his wallet. A five and two ones. And a twenty. The twenty Dana had loaned him on the Fourth of July was still tucked in the side pocket. He got out of the car and James stopped dribbling.

"James, do me a favor," Hanson said, holding out the twenty, "get a room for the night. Okay?"

James looked at the bill in Hanson's hand. "I can get a room for less than that," he said.

"Good," Hanson said, stuffing the bill in the pocket of his black jeans. "Have a big breakfast too, okay? Good night.

"Hey," he said, "last winter. When you walked all night. You ever run into a black guy, about my age, who always wore army fatigues? Guy named Millon?"

James smiled as if he was happy he knew the answer, and could be of some use to Hanson. "Sure. That's ole Marcelle. I seen him a lot. He bought me this ball."

"I gotta go," Hanson said, turning and walking back to the idling patrol car.

"Did you know," James called after him, "he won a Silver Star in the war?"

"Yeah, I did," Hanson said. "They don't just hand those out. He was a real hero."

"Get some sleep. Long day tomorrow."

"Yes, sir."

Hanson waved, got in the patrol car, and drove off, glancing in his rearview mirror at James waving back.

"Five Sixty Two's heading on in to the precinct," Hanson told Radio.

Copy. Five Six Two heading home.

He drove north up Mississippi Street, listening to a blues guitar coming from the Vet's Club where older people in the district went, people who had moved out from Chicago and Detroit to work in the shipyards during WWII, hoping for a better life. He slowed to see who was hanging out tonight, just as Fast Freddie came out the door. He smiled and tipped his hand, a subtle "Hello" no one else could see. "Look out, it's the po-lice."

A couple blocks farther up, Pharaoh was still on the job. Hanson slowed, pulled to the curb. "Pharaoh," he called, "what's happenin'?"

"Weather's changing," Pharaoh said, pushing his cart. "Look for thunder and lightning up on old Stormbreaker pretty soon."

"Runnin' late," he said, turning down an alley.

Hanson put the car in PARK. "Pharaoh . . ."

"I don't have no answers," Pharaoh began. His voice was swallowed up by the dark.

Hanson took Mississippi up to Killingsworth, then turned towards the river past the rose gardens where he could still smell the last of the dying blossoms in the cool air.

The road ran high above the big river, a long stretch of road back to the precinct lined with the new streetlights, where he'd told Dana, not long ago, "I can take the dog."

As he drove, looking down at the ships and tugboats and bridges, he could no longer keep from thinking about Dana, and wishing he was still alive. This was the drive they used to make together every night back to the precinct, talking about what had happened during the shift and who they should be looking for the next day. Now that he was on his way in, the radio was almost calming. All someone else's problem now. The radio traffic went on twenty-four hours a day, just like the river, sending cars out and bringing them back in every night.

He took the last curve, the precinct up ahead, looming in the dark industrial district like a fortress. Yellow light shone through the barred windows, and the flag, spotlighted in front of the memorial for officers killed in the line of duty, rippled in the breeze. Dana's name was on the big granite slab now, a brass plaque shinier than the others, bolted into the stone. But it wouldn't be long before the rain and snow and slow time turned it the same deep green as all the others.

He stopped halfway up the stairs, and walked back to the granite memorial, where moths fluttered in the spotlights and the snap link on the big flag rang against the pole above him like a dirge. He propped his shotgun against the stone and tapped Dana's plaque with his knuckles, then picked it up and walked across the damp grass and up the stairs.

Neal was at the club, already drunk. Everyone had been sympathetic after Zurbo's death, but it had gone on too long with Neal. He'd cornered Norman tonight, in one of the booths, and Hanson couldn't help hearing as he stood at the bar.

"He went out like a hero, man," he told Norman. "I should have been with him."

"He wouldn't have wanted . . ."

"He was my *partner*. If I'd been there instead of Duncan . . ."

"Then *you'd* be dead too. Would that . . ."

"What am I gonna *do?* What am I gonna do now?"

Hanson drank his beer down and walked over to the pay phone. He picked up the receiver, brought it to his ear, put it back down and left.

"*. . . out here beyond the wire. On radio watch. Mister Jones got the duty again tonight, people. Back in the world. I'll be taking requests at the top of the hour. Let me know if there's anything you need to hear. But now, here's Mississippi John Hurt, doin' 'Stagger Lee . . .'"*

John Hurt's guitar rolled and tumbled through Hanson's van on the way to the freeway.

"*My, my,"* Mr. Jones said, "*listen to that guitar. Sounds like somebody pleading for answers, lookin' for some kind of justice . . .*

"Po-*lice's* officers, how *can it be . . . you can ar-*rest *every-body but* cruel *Stagger Lee? That bad man, cruel little Stagger Lee . . .*"

Hanson took a left and headed back to town.

He knew where the station was. He'd driven past it before, late at night. He got out of the van and looked up at the lighted second-floor window. The heavy steel door boomed when he knocked, and a moment later opened a few inches.

"You got the *wrong* address," someone said, and closed the door.

He knocked again, harder.

"My *man*," the voice said when he opened the door. "What'd I just tell you?"

"I want to see Mister Jones," Hanson said.

"People in hell want ice water," he said, and slammed the door.

Hanson kept knocking. Finally, the door opened wide. Two big guys wearing sleeveless T-shirts and knit watch caps looked down at him. "We gonna have to put the police on your white ass?"

"Call the damn police," Hanson said. "Go ahead and *call* the motherfuckers. That's what people do when they can't take care of their own problems."

The one who'd spoken smiled. He looked at the other one. "Fine," he said, still smiling at Hanson. "I *needed* to wake up a little."

"Fuck you," Hanson said, and they came out the door.

"Hold on," someone inside said. "What's his name?"

"My name's Hanson."

"Let him go on up."

Hanson took the dark stairs to a dead-end landing and a closed door, wondering what to do next. Mr. Jones was talking, ". . . Seattle's own Jimi Hendrix, a veteran of the one-oh-first air-borne . . ."

"Go on in," a voice at the bottom of the stairs told Hanson, "he's expecting you."

Hanson opened the door.

Mr. Jones sat in a wheelchair, his back to Hanson. He was huge, what was left of him. The back of his head was ridged with scar tissue, and in the dim light from the transmitter dials, Hanson could see that his legs were gone.

". . . who made it home, but couldn't survive back in the

world," Mr. Jones said, lifting the record, a gleaming hook where his hand should have been.

He leaned back in the wheelchair, but didn't look around. "How you makin' it, brother?"

"Not so good."

"You listen to the show?"

"All the time."

"Good to hear that. Thanks for listening."

Hanson looked at his feet.

"Not many people get up here in the studio. You must of made a real impression on the brothers downstairs."

Hendrix's guitar snarled, growled, hesitated . . . Hendrix laughed, and strutted the guitar on down the street.

Hanson wiped his eyes with the heels of his hands.

"What can I do for you, brother?"

"How do you, you know, manage . . ."

"I got this show to do every night up here. It's people out there who depend on that."

"I came back without a scratch."

"Luck. That's all. Call it fate. Nobody's fault. Nothing you can do about it but be who you supposed to be. Figure out who that is."

"I better go and let you do your job," Hanson said, turning away.

"Wait one," Mr. Jones said, lifting another record onto the turntable with his hook. "Nobody says I can't play two in a row."

"Too late," Hanson said.

"Come on back and sit down for a minute. Here," Mr. Jones said, pulling a chair over next to his. "Pharaoh told me you might come by. Speaks highly of you. And I kind of wanted to talk, if you've got the time."

Mr. Jones turned in the wheelchair to face him. He held out his hook. "Tell me about that old dog . . ."

"We'll burn 'em when the weather cools off," Hanson said, pulling Fox's printouts from the big manila envelope Bishop had given him, feeding them into the woodstove. "What can they do?" he asked Truman. "Send me to Vietnam? Fire me so I don't get to drive around the ghetto all night beating up people for doing what *I'd* do if I was them? Fine. Fire me, motherfuckers. *Kill* me.

"Look at this," he said, reading one of the printouts. "That speeding ticket I got when I was sixteen. We're in trouble now," he said, laughing. "And this . . . high school records. That time I was suspended for fighting.

"College transcripts. Uh-oh, a 'C' in psychology," he said, tossing it in.

"Basic training. 'Expert' with the M-14, but only 'Marksman' with that plastic M-16. Infantry school. Look at this. Jump school. Rangers. Basic S.F. O and I. Jesus. Anti-Terror and Tradecraft at Hollabird. That shit was classified.

"Dog lab . . ." He wadded it up and tossed it in the stove.

"Orders for RVN," he said, flipping through the pages, sounding worried now.

"Okay," he said, "okay. I didn't think he could get into those files. It never fuckin' happened. No gaps in the record, either. I was officially in Da Nang then, a hundred miles away. And like Doc said, all that stuff got burned when the bad ole Communists took . . . Huh." The last page was an FBI form. Just a cover sheet with his name and date of birth. He tossed it in with the rest.

There was something else in the envelope. A letter, addressed to Bishop. From Falcone. Beneath the return address in Montana, Bishop had written a note to Hanson in pencil, "Read what she says about you . . ."

He looked at Truman, then began reading.

THIRTY-THREE

No one knows where the storms come from. Born in deep water beyond the curve of the earth, down some bottomless, unmapped canyon the sun never reaches, where eyeless fish no one has ever seen—all teeth and toxins, trailing blacklight lures—stalk each other through endless night, a bubble floats up, dense as a dead star, growing, soaring through crushing atmospheres of ocean, rising like a moon, exploding from the waves into a thousand miles of thunder and light, turning east, over beaches and highways to the Coast Range, uprooting trees and setting them afire on its way inland, towards the jagged face of Stormbreaker.

Hanson was sitting on one of the rock-hard benches on the second-floor hall of the courthouse, with half a dozen other cops from "A" relief, waiting to testify at an interfering/assaulting a police officer/riot trial in which most of the Barr family, filling the twelve-foot bench directly across the hall, were defendants—Reba Barr, the forty-eight-year-old grandmother, her daughter

Laticia, and Laticia's four sons from three different fathers. Her youngest son, Kenny, was sitting with his girlfriend, a baby in his lap.

The baby, adorable in a pink sun dress, her hair braided in corn-rows, didn't resemble anyone in the Barr family. Defendants often borrowed or rented a baby to take to trial, making a great show of fatherly affection for the jury.

The Barrs had broken Norman's collarbone at a family distur-bance call, and he had called in a code-zero. When the first cars got there, Norman was on the floor in a fetal position, trying to keep them from taking his gun away.

"Black man's day is coming," Kenny hissed at Norman, who took his notebook out and wrote down what Kenny said.

"Punk," Kenny said. "Write *that* down too."

The baby flirted with Hanson, tilting her head coyly, looking over at him from Kenny's lap. Hanson tried to ignore her.

"Where'd you rent the baby?" Bond said.

"I think it's this week's 'duty baby,' " Norman said.

"Can you say, 'goo-goo,' Kenny?" Bond said.

"Can *you* say, 'suck my black dick'?"

The baby squinted her eyes shut, then opened them wide at Hanson, who finally grinned at her, tilting his head.

Detective Farmer came out of the courtroom, and the cops, who had been leaning forwards, poised for a fight, sat back on the bench.

"Hanson?" It was one of the secretaries from the DA's office.

"That's me."

"You've got a phone call from another officer. She said it was urgent."

It was Bishop.

"Who?" Hanson said, trying to hear her through whistling static, afraid he'd lose the connection if he punched another of the blinking extension buttons.

Two cubicles down, a white doper in oil-stained blue coveralls was combing his long hair with his fingers, one dirty hand, then the other, arguing with his pudgy public defender, "The best we can *do?* Three to five? *Maybe* three? The *fuck* . . ."

She was one of those people who smile when they talk, no matter what they're saying "I feel terrible, too, but . . ."

Hanson ground the receiver against his head, hunched over the phone, squinting, as if that would help him pick out Bishop's words through static and the chirping in his ears. His back to the wall, he'd glance up when anyone came through the bronze doors down the hall, and he kept an eye on the doper, on his reflection in the glass of the cubicle, patterned with palm prints and thumb-prints, coiled loops and whorls and arches, tiny petroglyphs. ". . . not *your* fat ass looking at three to five."

"I might have done better, but with that confession," she said, her smile quivering a little. "If you just hadn't . . ."

"I fuckin' *know* that," he said, driving one hand, then the other through his hair, the obsessive gesture reminding Hanson of a coyote he'd seen in a traveling zoo somewhere, in a supermarket parking lot, pacing the far side of a tiny, shit-strewn cage, his shoulders and ribs rubbed bloody against the bars.

"I'm not . . ."

"Hang on just a second," Hanson said, holding the phone against his leg as he stood straight, turning towards the doper.

"Yeah, you are," he barked through the glass. The doper stopped moving, one hand in his hair, then slowly looked around at Hanson.

"You are stupid," Hanson said. "We know it, and you know it. Right?"

The public defender's locked-jaw smile went away, her mouth tight with anger, flaking dry lipstick as Hanson held up the phone.

"This is a very important call. Don't make any more noise. Please. The lady's cutting you the best deal she can," he said, bringing the receiver back to his ear, the public defender's face flushing at the word "lady."

"Bishop? I'm gonna try to get a better connection. If I lose you, please call right back. I'll wait."

He punched HOLD, punched another extension, and Bishop was there. "When?" he said, looking up at the huge bronze clock over the doors, blindfolded Justice in her toga, like someone's middle-aged wife taking initiation into the Elks Club Auxiliary.

"Thank you," Hanson told Bishop. "Yeah. I owe you," he said. He pulled the poorly fitting door of the cubicle open, shivering the glass walls down the way like dominos. "Thanks," he said to the doper, and jogged through the crowd towards the door.

"I got his badge number," the public defender said. "He was way out of line, talking to you like he did."

"Fuck you. I want to go back to my cell."

At the end of the hall, just across from the big doors, a crowd

was gathering where the legless WWII veteran who ran the news-
stand was watching a small black-and-white TV. A local reporter
faded in and out of the static like a ghost, superimposed on a
weather report bleeding in from another channel.

". . . just joining us, two police officers are dead and a young,
uh, black woman as well. All dead, apparently from gunshot, multiple gunshot wounds. The shootings occurred in one of the rooms
behind me, here, at the Desert Palms Motel, a location well
known for prostitution and drug dealing.

"That's all we know at this time, but . . . officer? Excuse me,
officer? Fine. Sure.

"Apparently, officers here on the scene are trying to protect the
crime scene, and tempers are . . . excuse me."

The reporter spoke to someone off-camera. Behind him school-
children and teenagers waved and grinned into the camera.

Hanson worked his way through the growing crowd, resisting
the urge to push people out of his way. He was less real to them
than the fluttering images on the TV screen.

"A suspect in the shootings, possibly badly wounded himself,
witnesses tell us, fled the scene in a yellow Trans Am, towards,
uh . . ."

Someone off-camera handed him a slip of paper.

". . . police have located the suspect vehicle, abandoned by
the, uh, apparently the . . ."

But Hanson was on his way downstairs to the parking garage.
Doc had killed Fox, Peetey and Asia.

A patrolman waved him past a patrol car blocking the street. The
misty breeze carried the sound of police radios, like evil whispers,
from packsets and patrol cars parked all around the block. For a
moment, Hanson imagined that the sound was only in his head,
metallic voices hissing instructions. He pulled to the curb and
walked the last half block to the SWAT van, the sweet sting of tear
gas in the air like pollen.

He stood behind and just to the side of the SWAT van, his arms
folded, looking down Missouri Street at a burning house. The
clouds were getting darker, boiling in from the west, the cold mist
turning to rain, and Hanson's face glistened as if he were sweating.

The last house left on the street, its backyard sheared off, a
forty-foot drop to the new freeway, it had burned before, the sec-

ond floor a charred tangle of roof beams and two-by-fours. The
SWAT team moved in behind the house, up from the freeway and
over the bank as if they had come from inside the earth, low
crawling in black coveralls, assault rifles cradled in their arms,
through gray-green, unmowed grass.

Tear gas billowed out of the downstairs windows, startlingly
white against the dark sky. A yellow tongue of flame flickered in
one of the windows, then faded back into the smoke. A tear gas
grenade, burning red-hot, turning the solid cake of CS into gas,
had set something on fire.

"Hanson!"

Hanson turned back to the van and looked at Lt. Brannon, the
hostage negotiator. "Lieutenant."

"What are you doing here?" Brannon said.

"I know the guy in the house. From the army."

A couple of SWAT team backups looked over from the shelter
of the van. They were drinking Cokes, their black submachine
guns propped against the van. "Hey, Hanson," one of them said,
"see all the excitement you're missing, not coming to work for
us?"

"Hiya, Mickey," Hanson said. "Yeah."

"Can you talk to this guy?" Brannon said.

Flames were steady against one of the windows now, burning it
black. As Hanson watched, it shattered in an eruption of smoke,
feeding more oxygen to the flames.

"I don't think he'll surrender," Hanson said.

"He ain't gonna surrender," Mickey said. "He killed a cop. He's
gonna burn or commit suicide."

"Come on, Mickey," Brannon said. "Okay?"

"Right, El Tee," Mickey said, "I forgot. We're gonna 'bring him
to justice.' "

Gray smoke framed the front door of the house and flames blew
out another front window.

"Hey," the other SWAT team member said, lowering a pair of
binoculars, "there's dogs up there. On the roof. See," he said,
pointing with the hand he was holding the Coke in.

"Jesus," Mickey said. "Fuckin' hot dogs pretty soon. Hey," he
said over his shoulder to Hanson, "you guys still got that Night
Dog thing going?"

Shrubbery on the side of the house, wet with rain, began to
steam.

"Hanson?" Mickey said.

Hanson was walking up the middle of the street towards the burning house. The rain had picked up, cold, stinging his face. He passed angle-parked patrol cars, cops crouched behind them, gesturing and calling out to him in fear and confusion and authority. The lieutenant stepped out to pull him behind a car, but Hanson unsnapped his holster and shook his head *no*.

Then he was past the cars, and he was okay again. It had been a long time since things had made sense, since his duty was clear. The flames hissed in the rain, and he shivered with cold and adrenaline.

One of the SWAT guys crouched behind the house was listening to his packset, holding it against his ear. As Hanson walked closer, the man with the radio gestured angrily at him.

Hanson smiled and began to sing, "Daisy, Daisy, give me your answer, do . . ."

The Tear gas was strong in the air now, mixed with the stink of burning wet wood and garbage.

"I'm half cra-zy, all for the love of you . . ." Fire filled the windows, and flames like inverted icicles climbed the walls. He kicked the front door open and stepped back as tear gas billowed out, burning his eyes and wet face. Snot filled his nose as he crossed the front room, past shoulder-high mounds of garbage marbled with bubbling plastic and Styrofoam, burning sofas, a duct-taped beanbag chair, and smoldering mattresses, carpets and clothing piled against the outside wall, around piles of green garbage bags into a hallway where a hypodermic needle crushed beneath his boot, his wet wool shirt steaming now. Down the hall a white door blistered and turned brown as he passed, and vertical brown stripes bled through the floral-print wallpaper like invisible writing.

The ceiling was burned away from the earlier fire that had taken the second floor, making it possible to see and breathe. Darker smoke from beneath the once-white door mixed with floor-hugging white smoke rolling in from the front room corkscrewed up *like caramel swirls in vanilla ice cream*, he thought, and out. He heard a clicking—*tic tic tic*—crouched and covered his head, looked up into beams and burning timbers. Dogs. Dogs above him on what remained of the second floor, where they had been living since the earlier fire. Dogs running the splintered, charred flooring, jumping roof joists, flames herding them back. Lightning flashes etched the black jigsaw of two-by-fours and fire blocking, dogs leaping through them. A frantic mongrel shepherd, ribs showing through wet gray fur, missed her footing, caught a rafter with her forelegs, and pulled herself back up.

The smoke got worse, swirling up through the roof, black and brown and gray. Hanson took another step and the floor was spongy beneath his feet, giving way where the old fire had dropped down and burned it. The house moaned, its timbers and floor joists shifting. It sighed and shifted on its foundation beneath Hanson's feet. He stood very still. Back behind him, in the first room, the garbage bags closest to the fire began to split, the heat rending them with wounds that spilled out bottles and Big Mac containers and last year's newspapers. Up on the roof the dogs were herded by the flames and smoke into an ever smaller island of safety. They ran from one end of it to the other, back and forth like sharks in a tank, snapping at each other because there was nothing else to fight.

Hanson stepped carefully around the charred part of the floor and down the hall to a bedroom door. He reached out for the doorknob then jerked his hand back from its heat. The hollow-core door was hot to the back of his hand. He kicked the door and it splintered free, opening halfway. Inside there was no flame, but the air quivered like the air above a summer freeway, like a silver mirage, fragile as the *idea* of a bedroom with its dusty and spotted curtains, broken bed and blind TV screen. Patches of the wallpaper blackened, a sad, lost-dream pattern with just a hint of flame around the edge of the blotches of black. The curtains burst into flame and a sheet of fire appeared over the filthy mattress.

The plastic-skinned lounger in the corner seemed to shrink and writhe, blistering and boiling as the window behind the curtains exploded outward, sucking the flaming curtains off their rods and out the window. There was a *whump*, a sound like distant artillery, and the door slammed closed as Hanson dove to the floor, the wave of superheated air blowing the door off its hinges behind him. He crawled the rest of the way down the hall to another bedroom. The door was cool to the back of his hand. He pushed it open a crack, then opened it wide.

It was dark inside, and rain was coming through a broken window, the wind blowing ragged window shades. Lightning flashed and lit the room for a moment. Doc was standing to one side of a window, looking out.

"Doc," Hanson said.

Doc spun around, a pistol in his hand. His hair was singed on one side. He tried to smile. "Didn't expect to run into you here," he said.

"I can get you out," Hanson said. "We can go together."

"Kill a cop, they kill you. I understand that," he said, coughing. "I respect that."

The fire was moving down the hall behind them, and smoke was coming into the room. Hanson walked to the doorway where a red glow threw shadows in the hallway. He shut the door.

Doc got his breath. "Thought that fire *had* me."

The house moaned again, shifting. Flames in the hallway sucked air out from beneath the closed door with a hiss.

"You carryin' that nine millimeter?" Doc said.

Hanson nodded. He pulled it from his belt, the grip hot in his hand.

"Don't want you to *kill* me. Just souvenir me a few rounds," Doc said, "I used mine up killing those fuckers."

The smoke was worse in the room. Hanson's eyes were stinging and watering, and his nose was pouring snot. His throat felt swollen, like he'd been breathing dust on a hot day. It made him think of the dry season in Northern I Corps and the red dust they had up there.

And that time when the two companies of Nungs had demanded that they hand over the Vietnamese commander. When he sat with the 3.2 rocket tube in his lap, artillery plotted on top of them, ready to start killing people, a *lot* of them. Ready to die, singing, " 'Daisy, Daisy, give me your answer, do . . .' " The happiest hour of his life.

"I'd like to go out, you know, *doing* something," Doc said. He looked at Hanson, and, in a different tone of voice said, "Die like a man."

Hanson popped the clip out of his Model 39, distant sirens audible now over the roar of flames.

"The fire department," Doc said, "they always a little late to get to this part of town."

With his thumb, Hanson popped the shiny half-jacketed rounds into the palm of his other hand. He held out his hand and Doc covered it with his own, scooping the bullets up. He loaded them into the clip of his pistol. As he was about to press the last bullet in, he stopped and handed it back to Hanson. "Better keep one for yourself," he said, dropped the clip into the pistol and slapped it home against his thigh.

"Damn," he said, his face white with pain and fatigue. He reached into his pocket and pulled out a little vial of cocaine which slipped from his fingers onto the floor.

"Gimme a hand with that?" he said, nodding at it. "I need a little bump."

Hanson picked it up and held a spoonful of coke to Dawson's nose.

Doc snorted it. "Hit me again, officer," he said.

"Much better," he said. He looked around the room, stuck the pistol in his belt and picked up an old television set that was tipped against one wall. "Just like teevee," he said, laughing and coughing, lifting the set above his head then hurling it through the window, fresh blood flowing through the material of his shirt.

"I can eat all the pain they want to give me.

"You the *last* one now," he said to Hanson, then looked out the window. The rain was pouring down, it was dark, and over-grown shrubs partially shielded the window. Doc knocked the loose glass off the side and bottom of the window and threw one leg over it, like a man about to slip over the gunnel of a lifeboat into the sea. He looked at Hanson, smiled, and said, "See you in hell.

"Comin' at you, motherfuckers," he yelled, firing as he went out the window and through the bushes.

The flame from his gun was orange-black against the dark sky.

The return fire sounded like a firefight, M-16s, shotguns, the *pop* of handguns. A few rounds hit the house, patterns of shotgun pellets and whining slugs splintering the walls. Hanson stood looking out the window as the fire died down, then stopped. His ears were ringing from the shots and from the roar of the fire behind him as he stepped out the window into the pouring rain. It had turned into a real thunderstorm. His face and arms throbbed like a bad sunburn and he could smell his own singed hair. He tipped his head up and let the rain wash the tears and snot off his face. He spit out brown phlegm, then opened his mouth to the rain that sizzled on his badge.

Doc was half on the sidewalk and half on the street. He'd al-most made it to the street. Two of the SWAT team held shotguns inches from his head as another cop in black coveralls handcuffed the bloody dead body, its arms broken by shotgun slugs. One of the SWAT team advance men was rolling on the ground, holding his leg where Doc had shot him, yelling, "God *damn* it, mother-fucker. God *damn* it!"

The heat reached out to Hanson's back, but he kept walking away, past Doc's body, down the street, arriving fire trucks shud-dering past him. A sergeant and lieutenant yelled at him—he saw their mouths moving—but couldn't hear through the ringing in his ears. He looked back.

The house was engulfed in flames, backlighting the clouds of smoke and sparks that rose into the dark, rain-filled sky. A dozen dogs raced through the ruins of the second floor, attacking each other, keeping the firemen at bay, their fur smoldering, still alive only because of the rain.

A big gray and black mongrel shepherd leaped from the roof, out of the sparks and smoke, landing in the yard near Doc's body. Its fur on fire now, howling in pain, one leg broken, it ran on three legs like a nightmare towards the SWAT team who shot it repeat-edly as it staggered past them and finally collapsed in the street at Hanson's feet. The exit wounds from the shotgun were terrible, but the dog was still alive, snarling, the smoking fur on its hind-quarters burned to black stubble. Then it convulsed and stiffened, legs twitching like a sleeping pet dreaming of pursuit. Muscle spasms pried its jaws apart and closed, apart and closed, blood frothing over its teeth. It was still breathing, the ribs straining with each breath.

The dog convulsed again and stopped breathing, its stiffened legs relaxed, and the pupil of its eye opened slowly, like a ripple in black water until the whole eye was liquid black, an onyx mirror, and Hanson saw himself in the dying, then dead, eye, alone and almost lost in fans of red and blue light from the police cars and fire engines.

HANSON TOOK A last look around his house. It was as clean as it had ever been; everything he owned, that he hadn't given away, was boxed and stacked in the living room.

"Too bad Mister Thorgaard didn't have time to pack up. Maybe if he had . . . hell, they'd have taken it to the dump *anyway*."

He opened the squeaking wood-stove door, lit a kitchen match, and threw it in. The academy photo of Falcone was still propped on the shelf above the stove. Hanson looked at it as the computer printouts of his life began to burn, smiled, then closed and latched the cast-iron door.

"I guess that's it, buddy. Time to go."

Hanson smiled, holding the screen door open for Truman. It was a beautiful day, a taste of autumn in the air, Stormbreaker sharp against the cloudless sky. "A good day for it."

They drove the blacktop road up Stormbreaker to where it ended at a green steel gate and a cattle guard. "Be right back," Hanson said, getting out of the van with a pair of army surplus wire cutters.

He took time to close the gate behind them, draping the ends of the chain behind the sign that said Authorized Personnel Only, then wrapped the wire cutters in a blanket, tucked them under the seat, and drove on. Truman sat stiffly in the passenger seat, not accustomed to riding in the van, which needed shock absorbers and a new muffler. He wasn't used to riding in a car at all, the movement disorienting, but Hanson could see that he was trying to be brave.

"This is the best thing," he said. "For both of us."

The stretch of road beyond the gate was steeper, the asphalt giving way to washboard gravel, and the shovel in the back of the van clattered as they continued up the mountain towards the tree line, leaving the heat behind like a fading memory of summer, the air thin and cool, rags of dirty snow on the north side of rocks, down in swales and scattered through the shadows of trees.

Finally, they had to stop at an earthen berm where the road ended. Hanson got the shovel out of the back and a small duffle bag. He opened the passenger door, and Truman listened, ears up, as he took his pistol out of the glove box and stuck it in his belt.

"End of the road," Hanson said, picking the dog up in one arm, carrying the shovel and duffle bag in the other. He climbed the berm and set the dog down.

"Pretty smooth going here," he said, and the dog followed the sound of his feet and voice towards the snow line. "I've put this off for too long. I'm just tired of all this shit.

"Look at that," Hanson said, a little out of breath. "Last year's snow. You doin' okay?" he said, looking back at the dog. "Let's go up to that . . . looks like a little pasture."

They climbed for another fifteen minutes to where the land leveled off. Hanson looked around. "We're out of the wind here," he said. "Smell that air. Plenty of water in the creek way up here. Listen."

The dog looked up at him where he stood, his head tilted slightly to catch the sound of water on the rocks.

"You know what? The chirping's gone. I can hear that creek as clear as can be." He laughed. "Perfect.

"You can see everything from here. Look, way down there, beyond those old-growth Douglas firs."

The dog looked in the direction he was pointing.

"That's our house. See it? This is a good place."

The dog watched as Hanson dug the hole, careful to square off the edges, three feet deep, a foot wide, and two feet long. He looked at the dog. "That should do it," he said, jamming the shovel into the earth.

He pulled the pistol from his belt, popped the clip out, reached in his pocket and took out a single 9mm round. "The one Doc left me," he said, loading it on top of the other twelve half-jacketed, 110-grain hollow points. He chambered the round and looked at Truman, then put the pistol back in his belt.

He opened the duffle bag and took out the box with "CON-SIDER THE LILIES OF THE FIELD HOW THEY GROW" around the sides, looked through the medals, badges, unit patches and snapshots, touched the beret to his cheek, then put it back and closed the box. "Adios," he said, setting the box in the grave he'd dug. He took his badge out of his pocket and set it on top of the box, tore the *katha* from his neck and tossed it in, then knelt by the grave, laid the pistol next to the badge, and picked up the shovel. He was about to dump the first shovelful of dirt in the grave, then tossed it away.

"Got carried away, there," he told Truman, bending down to pick the pistol up. "Shit, we don't want to face this world unarmed."

He buried the box, *katha*, and badge, smoothed the dirt, and, leaning on the shovel, looked out over the land protected by Stormbreaker.

The postcard from Falcone was sweat-stained, the writing

smudged, warped to the shape of his hip pocket. Hanson tapped it against his palm and put it back in his pocket.

"Come on, buddy," he said, "let's pack our shit and go to Montana."

The old dog trotted along beside him, up over the berm, and let Hanson put him back in the van.

ABOUT THE AUTHOR

Kent Anderson is a former police officer, a former Special Forces sergeant in Vietnam, where he was awarded the Bronze Star, and the author of the Vietnam novel *Sympathy for the Devil*. He lives in Idaho.